A WEDDING AT THE LITTLE BOOKSHOP BY THE SEA

ELIZA J SCOTT

Storm
PUBLISHING

Ebook ISBN: 978-1-83700-023-4
Paperback ISBN: 978-1-83700-024-1

Cover design: Rose Cooper
Cover images: Shutterstock

Published by Storm Publishing.
For further information, visit:
www.stormpublishing.co

ALSO BY ELIZA J SCOTT

Welcome to Micklewick Bay Series

The Little Bookshop by the Sea

Summer Days at Clifftop Cottage

Finding Love in Micklewick Bay

Christmas at the Little Bookshop by the Sea

Cupcakes and Kisses in Micklewick Bay

A Snowy Seaside Christmas

Life on the Moors Series

The Letter – Kitty's Story

The Talisman – Molly's Story

The Secret – Violet's Story

A Christmas Kiss

A Christmas Wedding at the Castle

A Cosy Countryside Christmas

Sunny Skies and Summer Kisses

A Cosy Christmas with the Village Vet

Christmas at Holly Tree Cottage

Heartshaped Series

Tell That to My Heart

To my wonderful editor, Kate.
Thank you for believing in my books.

ONE

FRIDAY 10TH APRIL

The afternoon had been the longest Florrie Appleton could remember, dragging into the evening like the tide creeping in. 'Where the heck's Lark got to?' she said, chewing at her bottom lip and tapping her foot impatiently. Such was her agitation, the mouth-watering aroma of fish and chips and the familiar Friday night jaunty tunes courtesy of the local folk band barely registered with her. 'It's not like her to be this late.' Her brown eyes went from the watch at her wrist – that told her it was seven forty-five – to sweeping the bar for the umpteenth time since she'd arrived at The Jolly Sailors pub twenty minutes earlier. She had something she needed to get off her chest, and she was struggling to contain the tension that had been building inside her since a worrying piece of information had reached her ears that afternoon. If Lark didn't get a wriggle on, it was in danger of spilling out in a great tidal wave at any moment, which wouldn't do; Florrie needed all of her best friends together for this. It wasn't as if she didn't have enough on her mind already. She turned to the door again. 'I just wish she'd hurry up.'

'I'm sure she won't be much longer,' said Stella, glass of Pinot Grigio in hand as she scrutinised Florrie fidgeting opposite her. They were sitting at their regular Friday night table together with

Maggie and Jasmine, embers glowing in the hearth of the nearby inglenook fireplace. Stella was looking effortlessly stylish – as usual – her fitted designer jeans doing an excellent job of showcasing her endless legs and her beige and cream striped sweater in the softest cashmere, complementing her long blonde hair and fair skin perfectly. And for all she was tall, it never stopped Stella from wearing the highest of heels, to which this evening's choice of ankle boots were testament. 'You okay, Florrie? You're looking a bit agitated there, it's most unlike you.'

Florrie nudged her glasses up her nose. 'I'm fine, just wondering where she is, that's all.' Even to her own ears Florrie was aware her faux casual tone failed to hide the snappy note in her voice. She pressed her mouth into an apologetic smile and tucked a stray lock of her chestnut bob behind her ear, conscious of the weight of three sets of eyes on her. She turned her attention to the cuff of her plum-coloured cardigan, feigning interest in an imaginary loose thread. *Stop fidgeting, woman!*

But the more she remonstrated with herself, the more het-up Florrie became. All the same, she needed to *stress* to her friends how strongly she felt about the situation before they got totally carried away and it was too late to do anything about it. A phone call or text message wouldn't do; they needed to see from her expression that she meant it. *Really* meant it. That she wouldn't budge on her decision, and that there'd be no wiggle room for even the slightest variation. And what's more, she needed to get across that no part of her would find any of what she'd heard remotely funny – not now, *definitely* not at the time, and not in the future. She had to be absolutely certain that they got the message. *Oh jeez!* Just thinking about it was making her worries escalate and her stomach churn even more furiously.

Calming breaths, Florrie. Calming breaths.

She inhaled slowly, releasing the breath steadily through her nose before repeating it, but was disappointed to find it did little good.

Though the rational part of her brain told her that her source must've got it wrong, that there was clearly some mistake or misunderstanding – surely she could rest assured that her friends wouldn't inflict something like *that* on her? – it still hadn't stopped the doubts sneaking in. And those doubts had mushroomed during the afternoon until they'd taken over every corner of her mind and now dominated her thoughts, which was surprising considering the other matter that was jostling for attention. Her anxiety levels were ready to shoot through the roof. Only when she was satisfied she'd got her point across would she be able to get on with enjoying her usual Friday night out with the lasses.

She glanced around the busy bar again, but there was still no sign of her friend. 'Ugh! Come on, Lark! Get your backside here!' She reached into her handbag that was beside her on the settle and pulled out her phone. 'I'll send her a text, see where she is.'

'What's the urgency, missus?' Maggie, who was sitting to Florrie's left, turned and gave her a full appraisal. 'You're getting your knickers into a right old knot there. I can actually feel the stress coming off you in waves.' Maggie was a bold splash of colour in her lime green fluffy jumper dotted with multi-coloured pompoms, betraying her arty background. Out of the group, she was the friend Florrie was closest to, despite knowing her for the least amount of time. They'd met at university in York where they'd instantly hit it off, with Maggie joining Florrie at her parents' home in Micklewick Bay most weekends. It was on such a weekend that Maggie had met her future husband, local man Bear Marsay, and had moved to the town to be with him once she'd finished her degree. They'd married not long after and had been loved up ever since.

'Please tell me it's nowt to do with Ed's mother and her sudden appearance in town?' said Jasmine, who'd not long since arrived herself and was still getting settled in her usual seat at the top of the table. Her freshly dyed red pixie crop glowed extra vibrant under the lights, complementing her Fair Isle jumper in shades of green, orange and beige.

'*What?*' Stella's head jerked in Jasmine's direction. 'Since when?'

'What's *she* doing here?' Maggie's shocked expression matched Stella's.

'No, no, this is nothing to do with that.' Florrie gave a quick shake of her head, the mention of Dawn Harte and her unexpected arrival that afternoon adding to the anxiety that was already swirling in her stomach.

'What makes you think she's in town, Jazz?' asked Maggie.

'I saw her heading – or should I say stomping – down Resolution Row.' Jasmine's expression darkened. 'You can tell she's a piece of work just by her walk, and don't get me started on the filthy looks she gives out, like she thinks we're all beneath her.'

'Sounds about right.' Stella's glossy top lip curled disapprovingly.

Jasmine gave a derisory snort. Earlier that day, she'd texted Florrie, saying she'd seen Dawn in town, warning her friend to be on her guard. But by then, Florrie had already had the shock of coming face-to-face with her future mother-in-law. Dawn Harte had landed at The Happy Hartes Bookshop – which Florrie owned and ran along with her fiancé, Ed – just after lunchtime, which was a good hour before Jasmine's text had arrived. She'd been armed with a bulging backpack and her domineering personality, announcing that she'd come to stay. Florrie had fired Jasmine a quick reply, thanking her for the warning and saying she'd fill her in with the details when they were all together at the Jolly.

Stella turned to Florrie, a troubled look on her face. 'Have you seen her yet?'

'And is Ed's dad with her?' asked Maggie, looking equally concerned.

'Yes, she called at the bookshop – luckily Ed was there, too, so I didn't have to face her on my own – and she's come alone; Ed's dad is still in London apparently.'

A loaded, 'Oh,' followed from Stella, Maggie and Jasmine.

'I know, that's what we thought, too,' said Florrie.

'I've been wondering what she's up to ever since I saw her,' said Jasmine. 'Any contact from her or her husband can only mean one thing: trouble.'

Florrie couldn't argue with that. Conscious of the worried expressions her friends were wearing, she hurriedly said, 'I'll tell you all more about it in a tick. What I want to talk about first has nothing to do with Ed's parents, so you can put your fretting about that to one side for the minute. I just wish Lark would hurry up and get here.' She didn't want to head down the Dawn Harte route right now; she wanted to get the problem at hand fixed before she tackled that. She blinked an image of the woman away, unable to stop the shudder that ran through her.

'Surely whatever it is you need Lark here for before you tell us, can't be anywhere near as bad as the news that Dawn Harte's in town,' said Jasmine.

Right now, it was a close-run thing in Florrie's mind. 'It's just something I have to—'

'So sorry I'm late, lasses.' Florrie's words were cut off by Lark's familiar gentle tones as the group were enveloped in a fragrant cloud of essential oils. Her long, blonde waves tumbled over her shoulders and her colourful metal bracelets jangled as she started unbuttoning her patchwork jacket in rich jewel shades. 'I'd nipped round to see my dad and Louisa after work and completely lost track of time.'

'Thank goodness you're here now.' Stella flashed a loaded smile as she inched along the settle, making room for Lark to slip in alongside her.

Relief flooded Florrie's veins, only for it to be quickly followed up by a generous dash of apprehension at hearing what her friends would have to say when she confronted them. She slid her phone back into her bag.

Once hellos had been exchanged and a glass of wine had been poured for Lark, Florrie cleared her throat and pushed up the sleeves of her cardigan. 'Before we get started, I really need to say something.'

'Ey up, lasses, looks like our Florrie means business,' said Jasmine.

'It sure does,' said Stella.

'Uh-oh,' said Maggie. 'Here goes.'

'What've I missed?' asked Lark, throwing a questioning glance around the table as she folded her jacket and lay it beside her on the settle.

'Nowt yet,' said Jasmine. 'We've been waiting for you to land so we could find out. Florrie's been like a cat on hot bricks ever since I got here and it has nowt to do with Dawn Harte landing in town.'

'What?' Lark's eyes grew wide as saucers, as attention turned to Florrie.

'I'll explain about that in a minute; there's something else I need to say first.' Florrie took a moment, lining up the words she'd rehearsed. She cleared her throat. 'So, this afternoon, while I was at the booksh—'

'Hiya, ladies, you all had a good week?' The chirpy tones of cockney landlady Mandy stopped Florrie in her tracks, sending a ripple of irritation through her.

<h1 style="text-align:center">TWO</h1>

With an inward sigh of frustration, Florrie waited while Mandy updated them on her broken wrist that was still in its plaster cast and keeping her from her cooking duties in the pub's kitchen. Florrie's heart sank even further when the landlady went on to tell them how the recent stint of sunny weather had been good for business, and described how a coachload of customers had landed unexpectedly and had the chefs run off their feet. *Please not now!* Florrie felt her impatience bouncing around inside her, so at odds with her usual easy-going demeanour.

When she was eventually done chatting, Mandy threw a couple of logs onto the fire, sending sparks shooting up the chimney and the aroma of woodsmoke into the air. Much as Florrie was fond of the landlady, she was relieved when she finally headed back to the bar, stopping to talk to other regulars as she went.

'I'm beginning to think we're never going to find out what's got our Florrie wound as tight as a spring,' said Maggie, as they all turned their attention back to their table.

'Yeah, come on, spill the tea,' added Jazz.

Doing all she could to push thoughts of her future mother-in-law out of her mind, Florrie took a moment to restore her focus before she spoke. 'So, this afternoon, your plans for my hen celebrations got back to me.' She swiftly swept her gaze around her friends, keen to catch their initial reactions, see what they'd reveal.

'Right,' said Stella, drawing the word out as she glanced between the others, her brow creasing in puzzlement. 'Not sure how that happened. We were all sworn to secrecy; it was meant to be a surprise.'

'A *surprise?* Shock more like,' said Florrie, making the creases in Stella's brow deepen.

'Okay, which one of you has blabbed?' asked Maggie. 'I've kept my trap tightly shut.'

'Not guilty.' Jasmine held up her palms. Her reaction was so convincing it made Florrie wonder if there'd been a mix up over what she'd heard, particularly since Jasmine's name had specifi-cally been mentioned.

'And I haven't breathed a word,' said Lark. 'Not even to Nate, well, only the bit he needs to know, and I stressed to him that he had to keep it secret.'

'Same here with Alex,' added Stella. 'And I'm confident neither of them would let anything slip, inadvertently or otherwise.'

Florrie's attention was pulled away from Jasmine as she tried to work out why there'd be something Nate and Alex 'needed' to know. Just as she was considering this, Maggie spoke.

'It's a real shame word's got out, especially after all the effort we've put in.'

Florrie could barely believe her friend's reaction. 'To be honest, I wouldn't call it a shame exactly. In fact, I'd say I'm relieved to have heard about it before it actually got the chance to happen. It's given me the opportunity to put a stop to it.' Ignoring the confused expressions around the table, she ploughed on. 'I just want to stress – *again* – that I don't want a big fuss, okay?' She pushed her glasses up her nose and glanced around at her friends, fixing them, one by one, with a warning look she hoped would leave them in no doubt that she was deadly serious.

Ah, right,' said Jasmine, in a way that suggested she'd just cottoned on to something. Florrie's gaze travelled back to her. Frustration flared through her when she saw her friend's mouth twitching in the way it did when she was struggling not to laugh. If that wasn't enough, her green eyes were twinkling mischievously which only served to confirm Florrie's worst fears. Clearly, her objections weren't coming out as forcefully as she'd hoped. Injecting a firmer tone into her voice, she continued, 'You all know how I don't like being the centre of attention; that I much prefer low-key stuff – it's exactly the reason Ed and I have settled for a small, intimate wedding. I'd be more than happy to have a quiet meal at Oscar's Bistro, just the five of us. In fact, the more I think about it, the more I think that would be quite nice.'

'"*Nice*"?' repeated Jasmine, the struggle with her laugh brought to an abrupt halt. From the look on her face anyone would think there was a bad smell under her nose. 'You can't settle for "*nice*" when you're celebrating getting married, Florrie. You've got to let your besties make some sort of fuss over you. Surely you wouldn't deprive us of that pleasure?'

Florrie groaned inwardly.

'I agree with Jazz,' said Maggie. 'The bistro's great, but we can go there any time; we've got to do something a bit different to celebrate such a momentous occasion.'

'Jazz and Mags are right,' said Stella. 'But I'm curious to know exactly what you heard, and also who you heard it from.'

'You can tell our Stella's a barrister; wanting to get all the facts lined up,' Lark said with a chuckle.

'Well...' Florrie's eyes flicked briefly to Jasmine – whose grin had made a reappearance – as she went on to explain how Leah, The Happy Hartes Bookshop's young assistant, had informed her that her best friend, Abbie, had been in the local supermarket when she'd overheard part of a conversation Jasmine had been having with a notorious local gossip, Pat Grievson, and that the words 'strippagram' and 'Florrie's hen party' had floated to her ears. Abbie had apparently reported it to Leah, who hadn't wasted any time in sharing it with Florrie.

'Then other customers started to mention it over the course of the afternoon, but what concerned me the most, was that some were saying they'd heard the stripper was going to turn up at the bookshop and... *perform* – if that's what you call what they do – right there, which is why I was so past myself worrying about it.' Florrie pressed her hand to her chest. 'Leah's a reliable source and she'd assured me that Abbie was, too, so I had no reason to doubt it was true.'

A collection of snorts ran around the table before all eyes turned to Jasmine. 'Oops! Sorry I blabbed,' she said, giving a cheeky smile.

'It's so not funny, you lot! It's totally not my kind of thing, you should all know that!' Such was her outrage, Florrie didn't notice the subtle flick of Stella's eyebrows in Jasmine and Maggie's direction, nor their equally subtle, non-verbal responses.

Putting her famous poker face to good use, Stella said, 'Look, flower, Ando's already agreed to be a strippagram for the occasion. He's looking forward to it; we can't just dump him; tell him he's surplus to requirements at this late stage, especially when he's said it's going to be the highlight of his year. We thought you'd be chuffed, especially cos he doesn't have the most exciting life, bless him.'

'Aye, Ando may be a bit of a daft lad, but he's got a good heart,' added Jasmine, clasping her hands to her chest. 'Which is why we thought you'd be happy to go along with it.'

'*What?*' Florrie's face paled as her heart went into freefall. It was even worse than she'd feared. She covered her face with her hands. 'No way! Ando? *Seriously?*' She didn't even want to think what him having a 'good heart' had to do with anything!

'Yep, seriously. He told me he was looking forward to it, too, Stells,' said Maggie. 'Collared me when I first got here, told me how he'd already worked out his routine; something involving those pickled eggs he was tirelessly trying to tempt our Jazz with before she and Max got together.' She flashed Florrie a wide smile as a loud snort came from Jasmine's direction. 'And I, personally, can't wait to see how he's going to incorporate his skateboard into the routine, but he's assured me it's going to be a very polished affair.' She scooped up her wine and took a sip, her eyes dancing as she peered over the top of her glass.

'Oh jeez,' Florrie muttered to herself as she let her hands fall away from her face. Her friends had created the most terrifying mental image; it was going to take a great effort to shift it from her mind.

With his battered leather jacket, ripped jeans and baseball cap worn back to front, Ando Taylor was a familiar sight in town, his attire more akin to the local teenagers he hung around with at the skateboard park than his peers in their forties. If he had a job, no one had a clue what it was since he seemed to spend most of his time skateboarding or propping up the bar at the Jolly. He was generally viewed as a harmless soul – if not a little misguided and prone to laziness. And, with the exception of Maggie – whose marital status appeared to have saved her from his unwelcome advances – he'd tried his luck with each of the women in the group, particularly when he was on the other side of several pints of Micklewick Mischief at the Jolly on a Friday evening.

He'd sway over to their table, his boozy breath making their noses twitch as he offered to walk home whichever of the friends was the subject of his attention at the time. It didn't appear to occur to him that his suggestion of rounding the evening off with a visit to his bedsit where they could dine on pickled eggs washed down with a glass or two of the home brew he'd named 'Gut Rot' wasn't remotely tempting. He'd never pushed further when his offer was declined; he'd simply stagger away, accepting their refusals. He'd finally given up when all of the friends had become happily settled in serious relationships. And though he'd been particularly persistent with Jasmine, everyone knew he'd had a soft spot for Florrie.

'And then there's the fact we've already booked and paid for him,' said Jasmine, once she'd recovered from her giggle-snort. 'Tell you what, for a hundred and fifty quid, Ando had better be bloomin' good or I'll be asking for a refund of my share.'

'Aye, me too.' Maggie was struggling hard not to laugh. 'I'm expecting him to deliver big time on what he's promised,' she said, before finally dissolving into a fit of the giggles.

'Ugh!' Florrie groaned, realisation dawning as she clocked the amused expressions her friends were wearing. 'You lot are terrible! Don't even joke about it,' she said, as the first ripples of relief kicked in.

'Who's joking?' said Stella, giving a hearty chuckle. 'Actually, didn't he say something about roping old Lobster Harry into it, too?' She feigned a questioning look. 'Buy one, get one free...'

'Aye, that's right; two for the price of one,' Maggie said through her laughter. 'Gotta love a cheeky little BOGOF bargain.'

'It would add a whole new dimension to proceedings, don't you think, lasses?' said Jasmine, mischief written all over her face. 'Mind, I'd put money on Lobster Harry keeping his raggy old gansey on for the performance.'

''Course he would, Jazz,' Stella said, feigning incredulity. 'He'd have to have it surgically removed otherwise, and I can't see him going to such lengths just for a few hours.'

Even Lark, who didn't usually partake in such persistent teasing, couldn't help chuckling at Stella's observation. Locals regularly joked that the craggy-faced, dentally challenged fisherman had never been seen without his tightly knitted gansey, even in the height of summer, and that he'd only replace the one he was currently wearing once it had become so threadbare it started to unravel.

Florrie rolled her eyes and clapped her hand to her forehead. 'Stop now! All of you! Not funny! At all!' The group collapsed into a riotous fit of the giggles, Florrie following suit, Jasmine's dirty cackle standing out above them all and attracting curious looks from nearby tables.

'Aww, poor Florrie,' Lark said in her familiar gentle tones. She reached across and squeezed her friend's hand, smiling kindly as she did so. 'We wouldn't do anything like that to you. Promise.'

''Course we wouldn't,' said Stella through her giggles. 'But, oh, your face was a picture.'

'Is there any wonder with you lot?' Florrie shook her head as the final traces of her fears ebbed away, allowing the jaunty tune courtesy of the folk band to register in her ears. She slumped back into the settle and took a sip of her wine, savouring the feeling of relief.

With the exception of Maggie, the women had been best friends since primary school. It was no exaggeration to say they'd been through thick and thin together, fiercely supporting one another as they'd dealt with the numerous challenges thrown at them over the years. Florrie would argue that every trial and tribulation they'd faced had brought them closer together, deepening their friendship, and strengthening their loyalty. It meant they could be completely honest about their feelings and worries, safe in the knowledge that they wouldn't be judged or ridiculed, or that they'd offend anyone. But that didn't mean they were exempt from being on the end of a good bout of bantering. As Florrie had just experienced.

When the friends' laughter had finally subsided, Stella asked, 'What the heck made you start a rumour like that, Jazz?'

'I was just trying to throw that dreaded gob-on-legs Pat Grievson off the scent, that's all. The nosy old bat was pretty much interrogating me about it when she collared me at the supermarket; like a rat up a drain, she was. And knowing how quickly gossip spreads round this town thanks to the likes of her, I knew if word of our *real* plans got out, it wouldn't take long before it reached our Florrie's lug 'oles. I thought dropping a cheeky little decoy into conversation with one of the town's biggest busybodies would work a treat and get her off the scent.'

'Seems it did the trick,' said Stella, her mouth twitching with a smile.

'Didn't it just?' Maggie agreed, chuckling.

'Threw me off the scent, all right,' Florrie said dryly.

'Tell you what, though, it wouldn't half add a bit of spice to the romance section of the bookshop if he'd *performed* – as Florrie so demurely put it – in that particular aisle,' Jasmine added with another raucous cackle.

'Ugh! Please don't. I doubt poor Jean would ever recover from the shock,' she said of the bookshop's septuagenarian assistant. 'Mind, she wouldn't be the only one.'

'Might be the highlight of her week for all you know,' quipped Jasmine. Florrie replied with an eye roll, though she couldn't help but laugh.

'So, lasses, here's a suggestion for you, what d'you think about giving our Florrie here a bit of a hint about what we actually *do* have planned?' asked Stella, glancing around at the others and steering the conversation in a direction Florrie found far more preferable. 'I don't mean to share the details, more like just enough info to help allay her fears once and for all, especially after the afternoon she's had fretting about it.'

'I'd be happy to do that.' Maggie nodded.

'Me too,' said Lark.

'Same here, especially since I've been the cause of her concerns – sorry, flower,' said Jasmine.

'No harm done.' Florrie gave her a warm, but knowing, smile.

'It's a fab idea, but how about before we do that, we let Florrie tell us about Dawn and why she's come to Micklewick Bay?' suggested Lark. 'I'm sure she'd rather get the bad stuff out of the way knowing there's something happy and positive to chat about after.'

'I'm good with that,' said Stella.

'Me too,' agreed Jasmine.

'Same here, if Florrie would prefer to do it in that order,' said Maggie.

'Actually, I like the sound of that.' Florrie noted how telling it was that even Lark, who rarely said anything negative about anyone, would refer to Dawn and her arrival as 'bad stuff'.

Feeling the weight of her friends' gaze upon her, Florrie's stomach clenched as her mind went back to the moment the bookshop door opened earlier that afternoon, and she looked up to see Dawn Harte standing there, a combative look in her eye. 'We had absolutely no idea she was coming so we were totally flabbergasted when she landed. But it was even more of a shock when she told us that she'd booked herself in at a local B&B and – I can hardly believe I'm about to say this–' Florrie grimaced. 'She said the reason for her visit was to *help* with our wedding preparations.'

A stunned silence followed as the four friends sat looking back at Florrie, mouths agape. The lively tune being belted out by the folk band was so at odds with the feeling of foreboding in her stomach.

'She *what?*' said Jasmine, once she'd recovered from the shock and was able to speak. 'Talk about dropping a bombshell.'

'She told us – quite forcefully, I might add – that she's here to "do her bit" for her son and "help" with our wedding plans.' In fact, the way Dawn had spoken, it had sounded more like a threat. Florrie had only met her future mother-in-law a handful of times which, if she was being honest, was enough since any contact with Ed's parents had invariably resulted in trouble and stress. And it wasn't just that; they hadn't kept their dislike of Florrie a secret, which was why she was suspicious of Dawn's motives for wanting to be involved with their wedding plans.

'After everything she's done, I'm not sure you should trust her, Florrie,' Stella said in a warning tone.

'Aye, same here,' Jasmine said firmly, her face flushing in the way it usually did when she was worked up about something.

'I have to agree,' said Maggie. 'I mean, her presence in Ed's life has been pretty sparse and any offer to help is so wildly out of character.'

'I know, which is why I've been struggling to make any sense of it, or work out what the real motive could be,' said Florrie. 'It's the same for Ed.'

'I'm with the lasses; I've got a bad feeling about this, Florrie,' added Lark, whose highly tuned intuition meant she was sensitive to bad vibes. Florrie knew that if Lark sensed something untoward about a person or place, it was worth taking notice of.

'And hasn't she left it a bit late in the day to want to help?' asked Stella. 'Your wedding's three weeks away, and you've got everything sorted. There's nothing left for her to help with.'

Florrie's mind drifted to their wedding plans. Stella had a point. Florrie was known amongst her family and friends for being organised; she left nothing to the last minute if she could help it. As soon as she and Ed had set the date for their wedding, she'd created a spreadsheet of everything that needed to be bought, the orders to be placed and venues to be booked. Every detail was included, no matter how small. Jasmine, being a celebration-cake maker, hadn't wasted a moment in offering her services to create their wedding cake. She'd invited Florrie and Ed to the home she shared with Max where the couple had spent a delightful couple of hours chomping on cake samples – ranging from traditional fruit, to lemon, to Victoria sponge, to gooey chocolate – as they'd pored over images of the designs Jasmine had created for other couples in order to choose their own. And while Florrie and Ed had agreed wholeheartedly on the gooey chocolate cake option, they'd been too spoilt for choice to be able to settle on a design, so they'd given Jasmine free rein to do what she thought best, much to her delight.

The couple had decided early on they'd like a book theme for the wedding, and had great fun sourcing items. Adding a personal touch, Ed had put his artistic skills to good use and designed their wedding invitations in the style of vintage library cards. And he'd gone one step further, making place settings that resembled the spines of old books. Both of which had delighted Florrie no end and added to her building excitement for their big day.

As for her wedding dress, Florrie had been feeling disillusioned by a recent unsuccessful shopping trip to York when she'd received a phone call from Lark, who owned Lark's Vintage Bazaar which sat across the road from the bookshop in the town's Victoria

Square. She sold vintage clothing and accessories – as well as crystals and her own blend of aromatherapy products. Lark had been beside herself with excitement, telling Florrie she'd just taken delivery of the most exquisite vintage wedding gown and asking if she'd pop in to the shop to take a look. 'I put it to one side straight away, it's *so* you! And I know you're just going to love it!'

Such was Lark's excitement, Florrie had rushed over to the store, desperate to see the dress for herself. And as soon as she'd set eyes on it, she'd fallen in love with its simple lines and exquisite lace that were very much her style. She'd hoped with all her heart it would fit as she'd disappeared into the changing room and slipped the delicate gown over her head. Florrie was thrilled to find that the only thing that needed altering was the hem which, with her being so petite, was a little too long. Lark had assured her it was something she could easily take care of, especially since she was no stranger to altering clothes for her shop.

'I have a bad feeling, too.' Jasmine's voice pulled Florrie out of her thoughts. 'The old cowpat's up to summat, without a doubt. There's no way, after everything her and her toxic husband have done to you and Ed, that she's come to "help". And besides, she has no business marching in bold as brass and telling you what she's going to do – especially when she's barely given her son a second glance for the whole of his life.' Jasmine's cheeks were now blazing. 'I don't believe it for a second. I reckon she's got an ulterior motive. I don't know why she thinks she has the right to turn up unannounced and start with all her toxic flippin' meddling. And don't get me on to the way she's treated you.' She set her mouth into a hard line, fury flashing in her green eyes. Only the very brave or the very foolish got on the wrong side of Jasmine.

A vision raced through Florrie's mind of Jasmine stomping over to someone she'd recently spotted sneaking a book into their pocket at The Happy Hartes Bookshop. The verbal savaging that had ensued meant the shoplifter had hastily replaced the pilfered item and hurried out of the shop, face burning. Florrie's lips twitched at the memory. Jasmine may be petite, but she could be a tornado of devastating proportions when she was angry, particularly when she was protecting or sticking up for those she loved. It didn't take much for her to adopt full-on mamma bear mode.

'Ey up, calm your jets, missus,' said Maggie, giving Jasmine a friendly nudge. 'Whatever it is Dawn Harte's up to, we'll do all we can to make sure the woman doesn't take over or interfere with Florrie and Ed's wedding plans.'

'You're not kidding. We've all got your back, flower,' said Stella, to which all of the friends agreed.

Florrie's heart squeezed at their show of loyalty. 'Thanks, lasses. Mind, I haven't told you everything.' Her eyes momentarily shifted to the server Immy who was negotiating her way to a nearby table, two plates piled high with steaming food in her hands, the delicious aroma wafting their way. Usually such a sight – and smell – would make Florrie's stomach rumble hungrily, but tonight, she appeared to have lost her appetite.

'Uh-oh, there's more?' said Jasmine, following Florrie's line of sight, her eyes widening as the plates were set down. 'I'll order our fish and chips soon.'

'About an hour after she'd left the bookshop to check in at her guesthouse, Dawn returned saying that she'd been misled by the B&B's website and that the room she'd been given was inferior and had no en-suite – she actually said it wasn't fit to stay in.'

Stella rolled her eyes and shook her head. 'Why doesn't that surprise me?'

'What's the name of the B&B?' asked Maggie.

'She just said it was down Resolution Row; didn't give a name.' In typical Dawn style she'd avoided giving any information she wasn't willing to share which only served to heighten Florrie's concerns.

Lark scrunched her nose up. 'I thought all the guesthouses down there were okay.'

'Apparently not. And worse, she started hinting heavily about moving in with us for the duration of her stay.' In fact, the hints had been so heavy, anyone would be forgiven for thinking they were made of lead! The prospect of Dawn staying with them at Samphire Cottage didn't bear thinking about.

'If I were you, I wouldn't let her over your doorstep.' The warning tone in Stella's voice sent a chill running through Florrie.

'That's going to be easier said than done,' she replied. Before Dawn had left the bookshop for the second time, she'd announced she intended to call in on Ed that evening, no doubt because she knew she'd find him alone at the cottage; it was common knowledge that Florrie joined her friends at the Jolly every Friday night. She only hoped he'd be firm and not let his mother browbeat him into agreeing to anything, or at least that he'd run any of Dawn's 'suggestions' by her beforehand. Florrie had enough experience of Dawn and her husband to know they were masters of wearing people down.

'I'm sure Ed'll be firm with her,' Maggie said, giving Florrie a reassuring smile.

'Aye, me too,' Jasmine said, her tone softening, though the look in her eyes told Florrie her friend wasn't totally convinced.

Lark reached over and rubbed Florrie's arm, her bracelets chiming as she did so. 'What a day you've had. I think now we've got that out of the way, it'd be a good time to go back to our hen party plans for you,' she said in her familiar gentle way.

'Good thinking,' Jasmine agreed, her cheeks still flushed.

'We'll let you do the honours, Stells, since it's you who suggested we do it,' said Maggie.

'Righto.' Stella fixed her gaze on Florrie, affection shining in her pale-blue eyes. 'So, we had a get-together to discuss what we should do to celebrate your upcoming marriage. And, since we all had lots of suggestions and struggled to settle on just one of them, we decided it would be a rather fine idea to go with each of our favourites.'

A crease appeared between Florrie's dark eyebrows. 'But—'

'Don't worry, they're all something you'll love; some very simple,' added Maggie, leaning in to their friend, evidently reading her thoughts. 'And there's nothing that could even remotely be construed as "making a fuss", I promise.'

'Mags is right. There's going to be four separate, totally wonderful, hen celebrations.' Lark beamed over at her, light from the wall lamp illuminating her blonde hair and creating a halo effect.

'*Four?*' said Florrie.

'Yep, all with belly laughs guaranteed – as is the norm when us lot get together,' said Jasmine. 'We've got some great stuff planned, and I swear there won't be a strippagram in sight. And none of them have owt to do with Ando Taylor or Lobster Harry, for that matter. I promise, cross my heart.' She mimed drawing a cross over her chest with her fingers.

'You all right, flower?' Maggie gave Florrie a gentle nudge with her elbow.

'Uh? Oh, yeah, I'm fine.' Florrie smiled. 'Just letting the relief sink in; enjoying a moment to savour it after my afternoon of utter panic.' Her reply made her friends chuckle. Taking in their smiling faces and the light-hearted atmosphere around the table, she switched off all thoughts of Dawn and focused her full attention on the conversation. She listened, her heart growing lighter as Stella shared – with much butting in from the others – that they'd already meticulously planned the days for the hen party celebration events. It made Florrie wonder when they'd managed to organise everything without her getting so much as a whisper of it.

'You'll only find out what we're doing on the actual morning – or maybe even the night before if we're feeling generous – but we'll share important details, like what to wear, anything you might need to bring with you, that sort of thing, well beforehand.'

'But what if I'm at work, I'll need notice to organise cover?"

'Like we said, it's all been taken care of.' Stella gave her a reassuring smile, her eyes twinkling.

Florrie blinked, absorbing it all. They'd really thought of everything.

'You're going to love what we've got planned.' Lark beamed

over at her, radiating her familiar air of calm. Florrie couldn't help but smile back. If Lark said she was going to love their plans, then Florrie was in no doubt that she would.

'Right then, with that said' – Stella clapped her hands together like she meant business, – 'the first hen event is this Sunday. So, soon-to-be Mrs Harte, we'll be picking you and Ed up at eleven a.m. sharp.'

'*Ed*?' Florrie asked, wondering how her fiancé was going to fit in with a hen party. 'But—'

'Don't fret, Ed's already up to speed with everything.'

This was news to Florrie, he hadn't breathed a word to her. 'But—' she tried again, only to be cut off by Jasmine this time.

'This one's our Lark's idea, and she thought it'd be good to kick off the celebrations with a joint hen and stag do. Mind, Ed's been sworn to secrecy, so no interrogating him when you get home, okay?'

'Okay,' Florrie agreed, feeling more than a little bewildered and wondering what the heck a joint do would involve. She reassured herself with the thought that if it was Lark's idea, then it wouldn't be anything completely 'out there'. Stella and Jasmine, however, she wasn't so sure. Her mind drifted, thinking it would more than likely be something to do with meditation and yoga, and copious quantities of essential oils and crystals would no doubt be included. That would be very Lark, not to mention very safe. Florrie breathed an inward sigh of relief. She quite liked the idea of having a moment or two's calm, especially with having Dawn's arrival to contend with. Maybe Lark, with all her extra-sensory perception and picking up of vibes from people had already known this? Florrie wouldn't be surprised. After all, it wouldn't be the first time her friend had got a sense of something that would happen in the future. Such feelings served her well with her business. Any item that had the slightest whiff of negative energy or gave Lark bad vibes wouldn't get across the threshold of her shop. It was positive, happy vibes only.

'And you need to wear comfy clothing, the sort of stuff that lets you move around easily,' Maggie said, chuckling at Florrie's increasingly confused expression.

'Yoga pants and a T-shirt would be ideal,' added Stella. 'And some flat shoes – no chunky boots.'

Florrie subconsciously wriggled her toes in her said chunky boots.

'Oh, and you'll need to bring something smart but casual to change into afterwards,' said Maggie.

'Right,' said Florrie, her confusion growing by the minute.

'But you'll totally love it, flower, and it'll help you forget your worries about Ed's mum for a while,' promised Lark. The look in her friend's pale green eyes told Florrie she was being sincere. It was sounding more and more like her meditation session suspicions were right – for part of it, at least. And having a few hours where she could forget about whatever it was Dawn was plotting couldn't come soon enough.

'Too right,' said Stella, raising her glass of wine. 'Cheers to us all having a great time on Sunday, lasses!' A wide grin spread across her face as the friends followed suit and a chorus of 'cheers' went up, sending a pulse of happiness through Florrie.

FOUR

SATURDAY 11TH APRIL

The air could only be described as bracing as Florrie and Ed made their way briskly along the top prom hand in hand, Gerty, their black Labrador, trotting jauntily on the end of a lead. Florrie was glad she'd wrapped up well in her thick wool duffle coat and red bobble-hat, which was doing a good job of keeping the biting wind at bay. They were taking their usual walk to work at The Happy Hartes Bookshop, one which she'd savoured ever since she was a young teenager and had first started working as the shop's Saturday girl.

They strode on, a clear blue sky above with just the odd cloud scudding by. The planters placed at intervals along the prom were brimming with brightly coloured spring flowers, the vivid yellow of the daffodils glowing golden under the sun. Florrie's gaze strayed to the view of the beach below as it always did. A small fishing boat was being thrown about by the choppy waves as it chugged its way out to sea. Further on, she spotted a gaggle of swimwear-clad women racing across the sand. The Goosebump Gals. They'd be taking their Saturday morning dip in the North Sea, Stella's mum, Alice, amongst them. 'Brr!' The mere thought made Florrie shiver. She released her hand from Ed's and linked her arm through his, hugging him close in a bid to suck up any stray warmth.

He turned to her, before following her line of sight, laughing. 'Not tempted?' he asked with a chuckle, amusement dancing in his navy-blue eyes.

'No! Never in a million years would you catch me so much as dipping my big toe in that sea at this time of year.'

'Don't blame you, though I'm surprised sport-loving Stella hasn't been tempted to join them.' He brushed his dark, floppy fringe off his face, his nose rosy from the cold.

'I'm not, our Stells might be into her running and keeping fit, but she likes her creature comforts and hurling herself into a freezing body of water with the Goosebump Gals doesn't tempt her in the least. Give her a sun-warmed ocean somewhere exotic and she'd be the first to dive in, but the sea off Micklewick Bay? Pfft! Not a chance,' Florrie said, shivering again. They watched as the women threw themselves into the sea, letting the waves wash over them, their resultant shrieks scooped up by the wind and blown across the sand. 'Oh, *blimey*. I'm even more nithered now, let's get moving.' She upped her pace, making Ed laugh some more.

It was a sound Florrie was glad to hear; he'd been quiet all morning, had seemed distracted which didn't bode well, especially with his track record. And though they were well organised, there were still a couple of things to tick off the to-do list – like pay the balance for the wedding flowers, and call in at the Jolly where they were having their wedding reception, and have a final run through the menu with Mandy. With their wedding now exactly three weeks away, the last thing Florrie needed was to try to work out what was going on behind those dreamy eyes of his.

It hadn't taken long in their relationship for her to learn that if anything was bothering Ed, he had a habit of going in on himself and clamming up. Much as she understood – and sympathised – that it was a habit he'd developed in childhood; a subconscious self-preservation mechanism to help him navigate a cold and uncaring home life and avoid attracting the negative attention of his parents (they had a lot to answer for in her book), it could still be frustrating. His lack of communication had, at times, caused problems in their relationship. Indeed, their romance had almost ended before it had got properly started because of it. It would send Florrie's mind into overdrive, and she'd come up with all sorts of explanations and scenarios as to the reason. And though it was a behaviour Ed was conscious of and was trying his hardest to change, it was so ingrained that finding out what was on his mind could still, at times, feel to Florrie like pulling teeth. For someone who preferred to talk her problems through, it was frustrating.

But, this morning, she knew his clamming up had nothing to do with what her friends had planned for their joint hen and stag celebration tomorrow. She'd quizzed him gently about that over their rushed breakfast. His face had broken out into a smile, pushing his frown away. He'd reached for her hand, telling her he was sworn to secrecy and that all he could say was that she'd love it. With that, he'd taken a last gulp of tea before nodding at the clock and saying they needed to get a wriggle on.

Which meant that there was only one thing – or rather, *person* – that had got under his skin since she'd left to meet her friends at the Jolly last night: his mother.

Florrie's stomach clenched at the thought of what Dawn Harte could have been bending her son's ear about. She wished the woman didn't trigger such hostile feelings in her; it was almost Pavlovian. She'd give anything to get on well with her future mother-in-law the way Maggie got on with hers, it would make life so much easier. But then, Chrissie Marsay was a totally different kettle of fish and thought of Maggie as a daughter. Unlike Dawn, who did nothing to hide her resentment of Florrie. It didn't help that Ed got on with Florrie's parents like a house on fire; they'd grown enormously fond of him and he them. With the young couple both being in possession of a calm and easy-going temperament, the only time Ed and Florrie bickered was when his parents got in touch, stirring up trouble. But what Florrie particularly disliked was how they treated Ed.

'So, other than quizzing me about what they've got planned for tomorrow, you didn't get the chance to tell me how your night went with the lasses. Were they all on good form as usual?' Ed asked, pulling her back into the moment.

Florrie fought against the urge to roll her eyes. The reason she 'didn't get the chance' was that Dawn was still holding court at Samphire Cottage by the time she'd arrived back home from the Jolly at almost eleven o'clock. And she was still there when Florrie had declared she was tired and heading to bed, Dawn's assertive tone rising through the floorboards, grinding away at Florrie's patience as she'd tried to get to sleep. Her bedside clock had told her it was well after midnight by the time she'd heard the front door closing, the sound of Dawn's car driving off up the road minutes after. Not wanting to end the night on a negative conversation – which Florrie knew it would invariably be – she'd pretended to be asleep when Ed had finally come to bed. But sleep had eluded her until at least two a.m. according to the clanging chimes of the bells of Saint Thomas's Church, her mind turning over how the conversation between Ed and his mum had gone, stress running on a loop around her body.

Her sleep deprivation had meant she'd turned her alarm off that morning and slipped back into the warm, comforting arms of slumber, as had Ed, making their usual leisurely breakfast a hurried affair involving only a few slurps of tea and the wolfing down of half a slice of buttered toast.

'The lasses were on excellent form, actually,' she said. 'They were having a whale of a time winding me up when I told them what I'd heard about their plans for my hen do.'

Ed threw his head back and let out a hoot of laughter. 'I can just imagine it. No doubt Jazz was the worst.'

'You're not wrong there, she can be a right wind-up merchant when she gets going.' She chuckled, remembering the impish look on her friend's face the previous evening. It was one Florrie had seen many times when they were children and Jasmine had been up to mischief. 'Mind, I have no idea why I convinced myself what

Leah was told was true, but anyroad, the lasses assured me I was way off the mark, which is a massive relief.' Florrie would usually be keen to share such an entertaining conversation, knowing how much Ed would enjoy hearing it, but this morning, she was reluctant to head down that route since she was unsure when they'd get a chance to discuss his mum's 'suggestion' – not to mention what other gems she'd hit him with last night. Florrie was eager to tackle it before they reached the bookshop and was frantically searching for the right words to bring it up without sounding like she was being critical. She was conscious that Ed would find himself in a difficult position, potentially being stuck between his fiancée and his mum.

The pounding of feet behind them made Florrie turn to see Davy Cropton on his morning run, his springer spaniel, Kev, trotting along beside him, bouncy with typical spaniel enthusiasm.

'Now then, folks,' said Davy in a familiar Yorkshire greeting, his face ruddy. 'Grand morning.'

'Hi, Davy,' Florrie replied, marvelling at his dedication; Davy was known for running come hail or shine.

'Hi, aye, it's nice and fresh,' said Ed.

Before long, they'd arrived at the wooden bench the couple had funded in memory of Ed's grandparents and Florrie's former beloved bosses, Bernard and Dinah Harte – or Mr and Mrs H, as she'd known them. It bore a brass plaque with a dedication engraved into it. Florrie and Ed had been thrilled to have it located in the very spot that looked out over the elderly couples' favourite view of Thorncliffe, the iconic, glowering bulk that dominated the seafront at Micklewick Bay. The landmark sat at the head of a precipitous line of cliffs that ran along this part of the North Yorkshire Coast. The seat was where the Hartes used to stop and take a moment on their daily trip along the prom, savouring the view which Mr H used to say looked different every day, depending upon the weather and the shadows that were cast over the clifftop and the broad expanse of sea. The elderly couple had continued their ritual when Mrs H had been forced to rely on a wheelchair to get about. They'd become a familiar sight, with Mr H pushing her along, chatting away.

It was easy for Florrie to understand why they'd loved the view so much; it was breathtaking and she adored it herself. And now she and Ed were continuing in his grandparents' tradition, taking a moment to sit on the bench every morning on their way to the bookshop, or even on Gerty's walk on the days the shop was closed. The couple agreed it was where they each felt closest to Mr and Mrs H, whom Florrie had regarded as honorary grandparents.

She slipped her backpack off and leant back into the seat, blinking as the wind rushed over the sea, making her eyes water. It didn't take long for the cold of the bench to start seeping through her trousers. She drew in a lungful of chilly air and cast her gaze along the long arc of golden sand. To the left was the newly created marina, the boats glittering in the spring sunshine. What would Mr H make of that? she wondered. He'd never been a fan of change, and the marina had certainly changed the fortunes of that once less than salubrious part of town. Her eyes travelled along the panorama, arriving at the pier, dark waves washing against its gangly metal legs, a handful of people taking a walk along the wooden planks, getting buffeted by the wind. Her gaze continued its travels along the rest of the beach, lingering on the cluster of characterful fishermen's cottages that made up Old Micklewick. They nestled together in the shadow of Thorncliffe where the town had its origins. It's where Lark's quirky home, Seashell Cottage, was tucked away amongst the ancient, cobbled streets. Occupying a prime position there was The Jolly Sailors inn, stoically facing out to sea and bearing the brunt of the inclement weather, just as it had done for the last four hundred years. It had a wealth of intrigue and skulduggery imbued in its walls, not to mention its rumoured secret tunnel to the grand home of local wealthy gentleman, Benjamin Fitzgilbert, who'd purportedly been in cahoots with Micklewick Bay's band of ruthless smugglers. The area around Old Micklewick was steeped in history, with its smuggling heritage – as the aptly named Contraband Cove around the curve of Thorncliffe was proof, along with the tales of the area's most notorious smuggler of them all: Jacob Crayke.

A building hidden beneath a network of scaffolding, with a variety of construction paraphernalia on the flagstone pavement before it, drew Florrie's gaze. It had a been a hive of activity for a good six weeks or so. 'It's great to see how quickly the work's coming on with the heritage centre,' she said, vocalising her thoughts, breaking the silence between them.

'Aye, it is.'

'Louisa told Lark it's ahead of schedule and should be finished a couple of weeks early,' Florrie added. The Micklewick Bay Heritage Centre, which was housed in the old chandlery building on the seafront, had originally been a small, uninspiring affair, but under the guidance and care of its new curator, Louisa Norton, it had been given a grant and had approval for its extension into the cottage next door, where she had plans for some exciting new exhibitions and displays, including one dedicated to Jacob Crayke.

'Louisa'll be chuffed about that, she's itching to get it up and running,' Ed said with a chuckle just as a herring gull started screeching from its perch on a nearby rooftop. 'And it's good to see her relationship with Lark's dad is still going strong. The last time I saw her with Silas, they were looking pretty loved up.'

'Yeah, Lark's so happy he's finally been able to move on from his grief for Greer. She was saying just last night how he has no regrets about moving back to Micklewick Bay, and how he's loving being a volunteer at the heritage centre.'

'He's a nice bloke; he deserves to find happiness again – Louisa, too,' Ed said softly.

'I agree, they seem well-suited.' She stole a sideways look at her fiancé, taking a moment to admire his handsome profile as he looked out to sea, her heart squeezing with love for him. Florrie knew he'd be as conscious of the fact that they'd been avoiding bringing up the subject of his mother as she was, finding anything to talk about but that. And, though she was reluctant to chase his smile away, she needed to know, needed to ask the question or it would torment her all day until Ed brought it up, which he would have to at some point, however disinclined he was. She knew he'd be mindful of upsetting or worrying her, but Florrie would rather know what she was up against. That way, she'd be able to deal with whatever it was, tackle it head on and be prepared for what Dawn was going to throw at her.

'So, how was your evening? How did things go with your mum?' She held back from asking him directly whether Dawn had touched on the subject of her accommodation, hoping he'd bring it up, but the anticipation of his response still caused her pulse to up its pace.

Just as she expected, his smile fell and he released a heavy sigh. He stretched out his long legs in front of him, his feet reaching the railings that acted as a barrier to the steep drop down to the bottom prom. He switched his attention to Gerty who was busying herself, sniffing the ground with great interest, and gave her a pat which was received with a wag of her tail. Behind them came the whirring sound of bike wheels as someone whizzed by in the cycle lane, causing Ed to turn. Florrie knew he'd be using these delay tactics to give him time to get his words in order; he'd be mindful to deliver them as softly as possible.

'Well, I'm sure I don't have to tell you, it wasn't the most relaxing Friday evening I've had.' He gave a wry laugh and rubbed his brow with his gloved fingertips. 'And, if I'm being completely honest, I actually can't ever recall having such a lengthy conversation with my mother, so that was kind of weird in itself.' He paused for a moment, as if contemplating this. 'As you know, she usually only gets in touch when she wants something – particularly so in recent years, what with the bookshop and everything... And it inevitably ends up with her ranting and shouting if I don't say what she wants to hear.' He paused again.

Knowing how long it could sometimes take for Ed to get to the point, Florrie held back from adding anything, waiting instead for him to continue when he was ready. She reached over and squeezed his hand, giving him a sympathetic smile. He turned to her, the corners of his mouth tipping up before he huffed out another big sigh. 'I felt bad, I mean, she's my mum, at the end of the day, but... I, um... I didn't know what else to say; it was so hard. I mean, the way she and my father have treated you is totally unforgivable, which makes it nigh on impossible to work out why she's got it into her head that we need her help in organising the wedding. Ugh!' He ran his hand over his face.

'Yeah, I have to agree, it is a bit puzzling.' She made sure to keep her voice neutral, though it wasn't easy, playing down how she really felt. Dawn's reason was absolutely baffling, not to mention worrying.

'We should be looking forward to getting married, not dealing with this, especially when I told her not to put herself out, that we had everything under control – which is true. I've told her we're keeping everything low-key so organisation has been more than manageable.' He brushed his hair back off his face. 'And on top of all that, I've no idea why where she's staying has suddenly become our problem.'

'No, neither do I.' Florrie had to agree. And it particularly rankled since up until fairly recently, Dawn Harte hadn't wanted to know her son and had treated him and Florrie with contempt.

Like her, Ed wasn't a fan of confrontation; they both preferred a quiet, peaceful life, rubbing along easily with everyone. Though, Florrie had to admit, she wasn't averse to standing up for what she believed to be right or if an injustice had been done, particularly if it involved supporting her family or one of her friends. But right now, she couldn't work out what Ed was trying to tell her. Had he taken the path of least resistance and told his mum what she'd wanted to hear and agreed to her staying with them? Her stomach started churning. *Please don't let Dawn have worn him down.* After all, his mother had been at Samphire Cottage for hours while Florrie was at the Jolly with her friends, which meant she'd had plenty of time to work on him. But surely, he'd run it by her first before agreeing to anything as monumental as his mum staying with them for who knew how long?

Ugh! Just thinking about it sent anxiety churning up her insides even more. And, as if that wasn't enough, Florrie had a nagging doubt Dawn's reason for coming to Micklewick Bay had nothing to do with helping them prepare for their wedding. Such an offer was so far removed from the woman she'd heard nothing good about from as far back as she could remember, not to mention her own experience of her since Ed had settled in Micklewick Bay a couple of years ago. There was no way it could be true. She'd be a fool to think so.

Florrie drew in a deep breath, secretly crossing her fingers and hoping with all her might Ed had been firm with his mother and told her she couldn't stay with them. 'So why do you think she didn't rant or shout?'

He turned, locking his eyes on hers. The look she saw there told her what she was about to hear would be the truth, though his troubled expression suggested he'd been wrestling with the question just as much as she had. 'I'm not a hundred per cent sure, to be honest. Maybe she's realised that her old ways don't work with us and arrived at the conclusion that it's time to try a different tack. Maybe it's her way of building bridges.'

'You think?' Florrie was unable to keep the incredulity from her voice. If that was the case, Dawn Harte had a gargantuan task on her hands. And she wasn't so sure Ed really thought that, either. Old habits die hard, after all; she couldn't see either of his parents going to such lengths any time soon.

'I mean, both her and my father seem to have lost a fair bit of their steam since the diagnosis of his heart condition and their move back to the UK – I'm still puzzled as to why they've been reluctant to share details about what the condition actually is, though knowing them, it shouldn't surprise me. I got the impression they'd accepted my grandfather's reasons for bequeathing the bookshop to us and not them.'

'Hmm.' Florrie couldn't argue with that. She turned her gaze back to the sea, mulling over Ed's words. His parents had definitely gone unexpectedly quiet after a sustained and relentless bombardment that included browbeating phone calls, demanding that Ed hand over the bookshop to them, telling him in no uncertain terms they were the rightful owners. At one point, they'd even enlisted the help of local unsavoury businessman, Dodgy Dick, to assist with their fight. But Florrie had just put them going quiet down to them finally getting the message that she and Ed were going to respect his grandfather's wishes and retain ownership of the bookshop.

That said, there'd always been a doubt lurking at the back of her mind that it could be resurrected at any moment. After all, they'd gone quiet before, and then all the tiresome drama had started up again when they'd got wind that Jack Playforth had signed a deal with his publishing house to write his autobiography. They'd taken exception to it, objecting in numerous aggressive tirades, saying that by giving Jack the go ahead to include mention of The Happy Hartes Bookshop in the telling of his story, it would risk exposing the Harte name to scandal.

It was only in recent years that Jack had discovered the identity of his birth mother and, even more intriguingly, that Mr and Mrs H had been involved in his secret 'adoption' by a childless couple. Teenager Jean Davenport had fallen pregnant, the father of her unborn child having washed his hands of her. As if that wasn't bad enough, her parents had threatened to disown her if she kept the baby. Devastated, Jean had confided in Dinah Harte, who, together with her husband, had stepped in and found Jack a loving home with a couple they knew who'd been desperate for a child for years.

The circumstances of Jack's 'adoption' had remained a secret until he'd traced a family connection back to Micklewick Bay. But what nobody knew was that Peter Harte had overheard his parents discussing Jack's 'adoption' one evening when he was still living at home. He'd been outraged, accusing them of taking the law into their own hands and telling them to never breathe a word of it to another living soul; he'd never be able to live with the shame if the details got out.

Knowing that Jack's impending autobiography would reveal

this long-kept secret, he and Dawn had done all they could to get Ed and Florrie to refuse Jack's request for full disclosure, saying it would cause untold damage to the Harte name. They'd finally had to accept defeat and their anger had eventually fizzled out.

Which is why Dawn's unexpected arrival had put Florrie on high alert. After all, it was more than a year since they'd last had any drama from his parents; the longest they'd gone since Ed and Florrie had taken the reins of the bookshop. It made her wonder if they were regrouping, checking the lie of the land before one final attempt at getting their hands on the bookshop. That thought sent a spike of alarm shooting through her. She wouldn't put it past them deliberately resurrecting their campaign again just before the wedding. No doubt thinking their son and Florrie would be too distracted to be aware of what was going on under their noses.

'My mum did mention something that's got me... um... well... thinking...' The cautious note in Ed's voice didn't escape Florrie. She turned to face him, her whole body tense.

'Oh?'

'Yeah, I can't remember her exact words' – Ed scratched his head – 'but having slept on it, it has made me wonder if she's come here to test the water about maybe...' He paused for what felt to Florrie like an age.

'About maybe...?' If she could've physically dragged the words out of her mild-mannered fiancé, she would.

'It's just a thought, and I'm sure I'm on the wrong path, so please try not to get stressed about it...' It sounded like he was trying to convince himself as much as Florrie. He gulped audibly and took another pause that seemed to go on even longer than the first.

Argh, Ed! Spit it out! Florrie felt ready to pop at any moment. Didn't he realise those words were guaranteed to get anyone stressed out? 'You've got me really worried now, Ed.'

'Sorry.' He winced. 'It's just, with some of the things she's been saying, it made me wonder if she and my father were toying with the idea of... of moving to Micklewick Bay.'

His words slammed into her, leaving her too stunned to speak, the implications charging around her mind. *Ed's parents, moving here? Please, no!* If this were true, then their peaceful, happy existence was over.

Their eyes met, and Florrie saw her fears reflected back in his.

FIVE

'But I thought your parents hated Micklewick Bay?' Florrie said when she finally found her voice. Her heart was thudding hard in her chest as shockwaves rippled through her.

'Yeah, that's what I thought, too. Haven't ever heard them say a good word about the place.'

After over three decades of living in sunnier climes, and eschewing everything to do with Micklewick Bay and the bookshop, Ed's parents had surprised those that knew them, giving up their nomadic lifestyle and settling in London. When asked why they hadn't opted for Micklewick Bay, Florrie had ignored the slight to her beloved hometown and felt an overwhelming sense of relief when Dawn had declared it too much of a 'behind the times little backwater where nothing of interest ever happens' and that it was a place that 'stifled their creativity' for them to entertain such a ludicrous idea.

As she absorbed Ed's words, something his mother had said about Ed's father yesterday started gnawing away in Florrie's mind. The almost dismissive tone in which it had been delivered, combined with the stony look in Dawn's eyes, was what had stood out and caught her attention. But since Dawn had steamed on in her usual overbearing way, there'd been no time for Florrie to loiter on it. So she'd brushed it aside, tucking it away for later. But now she had the chance to give Dawn's words some consideration, it only added to her confusion. If she remembered correctly, in answer to Florrie asking if Ed's father would be joining them, Dawn had snappily replied that he wasn't, and furthermore, he was going to have to get used to looking after himself whether he liked it or not.

Florrie couldn't help but feel Dawn was implying the inconceivable. Her breath caught in her throat. Had Dawn left Ed's father? If so, had she shared this news with Ed? Did Peter even know his wife was there in Micklewick Bay? Florrie glanced over at Ed, wondering if his thoughts had headed down this path, but it was impossible to tell, since so many other things could be attributed to his troubled expression.

Telling herself to calm down, that she was letting her worries get out of control, Florrie tried to steady her breathing.

'So, did she mention anything about your dad being keen to move here? Or what their plans would be? Or what had brought about such a change of opinion?' she asked, putting out tentative feelers. Not wanting to alarm Ed unnecessarily if she'd got the wrong end of the stick, she kept her voice steady and her thoughts about his parents' marriage to herself.

'Not really, no. All she said was that if the flat above the bookshop hadn't been converted into a tearoom, then her and my father would've had a ready-made home here.'

Realisation hit her in a flash. Dawn had no intention of moving to the town, which was a huge relief. She'd merely used reference to the flat's conversion, knowing full well it had been Florrie's dream to have a teashop within the bookshop. It was a thinly veiled dig, but one that she decided to ignore. Florrie refused to get drawn in to petty squabbles.

Ed was right, there was no denying Peter Harte's heart condition seemed to have taken the wind out of his parents' sails, which was hardly surprising. But assuming they were still together, it still made her wonder how they could go from having such a stormy marriage, fuelled by endless drama and high octane arguments – not just between themselves, but involving anyone who was unfortunate to get in their path – to this calmer version. Indeed, Florrie was surprised that such a stormy relationship had lasted at all. But they seemed to thrive on confrontation. They'd fought and bickered through almost four decades. It had been a case of them against the world, and that world appeared to have included their son.

Florrie assumed it was because Dawn and Peter were kindred spirits, their similar personalities and values drawing them to one another and keeping them together. Their bond had been stronger than any glue, that was for sure. Florrie's dad, Charlie, had joked on several occasions that it was because they hadn't found anyone else who'd put up with their bad behaviour and foul tempers, and Florrie had to concede, he had a point. But though she was relieved that Dawn had dialled down her hot-headed, angry nature over the last year, she couldn't help feeling wary that it could spring back to life at the click of her fingers. And she could never get her head around how they'd treated Ed. It was made more difficult because she'd come from such a warm and loving home.

Florrie regularly found herself wondering how they'd managed to produce such a mild-mannered, kind-hearted son. Though she'd quickly remind herself that he'd clearly inherited his grandfather's sunny, easy-going temperament, with a dash of schoolboy humour thrown in; she regularly saw reminders of good-natured Mr H in Ed's actions, even some of his mannerisms, and it warmed her heart. Thankfully, she hadn't witnessed the slightest trace of his parents' angry, confrontational behaviour.

Another thought struck. Did Ed mean that by talking calmly and using 'a different tack' Dawn had got what she wanted? *Ugh!* She sincerely hoped not. His parents had never made a secret of their dislike of Florrie. Nor had they hidden their resentful opinions on Mr and Mrs H's fondness for her. Their dislike had only intensified when Mr H had bequeathed the bookshop to Florrie and Ed, effectively snubbing his son. It was something the young couple had suffered for since.

'Right,' Florrie said, being careful how she responded. 'So, did she bring up her suggestion about staying with us?'

'Yep, she did.' Ed nodded. 'And I told her we didn't have room, that the spare bedroom was full of books and wedding stuff – which is true.'

'Oh!' Her head snapped round. This wasn't what she'd expected, especially since Dawn hadn't seemed annoyed when Florrie had returned home last night. That said, the chilly attitude she directed at Florrie was still in evidence, as was the cold look in her eyes that betrayed the fact she regarded her future daughter-in-law with utter disdain, which was another reason Florrie didn't want Dawn Harte living in her home.

'I could see it didn't go down well at first, but then she just nodded and said she'd look for another B&B. I have to say, her reaction was so unexpected, it's made me feel a bit wary, for want of a better word. At least if she'd started her usual yelling and shouting, I'd have known where I stood, and what was going on in her mind, but thinking about it now, her reaction is making me a bit uneasy.'

As his words sank in, wariness had started to seep through Florrie, too. She knew exactly what Ed meant.

'Well, at least you set her straight about not staying with us.'

'Aye, but then she switched her attention to the bookshop, saying what she'd do if she ran it. Rattled on about her ideas for the rest of the evening.'

Hearing this set fresh alarm bells clanging loudly in Florrie's ears. All she wanted was for her and Ed to be able to get back to being excited about their forthcoming wedding as they had been before Dawn had landed on their doorstep. She had a bad feeling about this. A very bad feeling.

SIX

Florrie was adding more books to the display of the latest novel by local romance author, Jenna Johnstone, *You Had Me at Chocolate Cake*. It had pride of place at the front of the bookshop; a stopping place for their customers before they lost themselves down the neat rows of bookshelves. The display was comprised of not only the paperbacks with their bright pink covers, but also a deep faux chocolate cake, complete with generously proportioned slices and fake crumbs scattered around, courtesy of Ed and his creative talents. The books had been flying out of the shop at such a pace that morning, it was the second time Florrie had restocked the table, not that she was complaining. She'd be sure to tell Jenna when she popped in with Jack later that morning to discuss the joint author reading they had planned for next week.

'Care to join me in the kitchen for a mug of tea and warm croissant freshly purchased from the bakery?'

Florrie looked up to see Ed heading towards her. Her eyes flicked to the clock above the counter to see it was five past eleven.

'Wow! Is that the time?' She'd wondered where he was going when he'd popped out ten minutes or so ago, but she'd been busy serving a customer. It was probably why she hadn't spotted him when he'd returned with a bakery bag in his hand.

'It is, and I thought since we barely had time to manage much breakfast, you might be feeling a bit peckish; I know I am.' He patted his stomach and flashed her the smile that was guaranteed to make her heart skip a beat. 'Thought you might need a bit of fortification before our eleven thirty meeting with Jack and Jenna. It'll no doubt spill over into your lunchbreak, so a cheeky little croissant will help stave off your hunger.'

Florrie had to admit, she was tempted. She glanced over at the counter to see Leah, the bookshop's young assistant, chatting away to a customer in her usual friendly manner, her glossy chestnut ponytail swishing as she nodded her head. Leah had opted to take a later lunch so she could meet up with her boyfriend, Marty, who was a trainee solicitor at Cuthbert, Asquith & Co across the square from the bookshop. The last rush seemed to have calmed down and Florrie was aware a couple of their regulars were currently browsing the aisles at a leisurely pace, while several customers had headed straight for the teashop upstairs. Gerty, the Labrador, was curled up in her bed by the counter, sleeping contentedly. Everything seemed to be under control. Her thoughts went to the meeting with Jack and Jenna.

'There's plenty of time to devour a croissant,' said Ed, reading her mind.

'And I can help Leah hold the fort, lovey,' said Jean, smiling fondly at Florrie and giving the younger woman's arm an affectionate squeeze. She'd been restocking shelves in the romance section nearby and was on her way to gather up more books when she'd overheard Ed. 'You might as well take advantage of this lull while it lasts; go and enjoy that croissant while it's nice and warm, especially if you didn't manage much breakfast. I'll finish the display here.'

Like all of the bookshop's staff, Jean was wearing the navy-blue Happy Hartes hoodie with its red font, teaming hers with a pair of smart dark blue slacks and dusky pink desert boots she'd just bought during a recent shopping trip with Jenna, and thought rather daring. With her neatly trimmed salt and pepper bob, rosy complexion and youthful outlook, you'd never guess she was approaching her eighties, and was regularly told she looked a decade younger which always had her beaming bashfully. And since she and her son, local author and poet, Jack Playforth, had invested in the bookshop, it seemed to have added an extra spring to her step.

Talk of food appeared to have prodded Florrie's appetite awake and her stomach growled loudly, making both her and Jean laugh. The meeting would no doubt mean she'd have to skip lunch and wolf something down later. 'After hearing that, I think I should take your advice, Jean. Mind, be sure to holler if you get a rush on.'

'Will do, petal. Now go on, off you trot, the pair of you.'

'Thank you,' said Florrie smiling. She'd caught Jean observing her and Ed that morning and suspected the older woman had sensed an air of discomfort between them and would be keen for them to put it right. Nothing much got by Jean, and she'd know it would have something to do with Ed's mother's arrival at the book-shop yesterday afternoon. And though Jean rarely said a bad word about anyone, there was one person she really didn't like, and that was Dawn Harte. Make that two – her dislike of Peter Harte was equally intense.

In the kitchen, which was tucked away at the back of the shop, Ed pulled out a chair at the small table. 'Madame,' he said, adopting a faux serious tone as, with a flourish, he gestured for Florrie to sit down. She did so, giggling as he made a performance of laying a paper napkin on her lap. His serious face broke into a smile before he took her face in his hands and delivered a warm kiss to her lips, making her heart tumble around in her chest.

'What's all this about?' she asked when he finally pulled away. She took in the neatly set arrangement, a small vase of flowers in the centre, wondering why he hadn't suggested popping up to the teashop.

She watched as he pulled out the chair opposite and sat down. 'I was conscious of things feeling a bit awkward when we were talking earlier and I wanted to grab the chance for us to have a chat, make sure you were okay. Plus, like I said before, I thought you might be feeling a bit hungry.' He reached for the teapot and set about pouring them each a mug of tea. 'I thought you'd prefer to talk somewhere a bit more private than the teashop, where there's a chance a customer could overhear our conversation.'

Since it had opened in the bookshop's converted living quarters last year, the teashop had become a great success, with both Florrie and Ed pleasantly surprised – and relieved – at how popular and well received it had been by locals. Bookshop customers were tempted upstairs by the clinking of china, not to mention the mouth-watering aroma of food that occasionally sneaked down and mingled with the smell of books. The tearoom had quickly become a place where friends regularly met before heading down to the bookshop and having a leisurely wander along the aisles of books. Florrie would go so far as to say, it had become an attraction in its own right, tempting those who declared not to be keen on books or reading. It had increased the bookshop's footfall and given sales a healthy boost on a scale neither Florrie nor Ed had expected.

'Oh, right, okay.' Florrie picked up the knife he'd set by her plate and sliced off a piece of croissant, concern prickling over her skin. Had he been speaking to his mum since they'd arrived at the bookshop? And, if so, did he have something to say that he'd rather wasn't overheard? She braced herself for what he was about to tell her.

'I just want to make sure you know that I haven't forgotten how difficult my parents have been with you, not to mention how badly they treated my grandparents; keeping their existence a secret from me for so many years is unforgivable.' His expression suddenly darkened.

Florrie put her piece of croissant back on the plate and reached across the table, resting her hand on his. Much as she wholeheartedly agreed with his assessment of his parents, she felt it best to remain quiet on that score. Instead, she pushed her mouth into an appreciative smile.

'I hope you understand that you come first to me, Florrie. In everything. Before I met you, I had no anchor, my life was meaningless. Empty. I just seemed to drift from place to place, feeling restless and unfulfilled. I was lonely, even though I hadn't realised that at the time. And then, fate intervened and brought me to Micklewick Bay, and to you.' He squeezed her hand and treated her to another one of his heart-melting smiles.

'Oh, Ed.' Florrie felt a lump form in her throat and swallowed it down. 'Mind, I'm not so sure it was fate, I reckon it was more like Mr H getting up to mischief and playing cupid; doing a spot of meddling from beyond the grave.' They both laughed at that.

'Aye, come to think of it, you do have a point. It was a crafty move on Grandad's part all right, naming us as the benefactors of the bookshop and throwing us together whether we liked it or not.' He popped a piece of croissant into his mouth and chewed, looking thoughtful.

'It so was.' Florrie smiled as an image of Mr H bloomed in her mind, a surge of love warming her heart.

Ed swallowed his mouthful. 'Anyroad, getting back to what I was saying. I want you to know that I'm not buying my mother's reason for her sudden arrival. Saying she's here to help with the wedding is so out of character it's ridiculous; she's fooling no one, especially when she's been so dead set against us getting married from the start.' He pushed another chunk of croissant into his mouth.

Florrie let his words settle. If anyone else had held such an opinion on their forthcoming nuptials, she would've been devastated, but it was par for the course with Dawn Harte, which she knew was why Ed had said it so casually, and why she hadn't taken offence. She looked on, taking in his earnest expression. Much as Florrie agreed with him, she was unsure of how to reply – if it even warranted a reply – and was glad when Ed continued.

'I want to reassure you that, though I can't stop them from coming to Micklewick Bay, I won't let her or my father interfere with our wedding plans, or our life together. I'm the happiest I've ever been, and I'm not about to let them change that. There's no way I want to lose you, Florrie. No way at all.' He leant across the small table and reached a hand around the back of her head, pulling her to him. His kiss that followed left her in no doubt he meant his words.

As he sat back in his seat, Florrie's eyes met his and she was touched by the sincerity she saw there. Her heart squeezed with love for him. She knew, despite the dysfunctional relationship he had with them, it wouldn't be easy for him to speak about his parents in this way. He had a good heart and decent values. Not for the first time did he remind her of his grandfather.

'Thank you, Ed. And will you promise that if you have any worries about anything at all, you'll come to me rather than keep them to yourself and start stewing on them? I know it's an old cliché, but a problem shared and all that.'

'I promise. I'm learning it's better to talk.' He flashed a lopsided grin as he took her hand.

Relief swept through her, her smile matching his. 'It's definitely better to talk; work through our problems together, especially if they're caused by other people.'

'I can see that now. I'm sorry it's taken me a while to grasp that fact. Having spent so long keeping my worries to myself, it's been a hard habit to break.'

'I get that.'

Growing up with cold and distant parents meant Ed had learnt to be emotionally self-sufficient. His childhood had been the polar opposite of Florrie's which had been loving and warm. Both were only children, and where Ed was treated as something of an inconvenience by his parents, Florrie had been the apple of her parents' eye. It broke Florrie's heart to think about how Ed had grown up, especially when he was such a warm, loving person.

'I want us to just focus on looking forward to our wedding.' He lifted her hand to his lips, kissing it softly. 'I love you, Florrie, and I'm not going to let anything get in the way of us getting married, or our enjoyment of preparing for it.'

'And I love you, too, Ed.' A smile crept over her face, her eyes looking onto his pools of navy blue. She pushed herself up and leant across the table. This time it was her turn to press her lips against Ed's, delighting in their soft warmth. He reached up and cupped her face in his hand, their kiss deepening, releasing a host of butterflies in her stomach. *Oh my days!*

'Ey up, I was under the impression there was a meeting going on in here,' came a familiar gravelly voice, making them jump apart.

'What the flippin'—?' Ed exclaimed, knocking his chair over with a clatter.

'Jack! It's good to see you.' With her face burning, Florrie went to gather the plates together, doing all she could to sound casual, and acting as if nothing was out of the ordinary. Though it was impossible to ignore the tingle in her lips left by Ed's meaningful kisses.

'Aye, but I'm not so sure your young fella would agree.' The author laughed, nodding in Ed's direction.

'Hey, it's always good to see you, Jack. Mind, I won't argue, your timing could've been a little, shall we say, better?' Ed grinned, having composed himself, setting his chair straight while Jack continued to chuckle.

'Ey, lad, there's nowt up with my timing.' He pushed the sleeve of his jacket back and looked at his watch. 'Ah, apologies, you're absolutely right, it's twenty past eleven; I'm a smidge early. Would you like me to come back in ten minutes, so you can carry on with your "break"?' He put finger quotes around the word, his eyes twinkling teasingly. 'Jen's in the shop, chatting weddings to my mother, so I could always go and join them.'

Now he'd mentioned it, Florrie could hear snatches of his

fiancée's melodic Geordie accent floating through from the book-shop as she chatted away enthusiastically.

Ed shook his head, laughing. 'No, you're fine to stay, Jack. The moment's gone.'

'Sorry about that,' said Jack, the mischief in his eyes at odds with his apologetic expression. 'Just call me Passion-Killer Play-forth; wouldn't be the first time.'

Ed chuckled while Florrie directed her gaze anywhere but Jack's way, the heat in her cheeks showing no evidence it was going to calm down any time soon. Reserved by nature, Florrie wasn't one for public displays of affection, even if they were inadvertent.

'Don't suppose there's any tea going spare in that pot, is there, lass?' Jack asked in his broad North Yorkshire accent. He was evidently keen to move the conversation on and help disperse Florrie's embarrassment. 'We've had a right busy morning – I'll leave it to Jenna to tell you all about it – but it's left me gagging for a cup of tea.'

''Course, there's plenty.' Florrie smiled, her embarrassment ebbing away. 'I'll pour a mug for Jenna, too. We can take our drinks through to the reading room, have our chat there.'

'Grand, I'd be grateful if you'd chuck in a biscuit or two, an' all. All this wedding talk hasn't 'alf got me famished as well as parched,' Jack added with a grin.

Jack's down-to-earth personality belied the fact he was a nationally revered author whose books had hit the *Sunday Times* bestsellers list several times over – his fiancée, Jenna's, too. She had a loyal following of readers, not to mention a book that had been optioned for a successful television series, with talks of yet more in the pipeline. Since the couple had moved to the town, they held regular author readings and book signings at the bookshop. The events were always a huge draw, not least because of their matching self-deprecating sense of humour that spilled over into copious giggles, much to the audience's delight. Indeed, Jack had announced their engagement at one such reading last year, when his comical description of him getting down on one knee had the audience crying tears of laughter.

Florrie followed Ed and Jack into the shop, relieved that the air between her and her fiancé was so much lighter after their chat. Jean caught Florrie's eye and the knowing smile that passed between them confirmed Florrie's suspicions: Jean had clearly had a subtle word with Ed about his mother's motives for turning up so out of the blue. She understood that Ed might not have realised that Florrie would need some reassurance. Florrie gave a smile and a quick lift of her eyebrows in acknowledgement.

It was fair to say Jean wasn't Dawn and Peter Harte's biggest fan, and not just because of how they'd treated Mr and Mrs H, blocking all contact for decades. She'd also witnessed the negative effect they'd had on Florrie and Ed's relationship, and she seemed determined not to allow it to happen again.

'Florrie, pet, it's good to see you,' Jenna said in her singsong voice, her softly highlighted hair framing her friendly face that was wreathed in smiles. In her mid-forties, she was over ten years younger than Jack. 'I can't wait to tell you our news.' She rushed over to Florrie and pulled her into a hug, delivering a noisy kiss to her cheek.

Her enthusiasm was infectious and Florrie couldn't help but smile back. 'Hiya, Jenna. Don't tell me, you and Jack have set a date for your wedding?' Florrie knew Jenna had been desperate to get a date fixed, and, unlike Florrie, the author was keen for a big, all-singing, all-dancing, elaborate do.

'Aye, that we have. I've just been telling Jean here our big day's been booked at Danskelfe Castle for the twelfth of June next year – I know it seems a long way off, but that was the first date they had free for the bigger wedding package. The venue's gorgeous, which is why it's massively in demand, but we really wanted to have our wedding there, so we're happy to wait. And, of course, we'll have one of Jazz's gorgeous wedding cakes. We've booked a follow-up appointment at the castle to discuss things in greater detail, like catering, flowers, décor of the dining room, music and so forth. I'm *so* excited!' Jenna said, rubbing her hands together enthusiastically, her exuberance bubbling over.

'Can't say we'd noticed,' Jack said dryly, though the happiness that danced across his face told them he was as thrilled as Jenna.

'Well, I'm chuffed to bits for both of you, I've heard how amazing they are,' Florrie said. And much as she genuinely meant it, hearing all that was involved in organising a wedding on such a big scale only served to make her glad she and Ed had been in full agreement that a low-key ceremony was more their style. Jenna's high-spirited personality, not to mention her huge family with endless cousins, and wide circle of friends, was far better suited to something more elaborate.

'Me too,' said Ed. 'And at least it'll give you plenty of time to find a suitable hat, Jean.' He grinned at her, making her chuckle.

'Eee, we could go shopping together, Jean. I know this totally fab shop in Newcastle that sells the most *amazing* headwear. We could stay over, make a real treat of it,' Jenna enthused. 'And I've noted you're wearing your new desert boots we bought on our last shopping trip – they look awesome on you, pet!'

'Thank you, lovey.' Jean beamed. 'I have to say, they're very comfy.'

'Bet you wish you'd bought the apple-green pair as well now, don't you? But no worries, we can pop back to the shop the next time you and me have a girls' weekend in the Toon. In fact, let's get one in the diary after Jack and me have finished our meeting.'

Jack hooted with laughter at his fiancée's enthusiasm. 'By 'eck, you don't hang around, do you, lass?'

'Not a blinkin' chance.' Jenna treated him to one of her warm smiles.

To say Jenna could be something of a whirlwind when she was excited would be an understatement. Florrie didn't know about Jean, but she sometimes felt like she needed a moment to catch her breath when Jenna was on a roll like this.

They were distracted as the bell above the bookshop door jangled cheerily and a dapper-looking gentleman stepped in. He was wearing a well-tailored tweed coat and neatly pressed trousers, a pair of highly polished brown shoes on his feet. The well-groomed look was topped off by a trilby hat set at a jaunty angle.

'Good morning,' the gentleman said, casting a warm smile around the group, his kind blue eyes shining.

'Good morning, Amery,' said Jean, her face lighting up with a smile. Her hand fluttered to her hair while the apples of her cheeks were suddenly tinted with a blush.

'Morning, Mr Wallace,' said Florrie, aware of the others observing with interest as Jean and Amery continued to beam at one another. She was clearly not the only one who could sense the sparks that had started dancing between them.

'Ey up, what's this, then?' Jack said, sotto voce. Florrie slid him a sideways look and a knowing smile.

A chorus of hellos, tinged with more than a hint of curiosity, followed as Jean made her way over to the counter. 'I'm afraid the book you ordered hasn't come in yet – we're expecting it tomorrow – but one came to mind yesterday that I thought you might like. I took the liberty of setting a copy aside for you. I hope you don't mind, but they've been selling rather quickly? R.J. Kingston's a newly published author but he's already gaining quite a fanbase. *Dark Night*'s been generating a lot of interest here and going from the sort of books you like, I think you'll enjoy this.'

'That's very kind of you, Jean, I'm always keen to find new authors.' Amery came to a stop before the counter where Jean now stood, tipping a friendly nod at Leah who, judging from her smiles, was enjoying this interaction as much as Florrie. 'Good morning, Leah,' he said, removing his trilby and revealing a headful of snowy-white hair that was neatly barbered and swept back off a strong forehead.

'Hi, Mr Wallace.'

Gerty heaved herself out of her bed and waddled over to him, sniffing his trousers. 'Hello there, Gerty.' He bent and gave her a pat and was rewarded with a wag of her tail. Satisfied that he had no dog treats lurking in his pockets, the Labrador lost interest and headed back to her bed where she flopped down with a 'Hmph', resting her head on her paws.

Amery turned his attention back to Jean. 'I finished Eleanor Farthing's book last night and I really must commend you on your recommendation; it was excellent, so cleverly executed – a real page turner.'

'I thought you'd like it.' Jean beamed, clasping her hands together and looking delighted with this news. 'Her books have been a favourite of mine for years, and I was thrilled when I heard they were to be republished. I devoured them all over again; they've definitely stood the test of time.'

'Couldn't agree more, I can see why the author has such a loyal readership.'

'Oh, that she most certainly has,' Jean agreed readily.

'Book talk aside, how are you this fine day, Jean? I must say, you're looking very well.' Florrie noted that, though he spoke with a North Yorkshire accent, it had a slight polish to it. A hint of his cologne wafted her way, a clean, traditional fragrance that smelled expensive. It put her in mind of the Penhaligon's cologne that Mr H used to wear when he and Mrs H had what he called 'date night'. It was something they continued until Mrs H passed away. Florrie regularly found herself hoping that she and Ed would enjoy the same sort of loving relationship into their old age as his grandparents had. Such thoughts had often found their way to thinking it was a shame that Jean, who'd never married, wouldn't get to experience such love and affection. But maybe that was about to change...

'Oh, thank you, Amery, so kind of you to say. I'm very well, thank you. And how about you? Have you had the opportunity to take a walk in the sunshine yet today?'

This was a side to Jean Florrie had never witnessed before; she was positively sparkling and it warmed her heart to see it. From the happy look Leah shot her, she was clearly thinking the same.

'Ah, well, books aren't my only reason for popping in today. I was wondering if you'd be free to join me for a stroll along the top prom at some point this afternoon? It's a beautiful spring day, with buds appearing on the trees, a hint of blossom on the ornamental cherries. It would be a shame to waste it.'

'Oh, well, how lovely. I'd very much like that.' Jean giggled like a lovestruck teenager, her hand going to her hair again. 'As a matter of fact, I finish here at one thirty, and, since I'm not building bears with Maggie this afternoon, I'll be free after that time. Would that fit in with your plans?'

'It fits in with them perfectly.' Amery was all smiles. 'Shall I meet you here at that time, or is there anywhere else you'd prefer?'

'Here would be wonderful.'

'Excellent. And I thought, if you're free, that is, we might be able to get a bite to eat at The Jolly Sailors. It's years since I was last in there, and I've been hearing amazing things about the food. And I'd love to hear more about this bear building you do.'

'Ah, that's for Florrie's friend, Maggie Marsay, she lives at Clifftop Cottage on Thorncliffe. She has the Micklewick Bay Bear Company and makes the most adorable teddy bears – interestingly, her husband's called Bear, well, it's his nickname. Anyway, ever since Maggie became a mum I've helped out so she could keep up with her orders; her bears are very popular and she has an exclusive range for Campion's of York. Remember them?'

'How wonderful! And, yes, I do remember them,' Amery exclaimed. 'I think I might like to get one of these bears for my little great-granddaughter; she just turned two last month.'

'They make adorable keepsakes; it's why a lot of Maggie's customers buy them.'

Conscious that everyone was looking on with interest – though Jean and Amery seemed so engrossed in their conversation, she couldn't help but wonder if they were oblivious – Florrie said, 'Right then, I reckon it's time we got on with our meeting. We'll just be in the reading room if you need us.' She looked between Leah and Jean before turning on her heel. 'Come on, folks.'

'Okay,' said Leah.

'Right-oh, lovey,' said Jean, reluctantly pulling her attention away from Amery.

'Spoilsport!' Jack chuntered as they made their way to the reading room, making Florrie chuckle. 'There's a fella out there hitting on my mother; it's only fair – and right – that I take the opportunity to give this Amery Wallace – fancy name, mind – the once-over before I give him my seal of approval to take my mother out without a chaperone. A stroll along the prom followed by some nosh at the Jolly? He sounds like a fast mover to me. Next thing we know, he'll be asking for her hand in marriage.' Though his tone and expression were serious, the sparkle in his eyes told them he was joking.

Ed let out a bark of laughter. 'Chaperone? Remind us, exactly which century are you from, Jack?'

'Hey, lad, you can't be too sure these days. Due diligence and all that.' Jack's dour resting face broke into a wide smile.

'Aww, bless her, your mam was absolutely glowing, Jack. I've never seen her look so happy.'

'I agree,' said Florrie.

'Aye, joking aside, it's grand to see her smiling like that. I know she's got an active social life, and keeps herself busy, but I do worry about her being lonely in the evenings. It's time she let a bit of romance into her life. It's never sat right with me that she kept relationships at arm's length after my biological father did a runner.'

'From what she's told us, I think her parents had quite a hand in that, Jack. They were very controlling,' said Florrie.

Jack heaved a sigh. 'Aye, you're right there, lass.' He looked thoughtful for a moment. 'Anyroad, what do you know about this Amery Wallace fella? Owt or nowt?'

'All we know is that he turned up in the shop a couple of weeks ago, asking if we stocked Samuel K. Bradley's books. He and Jean recognised each other and got chatting, heading down memory lane.' Florrie decided to keep to herself that she'd thought the usually reserved Jean had initially seemed uncharacteristically cheered by his arrival.

'And he kept popping in every couple of days, working his charm on your mum.' Ed grinned. 'I have to admit, he seems very nice; the perfect gentleman, and he's always so courteous, particularly so to Jean.'

'I haven't sensed anything dodgy about him, if that's what you're worried about,' Florrie added, spotting the flicker of concern that momentarily troubled Jack's dark eyes. 'From what he's told Jean, and what she's shared with us, he's originally from Micklewick Bay – was born here – but moved out of the area in the late sixties, early seventies. Apparently, his wife was from somewhere near Chester and wanted to move closer to her family, which is what they did.'

'Adding to what Florrie's just told you, Amery's a widower. His wife passed away last year, and he moved back here about a month ago.'

'So, there you have it, Jack.' Florrie smiled at him, hoping they'd helped to ease any concerns he may have. Though Jack had only found Jean a couple of years ago, after his adoptive parents had died, they'd quickly developed a strong bond, and she knew he was very protective of her.

'Well, for what it's worth, I think he seems a canny bloke and it's pretty obvious he's as smitten with your mam as she is with him,' chipped in Jenna. 'Good luck to them, I say. We all need a bit of romance in our life.'

'Hear, hear,' said Jack, throwing his arm around her shoulder.

'Now we've got all that out of the way, do you think we should make a start on the reason you and Jack are here?' asked Ed.

'Aye, good point, lad.' Jack chuckled. 'I hereby declare this meeting officially open.'

EIGHT

SUNDAY 12TH APRIL

'Right then, folks, climb aboard.' Maggie grabbed the handle of the Land Rover's heavy rear door, pulling it wide open. Bear had parked up in a space opposite Samphire Cottage while his wife had nipped across the road to let Florrie and Ed know they'd arrived.

'Thanks, Mags.' Florrie climbed in to see Lark and Nate sitting side by side on one of the benches that acted as rear seating and was rather basic by all accounts. The couple were wearing wide smiles. 'Hi, folks,' she said as she slid along the bench opposite, tucking her backpack containing her change of clothes between her feet. Ed followed suit.

'Hi, both,' said Lark.

'Now then,' said Nate, offering a Yorkshire greeting.

'All right?' Bear called from the driver's seat. 'Are you both belted up?'

'Yep, we're good to go,' said Ed, clicking his seatbelt in the dock. With that, Bear put the vehicle into gear and pulled out onto the road, setting Florrie's heart pumping with anticipation.

'So, Mags, are you going to tell me what you lot have got planned for today? My mind's been in overdrive, wondering what we're going to be doing since I first opened my eyes.' Florrie held back from saying how it wasn't the only thing that had occupied her thoughts. Dawn Harte had taken up a huge chunk of them. Since Ed's mum had driven off on Friday night, they hadn't heard a peep from her, which had been worrying. Florrie couldn't help but think the woman would be plotting and scheming somewhere in Micklewick Bay. Ed had offered a modicum of relief when Florrie had asked if he knew why they hadn't heard from her.

'Much as she was never bothered about our home being a tip when I was growing up, she was always very picky about hotel rooms or anywhere else she and my dad stayed. She'll be that busy going round town, inspecting all the B&Bs, she won't have had time for anything else,' he'd said.

Though Florrie hadn't been totally convinced, especially since he hadn't had so much as a text from his mother. Whenever she'd thought about it, it had made her feel unnerved, and she couldn't help but think Dawn would be plotting something to punish her son for telling her she couldn't stay at Samphire Cottage. From the stories Ed had told her, she knew that was just her style. Which was why Florrie had told herself that as soon as she found her thoughts creeping back to Dawn, she needed to push them away. Her friends had clearly gone to a lot of trouble to plan a day celebrating hers and Ed's upcoming wedding, and she wasn't going to spoil it, or take the edge off it or let them see her thoughts were occupied by something else and that she wasn't putting her all into whatever it was they had planned.

'Ahh, you'll find out our plans soon enough,' Maggie said in a jokey mysterious voice, making them all laugh and sending thoughts of Dawn trickling away.

'But like I said on Friday, flower, you'll love it.' Lark reached over and touched Florrie's arm. 'Oh, and while I remember, I've got something for you.' She reached into her patchwork tote bag and lifted out a small silk purse, handing it to her.

Florrie opened it to see a bracelet made of round, glossy crystal beads in dusky pink and pale purple. 'Oh, it's so pretty! Thank you, Lark.' She slid it onto her wrist, the beads cool against her skin. She was glad Ed was distracted as he listened to Nate who was updating him and Bear on the latest piece of furniture he was working on at his upcycling business on Endeavour Road. He'd know why Lark had given her such a gift and she wouldn't want him to feel uncomfortable.

'It's made of rose quartz and amethyst – two of my fave crystals, as you know; they help with stress levels. Thought you could do with them. And here's a lavender and chamomile pulse point for you to use whenever you need it.' She smiled, the look in her eyes was telling. Lark was a great believer in the healing power of crystals and aromatherapy and sold an extensive range in Lark's Vintage Bazaar. She regularly bestowed gifts on her friends when they were in times of need. Even ever sceptical Jasmine now swore by their benefits after she'd put them to use during a particularly tumultuous time last year. The bracelet would be to offer Florrie support and protection during Dawn's visit. And, boy, did Florrie get the feeling she was going to need it.

'You need to make yourself comfy, Florrie – well, as comfy as you can on the rock-hard bench seats of a Landie – we're in for a bit of a drive,' Maggie piped up from the front.

'Oh? Don't suppose there's a chance you can tell me where we're heading?'

'Nope. 'Fraid not.' Maggie turned and grinned. 'All I'll say is that the others are meeting us there.'

'Helpful.' Florrie caught Ed's eye and giggled. He gave her a wink and an affectionate nudge of the shoulder. 'S'alright for you, you're in on where we're going, which doesn't seem fair somehow,' she said good-naturedly.

Forty-five minutes later, Bear followed the route through the tasteful Georgian market town of Middleton-le-Moors, continuing along the winding road, the scenery becoming more rural and undulating as they drew closer to the turn-off for the North York-shire Moors. Light-hearted conversation filled the Landie, bubbling away and interspersed with copious amounts of laughter as old memories were relived. They landed on how the friends had teased Florrie mercilessly about their plans for the hen party while they were at the Jolly on Friday night.

'Ah, fellas, I wish you could've been there. Florrie's face was a right picture when Stells mentioned Ando and Lobster Harry joining forces as a strippagram,' Maggie had said, causing them all to fall about laughing.

'I heard you'd said something about Ando incorporating his pickled eggs into the routine,' Bear had added, his shoulders shaking with laughter.

'Oh, man, please stop before the terrifying mental image that's forced its way into my mind is permanently scorched there,' Nate had said, shaking his head.

'Aye, it'd be the talk of the town for a fair bit of time afterwards, that's for sure,' Bear had chuckled, the Landie rumbling on.

They'd been laughing so hard, Florrie's cheeks were still aching when Bear slowed the Land Rover in readiness to take a corner. She peered through the gap in the window between Lark and Nate, her brow crumpling in puzzlement as she noted the signpost for the villages of Danskelfe, Lytell Stangdale and Arkleby. The last time she'd been in this neck of the woods, she'd been taking Jasmine to Danskelfe Castle for her appointment with Lady Carolyn Hammondely to discuss the possibility of Jazz becoming their permanent wedding-cake maker. It had been the start of a much-welcome change in her friend's fortunes. Jazz had gone from baking celebration cakes as a side hustle to her two part-time jobs working in the local bakery as well as working shifts for the cleaning company owned by Stella's mum, Alice, to being a full-time wedding-cake maker. It was a role she loved, and she hadn't had a moment's regret.

Clocking Florrie's confused expression, Lark gave a gentle smile. 'We'll be there soon.'

'Still can't tell you though,' added Maggie as the Land Rover rattled noisily over a cattle grid.

'I have to say I'm intrigued as to why you'd be bringing Ed and me out here for a joint hen and stag party celebration, and I've honestly no idea what it could be,' Florrie said, catching snatches of the stunning scenery as they drove by. Vast swathes of moorland merged with the patchwork fields of farmland, edged with drystone walls and hawthorn hedges and punctuated by cosy looking farmsteads. Bear braked to allow a huddle of free-roaming sheep to amble their way across the road as if they had all the time in the world.

'Hurry up, ladies, we have somewhere we need to be,' said Bear, as one of the ewes stopped in the middle of the road, masticating slowly as it stared him out.

Maggie turned from her place in the front passenger seat, a look on her face that said mischief. Florrie had seen it many times before. 'All I'll say about us bringing you out here is that I hope you like pigs.'

'Pigs?' asked Florrie, incredulous. 'Why pigs?' She flicked a questioning look Ed's way, hoping to read his expression, but he was just laughing, as was Lark.

'Pigs are fabulous,' said Bear, a deep chuckle rumbling up through his chest.

'Being the son of a farmer, you're bound to think that,' said Florrie dryly.

'Fair point,' Bear conceded.

'I suppose we're nearly there so I might as well tell you,' said Maggie. 'We're going – brace yourself – pig herding! Ta-da!' She made jazz hands, a wide smile on her face.

'What?' Florrie asked, glancing around at everyone, wondering if she'd heard right.

Bear gave a couple of oinks, making everyone but Florrie laugh some more – her brain was too busy scrabbling about and trying to work out what pig herding would involve. It sounded messy and chaotic, and she was overwhelmed by the sinking feeling that it was something she wouldn't enjoy. Surely, it was another wind up? But, then again, they were driving through the countryside where there would no doubt be pig farms aplenty, so it did lend an element of truth to Maggie's words.

And if they really were supposed to be herding pigs, how big would the said pigs be exactly? She bit down on a sigh as some vague memory of a countryside television programme she used to watch with Mr H told her they could be quite large creatures, not to mention occasionally bad-tempered. *Oh, please no.* One thing was for sure, she didn't fancy getting on the wrong side of an angry pig that was bigger than her!

But she could hardly tell her friends she'd stand and watch while they got busy herding pigs when they'd organised the event specially for her and Ed. And, come to think of it, which one of her friends had come up with such an 'out there' idea? Jasmine and Maggie popped into her mind. It would be one of them, if not both. She could see how pig herding would appeal to their, at times, riotous sense of fun, particularly so Jasmine.

'I had no idea pig herding was even a thing.' She tried to inject a note of cheerfulness into her voice, not wanting to sound like a killjoy or that she was ungrateful for their efforts.

'Well, let me reassure you it really is a thing, isn't it, Bear?' Maggie turned to face her husband.

Florrie wasn't so sure 'reassure' was the word she'd use.

'Oh, aye, it is.' He nodded. 'It's another way for farmers to diversify. And, let me add for Larkie here's benefit, the pigs are very well looked after. In fact, I'd say they're as happy as pigs in sh —' Bear was stopped from finishing his sentence by a brace of pheasants that had darted out from the roadside, their colourful plumage glowing in the sun. 'Ey up, bloomin' wildlife out here could do with a bit of road sense.'

'And, from what I've heard, pig herding's a right laugh.' Maggie picked up where her husband had left off. 'Granted, it's a bit messy and smelly, but I believe the farm provides overalls. I thought we'd all get ourselves into the spirit and let our hair down, make sure we enjoy it.'

Thought we'd all get into the spirit? Enjoy it? Did her friends even know her at all? Just as Florrie was trying to work out what their immaculately groomed friend with never a hair out of place Stella would make of chasing a load of pigs around a pen, realisation struck like a lightbulb pinging on. 'Maggie Marsay, you're a terrible fibber! I know we're not going pig herding. There's no way in a million years you'd get Stella within a mile of a pig, never mind herding a whole load of them,' she said through her giggles. 'Nor Lark, for that matter. Lark always smells of aromatherapy oils – there's not a chance she'd want to swap that for pig muck!'

Roars of laughter filled the Land Rover, with Florrie and Lark bent double.

'That's a very good point,' said Lark, catching her breath for a moment.

'Ah, well, I clearly hadn't thought that one through, but it wouldn't half be a right laugh watching Stells tiptoeing around clarty mud and pig muck in her designer high heels while tackling a load of snorty pigs. Can you imagine the look on her face, especially if she slipped over?' Maggie was laughing so hard, tears were pouring down her cheeks, which only made the rest of them laugh all the more.

Florrie could see Stella's face clearly in her mind, the unimpressed look she'd wear. It made her laugh even harder.

'Oh blimey, we'll have to share this with her when we see her, she'll think it's hilarious.' Lark wiped tears of mirth from her eyes.

'Please stop now, if I laugh any more, I'm going to be in serious danger of cracking a rib,' spluttered Florrie.

'I'm not so sure how long my bladder can hold out. It's not what it used to be since I had Lucy,' added Maggie.

Bear shot her a concerned look. 'Let me know if you need me to stop. I've just hosed the Landie down. I don't need you piddlin' in your seat and undoing all my hard work.'

That set them all off howling with laughter again.

. . .

'Right then, folks, here we are,' Bear announced as the Land Rover nosed its way between two sturdy sandstone gateposts and into a large parking area. 'There's Alex's car over there, he's brought Stella, Max, and Jazz.'

'Where are we?' asked Florrie, scrunching her nose up and leaning forward to peer through the wide windscreen. They'd been so busy laughing and chatting she'd been totally oblivious to where they'd driven.

'Danskelfe Business Centre,' said Lark, as they jumped out of the back of the Land Rover. 'Though it looks a bit genteel to be described as a "business centre", if you ask me.' She was looking colourful in her stripy, loose-fitting harem pants she'd teamed with a lilac-coloured hoodie. She had a couple of skinny plaits either side of her face which were pulled back with the rest of her hair and tied in a long plait. Around her neck was an amethyst pendant Nate had given her.

Florrie's eyes swept around the well-appointed Georgian buildings of buttery sandstone, with their freshly painted wooden sash windows and doors, and lead planters brimming with spring flowers. She had to agree; it looked nothing like any business centre she'd ever seen. Amongst the hand-painted business signs she spotted a beautician's, a dance studio and a veterinary surgery. It sparked a memory of something Lady Caro Hammondely had said at Jasmine's meeting: she'd mentioned that as part of her plans to make the Danskelfe Estate more profitable, as well as helping to support the local rural economy, they'd been gradually converting the old unused buildings into affordable rental premises for local businesspeople. This was obviously such a place.

'Pretty nice spot to have your office, eh?' said Ed, squinting in the bright sunshine.

'Just a bit,' agreed Florrie, not that she would change where she worked; she'd always said the bookshop was her happy place and she couldn't imagine working anywhere else.

She was pulled from her thoughts by the sound of car tyres crunching over gravel. She looked over to see Jack at the wheel of his small four-wheel drive, Jenna beside him, wearing her familiar big smile and waving enthusiastically, with Jean in the back.

Jenna practically leapt out of the car once Jack had pulled up beside the Land Rover. She rushed over to Florrie and enveloped her in a hug. 'Happy hen party, pet. I bet you've been dead excited about what was planned.'

'Excited's a word.' Florrie shot Maggie and Lark a knowing look as Stella and Jasmine joined them.

'Oh?' Jenna asked, glancing at Maggie.

Once they'd exchanged hellos with Jasmine and Stella – the men had grouped together, looking at something Bear was pointing out on his beloved Landie – Florrie shared how Maggie had teased her about pig herding. Stella threw her head back and let out an amused cackle on hearing their description of her attempts at herding pigs. Like the others in the friendship group, Stella didn't take herself too seriously. 'Not gonna happen,' she said, shaking her head and smiling. 'They'll be selling ice creams in hell before you get me anywhere near a pig.'

After a round of excitable hellos, the group congregated near Alex's car, chatting away, an air of excitement in the air around them.

'Is anyone else coming?' asked Florrie, who was still none the wiser about what they had planned.

'We're just waiting for your mum and dad, and Leah and Marty, who are bringing Hayley and Josh,' said Stella, glancing at her watch. She even managed to look well-groomed in her yoga gear, her long legs clad in smoke blue yoga pants, a matching fitted jacket showing off her slim waist to its best advantage, while her long blonde hair was scraped back into a high ponytail. At five feet ten, she towered over Florrie's petite five feet two.

'Hayley's coming, too?' Florrie was pleasantly surprised by this news. Hayley had worked at the bookshop part-time before heading to university. Like Florrie, she'd been a Happy Hartes weekend girl. Florrie had been chuffed that the younger woman had kept in touch and still popped in for a catch-up when she was back from university.

'I'm sure they won't be long, we've got another fifteen minutes before the session's due to start.' She waggled her eyebrows.

'The session?' Florrie asked.

'Yup, "the session",' said Stella, 'and it has absolutely nothing to do with pigs, or the herding of them.' She pulled a relieved face. 'Still can't believe you actually fell for that.'

'I'm just too gullible for my own good.' Though Florrie smiled, she was beginning to feel distracted, wondering where her parents were – it wasn't like them to be late, they were usually the first to arrive for anything. It was a running joke with Florrie and her mum that her dad had 'punctuality-itis' as they'd coined it, teasing him that there was a cream for it, which he took in good spirits. But as far back as Florrie could remember, he'd been insistent they set off ridiculously early for everything, whether it be for appointments, trains or airports.

Florrie nibbled on a hangnail, telling herself her parents weren't late exactly, just late for them. She considered the idea they could've got lost en route. It was a distinct possibility since her dad abhorred the idea of a satnav and refused to entertain it. 'There's nowt wrong with a good old-fashioned road map. They've stood me in good stead for years,' was a regular cry of his. And besides, Florrie told herself, there were plenty of twisty-turny roads and tracks on the moors which made it easy to take a wrong turn, as Bear had done at one point on their way here, and they'd found themselves having to turn around in a farmyard.

She was toying with the idea of calling her mum – provided they had phone signal around here, of course – when she felt her mobile vibrate from the depths of her backpack. She slid it off her shoulder and fished around inside for it. Tapping on the screen, she saw her mum's name. Relief filled her chest. Her mum was probably texting to let them know they'd be with them soon, mindful they were running behind.

Florrie read the brief message, a prickle of unease creeping over her.

> Hi Florrie, didn't want to text before the lasses had a chance to tell you what they had planned for you. Am assuming you know by now. Unfortunately, your dad's feeling a bit off colour so we thought we'd better give your celebration a miss – don't want to pass around whatever it is he's got. We both send our love & hope you all have a wonderful time xxx

'Everything all right?' asked Lark, who was standing beside her and picked up on her friend's troubled expression.

'I think so... well... I've just had a text from my mum saying my dad's feeling under the weather so they won't be able to make it, which is a shame.' Florrie had thought he'd looked a bit peaky when she'd called in to see him last week.

'Oh, flower, that is a shame. I know they were looking forward to it.' Lark rubbed her hand up and down Florrie's arm, her bracelets jangling. 'He's probably picked up the stomach bug that's been doing the rounds. I know a lot of people have complained about having it. I'm sure he'll be right as rain soon.' She gave a kind smile.

'Hmm.' Florrie hoped that was all it was. Her dad was hardly ever ill and regularly described himself as being as strong as an ox. It was usually her mum she worried about, especially since she'd been so dangerously poorly with Stage 1B Hodgkin lymphoma when Florrie was in her last year at university. Florrie's big fear was that it would return one day, though she tried to remind herself that her mum took great care with her health since her brush with death. She ate well, exercised and took a great variety of supplements that Charlie joked would put her in danger of rattling if she took any more.

Florrie's mind went to the lift arrangements for that morning. It had puzzled her at the time, though she hadn't had much of an opportunity to dwell on it with all the hilarity on the way here. She wondered when they'd been arranged. She'd been surprised that she and Ed hadn't been put with her parents. That would've made more sense, and would've left Jenna, Jack and Jean to get a lift with Maggie and Bear along with Lark and Nate. The Landie boasted three spaces in the front and Jean could've sat in the comfier seat next to Mags rather than the smaller one in the middle where the gearstick was located. It would've meant taking one less car. Florrie guessed the travel arrangements would've been made in advance, which made her wonder if her parents had prior concerns about joining them before this morning, especially with her dad looking a little under the weather.

All of this was adding together and sending her mind running around in circles, but she was mindful of her friends looking at her expectantly.

Telling herself to stop overthinking, Florrie shared her mum's message with the rest of the group, which was met with disappointment. 'Won't be the same without your dad's jokes,' Max said, with everyone agreeing, asking her to send their good wishes and a speedy recovery for Charlie.

A few moments later Leah and Hayley arrived with Marty and Josh, the girls bubbling with youthful excitement. Stella called for everyone's attention, declaring it was time to make a move. 'Right, now we're all here, I can say, Florrie, it's time to prepare yourself for a couple of hours of...' She gave a dramatic pause while Bear obliged with a drumroll sound effect.

Florrie couldn't help but laugh at the expectation on the sea of faces looking back at her, all eager to catch her reaction. 'Come on, spill! It's killing me!' she said, giggling.

'Okay, we're going to be – count down with me, folks – three, two, one...'

'Salsa dancing!' the friends chorused loudly before giving in to a raucous round of cheers as the door to Danskelfe School of Dance opened and a young woman with a wide smile and long blonde hair appeared on the step.

NINE

'Welcome to Danskelfe School of Dance, everyone. My name's Anoushka Cartwright – though most people call me Noushka,' the young woman said in a soft moorland accent. 'And I can guarantee we're going to have the *best* fun this afternoon.' She smiled warmly at them.

Florrie's heart gave an excited lilt, the thought flittering through her mind that there was something familiar about Noushka. She looked over at Jasmine, the pair exchanging happy grins.

The group of friends had moved indoors and were now in the large, brightly lit dance studio, having divested themselves of their hoodies and jackets in the changing room. Black and white photos of dancers in action adorned the walls to the right and left of them above a line of ballet barres. Light flooded in through the large arched windows. Noushka stood before them with a wall of floor-to-ceiling mirrors behind her. She was wearing black dance trousers and a pink T-shirt emblazoned with the dance school's name and logo, tied at the waist, and sported black, heeled jazz shoes on her feet. Florrie would put her in her mid-twenties, and with her long flaxen waves and slim athletic figure, she put her in mind of Lark.

They were all standing in their couples – with the exception of Jean who was on her own, though Anoushka had assured Stella, who'd booked the session, that this wouldn't be a problem. A buzz of excitement filled the room.

Noushka beamed a warm smile at them. 'I *love* dancing the salsa; it's my favourite dance. It's so joyful and upbeat – you can't help but have a great time whether you're a learner or a professional; whatever skill level you are, it's lots of fun.'

'How about zero skill level and two left feet?' asked Bear, brushing his wild mop of chin-length hair off his face. He was built like a barn door and had hands like shovels. That, combined with his thick, bushy beard, meant he was regularly compared to a Viking. 'I'm not even joking.' He flashed Noushka an apologetic smile.

'Aye, I can vouch for that. He's no Anton Du Beke, that's for sure,' chipped in Maggie, making them all laugh, including their dance teacher.

'I have to admit to not being what you'd call coordinated, too,' said Max.

Noushka raised her palms, smiling kindly. 'I'm sure neither of you are half as bad as you think you are. And, like I said, you're here to have a great time and enjoy yourselves, which is what dance is all about, so just take the pressure off yourself and cut loose a bit. You'll be swinging those hips like there's no tomorrow by the time we're done.'

'Heaven help us with the size of mine,' quipped Maggie, who regularly grumbled about her curves and the struggles she'd had losing her post-pregnancy baby weight.

'There's nowt wrong with your hips, missus,' said Bear. 'They're perfect.'

'Bleurgh!' Jasmine mimed throwing up. 'Give over, you two.'

'Bear's right, Mags, you're gorgeous,' added Lark, smiling over at her.

'You so are,' agreed Stella. 'I'd give anything to have your curves rather than being straight up and down. I'm like a beanpole.'

'So' – Noushka flicked her hair over her shoulders once the banter had died down – 'before we get started, I'd just like to say *huge* congratulations to Florrie and Ed, who I gather are the reason you're all here today, to help celebrate their upcoming wedding. I'm so happy you chose to come here to do that, and I'll do all I can to make sure you have a fabulous time.'

Smiling, Florrie caught Ed's eye. 'Thank you,' they said together.

'That's very kind, we're chuffed to be here,' added Florrie.

'So, don't forget, this is all about having fun, not taking yourself too seriously, or getting stressed if you think you're doing it wrong. And, yes, some of the moves can be a bit tricky at first, but once you get the hang of them you'll be raring to go, I promise.' Noushka headed over to the back wall, all long, lean limbs, and picked up what looked like a remote control. Seconds later, the jaunty rhythm of salsa music filled the air, pounding through their feet.

'I'll just show you a few of the easy steps to get you started and while we wait for my assistant – and Jean's dance partner – to show up,' Noushka said as she put on a headset microphone, taking a moment to adjust the fit. 'I'll take it slowly at first until you get into the rhythm, then we can crank it up a few notches. I'll face the mirror so you can follow my steps. Okay, we'll start with the left foot first, on the count of three. One, two, three...'

They'd been following Noushka's instructions, with various levels of success, for a good five minutes when the door opened and in walked a man who Florrie couldn't help but think looked more than a little familiar. Her mind took off, searching for where she'd seen him before.

'Ah, good stuff, your dance partner's arrived, Jean,' said Noushka, her face lighting up. She quickly paused the music.

'Hello, everyone. So sorry I'm late, but my rather naughty Labrador decided it would be a good time to chew my shoes,' the man said in a soft Southern Irish accent that could melt the hardest of hearts. 'But, hey, these things happen, and the shoes had seen better days.' He gave a good-natured smile that crinkled his chocolate-brown eyes in the most appealing way. Coming to a stop beside Noushka, he put his hands on his hips. 'So, can someone point me in the direction of the lovely Jean?'

Florrie felt her mouth fall open. The man was the double of indie-folk singer Gabe Dublin. He even spoke like Gabe Dublin. Dressed like him, too. She stole a look at her friends to see that they were wearing matching expressions of astonishment. She turned her attention back to the man in question, taking in his floppy fringe and broad shoulders, the two-day stubble on his chin. Everything about him, even his posture, screamed Gabe Dublin. It couldn't be? Could it? It didn't make sense. Why would internationally famous Gabe Dublin be here, helping out in a dance studio in the middle of the North Yorkshire Moors? Surely he'd be living it up somewhere glitzy and glamorous, surrounding himself with equally famous people, or touring around Europe and the States?

Florrie blinked several times in quick succession, but it did nothing to change the message her eyes were sending to her brain. *Time for a trip to the optician's, Florrie, your eyes are clearly deceiving you.* Conscious that her mouth was still hanging open, she clamped it shut.

Noushka rested her hand on the Gabe Dublin doppelganger's shoulder with an easy familiarity. 'This is my boyfriend, Gabe, who's very kindly volunteered to be Jean's dance partner for the session.'

Florrie's eyes grew wide and she cast another glance around at her friends. It really was him! She caught Jasmine's eye, her friend mouthing, 'Oh my God,' as a ripple of surprise ran around the room. Seeing him out of context had totally thrown them all.

'Hi, folks.' Gabe gave a small wave. 'There's no need to look so shocked there, Jean. I know I don't look what you'd call graceful and elegant, but please let me reassure you that I've also been a pupil of Noushka's and she regularly has me brushing up on my skills, so I can say with a certain degree of confidence that you're in relatively safe hands with me as your dance partner. What I mean is, I don't stand on anywhere near as many toes as I used to.' He gave an amused grin. 'I'd all the elegance and coordination of a hippo with raging toothache when I first rocked up here, but I'm pleased to report, I've managed to shake off the toothache.'

That had everyone laughing, putting the group instantly at ease.

'Okay, so we'll have a quick recap on the steps we've just done, then we'll move on to the next stage,' said Noushka, getting things back on track. 'Gabe, if you could go and stand next to Jean, that would be great.'

'It'd be my pleasure,' he replied.

Jean looked like all her Christmases had come at once when Gabe took his position beside her. 'Hi there, Jean, it's grand to meet you.' He bent and kissed her gently on the cheek.

'Oh, and it's very grand to meet you, too.' Jean's eyes sparkled as her cheeks flushed pink.

'Looks like Amery's got a bit of competition,' Ed whispered in Florrie's ear as the music started up again, the pair of them sharing a smile.

The two-hour lesson passed in a blur of laughter and fun, with the friends declaring Noushka a wonderful teacher. She'd been patient, her instructions clear, and she had a kind way about her, a smile never far from her face.

Jean had been in her element with Gabe who'd made a fuss of her, bestowing copious compliments on her light footwork and natural sense of rhythm. And he wasn't exaggerating; Noushka had commented on how Jean seemed to pick up the steps quickly. Unlike Jasmine and Max who couldn't have been less coordinated if they'd tried. They'd spent most of the session tied up in knots, struggling to follow instructions, which had them snorting and giggling like a couple of mischievous school kids.

'They were exactly the same at school,' Stella had said, shaking her head and laughing when Noushka had tried to help out.

'Aye, some things never change,' Florrie had added.

. . .

All too soon, the session was at an end, much to the friends' disappointment.

'Thank you so much, Noushka, that was the best fun. I can't imagine a better way for Ed and I to celebrate our hen and stag party,' Florrie said, her cheeks flushed pink from dancing.

Noushka looked genuinely thrilled with the praise. 'I'm so happy to hear you enjoyed it. Offering sessions for hen parties is a new venture for me, and you're only the second group I've had, so your feedback's really helpful.'

'We've all had an amazing time.' Stella appeared beside Florrie. 'It'd be nice to think we could do it again.'

'Got something to tell us, have you, Stells?' Jasmine gave her an exaggerated nudge with her elbow. 'Are you and Al about to make an announcement?'

Stella rolled her eyes while Alex gave an amused chuckle. 'I didn't mean for that reason. It's just we've all had such a great time, it'd be good to think we'd be okay to book more sessions.'

'Yeah, yeah, we'll believe you, thousands wouldn't,' Maggie teased as she scooped up her dark curls that had escaped her bobble and fixed them back in place.

'You've all been great, we've had a fabulous time, haven't we, Gabe?' Noushka turned to her boyfriend.

'We have. I can't think of a better way to spend a Sunday after-noon than indulging in a bit of salsa with such an elegant dancing partner. Thank you for your patience, Jean – and apologies for stepping on your toes that time.' He took Jean's hand and kissed it, sending her all of a flutter.

'Thank you so much, lovey. It's been an afternoon I'll never forget.' Jean smiled bashfully, which sent a flood of affection rushing over Florrie.

'Ah, bless you. It's the same for me, too.' He gave her a lopsided grin before turning to Florrie and Ed. 'All the best for the future, folks, hope you have a fabulous wedding day, and thank you for allowing me to be a part of today's celebrations.'

'And I've just realised where I've seen you before,' said Jasmine, turning to Anoushka. 'You were in one of Gabe's videos.'

It was Noushka's turn to flush pink. 'I was. It was all very last minute; the girl who was booked was ill, so Gabe asked if I'd step in. He owed me one, which is why he helped out today.'

'And I'm sure glad I did.'

'And it's been awesome to have a couple of celebrities in my class, too.' Noushka smiled over at Jack and Jenna.

'It sure has.' Gabe beamed at them.

'Not sure why you're looking in this direction, are you, lass?' Jack feigned glancing around him, making everyone laugh.

Happiness danced through Florrie's veins. The afternoon had been totally surreal. Gabe Dublin – someone whose music she was a huge fan of; someone who she'd seen perform in concert – had actually been involved in her and Ed's celebrations. On top of that, he was a genuinely likeable and down-to-earth bloke. Talk about a pinch-me moment. She'd be reliving it for years to come.

'I'm guessing you're regretting that we didn't go pig herding,' Stella said dryly, taking in Florrie's happy smile. They were making their way over to the car parking area after getting changed into their smarter clothing.

'Yeah, she looks gutted, doesn't she?' said Jasmine.

Florrie turned to her friends, her backpack slung over her shoulder. 'Thank you all for arranging the *best* day for Ed and me. I'm buzzing with it all.'

'Yeah, thanks, everyone. I know I was in on the surprise, but it way surpassed my expectations, big time,' said Ed, as Florrie flung her arms around Lark, who was standing next to her. She proceeded to go round and hug all their friends.

'And what about our Jean, the star of the show?' Jasmine turned to the woman in question.

'Talk about fighting off admirers,' said Ed.

'Get away with you,' Jean replied, bashfully. 'Mind, I could listen to Gabe talk till the cows come home. He's got the most wonderful tone to his voice. Ooh, that accent...' She sounded almost dreamy and made everyone laugh.

'Right then,' said Stella, clapping her hands together. 'I know Jack, Jenna and Jean have to head back to Micklewick Bay, as do Leah and Hayley, but the fun isn't over for the rest of us yet.' A quick enquiry told Florrie that Jean was meeting 'a friend' while the two younger women and their boyfriends had been invited to a get-together with some of their former college pals.

'Stells is right about the fun not being over,' added Lark in Florrie's ear. 'We thought all that dancing would whip up an appetite, so we're off for Sunday dinner at The Sunne Inne in Lytell Stangdale.'

'No way?' Florrie's eyes widened in disbelief. The Sunne Inne's outstanding reputation had reached Florrie's ears in Micklewick Bay. As if this day hadn't been awesome enough already.

'Yes way,' said Jasmine. 'Now come on, you lot, no more faffing about. I'm that famished I could eat a scabby hoss between two mattresses.'

With that, they bid a quick farewell to those who were heading home, before walking to their respective cars.

In the Land Rover, Florrie had a quick rummage around her backpack for her mobile. She wanted to check for any further messages from her mum. It had crossed her mind several times during the course of their salsa lesson how much her parents would have loved having a go at learning some of the dance moves. She had no doubt they'd have thrown themselves wholeheartedly into it, particularly her dad. Not to mention how much her mum was a fan of Gabe Dublin's music – she regularly described him as having a voice that could melt chocolate. Florrie had to agree.

She fired off a quick text, the high-spirited chatter around her fading into the distance as she concentrated on what to say.

Hi Mum, hope Dad's feeling better and you're still okay. Had a fab time at the salsa lesson. Shame you couldn't have been there. Loads to tell you!!! Fxxx

Finding it difficult to type as the Landie bounced over potholes and bumps, not to mention the road being so twisty-turny, Florrie kept her message brief, deciding she'd call in on her parents later that evening. She hoped her dad was okay and her mum wasn't underplaying how unwell he was feeling so as not to spoil her and Ed's day. It had never left her mind that they'd kept her mum's illness a secret until she'd overheard them having a conversation about it. They'd been trying to protect her, not wanting her to worry as she faced her final year uni exams. She'd had to practically drag the details out of them. She'd made them swear never to do it again, but it still hadn't stopped a little doubt from lingering.

Tucking her phone back in her bag, her eyes slid to Ed's hands in his lap where he was holding his mobile. Florrie couldn't help but notice a text from his mother on the screen. It came as no surprise to see that she communicated in shouty capitals, and was demanding to know where he was. She caught a flash of something that included mention of his father, but before she could read any more, Ed swiped the message away and shoved his phone back in the pocket of his hoodie, releasing a weary sigh.

She bristled, as her heart simultaneously went out to Ed. How typical of his parents to put a cloud over such a happy day.

TEN

They piled out of the Land Rover that Bear had parked on the roadside in the village of Lytell Stangdale, joining the rest of the group where they'd congregated on the worn sandstone trod. Glancing around her Florrie could see why the village was described as chocolate-box pretty, with its quaint limewashed cottages topped by heavily thatched roofs and neatly tended gardens. From where she was standing, she could see a well-kept village green complete with pond and weeping willow dangling its branches in the water. She chuckled as a handful of hefted sheep ambled down the middle of the road towards them. Though she was aware it was a common sight in the moorland villages, it still managed to raise a chuckle from her and her friends.

Inside, the Sunne Inne was every bit as delightful as Florrie had expected, with its low, heavily beamed ceilings, thick, uneven walls and tweed soft furnishings in rich, moorland shades. A sturdy oak bar sat on the back wall, a row of gleaming beer pumps catching the light of the hand-forged wall lights. It exuded quality and cosiness all at once. Though the main lunchtime rush was over, the place was still thrumming with customers, the gentle murmur of chatter with the occasional laugh thrown in creating a jovial and welcoming atmosphere. The faint tang of woodsmoke hovered over the mouth-watering aroma of Sunday dinner that floated out from the kitchen. As if on cue, Florrie's stomach growled. Jazz was right, all that dancing and laughing had built up a huge appetite.

Stella, who was standing beside Florrie, leant into her. 'I'm told because the Sunday dinner here is so popular, the landlord and landlady decided to extend the lunchtime hours and continue serving it right through to the evening, which is why we've managed to get booked in.'

'Can't say I'm disappointed about that,' said Ed, who'd over-heard, his eyes glued to a couple of plates piled high with the said Sunday dinner in the hands of a young server who whizzed by on their way to a nearby table.

'Mmm. Same here,' said Florrie, following his gaze. 'Thank you so much for thinking of it and organising it for us.'

'Pleasure, flower.' Stella beamed.

After a brief discussion at the bar with a tall, wiry man with a plummy accent, and a pair of half-moon glasses perched on the end of his aquiline nose, Alex directed the group to a row of tables near to where flames danced in a large inglenook fireplace. A couple of dogs, who were baking themselves in front of the fire, barely looked up as the friends, drinks in hand, worked out who should sit where.

The group of people on the other side of the fireplace were engaged in friendly banter, the occasional loud bark of laughter coming from them. Amongst them, a glamorously dressed woman with a head of impossibly glossy purple waves with a distinctly fifties movie-star style caught Florrie's attention. She couldn't help but think her appearance seemed somehow incongruous in a pub in the middle of the North Yorkshire Moors.

The food was even more delicious than Florrie had expected — the roast potatoes were the perfect combination of golden and crispy on the outside and soft and fluffy in the middle, while the mashed potato was creamy and indulgent. And don't get her started on the Yorkshire puddings! They were like giant clouds smothered in lashings of beef and onion gravy that was in plentiful supply. And the toffee apple crumble with the most rich, velvety custard was to die for.

Florrie sank back into the banquette, Ed's arm curling over her shoulders, delicious flavours running around her mouth. The warmth of the pub and a stomach full of delicious food was proving to be a heady combination. She relaxed into Ed's embrace, a feeling of contentment and security wrapping around her, as she succumbed to a couple of long blinks...

'Uhh?' She was startled awake by a nudge in the ribs from Jasmine, who was sitting on the other side of her. 'What?'

'*Bloomin' 'eck*! You'll never believe who's just walked in.'

Florrie blinked, her friend's question taking a moment to sink in. 'Who?'

'Only Gabe Dublin and Noushka. And he's brought a guitar with him.'

Florrie's eyes pinged wide awake! 'No way!'

It took mere seconds for word of Gabe's arrival to get round the friends. They looked on as he made his way towards the group of people at the table next to them, his guitar in one hand, a pint of beer in the other. He evidently hadn't spotted the Micklewick Bay folk. Florrie felt a rush of relief; she wouldn't want him to think they were stalking him or coming to have a nosy at where he lived – assuming he called one of the local moorland villages home, that is. Anoushka had been waylaid and was chatting to a young woman with long auburn hair who was standing at the bar with a tall, blond man.

A low stool appeared and Gabe perched himself on it, leaning his guitar against the wall. The friends tried not to watch as he sipped his beer and chatted away amiably to his friends, the occasional lilt of his Southern Irish accent floating their way.

Before long, the man behind the bar – Florrie learnt he was called Jonty – called for everyone's attention and announced that they were going to be treated to a 'bit of a singsong' courtesy of Gabe who, from what she could gather, did live locally.

After an enthusiastic round of applause, accompanied by

whoops and whistles, the singer made his way across the room and perched himself on a barstool. 'Afternoon, folks,' he said, gently strumming his guitar, taking a moment to check the tuning of the strings. 'I apologise for interrupting your peaceful Sunday afternoon, but you're a captive audience and, hey, I couldn't resist!' He flashed a disarming grin, making everyone laugh. 'Oh, and I thought you might like to know that landlady Bea has a bagful of rotten tomatoes, so when you've had enough of my warbling, feel free to chuck 'em at me. I'll take that as a sign it's time to stop.' He chuckled, strumming at the strings of his guitar some more.

'Okay, then, I think some of you might know this one. And, if so, please feel free to sing along.'

Soon the bar was filled with Gabe's rich, smoky voice. Everyone in the room was spellbound. Florrie instantly recognised the song as his last single before he'd given up performing to concentrate on songwriting. 'My Rose-Shaped Heart' had hit the number one spot in the UK charts and stayed there for weeks. The lyrics of unrequited love, so tender and moving, combined with the emotive melody, brought a lump to her throat. As if that wasn't enough, the added hint of his soft Irish accent somehow made it feel all the more believable and tugged even further at her heart-strings. She sniffed quietly and blinked back a rogue tear, hoping no one had noticed.

'Thank you all for the best day ever,' said Florrie. The friends were standing outside the pub, preparing to head home, an upbeat air around them.

'Totally agree, thank you all,' said Ed, smiling. 'On paper it sounded fun, but – wow! – it far exceeded expectations.'

'It so did,' said Florrie, feeling the nip of the chilly wind that had picked up since they'd first arrived in the village. The temperature high up on the moors was a good few degrees cooler than by the coast.

'Didn't it just?' said Jasmine. 'I mean, *Gabe Dublin*... who'd have even thought?'

With cheeks kissed and hugs bestowed, the friends headed to their respective cars. 'I'll be in touch about the next thing we've got planned for your hen celebration. It's later this week – after work – and this one's my idea,' Jasmine called across the road.

'Thanks, Jazz. Looking forward to it.' Grateful as she was, Florrie was too tired to even think about what it might be.

In the Land Rover, passing the beautiful, rugged moorland scenery, Florrie sat back, allowing the events of the day wash over her. To say it had been a far cry from what she'd originally feared her friends had planned for her would be an understatement. It had been wonderful. She knew it would be something they'd be talking about for years to come.

ELEVEN

It hadn't escaped Florrie's attention that Ed had been quiet on the way home. And though she'd seen him check his phone several times, she hadn't been able to catch a glimpse of the screen to see if there'd been any further communication from his mother. She'd tried to suppress her worries by telling herself his quietness was more than likely down to him being tired after their busy day, but a feeling deep in her gut told her otherwise. It was the same problem it had been whenever he'd gone quiet like this: his parents.

Arriving back at Samphire Cottage, Gerty greeted them with such great enthusiasm, anyone would think they'd been away for six months, which seemed to brighten Ed's mood in an instant. In fairness, it was impossible to feel down when Gerty was around, with her upbeat nature and impossibly waggy tail.

'Hello, Gerty-Girl, have you missed us?' Ed gave a happy chuckle as he bent to give the Labrador's black velvety ears a thorough ruffling, which appeared to increase the tail-wagging.

Florrie followed suit, tickling Gerty under the chin and promising her a biscuit for being so well-behaved while they were out.

'What an amazing day, I can't remember the last time I laughed so much,' she said, looking up into Ed's dark blue eyes, her heart fluttering. She pushed her glasses back up her nose. 'I've no idea how you managed to keep all that a secret, I'd have been bursting to tell you.'

He laughed, wrapping his arms around her and pulling her to him, sending a rush of love through her. 'You're right, it has been an amazing day.' He kissed the end of her nose. 'And I'm very happy to hear you enjoyed it. And I didn't find it too bad keeping it secret; mind, I didn't know all of the details, and none of us had a clue about Gabe Dublin – I think I might've struggled keeping that to myself.'

'It's still sinking in.' She laughed. 'I wonder if Jean's still floating around on cloud nine? He thoroughly charmed her. And I wonder if her "friend" knows about her dance partner?'

Ed chuckled. 'Ah, bless her. She was actually the best salsa dancer out of all of us. That lady sure has rhythm.'

'Doesn't she just?'

'And I don't think Amery needs to be jealous, especially when he hears she was leaving Gabe to head back for her date with him – assuming we can call it a date, that is.'

'Hmm. I'd probably be a bit careful with that one until we hear how Jean refers to it. I wouldn't want to make her feel uncomfortable, especially with it being such new and unfamiliar territory to her.' Although she was in possession of the facts concerning Jack's father, in all the years Florrie had known Jean, she'd never been aware of her being in a relationship with a man.

'Aye, makes sense. I'd hate to make her feel uncomfortable and put her off.' Ed nodded thoughtfully. 'It's a shame your parents couldn't make it. It would've added an extra level of fun with your dad strutting his stuff the way he does.' He grinned at her, his smile making his eyes crinkle.

'He'd have taken up a lot of room, though.' Florrie giggled as a picture of her dad at a fundraising event filled her mind. It had involved an evening disco and he'd thrown himself – and Florrie's mum – into it wholeheartedly. 'No one could ever accuse him of not being an enthusiastic dancer. He's worse with eighties music, mind. Let's not forget how he entertained everyone with his moves to "The Only Way is Up" by Yazz or that one by Dead or Alive at the fundraising disco last January. His dancing was totally wild.'

Ed laughed, too. 'True, he excelled himself dancing to "You Spin Me Round".' He released a happy sigh. 'Though today wasn't the same without your parents, it was still a fabulous way to kick off our wedding celebrations.'

'It was wonderful.'

He bent and pressed his lips against hers, his kiss deepening until Gerty started to whimper, apparently feeling left out. Ed reluctantly pulled away, his hands sliding down Florrie's shoulders, giving them a squeeze.

'I think I'll take Gerty for a leg-stretch along to my parents. Kill two birds with one stone, see how my dad's doing, and give Gerty some exercise.' For all they'd asked their neighbour, Mrs Fergus, to let the Labrador into the garden for a toilet trip and a bit of company, Florrie thought they'd both benefit from the walk to her parents' house – Gerty for the exercise, and herself for the fresh air since she was in serious danger of snuggling up on the sofa and falling asleep.

'Aye, good plan. I was thinking I should maybe pop down to the bookshop, crack on with my work in the windows.'

'Ooh, yes!' Florrie's face lit up as she suddenly remembered the unveiling of the window displays that were scheduled for next week to coincide with Jack and Jenna's author reading event. 'Am I allowed any hints as to the subject matter?' She stood on her tiptoes and kissed him, following up with a hopeful look.

'Nope, and don't think those delicious kisses will make me tell you either. Though, maybe you could give it another try, just in case...' He lifted an eyebrow and gave a lopsided smile that made Florrie's heart skip a beat.

'Always worth a try.' She reached up, her pulse racing as his lips brushed hers.

Since Ed had arrived in Micklewick Bay, he'd taken charge of the displays in the large windows of the double-fronted bookshop.

An artist by trade, he'd put his creative skills to good use, designing captivating scenes complete with moving components. They'd become a popular local attraction – particularly at Christmas, with not just the local children being enthralled by them. The theme always remained a secret – even to Florrie – hidden away behind thick, black curtains, before they were officially unveiled by Jack Playforth.

'Tempted to give up any clues?' she asked, reluctantly bringing their kiss to an end.

'Hmm...' Ed feigned taking a moment to consider her request. 'It's still a no, I'm afraid.'

'What? As kisses go, I reckon that gets a good eight out of ten.'

'I'd have to agree with that; I'd even nudge it up to a nine. You're still not getting a word out of me, though.'

'Gah! Spoilsport!' She wriggled out of his arms. 'In that case, all kisses are off until further notice.'

'Harsh!' he said, them both laughing.

'S'just me,' Florrie called as she stepped into the hallway of her childhood home, its familiar comforting smell curling around her nose. Usually on a Sunday the air would be filled with the rich aroma of her mum's delicious roast dinner, but not today. It acted as a reminder that her dad was feeling unwell and, no doubt, off his food, which was most unlike him.

'Hello, lovey.' Her mum appeared around the kitchen doorway, looking pleased to see her daughter, a tea towel thrown over her shoulder. 'That's good timing, I'm just making a cuppa, d'you have time for one?'

'Love one, thanks, Mum.' There was always a pot of tea on the go at her parents' house.

'So you all had a lovely time salsa dancing, then?'

'We did, thanks, though you and Dad were missed by everyone.' Florrie bent to unfasten Gerty's lead, the Labrador trotting off in the direction of the kitchen. 'How's Dad?' she asked, straightening up and hooking the lead over a peg next to the coats before slipping her jacket off and hanging it up.

'He's had a lie down and is looking a bit brighter, which is good. Said he fancied a cup of tea and a plain biscuit.' Paula headed towards Florrie, hugging her warmly and pressing a kiss to her cheek.

'So, what's up with him? It's not like him to be poorly.'

'I know.' Paula's brow crumpled with a frown. 'Said he's been feeling dizzy which has made him feel sick, described it as being like carsickness.'

'Oh, poor Dad, that sounds awful.' Florrie followed her mum down the hall. 'Mind, much as it's a shame you missed the salsa lesson, I'm not sure it would've been a good combo for him with it involving a fair bit of spins and turns.'

'That's what we thought, too.' Paula stopped outside the living room door. 'Two ticks, lovey, I'll just fetch the tray with the tea things. You go and see your dad,' she said, nodding in the direction of the living room.

There, Florrie found her dad stretched out on the sofa, a pillow puffed up behind his back and a fleece blanket over his legs. 'Hi, Dad, how're you feeling?' she asked, injecting a cheery note into her voice. She was struck by how pale he looked, with not even the slightest hint of his usually ruddy cheeks. And the last time she'd seen him with such dark circles under his eyes was when her mum had been so very poorly and the worry was eating away at him. It felt strange to see him incapacitated like this. He was always fit and healthy; never still, always had to be busy doing something. Her mum regularly said he had ants in his pants. His job as a builder meant he'd always been toned and muscular. And he never usually ailed anything worse than the occasional head cold.

'Hello, love, it's grand to see you.' He pushed himself up on his elbows, giving a watery smile. 'I have to say, I've felt better. If I stand up, I get that dizzy, I end up walking around like I've had an afternoon session at The Cellar, guzzling a load of Micklewick Mischief. Even turning my head makes me feel right rotten.'

'That doesn't sound good, Dad.' From his description, Florrie didn't think he'd picked up the stomach bug Lark had mentioned.

'I've been making him ginger tea, which is good for settling dicky tummies,' said her mum, who'd joined them, setting a tray of mugs down on the coffee table beside her husband.

'Aye, but it does nowt for dizzy spells,' added her dad.

'It's been going on for a few days, so I've made him an appointment at the doctor's.' Paula went to puff up the pillow behind him.

He huffed out an impatient sigh. 'I don't know why you're making a fuss, love. You know I'm not happy about wasting a doctor's appointment on me. I'll be right as rain in no time. Like I keep saying, it'll just be something I've picked up somewhere and not worth fussing over.'

'Typical man.' Paula shook her head and rolled her eyes.

'It's not a waste of time, Dad. You can't go to work, climbing ladders or using heavy equipment or machinery if you're feeling dizzy. It's dangerous.' Though she felt strongly about getting her point across, Florrie wasn't keen to dwell on the thought of her dad putting himself at risk at work, knowing he was the sort of man who didn't like to let his clients down, and would push himself to ensure jobs were finished on schedule. Chas Appleton & Son Traditional Builders was a third-generation building firm that had an excellent reputation in Micklewick Bay and the surrounding areas, and it was one that Charlie had strived to continue.

'That's exactly what I've been telling him,' said her mum. 'See, Charlie, our Florrie agrees.'

'Aye, well, I'll go, see what the doctor says. Hopefully, she can give me summat to put me right and stop you fretting about me and pouring this ginger tea muck down my neck.' Though he was joking, his reply seemed to satisfy his wife and daughter.

Florrie stayed at her parents for an hour, chatting over a cup of tea, refusing the offer of a biscuit. She was still so full from her Sunday dinner, she couldn't imagine ever feeling hungry again. She shared all the details from her afternoon with her friends, her parents listening in disbelief as she told them about Gabe Dublin.

'I'm right sorry I made us miss it, lass.' Charlie threw his wife an apologetic look. 'You'd have had a whale of a time.'

'Hey, no need to apologise, you weren't up to it, love.' Paula reached over from the armchair beside him and patted his hand.

Florrie was glad to see a sparkle had returned to her dad's eye. She'd been right to call in on her parents, it had eased her worries, seeing that her dad wasn't as ill as she'd convinced herself he was.

'Have you heard any more from Dawn Harte?' Paula asked, not bothering to hide her dislike of the woman. Florrie had filled her mum in on Dawn's arrival over the phone the day before.

'No, but I think she was trying to get in touch with Ed while we were out today. I've no idea what it was about, though.' Florrie wondered if he'd return his mother's calls, or replied to her texts while she was out.

'Well, don't let her browbeat you,' said her dad firmly. 'You know what Ed's parents can be like.'

Didn't she just? They had the power to burst the happiest of bubbles. She hoped that wouldn't be the case today, hoped it would be allowed to finish on a high.

TWELVE

MONDAY 13TH APRIL

'I really like these pens, I think we should place an order for—'

Florrie's conversation with Leah was brought to an abrupt halt as the door burst open and Dawn stepped into the bookshop on a wave of self-importance, sweeping aside the calm atmosphere in one fell swoop.

'How very *parochial*,' she announced in an officious voice, giving a disapproving sniff.

Florrie and Leah exchanged concerned glances. 'Hello, Dawn.' Florrie set her pen down on the counter where she and Leah had been perusing a brochure of stationery. She valued her young assistant's opinion on such things, especially when choosing stock that would appeal to younger customers.

If Dawn had heard Florrie's greeting, she chose to ignore it, and instead proceeded to look around, a scornful expression on her face as she gave her surroundings a quick appraisal. Anyone would think it was the first time she'd set foot in the bookshop rather than it being her first port of call when she'd arrived in the town on Friday. Granted, she hadn't hung around for long then, when it had been busy with customers.

'After all Ed's told his father and I about this place, waxing lyrical about the *improvements* you've made, I was expecting something far more *impressive* than this,' Dawn said in a scornful tone as she made a show of glancing around the space.

Florrie exchanged another glance with Leah, her hackles standing on end. From the look in her assistant's eyes, they were thinking the same thing.

'You didn't see what it was like before, Mum.' Ed spoke in a much gentler tone than the one Florrie would've used.

He'd been working in the window when his mother had arrived, and had jumped out on hearing her voice, tripping over the curtain in his haste. He had flecks of white paint in his hair and a generous dusting of glitter on his face. 'I mean, for a start, there's the staircase, and now the teashop. They're major improvements.' The couple hadn't just updated the bookshop's dowdy décor; they'd managed to balance it with a traditional aesthetic that suited the Victorian age of the building, while making it a more pleasant place to spend time browsing the shelves.

A striking reclaimed staircase, with its highly polished handrail and ornate cast-iron balusters, now curved around the wall to the right and led to the first floor where the former bookshop accommodation had been converted to more bookshop space with the tearoom occupying the large room at the front. Though it was a functional structure, the salvaged staircase added a welcome touch of character to the bookshop, especially since Florrie and Ed had utilised the space below to great effect. They'd created a cosy area where customers could take a moment to relax whilst perusing a book in the brace of squishy armchairs they'd placed there. There was a small table set before the seats, topped with leaflets promoting, amongst other things, the shop's loyalty card, new titles they would be taking delivery of, and the various events the bookshop held.

'And we've updated the tills, linked them in with a sophisticated point of sale system and stock management software; it's all very efficient. It's a far cry from the antiquated till that regularly conked out, and handwritten order book my grandfather used to have.'

'Hmm.' Dawn spun around on her heel, fixing him with a cold stare. 'That's all very well, but it's hardly ground-breaking, is it? I could never understand why your grandparents were so attached to this place, and I've no idea why you're so keen to follow in their footsteps and be a *shopkeeper*.' She shook her head and rolled her eyes derisively. 'You had a perfectly good career as an artist, which you seem to have had no qualms about throwing away.' In typical Dawn style, she wasn't holding back.

This was one of those moments when the usually quiet and unassuming Florrie wanted to leap to the defence of someone she cared about and tell the offending individual exactly what she thought. But something told her doing that wouldn't help the current situation. She didn't want to add fuel to his parents' dislike of her, knowing it would only make things worse for Ed. So, as difficult as it was, she bit down on her outrage and remained quiet.

'I mean, this town, for starters,' Dawn continued. 'It's stagnant, insular. Where's the opportunity? Where's the—'

'Well, I love it here, Mum, and I love the bookshop. Florrie and I are finding new ways to improve it all the time, which is why *we're* staying put,' Ed replied, his calmness a contrast with his mother's harsh, overbearing manner. 'I'm the happiest I've ever been. Florrie and I have a good life here. This is where my roots are.'

'Your *roots*? Really? I'd be interested to hear what your father has to say about that.' Dawn gave a mocking laugh before casting Florrie a disdainful look. 'Very well, I suppose it's your choice.' She muttered something indiscernible under her breath before saying, 'I've been giving your wedding some thought and have a few ideas to put forward. After all, you are my son and I daresay your fiancée's parents have been heavily involved. And while I'm here, I can give you some ideas on how you can improve things in this place.'

Gerty, who'd been observing the interaction from her bed by the counter, raised her head from her paws as a low growl started emanating from her. Dawn shot her a look of irritation.

'Go, Gerty,' Leah said under her breath.

Florrie's face drained of all colour, her expression betraying her feeling of utter horror.

'Yes, *Florrie's* mum and dad have been helping, but we've done most of the organising ourselves. There's not been that much to do with us keeping things low-key; we've pretty much got things sorted.'

'In that case, I'll help out here in the bookshop for now,' Dawn said in a tone that wouldn't brook any argument. She jabbed her hands on her hips and pinned Florrie with her gimlet gaze as if daring her to respond.

'Oh my God, please no,' Leah said under her breath, as a customer made his way to the counter. From the awkward expression on his face, he'd clearly heard the interaction, but then, Dawn's voice was so loud, there'd be no missing it, it would've reached every corner of the bookshop.

'Where's your mum?' Florrie asked later that morning when she'd returned to the bookshop, droplets of rain glistening on her bobble hat and the shoulders of her duffle coat. She'd taken Gerty to the local veterinary surgery for the Labrador's annual vaccination boosters and had been out longer than she'd hoped thanks to the vet running late. It was instantly evident that Dawn was no longer in the building as the usual calm atmosphere had returned. It was almost as if the bookshop had breathed a sigh of relief along with Leah and Ed.

Florrie and Ed had agreed that with the current situation, it would be best if she took Gerty to the vets while he remained at the shop, rather than leave Leah, or even Leah and Florrie, with Dawn. Even though they knew the appointment wouldn't take long, Ed had, in a roundabout way, said he felt uncomfortable leaving them on their own with his mother. Florrie was grateful for this, especially since they were still yet to fathom the real reason for Dawn being there. Her capricious moods – of which there had been many – hadn't helped either and could change at the drop of a hat. They seemed to swing from her original disdain to feigning interest in the wedding. Florrie couldn't decide which was worse, especially when Dawn had started showing an interest in her wedding dress, even pushing to see it.

'It's not an unreasonable request, your mother will know what it looks like. It's only fair that I do, too.' Taking in Florrie's shocked expression she'd said, 'Well, it is! And there's no need to look so outraged. What harm could it do for me to take a look? It's not as if I'd tell all and sundry what it's like. And don't tell me you hold with all those ridiculous, old-fashioned superstitions about it being bad luck for anyone else to see it. We all know that's a load of clap-trap.' Dawn had craftily made sure to make all of her comments out of Ed's earshot while he was busy working in the window. And though she'd attempted a smile, there was no disguising the chal-lenging glint in her eyes.

Ed's mother had continued to push to see the dress until Florrie had taken Gerty and left the bookshop for the vets, her insides churning, her stress levels climbing skywards. Which was probably why the relief at not hearing her future mother-in-law's voice on her return was so welcome.

She looked at Ed, taking in his expression. If she didn't know better, she'd swear he was looking more than a little sheepish.

'Has something happened?' Florrie asked. She had a horrible feeling she wasn't going to like what she was about to hear. Her eyes switched to Leah at the counter. The young girl, who was out of Ed's eyeline, pulled an exaggerated scared face.

'Er, no. Everything's fine. She's... um. She's at Samphire Cottage,' he said.

'Samphire Cottage?' Surely she couldn't have heard right? Florrie's mind went straight to her wedding dress that was hanging on a hook on the back of the door in the cottage's tiny box room – the room where Ed's mum had wanted to stay. Granted, it was hidden beneath a garment cover, but knowing Dawn, she wouldn't put it past her to take a look. It made her suddenly wish she'd taken her mum up on her offer of keeping it at their house.

Ed cleared his throat. 'She's doing us a favour. I got a text saying the new kettle was going to be delivered – it's a day early and there's been a mix-up with the address. I think I must've forgotten to change the delivery option to here rather than home after I put my card details in.' Watching Florrie's frown deepen as she processed this information, he continued, 'And since I was covered in paint, and Leah was busy with a load of customers, my mother offered to go and wait in for it – I'd just picked up the notification email; the kettle was due for delivery any minute, so she drove there.'

'Right.' She could just imagine that Ed had been steamrollered into agreeing to it by his mother.

The implications started racing around Florrie's mind. Dawn was currently in possession of a key to their home, had free range of it, was able to peer into cupboards and drawers, nosey around the rooms – not that they had anything to hide, but it still made her feel uneasy. Though she was Ed's mother, she was still no more than a stranger to Florrie.

'How long ago was that?'

'Um' – his gaze went to the clock above the counter – 'about half an hour ago; fifteen or so minutes after you went out.'

Samphire Cottage was no more than a five-minute drive away. If delivery had been as imminent as Ed had implied, why had Dawn not returned?

'Okay.' Florrie didn't know what else to say, Dawn was his mum after all. He was in a difficult position, and she knew he'd feel just as concerned as she did about Dawn being in their cottage on her own, especially when she'd never been willing to set foot in it before. The last thing Florrie wanted to do was to make him feel any worse about it. There was always a chance the delivery driver had got lost and had been late. She held back from saying her mum was at home, which wasn't far from Samphire Cottage. It would've made more sense for her to pop round and take delivery of the kettle, which is what Florrie would've suggested if she'd been there. Paula would've been happy to help, and she had a key, after all. And now, so did Dawn. 'I'll just go and dry Gerty off. That mizzle's heavy; we got a bit soggy, didn't we, lass?' Gerty looked up and wagged her tail.

'That flippin' woman's been a *total* nightmare,' Leah said quietly, when Florrie returned and Ed was back working on his window displays. 'She's a right cow, and the way she talks to Ed is just awful. I mean, he's her son, but she sounds like she can't stand him. I wanted to say something so many times and had to bite my tongue cos I know it's not my place, but... ugh! She has no right to talk to him like that. I don't know how he puts up with her.'

'No, neither do I.' Florrie gave a sigh and started chewing on her bottom lip. She suspected it had probably become the norm such that neither mother nor son noticed it any longer. Though, on reflection, Ed had seen how she interacted with her own parents and had often commented on the supportive and loving dynamic they shared, not to mention the respect they had for one another. And, from the conversations they'd had over the last couple of years, she knew he'd compared it to his relationship with his own parents. She assumed he continued to put up with it since to tackle his parents about it would run the risk of incurring their wrath, particularly his mother's. Dawn had a reputation in the Harte family for her volatile temper and anger issues – though Florrie didn't know her well and hadn't actually met her to speak to until last Friday when she landed at the bookshop, it was the first thing that sprang to mind whenever Dawn Harte was mentioned.

She rubbed her brow frustratedly.

'We're going to have to go around and check the bookshelves cos she decided we'd got it all wrong and started rearranging things as soon as you went out,' added Leah. 'Honestly, she was moving that fast she was like a tornado. I don't know if you noticed, but she's taken Jenna's books off the main display table and put them under the counter. Said they were drivel and that no one was inter-ested in "romance rubbish" as she called it. Said books on travel were far better and that people round here needed to broaden their minds and explore the world – or words to that effect.'

'She *what*?' Florrie turned to see the table unimaginatively piled with hardback travel books where Jenna's display had been. Rage surged through her with such force, she was struggling to rein it in. 'That woman has overstepped the mark, big time. She clearly has no idea what a popular genre romance is, or how offensive that is to our romance readers who are amongst our most loyal customers. And Jenna's books are probably our biggest sellers.'

'That's what I told her, but she wouldn't listen. She just steamed on regardless. She was literally stomping about that hard the floorboards were bouncing and the bookshelves shaking.' Leah gave a quick demonstration on the spot complete with an exaggerated determined facial expression. Florrie couldn't help but laugh. 'She had a right face on her and just started ranting about how we needed to make the bookshop more highbrow if we wanted it to be a success, and that everything about it was generations behind the times. I tried to stop her, but she's bloomin' scary when she gets going. I'm really sorry.' Leah gave an apologetic look. 'Customers were looking, it was really embarrassing so I thought it best to stay quiet.'

Florrie rested a hand on Leah's shoulder. 'Don't you go apologising for what Dawn's doing. I'm glad you didn't say anything; I wouldn't want her to be horrible to you, especially in front of customers, which she would have no qualms about, and I know would've made you feel even more embarrassed. She doesn't take being challenged very well. Though, bizarrely, she seems to like nothing better than a disagreement.' From what Florrie had gathered over the years, Dawn seemed to thrive on confrontation, and she wasn't going to allow Leah to bear the brunt of Dawn's bad temper. She was a sweet-natured girl and didn't deserve that.

'Yeah, I kind of got that.'

. . .

Florrie couldn't wait to get home after work. They'd locked up and left the bookshop as soon as possible. It was definitely a case of best foot forward as they made their way along the top prom, with Ed jokingly asking if she was training for a run.

But though he didn't say it, she knew he'd realise the reason for her haste: Dawn still had Ed's house key; she hadn't returned to the bookshop, and what's more, they hadn't heard a word from her. Florrie's mind had been working overtime, her stomach churning for the rest of the afternoon.

When they were finally back home, Florrie kicked off her shoes and raced upstairs, citing needing the loo as her reason. She arrived on the compact landing to see the door to the spare room standing ajar, which she was certain wasn't how it had been left that morning. Florrie had got into the habit of keeping it closed since she'd started using the room to store her wedding dress and accessories, not that she thought Ed would go looking for a second, but just in case he forgot it was temporarily out of bounds and ventured in by mistake.

But seeing it like this sent suspicion curling around inside her. She pushed the door open and tentatively stepped inside. Though nothing leapt out as being different, Florrie couldn't shake the feeling that Dawn had been snooping in here, no doubt checking that they were telling her the truth about not having enough room for her to stay. She'd very probably found her dress in the process. Florrie shuddered as unease rippled up her spine.

'Everything okay?' Ed looked up from pouring boiling water into the teapot as Florrie walked into the kitchen. 'Thought we'd use the old kettle one last time before we put it into retirement.' The smile he flashed pushed through her feelings of annoyance with his mother.

'Yeah.' She smiled back. It wasn't his fault his parents behaved the way they did, and since she couldn't be one hundred per cent certain that the door had been closed when they'd left that morning, she decided to keep it to herself. What was the point of piling more worries onto Ed, when she knew he was feeling bad enough about his mum's attempts at taking over at the bookshop. Florrie was still riled at Dawn removing Jenna's display, but their wedding was just around the corner and she didn't want to spend the run-up squabbling with him because of his parents. If only he hadn't given his mother the key to their home, she thought for the umpteenth time that day.

THIRTEEN

TUESDAY 14TH APRIL

'How's your father doing, lovey?' Jean asked, handing Florrie a mug of tea. The bookshop had been busy all morning and they were taking advantage of a quiet spell before they were hit with the lunchtime rush.

'Thanks, I'm ready for this.' Florrie took the mug and set it down on the counter. 'My mum said he was feeling a bit better when I spoke to her last night. The doctor diagnosed him with labyrinthitis and prescribed some antibiotics which should, hopefully, kick in soon.' She gestured, crossing her fingers. 'Looks like he'll be off work for a while, though, which he's not happy about.'

'That I can believe.' Jean chuckled. 'Well, at least he knows what's wrong with him now.'

'I just hope he'll be better in time for the wedding. Apparently, the doctor told him it could take up to six weeks to be fully recovered.'

'Ooh, goodness, that is a long time. Mind, knowing your dad, he'll be right as rain before you know it.' Jean gave her a reassuring tap on the arm. 'He's in good hands being looked after by your mum. She'll have him back on his feet well before he needs to walk you down the aisle.'

'I hope so.' It was another thing to add to her worries. 'Mum said she'd push him down in one of his wheelbarrows if necessary.'

'That would be worth seeing.' Jean's hearty chuckles made Florrie laugh, too.

The two women were alone in the bookshop since it was Leah's day off and Ed had taken Gerty for a walk and was picking up some glue at the local DIY store while he was out – apparently it was something he needed for the display. There'd been no sign of Dawn that morning and Ed said he hadn't heard from her. Florrie was torn between feeling relieved that his mum wasn't there and unease, wondering what she'd do next. On paper, it seemed wrong that she was happy for her mum to have a key to Samphire Cottage, yet felt beyond irritated that Dawn had managed to get her hands on one. But those who knew their backstory would fully understand Florrie's misgivings.

There was also the fact that Florrie had bought the property before she'd met Ed and it was still in her sole name – it was something she was keen to rectify once they'd got married, unless they decided to move, which was something they'd touched on once or twice. She'd given both her parents a key right at the start, telling her dad to hang on to the one he'd used to let himself in while he was doing the building work on it and Florrie was still living at home with her parents. Dawn, on the other hand, had never wanted anything to do with Florrie, and hadn't spoken two words directly to her until she'd turned up at the bookshop last Friday.

'How about her majesty?' asked Jean. There was no love lost between Jean and Ed's parents either.

Florrie rolled her eyes and updated her friend on the events of the previous day, Jean's expression morphing from disbelief to outrage.

'She has no business coming in here and taking over! It's not five minutes since she and her husband were trying to browbeat you and Ed into selling the place and giving them the proceeds. It was disgraceful! Bernard'll be turning in his grave. She's up to something, mark my words. You need to watch her, lovey.'

Florrie's heart lurched. Jean had vocalised her own concerns.

'As you know, Bernard rarely used to speak about the situation with his son and daughter-in-law, but on the occasions he did, he used to say that he got the impression Dawn worked away behind the scenes, pulling the strings while Peter did most of the talking.' Jean took a slow sip of her tea, thoughtful for a moment. 'Does make me wonder why Dawn's suddenly planted herself at the centre of things. It's very much out of character.'

'Yeah, that's what I thought, too,' said Florrie. Though it was good to know she wasn't being paranoid, it only added weight to her fears about Dawn's reasons for being in the town.

'All I know is that they're a right toxic pair, her and her husband, and I wouldn't trust either of them as far as I could throw them.'

Florrie couldn't argue with that.

Their conversation was brought to an end by the return of Ed and Gerty. Fresh salty air clung to the pair of them. Ed was ruddy-cheeked while the Labrador was panting. Once released from her lead, she trotted off to the kitchen, no doubt to avail herself of the water bowl that was kept in there.

'That's what I call good timing, young Edward.' Jean beamed at him. 'There's some fresh tea in the pot; I'll just go and pour you a mug.'

'I'll go, there's no need for you to trouble yourself, Jean.'

'It's no trouble, lovey. Two ticks.' She set her mug down on the counter and headed off to the kitchen.

'Good walk?' Florrie asked, looking up at him, his blue eyes shining from the exercise.

'Bracing.' He grinned, pulling off his gloves and stuffing them into his pockets.

'Did you manage to get what you needed from the DIY store?'

'I did. And you might be surprised to hear I finally caught up with my mother. Got my key back, too.' The way he hitched his eyebrows suggested he shared Florrie's surprise.

'Oh, right.' This was good news. 'Did she say why she didn't come back to the shop?'

'She did.' Ed nodded, unravelling his scarf from round his neck. 'Apparently, after she'd taken delivery of the kettle, she'd gone for a walk and bumped into someone she used to know. They got talking which led to them organising a meal for later in the evening so they could continue their catch-up. Would you believe this person – it's a woman, by the way – is on holiday here in Micklewick Bay? What's the chances of her being here at the same time as my mother, not to mention them bumping into one another? Talk about a coincidence.' Ed gave a chuckle as he unbuttoned his jacket.

Myriad thoughts raced around Florrie's mind, questioning if it really was a coincidence, wondering as to the identity of the person. She was thankful they could rule out local unsavoury businessman Dodgy Dick who Ed's parents had at one time enlisted to wage a campaign of bullying and intimidation in the hope of forcing Ed and Florrie to hand over the bookshop; he was local and had lived here all his life. And besides, the last she'd heard, he and one of his equally undesirable colleagues were doing a stint in prison. Yet something about this set a niggle gnawing away in the pit of her stomach.

'I wonder who it was?' she said, thinking it was better to keep her thoughts to herself for now.

'She didn't say. When she eventually answered her phone, I told her I needed my key, so she agreed to meet me on the top prom so she could hand it over. She was in a bit of a rush, said she didn't have time to stop and chat, so any forthcoming information was sparse. Oh, and she's still at her original B&B; didn't say why she hadn't moved to a different one and I forgot to ask.'

Florrie wondered if it all sounded as odd to Ed as it did to her. Her gut was telling her something was off, and her gut had never let her down yet. As if sensing her concerns, Ed pulled her into his arms, hugging her close and dropping a kiss on the top of her head.

Florrie inhaled the scent of fresh sea air that was still clinging to him, felt the chill of it on his clothing.

'Here you go, Ed, lovey.' Jean returned, all smiles with a mug in her hand. 'It's still nice and hot.'

'Thanks, Jean.' Ed flashed her a grateful smile as he released Florrie from his embrace and took the mug. 'So, how're things going with you and Amery, if you don't mind me asking?' He blew on his tea, his eyes peering over at her questioningly.

Florrie watched as Jean's cheeks flushed pink and her eyes lit up. 'Well, I don't mind telling you he's the perfect gentleman and has lovely old-fashioned manners.' Florrie hadn't seen her friend look so animated before.

'I'd expect nothing less of the man who's stepping out with our lovely Jean,' said Ed.

'Same here,' Florrie added.

Jean gave them a warm smile. 'I think I mentioned we used to know one another many years ago, and I don't mind admitting I used to have quite a crush on him when I was a young lass – most of the girls at school did – but he was a couple of years above me so he was completely oblivious to my existence!' She giggled at that.

'I kind of get the impression that's changed quite a bit,' Florrie said, her eyes soft with affection for her friend.

'I was surprised he even remembered me, to be honest,' Jean said bashfully.

'So, when's Amery next wining and dining you?' Ed asked.

'Well, he's coming to Jack and Jenna's reading on Thursday – he bought that ticket Josie Bedford had to return with her having to go in for her operation, poor lass – and he's booked us a table at Oscar's Bistro for afterwards.' Jean glanced between them, unable to contain her smiles.

'How lovely.' Florrie's grin was almost as wide as Jean's. She was thrilled at the prospect of her friend enjoying a bit of romance. 'What's wrong?' She was taken aback to see Jean's smile had suddenly fallen.

'The only thing is, I haven't told him about Jack and... and how

I had to give him up.' She cast a troubled glance between them. 'I'm worried he might think I'm a terrible person and hate me for it. Goodness knows, I hated myself for it long enough.'

'Oh, Jean, I'm sure he won't hate you.' Florrie reached over and rested her hand on her friend's arm. 'I don't know anyone who wouldn't feel anything but compassion for what you went through, don't you agree, Ed?'

'Wholeheartedly.' He nodded. 'And put it this way, Jean, if he doesn't understand, or doesn't like it, then he's not worth knowing, and he can sling his hook right out of Micklewick Bay and get himself back to Chester. In fact, I reckon Florrie would do a pretty good job of chasing him out if she got so much as a sniff of him thinking like that.'

'You'd better believe it,' Florrie said firmly. She and Ed had become protective of Jean since she'd shared her heartbreaking story with them.

That made Jean's smiles reappear. 'Yes, I daresay you're right.' She laughed. 'I'm dreading telling him, but I know I'm going to have to do it soon.'

'Get it over and done with, Jean, and the sooner the better. It'll be a huge weight off your shoulders. Then you'll be able to stop fretting about it and just get on with having a lovely time together.' Florrie leant into her friend. 'And I don't mind telling you, I've got a really good feeling about this.'

'Aye, me too,' said Ed. 'It's easy to see he thinks a lot about you from the way he looks at you.'

'Really?' Jean pressed her hands to her chest, her eyes lighting up.

'Really,' Florrie and Ed said in unison.

'Oh, that's given me a real boost, it has. In fact, I think I'll give him a call once I'm done here and before I head up to Maggie's, ask if we can meet to have a chat, get it over and done with before Thursday. That way, if he decides he doesn't want anything to do with me, it won't spoil our Jack and Jenna's evening. Unless you think that's pushy of me?' Concern furrowed her brow as she glanced between them.

'It's not at all pushy, Jean. It sounds like a good plan to me,' said Florrie.

'I agree,' said Ed. 'In fact, there's no time like the present. Feel free to call him now. You can do it from the kitchen where it's nice and private, we'll keep out of your way.'

Jean's hand went to her mouth. 'Oh, my goodness, that does seem very sudden.' Florrie looked on as a mix of emotions crossed Jean's face. 'You're right, Ed, there's no time like the present. I'll do it this minute.'

'Go, Jean,' said Florrie, just as the bell above the door jingled and Amery stepped in.

'Good morning, folks,' he said, his distinctive cologne wafting over to them. He directed his bright blue gaze at Jean as he removed his trilby.

'Good morning, Amery, I wasn't expecting to see you today.' Jean looked suddenly flustered.

Florrie and Ed returned Amery's greeting, exchanging a look of surprise.

Gerty appeared, wandering her way from the kitchen. Spotting Amery, she trotted over to him and started sniffing at his trousers.

'Hello there, Gerty, it's good to see you again,' he said, bending to ruffle her ears. The Labrador gave an enthusiastic wag of her tail before heading to her bed.

Smiling broadly, Amery turned his full attention to Jean. 'Jean, my dear, I was hoping you'd be here. I wanted to tell you how much I enjoyed R.J. Kingston's novel, such clever plotting and well-drawn characters; kept me guessing right up to the end. I finished it late last night and am now eagerly awaiting publication of the next book in the series.'

'I thought you'd enjoy it.' Though Jean smiled, Florrie could see the hint of uncertainty in her eyes. She hoped Amery hadn't detected it and got the wrong impression.

'I did. It was another excellent recommendation of yours, and now I've come to take a couple more Eleanor Farthing books off your hands.'

'Ah, good choice,' said Florrie. 'Jean and I are huge fans of her books. She's having a bit of a renaissance since the BBC announced they were making a new series based on her novels. I think they're set to air in the autumn.'

'Something to look forward to,' Amery said. 'The books aren't the only reason for my visit. I wondered if you'd be free to take a walk with me at some point today, Jean?'

'Oh, I... um, well...' Jean's eyes darted to Florrie.

Seeing Amery's smile falter, Florrie stepped in. 'I know you've got a busy afternoon with Maggie, but why don't you slip away now? It's not like we're rushed off our feet.'

Amery looked on expectantly as he waited for Jean to reply.

'It's a grand day out there, Jean, you might as well make the most of that gorgeous sunshine. You never know when it's going to start chucking it down,' said Ed.

'I agree,' said Florrie.

Jean seemed to take a moment to fortify herself and said, 'That sounds like a lovely idea, Amery. I'll just get my coat.' She briefly caught Florrie's eye. 'There's something I'd like to talk to you about, actually.'

While Jean disappeared to get her coat and hat, Florrie served Amery with a couple of Eleanor Farthing books, the pair making small talk about the upcoming television series. Ed, who'd hung back from resuming his work on the window displays so he could say goodbye to Jean, chipped in every now and then.

It wasn't long before Jean reappeared, bundled up in her warm wool coat and woolly hat. Just as the couple were about to leave, Florrie went to give her friend a hug. 'Good luck, lovely,' she whispered in her ear. 'Everything will be fine, trust me.' She squeezed Jean tightly before releasing her.

Jean gave her a hopeful smile. 'Thanks, lovey. I really hope so.'

'Let us know how it goes.'

'Will do.'

Florrie and Ed watched as Amery, ever the gentleman, held the door open for Jean, bidding them a warm goodbye.

'I'd be amazed if Jean has anything to worry about there,' said Ed as the door clicked shut and the couple stepped out into Victoria Square. 'He seems to hold her in quite high regard.'

'He does. I'm keeping everything crossed it goes well.'

Before Florrie had time to contemplate this further, her mobile pinged to life on the countertop.

'Right, I'll take that as my cue to get back to my work on the window display. I need to make sure everything'll be snag-free for Thursday.'

'Sure I can't take a peek?' Florrie asked, a mischievous smile on her face.

'I'm sure,' he said with a laugh. 'You'll have to wait till Thursday like everyone else.'

Florrie stuck out her bottom lip in an exaggerated display of disappointment. 'That's so not fair.'

Her pitiful expression had Ed shaking his head with laughter. 'Too bad,' he said, as he undid the fastenings of the curtains and climbed back into the window, retying them tightly.

Florrie reached for her mobile to see the text was from Jasmine.

Hi Florrie, hope all's well and The Dragon isn't causing you too many probs. Just a quick reminder about tomorrow's hen do celebrations. It starts at 6pm so one of us will pick you up at five forty. You'll need to wear something you don't mind getting messy!! Let us know where you want picking up – the bookshop or home. Jxx

Florrie couldn't help but laugh at the dragon and scream-face emojis that decorated the text. Though, with everything that had been going on recently – particularly with Ed's mum and whatever it was she was up to, not to mention her dad being poorly – Florrie hadn't had the time to give much thought to her friends' plans for tomorrow evening. She couldn't begin to imagine what it would be – hopefully it wouldn't be anything like pig herding, with Jazz saying to wear something she wouldn't mind getting messy. Then again, if they were picking her up twenty minutes before whatever they'd got planned was due to start, it was highly unlikely; she didn't know of any pig farms they could reach in that time. Whatever it was, the salsa dance class would take some beating.

Smiling, she typed out a quick reply.

> Hi Jazz, thanks for the reminder. I'm intrigued but looking forward to it – as long as it doesn't involve pigs!! Am I okay to get picked up from home? Will update you on 'The Dragon' tomorrow evening. Fxxx

Seconds after she'd pressed send her mobile pinged. She let out a bark of laughter when she saw Jasmine had replied with a line of pig emojis. The feeling that it would be good to have some time with just her four friends washed over her. She was keen to have their take on the weird situation with Dawn.

FOURTEEN

Florrie was greeted by a welcome rush of warmth and the delicious aroma of her mum's lasagne as she pushed open the door of Samphire Cottage. She loved her little home and was always happy to return to it. Florrie had got it for a song, but there'd been no denying the two-up, two-down that sat at the end of a quiet Victorian terrace had been in dire need of renovation. Luckily, her dad had come to the rescue, carrying out the necessary work and saving her a small fortune. She'd had fun sourcing furniture and putting her own stamp on the place and, naturally – being a serious bookworm – there were bookshelves everywhere. She'd created a haven where she loved to relax and unwind. And it had felt even more like home when Ed moved in.

'Hello, I'm back,' she called as she hung up her coat and hat on the line of hooks by the door. The words had just left her mouth when Gerty appeared, hurling herself down the short hallway, her tail wagging frantically. 'Hello there, lass. It's grand to see you, too.' Florrie chuckled as she leant down and ruffled the Labrador's ears. Gerty's greetings were always guaranteed to be full of enthusiasm. 'Shall we go and see what your dad's up to?'

Florrie found Ed setting the small dining table in the kitchen, the fairy lights strung along the blue painted dresser adding a cosy air to the room. 'Mmm. Smells delicious,' she said, smiling. Her mum had dropped off a couple of two-person meals for the freezer last week – something she regularly did – and Ed had lifted the lasagne out the previous evening, giving it time to defrost in readiness for their evening meal.

'It's just about ready. All we need to do is pop the garlic bread in; should be good to go by the time you've got changed.'

'Sounds fab!' She headed over to him and pressed a kiss to his lips, savouring his warmth.

'Blimey, your nose is freezing.'

'I'm not surprised, it's really chilly out there, the temperature's plummeted. I reckon there'll be a ground frost tonight. My dad was telling me it's set to be one of the coldest Aprils for decades. Hopefully, thing's will've warmed up by the time we get to May and our wedding.'

'Yeah, let's hope so. How were your parents? Is your dad any better?' Ed lifted the garlic bread out of the fridge; he'd picked it up from the deli earlier that day. When they were on their way home after work, Florrie had split off from Ed and Gerty, taking the road that led to her parents' house while he'd headed back to Samphire Cottage so he could get the evening meal underway.

'He's still looking pale, but he says he's feeling a bit better; not as dizzy, which is good. And he's determined to help out on Thursday night with the reading and window reveal like he usually does. Not sure my mum's too keen on that, though. When we were on our own, she mentioned that she thinks it's too soon for the tablets to have properly kicked in. Reckons it's wishful thinking on his part.'

'Oh, poor Charlie.' Ed pulled a sympathetic face. 'It'd be a shame if he couldn't join us; wouldn't be the same without him. We could give him and Jack a stool each to sit on while they're on the door, rather than your dad having to stand for long. And maybe it'd reassure your mum if we tell her we'll keep a close eye on him – without making it obvious to your dad, of course. We wouldn't want to make him feel like he's not up to it.'

'Oof! Heaven forbid.' Her eyes widened. 'They say hi, by the way. Asked after your mum, too.' That wasn't strictly true; they hadn't so much asked after Dawn, more that they were keen to know what she'd been up to, and wondered if Florrie had found out what she'd been plotting.

'That's kind of them.' His mouth turned up in a quick smile. 'Am I okay to put this garlic bread in the oven now?'

Florrie took the hint. 'Yep, I'll go and change out of my work stuff. I'll be back in a flash.'

Upstairs, Florrie quickly slipped into her loungewear and hung up her trousers and Happy Hartes Bookshop hoodie, hooking the hanger on the handle of the wardrobe door. As she smoothed her hair in the mirror, her gaze snagged on the collection of crystals she had set out on the dressing table, her brow creasing with a frown. They were a gift from Lark in a bid to give a layer of protection and calm the last time Ed's parents had been causing problems. Florrie had the crystals set on a small wooden tray and had them arranged in a particular order, with the large piece of amethyst at the back, the other crystals, a mix of rose quartz, onyx and fluorite, to the front.

She wasn't OCD with her home by any stretch of the imagination, but she liked to keep it tidy, and she could've sworn the bowl of crystals weren't like that when she'd left the room this morning. It was as if they'd been tipped out and dumped back in haphazardly. Her mind went to the last time they'd returned home and found things knocked over at Samphire Cottage. They'd been relieved to discover it had been next-door's cat, Clarence, who'd sneaked in through the open kitchen window and helped himself to a prowl around the cottage.

Gripped by a feeling of alarm, she rushed to the spare room. Like yesterday, the door was ajar. Florrie knew for a fact it had been closed when they'd left that morning since she'd made a point of checking it. She glanced around the room, her heart thudding as the feeling that someone had been snooping around crept over her, and worse, that something told her it wasn't Ed. Her gaze stopped at the small desk tucked beneath the window, her attention instantly grabbed by one of the drawers where a clutch of papers were poking out, preventing it from closing properly. Her stomach flipped over.

'Oh no!' she said quietly. She'd never leave it like that. It's where she kept the folder that contained the correspondence and invoices for all their wedding-related items. The spilt crystals might be explained away as another visit from Clarence, but the open drawer was a different matter. 'We can't blame next-door's cat for that,' she said to herself.

She rushed over, pulling the drawer fully open, her heart steadying when she saw the wedding file was still there. She flopped down onto the seat, pressing her hand to her chest as her mind tried to make sense of it all. Yes, Ed had been in the house on his own, but she knew instinctively he wasn't responsible for her things being disturbed. Someone else had been in their home and Florrie had a strong feeling that someone was Dawn Harte. Another thought crept into her mind, building as she processed it. The crystals hadn't been disturbed yesterday – she would've noticed straight away if they had. The same went for the papers that were sticking out of the drawer – other than the feeling that someone had been in the room, nothing had looked out of place yesterday, nothing leapt out as being different, and the drawers had definitely been shut. Dawn had given Ed his key back earlier that day which meant...

Florrie let the thoughts permeate for a moment, her heart thumping...

It meant either Dawn had been back to Samphire Cottage before she'd returned Ed's key, or Ed had been searching for something. She felt the latter option highly unlikely, especially since he'd only recently asked if he could have the ruler from the pot on the desk, rather than fetching it himself, knowing she'd prefer him to avoid going in while her wedding dress was in there. Every bone in her body was telling her she could trust Ed, that it wasn't him.

He was as honest as the day was long. His mother, however, was a different matter.

'Tea's ready.' His voice travelled up the stairs, pulling her out of her thoughts. Florrie knew she had no choice but to mention something. The only problem was, she wasn't sure how to bring it up in the conversation. She was reluctant to add to his guilt for letting his mum have a key.

'Coming.' She tucked the wedding folder back into the drawer and made to leave, her eyes roving over the garment cover that contained her wedding dress on the back of the door. At first glance, everything looked okay, but Florrie made a mental note to give it a check over after they'd eaten and before she hopped in the bath.

Back in the kitchen, Florrie found Ed serving up two generous portions of lasagne alongside a selection of vegetables as Gerty watched with hopeful eyes from her bed, drool forming at the corners of her mouth. Florrie couldn't help but laugh. 'What are you like, Gerty? I'm not sure lasagne will do your insides much good.' The Labrador responded with a woeful whimper.

'Right then, time to eat,' said Ed, setting their plates down on the table, steam rising from them.

'Mmm. That looks fab.'

'Can't beat a plateful of Paula's lasagne on a nippy evening, although I have to be honest, it's a close-run thing with her shepherd's pie, especially when it's got loads of cheese grated on top.' He grinned over at her. 'She's a total star, your mum, dropping off meals like this.'

'She is.' Though she agreed with Ed, Florrie had to force a smile. His comments had made her even more conscious of how to broach the subject of the possibility of his mum snooping around their home. And though she didn't expect him to hit back all defensive as he'd always been honest about his less-than-perfect relationship with his parents, she knew he'd be mortified at the suggestion, and that, somehow, felt worse. She couldn't imagine having to face hearing something like that about her own mother, but then again, her mum had never put her in a position like this. Her heart went out to Ed. He was a good man, and really didn't deserve this.

'Have you heard anything from Jean?' he asked, breaking into her thoughts, a forkful of lasagne poised in front of his mouth.

'Mmm.' Florrie nodded enthusiastically, grateful for the change of subject. She finished her mouthful before answering. 'I have. She called as I was on my way back from my mum and dad's, told me everything went really well, which is great. She said Amery was very understanding and kind, didn't blame her for any of it. She sounded like she was back on cloud nine. I was so relieved for her, bless her.'

Ed sat back in his seat, a smile spreading across his face. 'Ah, that's so good to hear. I was sure he'd be okay about it, but I can totally get why Jean was anxious to tell him.'

'Mm, me too. It was a big thing for her, and not exactly something you can just throw into a conversation.'

'Well, she's done it, and it sounds like everything's going to be fine. She'll be glad she's got it off her chest.'

'That's definitely how she sounded.' Florrie wasn't so sure she was going to feel as relieved as Jean when she got her own worries off her chest, but, like Jean, she knew she needed to bite the bullet.

Here goes.

Florrie set her fork down, dread pooling in her stomach, the prospect of upsetting Ed overriding her annoyance at the thought of Dawn creeping around their home. Florrie would prefer it if he'd been the one looking around the spare room and rearranging her bowl of crystals, but she knew, deep down, it wasn't Ed. Adopting a light-hearted, jokey tone, she said, 'You haven't been looking for anything in the spare room recently by any chance, have you?'

Ed looked up from his lasagne wearing a puzzled expression. ''Course not, I know your wedding dress and other wedding stuff's in there. I haven't been in since we had a conversation about it a couple of months ago. Why?'

'Um...' She took a moment, choosing words that wouldn't

sound picky. 'And you know the little bowl of crystals on the dressing table?'

'The ones Lark gave you?'

'Yeah, those.'

'What about them?'

'This is going to sound daft, but you didn't knock them over when you got back earlier, did you?'

'Is this a trick question, or something?' He searched her face as if trying to read her expression. 'But, no, I haven't touched them. I just got changed and came straight back downstairs. Why d'you ask?'

Florrie drew in a deep breath. 'It's just yesterday and today, I found the door to the spare room ajar when, as you know, we've recently been keeping it shut – and I know for a fact that it was properly closed this morning cos I double-checked before we left. And when I was getting changed tonight, I noticed the crystals weren't how I usually arrange them in the bowl.' She cringed inwardly, knowing how petty that sounded.

'You think someone's been in the house while we've been out?'

She nodded, hoping Ed would join the dots and save her from having to put her suspicions into words.

'Have you noticed anything else?'

Florrie nodded again as she told him about the drawer in the spare room.

'Right...' Realisation flickered across his face. 'My mother. It must be her. But wouldn't you think she'd have had a poke around yesterday, rather than coming back today?'

'You'd think so, but I'm pretty sure those crystals were how I usually have them when we left this morning; I would've noticed if they weren't. I know my eyesight's not the sharpest, but that's the sort of thing that draws my eye.'

'Yeah,' Ed said in agreement. 'I wonder what she was looking for?'

'Well, she was pretty keen for me to show her my wedding dress the other day. Maybe, cos I was reluctant, she thought there'd be no harm taking a peek while she was here.' She was mindful to word it as softly as she could even though the thought made her hopping mad.

Ed puffed out his cheeks. 'If she has, then she's well out of order, and I daresay she didn't know where you keep it so she'd have had to snoop around to find it. It's not as if I can defend her and say it's not the sort of thing she'd do, because, in all honesty, I wouldn't put it past her.' He slumped back in his seat, raking his fingers through his hair. 'All I can say is I'm really sorry for being such an idiot and giving her the key. It was an on-the-spot decision, and I couldn't come up with a reason to refuse quickly enough, but if I could turn the clock back I would've been firm with her. Told her Mrs Fergus would pop in and wait for the flaming kettle for us like she's done with other stuff.'

Florrie's heart ached for him. She reached across and took his hand, wrapping her fingers around his. 'It's not your fault, Ed, and you're definitely not an idiot, so please don't say that; you were under pressure of time. Your mum's the one who's in the wrong here, not you. You can't be held responsible for her actions, and I know how forceful she can be when she sets her mind to it.' Florrie had heard Dawn's voice in the background plenty of times when Ed had been on the phone to his parents. Forceful was an under-statement; overbearing more like, and just the sort of person Florrie did her best to avoid. 'And at least you've got your key back now so it's not as if she'll be able to do it again.'

'True.' He nodded wearily. 'It wouldn't be so bad, but she's never shown an interest in where we live, or getting to know you. I just don't get it. And I know she's my mum, but I really wish she'd stayed down in London with my dad and only come up for the wedding. I can't shake the feeling she's up to something, but I can't work out what it is.'

His words sent a shiver running up Florrie's spine.

FIFTEEN
WEDNESDAY 15TH APRIL

Despite Ed having his key back, Florrie still felt the need to check around the house before they left for work that morning. She made sure to do it discreetly so as not to attract his attention and make him feel worse about his mum. The thought that someone had been snooping around their home had unsettled her sufficiently that she'd even used her phone to take a photo of the desk in the spare room, with its drawers closed and the notebooks, pot of pens and faux plant all neatly arranged on top. That done, she took a couple of shots of her wedding dress in its garment bag – after checking it last night, the only thing she'd found untoward was that the zipper hadn't been closed properly, something she always made sure to do – as well as the box of wedding accessories – which included her shoes – she'd set beside the bookcase. Logic told her no one else had sneaked into their home and that it had been Dawn taking advantage of having Ed's key, but all the same, she felt better for having done it.

'What a beautiful morning,' Ed said, his breath hanging in a plume of condensation as they headed down the short path of Samphire Cottage, a clear blue sky above, the air crisp and fresh. The pavements and hedges sparkled in the bright spring sunshine.

'It is.' Florrie closed the gate behind them, slipping her gloved hand into his. She inhaled a lungful of cool, salty air. 'And I was right about the frost, but I love days like these, they make you feel invigorated,' she said brightly. 'Especially when there are signs of the gardens springing back to life everywhere.' Spring always arrived late in North Yorkshire and this year's in particular appeared reluctant to release its chilly grip.

Soon, they turned the corner onto the top prom, Gerty trotting along on the end of her lead, setting a jaunty pace, the cries of seagulls filling the air as they wheeled overhead. 'Looking forward to this evening with the lasses?' Ed turned, glancing down at her, his eyes warm.

'I am, actually.' She beamed up at him, her heart lilting at his smile. 'Still haven't a clue what I'll be doing, but I don't think it can be too far away if I'm being picked up just after half five for a six o'clock start. I'm not sure what time I'll be back, though, so you might need to eat alone tonight.'

'Don't worry, I've been filled in on all the details.'

'Care to share any of them?'

'Nope.'

'*Please.*' She fluttered her eyelashes at him, making him hoot with laughter.

'Nope.'

'Oh, well, it's always worth a try,' she said, feigning disappointment. 'So are you looking forward to your stag night with the lads on Saturday? I assume everything's organised?'

'Sure am. And, yep, Bear's got it all in hand; organised the minibus, booked us a table. You can't beat a bloomin' good curry and a few beers with your mates.'

'I reckon you've got off lightly, unlike me with all the torture of strippagram and pig herding teasing. Not so sure why I deserved it,' she said with a smile.

'It's cos the five of you go back a long way, you know how to wind each other up. I haven't known the fellas all that long, and Max is new to the group. We didn't want to scare him off.'

'Doubt you'd do that – have you seen the way he looks at Jazz? Besotted doesn't come into it.'

'Yeah, I guess you have a point.'

Florrie heaved a happy sigh. If anyone deserved happiness, it was Jazz. It was so good to see everything working out for her friend, especially after the tough few years she'd had since the kids' father had died. She'd had to become both mum and dad overnight, working all hours to make sure they didn't go without. But now, she was radiating happiness and thriving in her relationship with Max Grainger who, it was clear to everyone, loved her deeply.

Before they knew it, they'd arrived at Mr and Mrs H's bench. Sitting down, Ed threw his arm around Florrie's shoulders, delivering a kiss to her cheek. She snuggled in closer to him, delighting in his warmth as she gazed out to sea. She loved this man with a passion she hadn't thought she was capable of. He was kind and considerate, and he had the biggest heart with so much love to give. It was something Florrie struggled to understand after the cold childhood he'd experienced with very little parental affection thrown his way. It made her wonder how his parents could be so frosty to the loving little boy he must've been. They sat in silent contemplation, Florrie's thoughts wandering to Ed's grandparents, wishing they were still here to see them getting married. Her own grandparents having died before she was born, Bernard and Dinah Harte had stepped in and filled that role, and there wasn't a day that went by when she didn't miss them. From the sigh that emanated from Ed, she wondered if his thoughts were heading down a similar track.

'You know, I've been thinking about giving surfing a try.'

'You have?' Evidently his thoughts were on a very different path altogether!

'Yeah, I was talking to Jeff Palmer when I met Bear down at the Jolly a couple of weeks back. As you know, he's an avid surfer, said he'd show me the ropes if I fancied.'

Florrie turned her attention to the sea, trying to imagine running into the waves in a wetsuit. Though the sun was shining, the water, with its ripples of frothy white horses, still looked bitterly cold. 'Rather you than me,' she said with a shiver.

'Fair enough,' he said, laughing. 'Right, time to move, my backside's in danger of freezing to this bench.' Ed removed his arm from Florrie's shoulders and pushed himself up, offering her his hand.

'Not so sure your grandparents would be too keen on that,' Florrie chuckled, letting him pull her up.

They walked along, heading towards Skitey Bank that twisted and turned its way down to the bottom prom and the road that led to Old Micklewick. To the right, the grand Victorian houses loomed over them, a legacy of when the town was in its heyday and families made wealthy from local industry further up the coast holidayed there. It regularly boggled Florrie's mind that these five-storey houses were actually built as holiday homes, with their panoramic views of the sea dominated by the brooding mass of Thorncliffe. The properties even included servants' quarters, and though they'd long since been converted into apartments, they clung onto a haughty air like an old dowager from times gone by.

As they took the turn onto Endeavour Road that led to Victoria Square, it gladdened her heart to see the refurbishment of The Micklewick Majestic was well underway. The once exclusive hotel had been a major attraction for the town until its owner had fallen on hard times and the building had been left to fall into disrepair. But its fortunes had changed when it was bought by Jasmine's partner and property tycoon, Max, who had ambitious plans for its renovation.

Florrie looked up from the counter where she was checking stock levels of Jenna's latest book in readiness for tomorrow's author event as the bell above the door chimed and Lark appeared. Her friend was a blast of colour in her patchwork coat and purple flared velvet trousers. 'Hi, Lark. How's things?' Gerty made a beeline for her, wagging her tail as she went.

'All fine and dandy, thanks, flower. How about you? And how's this gorgeous girl?' She bent and made a fuss of the Labrador which was met with much tail wagging.

With Gerty satisfied that Lark didn't have a stash of dog treats secreted in her coat pockets, she plodded back to her bed and flumped down, resting her head on her paws. Florrie gestured to the window, signalling to Lark that Ed was working behind the curtain; she didn't want her friend to mention his mum and risk making him feel uncomfortable. Lark nodded, indicating she understood, then mouthed, 'Where's Dawn?'

Florrie gave an exaggerated shrug, raising her palms, mouthing back, 'No idea,' to which Lark nodded in acknowledgement. 'All's good here,' Florrie continued. 'I'm looking forward to whatever you've got planned this evening.'

Lark beamed. 'Ah, I'm happy to hear that, and I say with confidence that you're going to love it.' Arriving at the counter, she unhooked her patchwork tote bag from her shoulder and fished around inside. Lowering her voice, she said, 'I gather you've been having a bit of a rough time of it so I thought you might need some more supplies.' She set out a lavender and rose geranium room spray along with a stout bottle of bubble bath infused with lavender and chamomile essential oils. It was from her homemade aromatherapy brand that she sold in Lark's Vintage Bazaar.

'Aww, that's so kind, Lark.' Florrie pressed her hands to her chest. 'Thank you.' She was regularly touched by her friend's kindness. Lark had given her some of the bubble bath last Christmas and Florrie had loved it, regularly finding herself drifting off as the soothing aromas had filled the bathroom and worked their magic.

'How've things been?' Lark's usual speaking voice was soft, but now she kept her tone extra low. 'I saw Dawn arrive at the shop the other day. She has a very determined walk. Looked like she was on a bit of a mission.'

'Er, yeah, you could say that. I'll tell you about it tonight; I'd value everyone's opinion.'

'Fair enough, as long as you're okay.' Lark's expression told Florrie she wasn't completely convinced, but then again, she and the rest of the group of friends were all too aware of Dawn and Peter Harte's track record. It included the attempted sabotage of an author event, which had been circling around Florrie's mind with the latest one inching closer.

Their conversation was brought to a halt by Mrs Plews coming to the counter with a handful of books.

'Right, I'd best scoot, but I'll see you after work.' With that, Lark flashed her a wide smile and dashed off, flicking her long blonde plait as she went.

Once Mrs Plews was dealt with, Florrie returned to her task of checking Jenna's book on the stock level management system. Installing the software had been a godsend as far as keeping up with stock and reordering was concerned. It had saved Florrie hours of time, leaving her free to focus on other ways of improving the bookshop. She'd just got started when the shop door burst open and Dawn arrived in her inimitable way, making Florrie start.

The woman knew how to make an entrance, that was for sure. Dawn glanced over at Florrie, wearing what could only be described as a smirk. Behind her strode a tall woman Florrie had never seen before. The stranger had a mass of glossy dark waves offset by her berry-coloured long velvet coat. She wore an aloof expression as her eyes, framed by impossibly long eyelashes, tracked around the bookshop, the faint hint of a sneer pulling at her mouth.

'Where's Edward?' Dawn asked in her usual officious tone, completely bypassing any pleasantries.

Hello to you, too, Dawn. Florrie groaned inwardly – so much for not letting Ed's mother get to her. 'He's working on the display in the window.' Florrie could easily see how Ed had been intimidated into giving his mother his key. She was a force to be reckoned with, a woman used to getting her own way. Florrie had never encountered anyone like her before.

'Right, well, I need him out here.' She marched over to the window, vigorously shaking the curtain that hid the display. 'Edward, I need you to get yourself out here. Now.'

The way she spoke to her son made Florrie bristle. Anyone would think he was someone she disliked or that she was a sergeant major, barking out orders at a bootcamp.

Florrie glanced at the younger woman, feeling awkward. The sooner she served her and got her out of the shop, the better. She didn't want to risk a potential new customer being put off by Dawn's behaviour. 'Can I help you?' she asked, fixing a friendly smile to her face.

The younger woman gave a scornful laugh. 'I very much doubt it.' Her condescending tone knocked Florrie off kilter.

'What's up?' Ed appeared from behind the curtain, stopping dead in his tracks. Florrie watched as the weary expression he was wearing on hearing his mother's voice was replaced by a mix of shock and disbelief, the colour draining from his face. He glanced first at his mother and then to the other woman, then back to his mother. There was no mistaking he was shaken to the core. Finally finding his voice, he said, 'Luella?'

Luella? Florrie's mind scrambled to remember where she'd heard the name before, but her brain was too fuddled by the strange situation that was unfolding, making it impossible to grasp hold of.

'Hi, Eddie,' Luella said, in what Florrie thought sounded like a transatlantic accent. 'It's been a while.' She giggled as she gave him a coy smile, wiggling her fingers in a wave.

Eddie? It was the first time Florrie had ever heard anyone address her fiancé as 'Eddie'.

Florrie looked on, trying to make sense of this odd scene playing out in front of her, noting how uncomfortable Ed seemed. In that moment, realisation struck and she remembered where she'd heard the name Luella before. Her hand flew to her mouth. '*Oh my gosh!*' she said with a gasp. It was his ex-girlfriend!

SIXTEEN

Florrie had known about Luella before she and Ed had got together. She was the woman he'd been dating right before he first came to Micklewick Bay a couple of years ago. If her memory served her correctly, Luella hadn't taken Ed breaking up with her too well and had trashed his London flat while he was here. Memories started tumbling into her mind, clashing around chaotically: Mr H mentioning an ex of Ed's that put him in mind of Dawn and how they shared an aggressive temper and were prone to throwing and smashing things. Him describing them as manipulative, that they had a conversational style that was to shout and dominate. It was rare for Mr H to say anything negative about anyone, which was why his comments had struck such a chord with her.

Florrie's pulse started whooshing in her ears and her stomach churned so violently it was making her feel physically sick. If she was feeling this way, she dreaded to think how Ed must be affected by it all. Her heart went out to him.

'B... but... but... What are you even doing here?' Ed pushed his fingers into his hair, looking at Luella in disbelief. 'How did you find out where I live?'

'Your mom told me.' Luella's smile widened as she hitched her oversized bag further onto her shoulder, seemingly oblivious to the chilly tone that laced Ed's words.

He pressed his hand to his forehead, glaring at Dawn, his breathing shallow. 'Would you like to tell me what's going on, Mother?' he said. From the way he spoke, it was clear he was trying to keep his anger from his voice.

'Calm yourself down, boy. I can assure you, nothing's going on,' Dawn said, adopting her familiar overbearing tone. 'Lu's the friend I bumped into the other day – remember, I told you it was the reason I didn't get back here with your key.' Dawn treated him to a rare smile that had no warmth to it. It crossed Florrie's mind that it could easily be mistaken for a snarl.

'You appear to have omitted an important detail.' He set his mouth in a hard line.

Dawn steamed on, evidently choosing to ignore what Ed was getting at. 'You know very well you'd be disappointed if I didn't let you know Lu was in the area. And, since she said she was keen to catch up with you, it made sense for me to bring her here, rather than that poky house you share where there's hardly room to swing a cat.' She side-eyed Florrie, as if to make sure her thinly veiled barb hit its target.

Florrie's eyes widened at the thought of Dawn turning up at Samphire Cottage with Luella. That would've been unbearable on so many levels. And, ludicrous as it sounded, she wouldn't put it past Dawn pulling a stunt like that.

'Mother, that's hardly helpf—'

'I felt sure you'd want to catch up with her, too, see how she's been doing. After all, you and Lu were *very* close for a long time, and you're well aware of how fond your father and I are of her.' Dawn was talking so fast, she barely drew breath.

Ed shook his head in disbelief, raking his teeth over his bottom lip.

Before he could speak, Luella picked up from Dawn. 'We ran into one another in London, and your mom described Migglewig Bay – *seriously weird* name, by the way – and I couldn't even begin to imagine you living in such a funny little place or working at a *bookshop* of all places, especially with you barely being able to read, so when Dawn said she was popping up for a visit and that I should join her, I thought, hey, why not?' She treated him to an extra wide smile.

Florrie's anger blazed at the cruel reference to Ed's dyslexia.

'So you didn't just "run in" to Luella, you asked Luella to join you?' He turned to his mother, giving her the full weight of his accusatory glare.

'Semantics, boy.' Dawn waved a dismissive hand at him. 'What does it matter anyway? She's here now.'

'Aren't you pleased to see me, Eddie?' Luella asked, batting her incredibly long eyelashes at him. They were so long, Florrie felt sure they must be false, not that she was an expert on these things; any make-up she wore she kept to a minimum.

She was still trying to get her head around it all when Dawn turned to her, a cold glint in her eye, and said, 'I don't suppose Edward will have told you all about Luella, his girlfriend of not so very long ago. His father and I always say she was the one that got away – we were devastated when they broke up.'

The dig wasn't wasted on Florrie. 'Yes, I know who Luella is,' she said, determined to keep her voice steady, wondering all the while what Dawn was doing bringing her here. She was amazed his parents knew the names of any of Ed's previous girlfriends; they usually took such little interest in his life, unless it was trying to get him to hand over the bookshop to them. Florrie knew the only reason her own name stuck was because of the bookshop connection. They wouldn't give two hoots about her otherwise.

'Mother, this is seriously out of order. I'm not sure what purpose you thought it would serve, bringing Luella here, but you had no right.' Though Ed spoke quietly, there was a steeliness to his voice, and Florrie had never seen him look so angry. 'We need to talk, and not just about this, there's something else; I'm sure I don't need to tell you what it is.' He turned to his ex-girlfriend.

'You should never have listened to my mother, Luella; you shouldn't have come here.'

His ex's face darkened with a scowl that matched the one Dawn was now wearing. 'That's not very kind or friendly, Eddie. I've come all this way to see you, and that's all the greeting I get?' She pushed her mouth into a moue, her eyes flashing angrily at Florrie.

It was all the trigger Ed needed. 'Right, both of you, come with me.' In the next moment he'd placed his hand on Luella's elbow and guided her out of the shop, his mother stomping over the floorboards after them. Dawn shot Florrie a contemptuous glare before slamming the door shut with such force the whole building shook.

The bell was still jangling when Leah returned from the teashop a few moments later where she'd taken her lunchbreak, Marty in tow. 'Wow! That was one heck of a door slam. We could feel the vibration as we were walking down the stairs. Did someone have their knickers in a knot?'

'It was Dawn,' said Florrie, still feeling unnerved by the hatred in the parting expressions the two women had treated her to.

'*Dawn?* What happened? Are you okay?' Leah's eyes were full of concern.

'I'm fine, thanks, Leah. It looks as though she'd arranged for Ed's ex-girlfriend to visit the town and would you believe she actually brought her to the shop?'

'Wow! That's weird,' said Marty.

'She did what?' asked Leah, incredulous. 'She's seriously delulu, that woman.'

'Yeah, that's one way of putting it.' Florrie looked out onto the street, wondering where Ed had taken the two women, memories of what he'd shared of his relationship with Luella running through her mind. Toxic was how he'd described it. Said she reminded him of his mother, with her touch-paper temper that could be ignited by the simplest of things. Florrie felt a dart of worry shoot through her. She hoped he'd be okay, dealing with the two hot-headed, volatile women on his own, that he wouldn't be bullied into anything. Not for the first time did she wish Mr H was still here. He'd had a gentle strength, and was the wisest man Florrie had ever known. He'd have the right words at his fingertips and would've offered Ed some much-needed support. And there would've been no way Dawn would've waltzed in and tried to cause such disruption the way she had.

Florrie reached for the aromatherapy room spray Lark had dropped off earlier and gave the air around her a generous spritz, even giving herself a quick squirt for good measure. Right now, she needed all the help she could get.

'Try not to worry, I'm sure everything'll be okay,' said Leah, offering a kind smile, rubbing Florrie's arm.

'I can hang around until Ed comes back, if you like?' Marty said earnestly, looking impossibly young in his suit and tie. 'My dad'll be cool with it.' Marty's father was Sam Asquith, a senior partner at Cuthbert, Asquith & Co, and Florrie wasn't so sure he'd be 'cool' with his son taking an extended lunchbreak on her account. And though she was touched by the young lad's offer, she'd rather avoid him getting caught in any potential crossfire of whatever was going on with Dawn and Luella. Come to think of it, she wouldn't want anyone to get caught in the crossfire; if the two women returned to the bookshop, she'd make sure all customers had left, then she'd turn the sign to closed and bolt the door.

'It's fine, Marty, but thanks for your offer, I really appreciate it.' She gave him a grateful smile.

'Okay, but you know where I am if you need me.' He turned to his girlfriend. 'If Ed's mum comes back and kicks off, just call me and I'll come straight over. Moral support and all that.'

'Will do, Marty.' Leah nodded gravely.

After dropping a quick kiss on his girlfriend's cheek, Marty left the shop, Leah gazing after him with puppy dog eyes.

'He's a nice lad,' Florrie said.

Colour flooded Leah's cheeks and her mouth tipped up in a smile. 'Yeah, he is, and his parents are really cool, too. Unlike someone else's we know.' She gave Florrie a loaded look.

SEVENTEEN

It was almost two hours later when Ed returned to the bookshop, looking dishevelled and exhausted. Though her heart leapt with anxiety, Florrie was relieved to see he was on his own.

'How did it go?' she asked, rushing over to him, searching his eyes for clues.

'Ugh!' He dragged a hand down his face. 'I hate to say it, but I think it's kicking off again.'

Her heart plunged. 'What? But I thought they were okay with us having the bookshop?'

Ed shook his head, rolling his eyes wearily.

Florrie caught Leah's eye. Holding up two fingers, she mouthed, 'Two minutes,' then pointed in the direction of the kitchen.

The young assistant nodded and mouthed back, 'Good luck.'

'What happened? Where did you go?' Florrie asked, gently closing the kitchen door behind them.

Ed puffed out his cheeks, exhaling noisily. 'We went to the B&B where my mother's staying with it being not too far from here. I didn't want to go to Luella's guesthouse, and I didn't know where else to take them where we could talk in private; I certainly didn't want to go to our home.'

Florrie was inordinately relieved to hear that, though it didn't stop her heart from banging hard against her ribcage. 'So what did your mum say?'

He rested his hands on her shoulders, looking intently into her eyes. 'Before I go any further, I want you to know that whatever ridiculous lengths they go to they're never going to change my feelings for you. I love you more than I can ever say – which isn't hard considering how inarticulate I am – but I just want you to know that.' He gave a lopsided smile. 'It looks like their old resentment of my grandfather bequeathing us the bookshop has reared its ugly head again, and from what I can gather, us getting married has been the catalyst.'

Florrie felt her knees buckle. She pulled out a dining chair and sat down. She could hardly believe this was happening less than three weeks before their wedding.

Ed took the chair beside her, reaching his arm across her shoulder and pulling her close. She inhaled his familiar comforting scent: a mix of his woody cologne, the bookshop and a hint of paint.

'But I thought they were okay with us having the bookshop now, especially with Jean and Jack having shares in it. Didn't your dad tell you as much when you went down to London to speak to him the last time there was trouble? They've been quiet about it for over a year.'

'I know, and he did, yeah. But it would seem things have changed, though my mother didn't go into too much detail in front of Luella. I called my father and he finally answered when I told him Luella was here. I figured that if I sounded angry about it, he'd ignore my calls – which is what he's been doing since my mother landed in town – so I made out I was really chuffed to see her and – surprise, surprise – he rang back straight away. I did a bit of subtle digging while I was talking to him, and it looks like it's the same old problem of money running through their fingers. They're in debt again thanks to some investment they made which didn't quite work out, or at least that's what he tells me. Anyroad, our impending wedding seems to have got them running scared and I got the impression they think once we're married it'll make it even less likely for us to hand over the bookshop, or sell it and give them the proceeds. He told me that he and my mother thought we'd never last and that you'd hand over your share of the bookshop to me, and that I'd eventually "see sense" as he put it, and sign it over to them.'

'Oh, Ed, this is getting so old.' She rested her elbows on the table and put her face in her hands.

'I know. I've told both of them it's never gonna happen. I mean, can you imagine if we did what they wanted? They'd have it sold and the money spent in no time, with nothing to show for it. All my grandparents' hard work would be gone just like that.' He clicked his fingers. 'The bookshop's been in the Harte family for generations.'

'It has, ever since the shops were first built,' Florrie added, her voice muffled by her hands. 'It's only ever been a Harte's bookshop.'

'Which makes me all the more determined for it to continue as a Harte's bookshop, and even more so with you.' He took her hand in his. 'You and me, Florrie, we're a team. Together, we've brought the bookshop up to date and I know my grandparents would be proud of everything we've done. The teashop has been a genius idea as has Jean and Jack's investment. I want to build something we can be proud to pass on to our children, to safeguard its future, and keep it in the Harte family for more generations to come.'

As Ed spoke, the emotions Florrie had been battling since Dawn's arrival in town swirled together, mingling with her concerns about her dad, intensifying and gaining pace. She fought against them as they rose in her chest, clogging her throat. She pressed her lips together in a bid to keep them under control, but as soon as he'd finished speaking, it was as if the dam had burst and a sob escaped as she dissolved into hot tears.

'Hey, sweetheart, don't cry.' Ed wrapped both arms around her, squeezing her tight, pressing a kiss to her head.

Ed's words meant more to her than she could ever say. On top of that, he was communicating with her, sharing his thoughts and views instead of adopting his usual tack of going in on himself and trying to resolve problems on his own. Having his support, him articulating that they were a team, made her feel safe and secure in a way she hadn't realised she needed from him. It somehow seemed to galvanise their relationship.

'We've got this, okay?' he said softly. He sat back, taking her face in his hands, wiping her tears with his thumbs. 'Nothing's going to come between us, and nothing's going to make us give up the bookshop. I've told Luella she should go home, that I'm in love with you, that my mother had no right to meddle; made sure she was in no doubt that I had nothing to do with her being here, had no knowledge of it.' He placed a tender kiss on her forehead. 'So, I suggest we just block out all their noise and get back to looking forward to getting married. Deal?'

'Deal.' Florrie nodded, her heart feeling lighter.

EIGHTEEN

A knock at the door of Samphire Cottage just after five forty made Florrie jump to her feet. 'That'll be one of the lasses,' she said, reaching for her bag that was hooked on the back of one of the kitchen chairs. She'd already got her hat and coat on in readiness for heading out.

'Have a fantastic time,' Ed said, planting a warm kiss full on her mouth. The strength of it made Florrie's heart flutter.

'Mmm. I will,' she said, kissing him again. 'And I'll look forward to catching up with you when I get back.'

'Sounds good to me.' His eyes twinkled at her, making her heart flutter some more. After their chat at the bookshop, it had felt like a weight had lifted from her shoulders, knowing they were united in taking a stand against his parents. They were a team, and it felt good.

Florrie opened the door to see Stella smiling back at her in the soft dusk light. 'Now then, missus.' Her friend was looking glamorous in a black shearling coat and a pair of black flared jeans. 'Your chariot awaits.'

'Hi, Stells, I wondered who'd be picking me up.'

'Hi, Stella,' Ed said from behind Florrie. 'Have fun and I'll see you when you get back.'

'Thanks, Ed. We should have Florrie back around elevenish.'

'So, are you allowed to tell me what we're up to tonight?' Florrie asked after they'd said their goodbyes to Ed.

'Not until we get there.' Stella threw a smile over her shoulder as they made their way down the path and out onto the street. 'All I can say is that we're picking up Jazz en route, and it won't take long to get there.'

'That's so not helpful, Stells, but as long as it's got nothing to do with pigs and the herding of said creatures, then I'm happy.' Florrie chuckled as she climbed into Stella's stylish four-wheel drive.

'Yeah, you and me both. So, how's things with Dawn?' Stella asked as they headed down the road.

'Oof! Blimey. How to answer that one!'

Stella stole a quick look in Florrie's direction. 'That doesn't sound too good. Please tell me the obnoxious woman's not up to her old tricks and causing trouble.'

'I wish I could, but that would be a lie. If where we're heading this evening is the sort of place we can chat, then I'll tell you there – a lot's been happening and I wouldn't want you to have to hear it all over again – but if not, I'll save it for Friday at the Jolly.' She watched as Stella took the turn for the lane that led to Jasmine's house.

'You'll definitely have the opportunity tonight. And we don't want you keeping it all in till Friday.'

After scooping up Jasmine, they headed into town where Stella took a turn on to Endeavour Road. A moment later, she announced, 'Here we are.' She flicked the indicator and effortlessly reverse-parked into what seemed to Florrie like a space that was far too small.

'I don't know how you do that, Stells. I need a space that would fit at least two double-decker buses before I'd even consider it.'

'Wish I could take the credit, but the sensors on the car help a lot.' She flashed a grin at her.

'I'll take your word for it.'

'You seriously can't be worse than me, Florrie,' said Jasmine. 'I managed to scrape the front of my car on a drystone wall when I was trying to park up at Danskelfe Castle last week.'

'Oops!' Florrie replied.

Out on the pavement, her gaze ran along the row of shops, including Nate's recycling business which was now in complete darkness.

'Follow me,' said Stella, all businesslike.

Florrie did as she was bid, trotting behind her friends who stopped at the doorway of Pippa's Paint Pots, the newly opened pottery painting shop.

'We're pottery painting?' she asked.

'We sure are.' Jasmine grinned. 'This is Maggie's hen do suggestion.'

'After you, madame,' said Stella, holding the door open for her.

Stepping inside, she was greeted by a bubbly atmosphere with an upbeat playlist burbling away in the background. Florrie spotted Lark and Maggie already settled at a table, chatting away. They were wearing brightly coloured PVC pinnies with the shop's name and logo. Maggie looked up and waved excitedly, Lark following suit. Their smiling faces and the warmth of their greeting sent a wave of happiness washing over her.

'Come and park your bum, missus,' said Maggie. 'Since you're guest of honour, we thought you should sit at the head of the table.'

'And you've got to wear what's in here – no arguments,' said Jasmine, smiling as she passed a gift bag down the table once they were seated.

'Oh, okay.' Florrie took the bag that bore the word 'Congratula-tions' in large gold letters, and peered inside to see it stuffed with bright pink tissue paper.

Before she had a chance to lift anything out, a smiley-faced young woman appeared at their table wearing a name badge that told them she was called Casey. 'Now you're all here, can I get you some drinks?' she asked.

'Ooh, sounds good,' said Lark, beaming up at her. 'I've been hearing wonderful things about the hot chocolates here, so I think I'll have one of those with all the trimmings, thanks.'

'Can you make that two, please?' said Jasmine.

'Two house special hot chocolates,' said Casey, as she wrote down their order.

'Actually, I'll have the same, thanks,' said Florrie, thinking they sounded delicious.

In the end, all of the friends were tempted by the house special hot chocolates.

'So, what's been happening, flower?' Stella asked as soon as Casey had left their table and was out of earshot. All eyes turned to Florrie.

'Actually, can we let Florrie see what's in the gift bag first?' Lark said gently.

'Good point,' agreed Jasmine. 'We can't go any further until... well, you'll see.' She threw Florrie a wink.

'I hope there's nothing risqué in here. I know what certain people round this table can be like, mentioning no names... Jasmine and Maggie.' That set the friends off laughing, Jasmine's dirty cackle standing out above the others.

Removing the tissue paper, Florrie reached inside the bag and lifted out a sparkly, plastic tiara with the word 'BRIDE' emblazoned across it in pink faux gems. Her face broke out into a beaming smile. 'Aww, lasses.'

'You've got to wear it,' said Jasmine.

'Of course I will.' Florrie slid the tiara onto her head. 'What d'you think?'

'Very stylish, flower,' said Stella.

'There's more,' said Lark.

The other items included a bright pink sash with 'THE BRIDE' splashed across it, a pair of pink, flashing 'Bride' earrings and a matching flashing 'Bride' badge. 'Thanks, lasses, I love it all,' Florrie said, adjusting her tiara which was catching on the arms of her glasses.

'You're looking very eye-catching there, petal,' said Maggie, as

Florrie pressed the button on her badge so it flashed along with her earrings.

'Hey, never let anyone tell you we're not classy birds with discerning taste in gifts for our friends.' Jasmine gave one of her cheeky grins. 'Oh, and you've got to wear them on our next hen event, which is on Sunday.'

'Oh, right.' Florrie had just started to ponder what that event might be when Casey arrived with their hot chocolates.

'Here you are, lasses.' She was greeted with sounds of approval as she proceeded to hand out five generous-sized mugs spilling over with whipped cream and marshmallows finished with grated chocolate and a flake. 'Enjoy,' she said as she left them to dive in.

'Not sure how I'm going to tackle this,' said Lark as she eyed the generous mountain of whipped cream that sat on top of her drink.

'You're going to have to dig your way in with one of these,' said Maggie, waving a teaspoon at her.

'Good plan.' Lark scooped up her spoon.

'Right then, Florrie, you, Jazz and Stells need to choose an item to paint. They're on the shelves over there,' said Maggie. 'Once you've done that, Pippa said she'd come over and tell us what we need to do and share some tips.'

'Ah, right, okay. Come on, you two, let's go and choose something.'

'Good plan. Mind, I don't need to warn you in advance, lasses, since you already know my artistic skills are pretty limited, verging on zero – so don't forget to keep your expectations suitably low.'

'There's no of fear of that, don't forget we were at school with you, Stells. We haven't forgotten your shameful efforts in art class. That time we had to do portraits of the person opposite is etched on my mind forever, with me being the unfortunate soul sitting at the other side of the table from you. My self-confidence still hasn't fully recovered since you drew me looking like Mr Potato Head,' said Jasmine dryly, making them all howl with laughter, yet somehow managing to keep a straight face herself. 'Who knew my nose was somewhere round by my right lug 'ole? And as for my mouth, it was like some sort of squidged banana-shaped thing; I've never seen anything like it in my life. You'd never think it was one of my besties who'd drawn me, more like my arch enemy.' She shot Stella a look of mock offence.

'Please stop, Jazz!' Stella pleaded. 'I'm not sure my bladder can hold up for much longer.' But Jasmine appeared not to have heard.

'You have no idea how lucky you are to have escaped such horrors, Mags. Honest, she had me looking like some giant troll with an oversized head, the sort that gives kids nightmares for the rest of their lives.'

'I still struggle to sleep for it now,' said Florrie, giggling.

'Harsh,' said Stella, though she appeared unable to stop herself from laughing.

'But fair,' added Jasmine.

'Oh, poor Stells,' said Lark, giggling.

'And what made you think I had three eyes?' Jasmine asked, feigning outrage. 'I'm not some creature from Greek mythology, you know.' That had them all cackling loudly.

'I didn't deliberately give you three eyes, it's cos I'd drawn one in the wrong place so had to rub it out, but I couldn't get it to disappear completely, which is why you had a faint smudgy one. I hoped no one would notice.'

'Well, you hoped in vain. It was like the lovechild of Mr Potato Head and some mythical sea creature! Not pretty. Oh, and remind me again how you explained away the fact that you'd given me a moustache?'

Stella was laughing so hard, she was bent double. 'Same reason as the third eye. I'd had to rub something out; it left a bit of a shadow.'

'Yeah, you're not wrong – a five o'clock shadow,' quipped Jasmine. 'And that's not the worst of it, Mags.' Jasmine reached over and tapped Maggie's hand for emphasis. 'The teacher only went and put it up on the wall in the entrance area with all the other portraits for the *whole* school to see. And some of the kids even guessed it was me! Can you believe that? Scarred me for life, it did.'

'Oh my days, Jazz, you really need to stop before I piddle my pants,' said Maggie, wiping tears of laughter from her eyes.

'What is it with you lot and your bladders? Don't you ever think of popping to the loo before you leave the house?' Jasmine shook her head.

'My bladder still isn't right since I had Lucy, so I've got an excuse,' said Maggie. 'What's your excuse, Stells?'

'On that happy note, shall we go and choose something to paint?' Florrie pushed her chair back and stood up, her cheeks aching from laughing so hard.

'I think that's a very good idea,' agreed Stella, still chuckling.

'Me too,' said Jasmine.

A few minutes later, Florrie returned to the table with a chunky mug, as did Jasmine, while Stella had chosen a small tea plate and was muttering something about not having a clue how she was going to decorate it. Florrie couldn't help but laugh at the face her friend was pulling.

They'd just got settled in their seats when Pippa arrived, detailing her instructions and sharing tips in a cheerful manner, explaining that they needed to keep it in mind that the paint colour would deepen once their pots were fired. 'I think that's everything,' she said. 'Enjoy yourselves, ladies, and shout up if you have any questions.' That done, the friends selected their paint and tools in a babble of excitable chatter, Florrie deciding to go for a simple design of a sky-blue background with large dots in contrasting shades.

Lark picked up the conversation Stella had started earlier. 'So, Florrie, what's been happening? I'm sure I saw Dawn head into the bookshop this morning. Looked like she was chatting to a tall woman – I got the impression they were together.'

Florrie's happiness of moments ago scattered and her mood sank like a lead weight. She glanced around the room to make sure no one would be able to hear their conversation. Noting that the level of background music and chatter would make it difficult for anyone to eavesdrop, she took a fortifying breath. 'Well, you're right about both things. Dawn did come into the bookshop, and she was with the tall woman; it was Ed's ex-girlfriend, Luella, and – I can hardly believe I'm saying this – Dawn had invited her to Micklewick Bay.' Saying it out loud made the situation sound even more ridiculous.

A collective gasp ran around the table. Lark's hand flew to her mouth as Stella tutted and shook her head.

'Why would she do that?' Lark asked.

'You could ask the same of everything she and her husband have done right through Ed's life,' Florrie said wryly.

'Fair point,' agreed Stella.

Florrie swallowed as she went on to share what had happened since their Friday catch-up at the Jolly. By the time she'd finished, her stomach was in knots. She swept her gaze around the table to see four stunned faces looking back at her.

'You've got to be kidding me,' said Maggie in disbelief. 'I mean, are they for real?'

'I thought they'd finally accepted that Mr H had wanted you and Ed to have the bookshop. Didn't they tell you as much well over a year ago?' asked Stella.

Florrie nodded. 'They did – well, Peter told Ed when he went to see him in London two Christmases back.'

'Says exactly what sort of people they are that they decide to resurrect it just weeks before you're due to get married. And if that's not bad enough, they stoop even lower and drag an ex-girlfriend into it, hoping to tempt Ed away from you.' Jasmine shook her head in disgust, her cheeks flushing angrily. 'He's their son, for God's sake! Who does that?'

'They've really gone too far this time, Florrie.' Lark gave her a sympathetic look. 'They're beginning to sound deluded.' These were strong words coming from Lark who rarely said anything bad about anyone. 'But it's reassuring to hear Ed's standing up to them, leaving them in no doubt that you're not going to be bullied or manipulated into doing what they want. And that it's you he loves. I hope that makes you feel better?'

Florrie nodded. 'It does, actually. It seems different from before, when he used to go quiet and ignore their calls, or – worse – disappear. He faced them head-on this time which will, hopefully, make them back off.'

'I'd love to help them back off, send the old witch packing out of town as fast as her broomstick can carry her.' Jasmine's eyes shone angrily. 'Mind, there's somewhere I'd like to shove it first.' The look of utter distaste on Jasmine's face made the friends laugh.

'Oh, Jazz, I do love you,' said Florrie, her heart filling with affection for her friend.

'Just know we're here for you if you need us. I'm happy to nip over to the bookshop if Dawn or this Luella turn up; I don't want you to have to deal with them on your own,' said Lark.

'Same here,' added Jasmine. 'I'd be more than happy to down tools and come and give you some moral support.'

'Me too,' said Maggie.

'Much as I'd really love to, I think I'd struggle to get Judge Hoskinson to adjourn the trial while I race over here from York. I'll be with you in spirit, though.'

'Thanks, lasses,' said Florrie.

'Oh, Jazz, that looks gorgeous!' Lark exclaimed, looking over at the mug Jasmine had in front of her, clearly sensitive to the dip in Florrie's mood.

'It's really pretty, Jazz, you're so creative.' Florrie took in the bold-coloured poppies Jasmine had painted onto the mug, grateful to have attention directed away from her and the chance of a change of subject.

'Come on then, Stells, let's see your efforts.' Maggie peered over the table and let out a loud guffaw. 'Oh, wow!'

'What the bloomin' 'eck is it?' asked Jasmine, who was sitting beside Stella.

'I don't mean to be unkind, but I'm not sure.' Lark stretched her neck, her brows drawn together. 'Is it meant to be a face?'

Stella held up the plate she'd been painting, showing it around for them all to see. It was met with much squinting and head tilting as the friends tried to work out what it was.

'Oh no! Stella's portraits strike again,' said Florrie.

'If you close one eye and squint, it has an almost Daliesque quality to it.' The corners of Maggie's mouth twitched with amusement.

'You think?' asked Lark, not sounding quite so sure.

'Lark's right, it's a person – slightly offended you can't tell who, though. Thought the bright red hair would give it away,' said Stella, perusing her handiwork. 'Thought I'd have another go at painting Jazz, see if my artistic skills have improved over the last twenty or so years.'

'No way! This is victimisation! My feelings are in tatters.' Jazz feigned outrage.

'And if you're comparing me to a creative genius like Salvador Dali, then I guess I have my answer.' Stella treated them to a wide grin. 'Good to know if my career fails at the bar, then I can always fall back onto my art.'

'I suggest you do all you can to make sure your legal career never fails,' Florrie joked.

'I'll second that,' quipped Jasmine, as the group fell into more hilarity.

'It sounds like you were all enjoying yourselves earlier,' said Pippa, smiling. The friends were standing at the counter of Pippa's Paint Pots, settling up for their session.

'We were, it was brilliant. And the hot chocolates are to die for,' said Florrie.

'That's good to hear, thank you. I hope to see you again.'

Out on the street, the chilly air, nipping at their cheeks, stood in stark contrast to the warmth of Pippa's shop.

'Thanks for organising such a fab evening, lasses. I've loved every minute.' Florrie beamed round at them, her eyes shining with happiness.

'And the good news is, it's not over yet,' said Jasmine, her hair glowing red under the vintage streetlight. 'We're heading back to Stells' place where we're going to stuff our faces with pizza and cheesy garlic bread from Pepe and Chiara's.'

'Really?' Florrie was delighted to hear this.

'Really,' said Stella. 'I'm going to drive us all back to my apartment where we'll order the pizzas and garlic bread and get it delivered. And, best of all, Jazz has made one of her wickedly indulgent chocolate cakes for pudding.'

'Mm-hm. To steal the title of Jenna's latest book, you had me at chocolate cake.' Florrie grinned.

NINETEEN
THURSDAY 16TH APRIL

It was approaching lunchtime, and Florrie had barely seen Ed all morning; he'd devoted the bulk of his time to the window display since they'd arrived first thing, which had been an hour earlier than normal to allow them enough time to prepare for Jack and Jenna's reading and the official window unveiling later that day. She'd pleaded with him again, asking to let her take a peek behind the curtain, but his answer was still a disappointing no, followed up with an amused smile. 'You don't have long to wait now,' he'd said. 'So what's a few hours more?'

'It's agony, that's what it is!' she'd declared.

There'd been a steady flow of customers throughout the morning and though Florrie was glad of her mum's help, she'd been worried about her dad being left on his own in case he took a tumble. 'He'll be fine, lovey, he says he's feeling a bit brighter this morning; I wouldn't have come otherwise,' Paula had said as she'd bustled in ready to help. 'He's got his phone beside him, and I managed to get a parking space right outside the shop so I can whizz straight back home if he needs me. Ruth from next door said she was going to pop in and check he's okay, make him a cup of tea. And besides, I think he'll be glad to have a bit of time on his own without me fussing over him. Your dad has a long fuse, but I think his patience is starting to wear a bit thin,' she'd added with a chuckle. 'Mind, he's looking forward to helping out with Jack this evening, which is why he's agreed to take it easy for the rest of the day.' Paula's words had gone a considerable way to easing Florrie's concerns.

It wasn't just worries for her dad that had been on her mind. Every time the bell jangled, Florrie's heart had jumped in her chest, fearful she was going to look up and see Dawn or Luella, or both. But so far, there'd been no sign of them. And the longer the morning went on, the more Florrie was hopeful they'd taken Ed's words on board; maybe even headed back to London, though she told herself that was wishful thinking.

She was beginning to wonder when she was going to be able to get a chance to give the reading room a check over when Jack landed unexpectedly.

'Now then, folks, by it's a grand day out there,' he said in his broad, gravelly accent.

'Morning, Jack, it is. Let's hope it stays that way for this evening,' said Florrie.

'Aye, too right. I've just dropped Jen off to get her hair done for the event, so I thought I might as well pop in, see if there's owt I can help with; make myself useful, like.'

It was so like Jack to offer to help and muck in. Despite his fame – he was increasingly getting referred to in the press as a 'national treasure' though whenever anyone mentioned it to him, he joked that it was a typo that had been latched on to and what they really meant was 'national disaster' – he didn't have a starry bone in his body and had never shown so much as the tiniest hint of diva behaviour. His dour resting face – which was solely responsible for his reputation of being grouchy and moody – belied his cheerful disposition. He was always quick to crack a joke – usually at his own expense – and enjoyed a good belly laugh. And since he'd moved to Micklewick Bay, he'd been taken to the townsfolks' hearts and regarded as one of their own. It was a position he was enormously proud of and never took it for granted.

'Tell you what, why don't I start by sticking the kettle on and making us all a cuppa?'

'Ooh, music to my ears, Jack lovey. I could do with a cup of tea before I head back home,' said Paula. 'Unless you'd like me to do it, of course?'

'Not at all, you look like you've got your hands full there.' He switched his gaze from Florrie to where Paula was adding more books to the display table they'd placed next to Jenna's in readiness for the reading. This one was for Jack's books, and Ed had instructed Florrie's mum how best to utilise the props he'd given her specifically for that display. 'I'm happy to be the bookshop's teaboy this morning.' Jack grinned before heading off to the kitchen with Ed calling after him that he could do with a cuppa, too.

'Righto, lad!' Jack called back.

Jean arrived not long after Jenna whose warm chestnut locks were looking extra glossy thanks to the caramel highlights that had been threaded through them. The two women joined Jack in the reading room with the two authors setting out chairs for the audience, while Jean stacked copies of their books next to the till on the wall at the front of the room. Once that was done, Jack and Jenna headed home to prepare for the reading.

The afternoon whizzed by and before they knew it, the sound of the church bells announcing five o'clock chimed in the distance. Leah didn't waste a moment. She dashed over to the door, turned the sign to closed and slid the bolt across. It was always a quick turnaround when they had a window reveal, with only an hour until things got started. In the early days of the window reveals, Florrie and Ed would head back to Samphire Cottage – they always drove to and from the bookshop on such days – grab a quick bite to eat, then head back, minus Gerty since the Labrador found all the fuss and influx of people unsettling. But today, they'd agreed that just Ed would drive Gerty back to the cottage so he could get changed out of his paint-spattered clothes – being a perfectionist with his work, he always found a last-minute tweak for his window scenes. He'd leave Gerty at home, then head back to the bookshop where he and Florrie would quickly wolf down some food and wait for the rest of the staff to arrive.

'If it's okay with you, I think I'll stay here,' said Leah.

''Course it is, you can keep me company while Ed takes Gerty home,' said Florrie. 'And there's no need to ask.'

'Thanks.' Leah smiled, looking relieved. 'Thing is, if I go home now, I'll only end up getting stuck helping Tilly with her homework and I really don't want to be late for when all the fun starts here. I mean, I don't mind helping her, but she always leaves it so last minute and it can get quite stressful, especially if I have to be somewhere. I've told her I'll help when I get back; it's not as if a couple of hours is going to make much of a difference.'

'True.'

Leah still lived at home with her parents and was regularly expected to help her younger sister with her homework which had often made her late for going out with her friends or Marty. Florrie was fond of Leah and felt that Tilly leant a little too heavily on her older sister – from what she could gather it was subtly encouraged by their parents – and took advantage of Leah's good nature. But, tempted as she frequently was to gently guide her away from doing so much, and in the process hopefully weaning Tilly off her reliance, Florrie felt it was ultimately none of her business, so kept her thoughts to herself.

'Have you got something to eat?' she asked.

'Yeah.' Leah nodded. 'I grabbed a piece of quiche and some salad from the tearoom and put it in the fridge in our kitchen.'

'Good thinking. Ed and I did the same; I was going to say you could share ours if you didn't have anything,' said Florrie, giving Leah a warm smile. 'Maybe we should have it now while it's quiet instead of wolfing it down two minutes before things get started – wouldn't be the first time,' she said with a chuckle. 'Ed can grab his when he gets back.'

. . .

By the time Ed returned, a substantial crowd had gathered on the pavement in front of the bookshop. The air was alive with high-spirited chatter and anticipation. A small cheer went up as he reached the door, and an even bigger one followed when Jenna, Jean and Jack arrived not long after.

Florrie was thrilled to see her dad looking brighter. He'd arrived with her mum about ten minutes after Ed had left, and though he was still looking pale, he seemed more like his chirpy self, chatting away to Jack where they were perched side by side on their seats next to the door. It was their usual place when the book-shop was holding an evening event, checking to make sure only people with tickets gained access to the shop, the two men jokingly referring to themselves as 'bouncers'.

'Ey up, there's the film crew,' Charlie said, peering out through the glass of the door before adopting a David Attenborough-style tone. 'We're here, on the wild plains of Victoria Square in the North Yorkshire town of Micklewick Bay, cameras poised, ready to film the huge variety of wildlife that inhabits the area. It's a place where the locals gather together in a ritual unique to the region and known as The Great Window Reveal. This fascinating display of behaviour happens only a handful of times a year and we feel incredibly privileged to have the opportunity to film it.'

Everyone fell about laughing, particularly so Florrie, who was thrilled to see her dad back on form.

'The crowd seems bigger than ever,' said Paula, peering out beside her husband. 'Ooh, and there's the reporter from the local newspaper, too. See, Charlie?'

'Aye, I can see, lass.'

Word of Ed's amazing displays had spread quickly when he'd first taken over decorating the windows of the double-fronted Victorian shop. They'd garnered such interest that the local news-room and newspaper sent reporters to record the unveiling. Florrie always made sure to announce it, together with Jack and Jenna's reading, on the bookshop's social media pages, as well as dotting leaflets and posters advertising it not only around the bookshop, but the tearoom, too; she was aware that some of their older clientele had no interest in the internet or social media. It went without saying that the two authors' events sold out within minutes.

Jack checked his watch. 'Right then, Ed lad, it's nearly six o'clock and folk are starting to look a bit nithered out there. You just say the word, and as soon as you're ready, I'll get my butt outside, feed myself to the lions – to continue in the spirit of Charlie's wildlife documentary theme.' He grinned at Charlie, the pair chuckling like mischievous schoolboys.

Charlie didn't waste a moment, picking up on Jack's cue. 'And here we see the alpha male preening himself as he prepares to strut his stuff in front of his adoring minions who've been waiting patiently in what can only be described as inhospitable conditions.'

'Strut my stuff. Ah, I love it!' Jack gave a throaty cackle.

'Give over, Charlie, you daft thing,' Paula said, laughing, catching Florrie's eye, an unspoken message conveying their happiness that he was back on form passing between them.

'Two ticks,' said Ed. He had a quick check of the sockets where the electrics linked to the display were plugged in, then loosened the ties of the curtains that hid his work. 'Right, we're good to go.' He looked over at Florrie, the pair exchanging an excited smile. This was the first display she'd never had a preview of and she was intrigued to see what it would be. She'd have to wait until the crowd had dispersed before she'd get the chance.

'Right then, folks, let's get the evening underway.' With that, Jack opened the door and stepped out onto the chequered tiles of the bookshop's entrance. In an instant, a roar went up from the crowd, accompanied by a round of applause and much cheering and whistling.

'Good evening, everyone. Thank you for coming and for your patience.' But his words were lost in the cacophony. He tried again, this time holding his hands up in a bid for them to quieten down, laughing happily as he did so. 'Well, that was quite the welcome, but I know it's not for me, and that you're all here to see what delights are lurking behind these curtains. And I can tell you this, so are the rest of us here at the bookshop. Ed's been working on it solidly and none of us has a clue as to the theme. Anyroad, that's enough of me wittering on, but before we start the countdown, can we make sure we have all the little 'uns at the front so they can see what's going on?'

In the doorway, Florrie peered over Jack's shoulder, excitement swirling inside her. Light was already fading as dusk inched its way over the sky. She caught sight of Jasmine and Max, standing behind their mix of kids, Zak, Chloe and Connor. Jasmine beamed a wide smile at her, giving a happy wave, which Florrie returned. As she scanned the crowd, checking for a glimpse of their other friends, her gaze snagged on an unexpected face. Her heart jolted and her breath caught in her throat. *Please, no!* She blinked quickly, but the face was gone. Her eyes darted back and forth over the crowd, searching the sea of faces that were eagerly looking towards the shop. Had she been seeing things? she wondered. Surely, if she was still in town, Luella wouldn't have the brass neck to come to the unveiling of the bookshop's window displays after Ed had been so blunt with her, would she? Florrie would've hot-footed it out of town in a blaze of humiliation if an ex had told her in no uncertain terms that they were finished and she was foolish for turning up at his new home. There was no way she'd ever want to look like she was clingy and desperate or feel like some sort of stalker.

But then, there was Peter and Dawn's influence to factor into this odd situation which was probably why she'd woken with the nagging worry that they were going to make an appearance that evening. It didn't help that Ed had said he'd heard nothing from either Dawn or Luella all day. She'd at least hoped he'd get word that they'd left town and were heading back to London. Only then would she be able to relax sufficiently for the fingers of concern to loosen their grip and allow her to properly enjoy the evening.

'Right then, I think we're all sorted, so, without further ado, I'd be very grateful if you could join me in a countdown.'

Jack's voice broke into her thoughts, and she made the hurried decision to sweep all concerns of Ed's parents and Luella from her mind and focus on what he was saying.

'From five, here we go! Five... four... three... two... one!'

A great roar went up as Ed flicked a switch at the rear of the window on the right-hand side, and the curtain slowly swept back. The anticipation in the air was tangible. It was as if a collective breath was being held as the crowd fell silent, instantly followed by an 'ahh' as the full view of the window was revealed, showing Ed's creative talents in all their glory.

An enthusiastic round of applause rang around the square with yet more cheers and whistles. The mood of the crowd was infectious, and Florrie found her heart dancing with anticipation. It didn't help that she was certain she kept hearing her name being mentioned out on the street.

But what she couldn't see from her position in the doorway was that the crowd were gazing upon a bride and groom in miniature form that bore more than a passing resemblance to her and Ed. The bride, whose brunette bob was a carbon copy of Florrie's, was wearing a pair of tortoiseshell glasses and was dressed in an empire line, floor-length gown in ivory silk, the short sleeves and neckline finished with an antique gold braid trim. Mini Florrie's bouquet was made of paper roses, their petals cut from the pages of damaged books that Ed had retrieved from the skip for paper at the recycling centre in Lingthorpe. He'd even fixed a diamanté tiara to her head, the faux diamonds twinkling in the light. The 'couple' were standing at opposite ends of the window before a backdrop that included a scaled-down version of the bookshop's frontage. It was set against a background of Thorncliffe, a bright blue sky above with occasional puffy white clouds. Clifftop Cottage – home to Maggie and Bear – was visible on the fields of the cliff, and even the Jolly was included, nestling in Old Micklewick –where the couple were holding their wedding reception. Ed had skilfully managed to include great detail without making the backdrop look cluttered or clumsy. Standing between 'Florrie' and 'Ed' was a black

Labrador who was a dead ringer for Gerty, a basket of spring flowers clenched between her teeth.

Seconds later, the bride and groom started to move slowly towards one another, the sound of church bells chiming joyfully in the background. 'Gerty's' tail began to wag as her head bobbed up and down. With the Labrador between them, the bride and groom came to a halt before bending towards one another and sealing the scene with a lingering kiss. In that moment, a cascade of faux rose petal confetti started to fall from above.

The next moment, the loudest roar of the evening rang out, the happy sound ricocheting off the buildings and bouncing around the square.

Jack, who'd been watching the display from the side of the window, turned to Ed. 'By 'eck, I reckon you've excelled yourself there, lad. Your missus-to-be is going to be chuffed to bits with it.' Switching his gaze to Florrie, he said, 'Wait till you see this, it's nowt short of bloomin' fantastic.'

Florrie's heart skipped a beat. She looked across at Ed who was wearing the widest smile. She knew he'd secretly be relieved that everything had gone without a hitch. 'Go and take a quick look; it's already on repeat, but I can set it to play from the start,' he said to her, the remote control poised in his hand.

'Are you sure? I don't want to delay the reveal of the other window.'

'Get yourself out here, lass, no one'll mind,' said Jack. In his next breath, he addressed the crowd, gesturing for them to lower their voices, which took a while. 'I think we all know, the bride and groom in the window here are The Happy Hartes Bookshop's very own Florrie and Ed, however, as I mentioned earlier, our Florrie hasn't seen it yet with all the cloak and dagger secrecy during its creation. She's been waiting here like patience personified, so I'm sure you kind folk of Micklewick Bay wouldn't mind if she came out here and took a quick shuftie right now, am I right?'

His question triggered a cacophony of words of agreement mixed with calls of 'Florrie! Florrie! Florrie!'

Jack held out his hand to her. Feeling suddenly bashful at being the subject of everyone's attention, she took it and let him lead her outside as a chorus of 'I'm Getting Married in the Morning' struck up from the gathering. Feeling her cheeks burn, she stepped out onto the pavement and turned to face the window just as Ed pressed the button for the moving parts to start from the beginning.

Florrie watched the scene play out, pressing her hands to her chest, a gasp escaping her mouth. 'Oh wow!' She laughed, delighted to see herself and Ed in scaled-down form. 'It's *fantastic!*' After the festive displays he'd created last Christmas, with everyone saying they were his best yet, she couldn't imagine how Ed was ever going to top them, but this, with its personal message, had done just that. 'Oh, look, Gerty's there, too.' Her eyes dancing with happiness, Florrie took in the detail of the mini Labrador's gold braided collar made from the same trim that featured on mini Florrie's dress, the colourful spring blooms in the basket Gerty was holding, not to mention the dog's shining amber eyes, so like the real thing.

'Pretty amazing, isn't it?' said Jack beside her. 'He's a talented lad.'

'It is amazing, and he is.' In that moment she found herself wishing Mr and Mrs H were here to see it; she knew they'd be in raptures over their grandson's artistic flair and imaginative creations. They'd have lavished praise on him, their faces glowing with pride. They were the polar opposite of his parents who, Ed had told her, used to refer to him as useless and disappointing. The scars of those words were still visible today, though it gladdened Florrie's heart to know that they were gradually fading.

A frown fleetingly troubled her brow as it crossed her mind that it was a shame his mum and dad didn't feel able to visit the town without an agenda, that they let their bitterness cloud their view such that it stopped them from seeing their son's talent, and taking pride in him and the praise his work received. Surely they would get enormous pleasure from that? But now, she told herself, wasn't the time to dwell on Peter and Dawn Harte. There was another window to be revealed and an author reading to enjoy.

Florrie slipped back inside the bookshop, rushing over to give Ed a hug. 'It's gorgeous! I love it!' She kissed him hard on the mouth, making him laugh.

'Glad you approve.' His smile and the sparkle in his eyes told her he was thrilled. 'I think you'll like the second window, too.'

'Can't wait to see it,' she said, happiness racing through her.

'Are you all ready to see what's behind the curtain of the next window?' Jack's voice rang out into the square and was quickly followed by a resounding yes, the enthusiasm making him laugh. 'Okay then, let's count down same as last time, folks. Five! Four! Three...'

The curtain swept back and another gasp ran around the gathering as everyone took a moment to absorb the rustic scene before them with hints of time gone by. This one was of rugged moorland, complete with swathes of rich purple heather in full bloom. It included a weathered moorland cross, the words carved into it being swallowed up by lichen. The backdrop created a scene that led the eye to believe they were at a point high up on the moors, with unspoilt views all around, a clear blue sky above. A young woman in a long Georgian style dress of floral cotton was standing upon a mossy sandstone crag, her hair loose around her shoulders, wispy curls framing her face. She held a small piece of paper in one hand and what appeared to be a quill in the other, while a leather-bound novel bearing a well-known title was set on the ground beside her. A worn signpost was pointing towards an austere looking house of grey sandstone behind her. It bore the words 'Top Withens', painted in a cursive hand.

The group watched as the scene came to life and a faux pheasant glided behind the girl, its cackling cry spilling out into the square, while flimsy wisps of cloud floated by in the background. In the next moment, the girl lowered her head as her hands slowly began to move together until the quill was resting on the paper. As she was moving, a breeze appeared, gently blowing her dress and the tendrils of her hair. Despite its undeniable air of melancholy, the scene was utterly mesmerising.

'Oh wow! What a showstopper that is!' declared Jack. 'There's no mistaking what this scene's all about. Florrie, I think you need to get yourself out here again, flower. This is right up your street.'

'I'll set it to start from scratch like the other,' said Ed.

Florrie didn't need telling twice. She hurried out onto the pavement, her heart leaping as her gaze roved excitedly over the scene. '"Top Withens",' she read aloud, her gaze sliding to the girl, then the copy of *Wuthering Heights* resting amongst the bracken as realisation dawned. 'Oh my days, Jack! It's Emily Brontë! And Top Withens was reputedly the inspiration for *Wuthering Heights*!'

'Aye, you're right,' said Jack, taking a closer look at the scene.

Tears started spilling from Florrie's eyes. Ed had created this just for her; she must've mentioned to him hundreds of times that Emily Brontë's novel was her favourite book of all time. What had she done to deserve such a wonderfully thoughtful man? She could look at this beautiful recreation of the moors around Top Withens forever!

She rushed back inside, throwing her arms around Ed. 'Thank you, Ed! Thank you! It's absolutely wonderful!'

'Thought you'd appreciate the nod to *Wuthering Heights*.'

'I do, I'm over the moon. Oh, Mum, you should go and take a look, it's amazing! Both windows are.' Florrie had inherited her love of books from her mum who'd been bringing her to the bookshop from being a tiny babe in arms, and when it was simply known as Harte's Bookshop.

'After seeing how excited you are, I don't think I'll be able to resist, lovey.' Paula chuckled as she sneaked out of the bookshop to take a look. From her reaction when she returned, Paula was as delighted by Ed's handiwork as her daughter.

The window reveal over and done with, Jack and Paula returned inside the bookshop, closing the door and sliding the bolt across. It was decided that the rest of the team would take a look after the reading and when the crowd had thinned – which they all agreed was the biggest one they'd drawn so far.

'It's just gone twenty past six, so I reckon we've got time to catch our breath and grab a quick cuppa before we open the door and start letting folk in for the reading,' said Jack. 'I could do with wetting my whistle after all that yelling trying to get folk to quieten down.'

'Sounds like a good plan to me, son. I'll go and put the kettle on.' Jean patted his arm and gave him a smile as she passed en route to the kitchen. 'We'll have to be quick, mind.'

'Wait up, Jean pet, I'll give you a hand,' said Jenna, trotting after her.

'By 'eck, they're a right lively bunch out there, Jack. There's no wonder you had to shout to be heard,' said Charlie. 'You could do with one of them megaphone things.' Both men chuckled at that.

'Aye, I might look into getting one for next time, save the old vocal cords.'

Florrie was pleased to see her dad still seemed to be doing okay and suffering no ill effects from being up and about this evening after spending so many days on the sofa at home. She'd spotted her mum keeping a close eye on him, which was reassuring, especially since she'd mentioned to Florrie he was still experiencing some dizziness caused by the labyrinthitis, although Paula had stressed that the spells weren't as severe or as frequent. Florrie had been relieved to hear that, especially since she knew his worries about not being able to walk her down the aisle were still preying heavily on his mind. She hoped this evening would go some way to assuaging his concerns.

TWENTY

'Have you got your voice limbered up, lass?' Jack asked Jenna, grinning broadly.

'I have that, pet, and I'm raring to go.' She grinned back, rubbing her hands together. The Happy Hartes team were loitering at the front of the shop, waiting for the two authors to say the word before the door was opened and the next stage of the evening got underway.

Jack turned to Florrie and Ed who were standing side by side, Ed's arm thrown around her shoulders. 'Happy to let folks in, you two lovebirds?'

They both laughed and told him they were.

'Right, team Happy Hartes, time to get to your stations.' Jack spoke in a mock army sergeant voice.

'You okay there, lovey?' Paula rested her hand on Charlie's shoulder.

'Aye, I'm fine, lass.' Charlie rolled his eyes good-naturedly at Jack.

'Don't fret, Paula, I'll watch him like a hawk,' Jack said, winking at Charlie. His words seem to satisfy her and she hurried over to the reading room where Jean was waiting by the door in readiness to take tickets. Jenna scuttled over to the counter where

Leah was stationed to advise any customers keen to purchase books that they could do so after the event. Jenna and Jack always walked into the reading room together, once the audience were in their seats. Florrie and Ed made their way over to the reading room, waiting to greet the audience.

A thrum of excitement ran through Florrie. She loved Jack and Jenna's readings, the way the couple bounced off each other; their affectionate banter went down well with everyone and a great night was always guaranteed. She regularly pinched herself that their humble little bookshop was so wholeheartedly supported by such well-respected authors. Even better, Jack and his mum were partners in their business – granted, they had a small number of shares, but it still felt good to know they had their support and backing.

She stole a quick look around the room, pleased with how they'd decorated it for the evening. The style Florrie and Ed had chosen for the space when they'd renovated the former storeroom was that of a vintage study. They'd invested in two second-hand, sturdy wingback leather armchairs, dressing them with plump tweed cushions and wool throws. They'd placed these either side of a vintage desk upon which they'd arranged a pile of old books. For this evening's purpose, however, the old books had been replaced by copies of Jenna's latest novel set alongside a huge faux chocolate cake that was surrounded by faux chocolate cupcakes. A large vase of flowers in pinks, purples and cream sat at the opposite end, softening the study vibe and lending a feminine feel to the room, while a selection of lamps dotted about added a cosy vibe. One of their best-loved readings was the time the couple had selected one of Jenna's novels and Jack had taken the role of the male protagonist. It had gone down a storm, his dry delivery adding to the light-hearted humour of the story. Tonight, they would both be reading an extract from *You Had Me at Chocolate Cake*, followed by Jack reading from his book of poetry he'd written in North Yorkshire dialect.

It wasn't long before people started to filter in and a buzz of quiet excitement filled the room. Florrie looked on as people took their seats.

'Now then, flower,' a voice said in Florrie's ear, which she recognised instantly as belonging to Stella.

'Hiya, Stells, thanks for coming. You too, Alex.' Florrie nodded to Alex who was standing behind her friend. From her quick appraisal, she noted Stella was still in her court suit, her hair tied back in a neat chignon, the way she wore it to work.

'Wouldn't miss it for the world.' Stella smiled. 'I came straight from chambers; stopped off briefly at home and scooped up Al – saves us clogging up the streets with two cars.' Turning to Ed, she said. 'Fantastic window display, Ed. You've really excelled yourself this time with the *Wuthering Heights* and Top Withens reference.'

'I know, I couldn't believe it,' said Florrie, beaming at her friend.

'They're both amazing, mate,' added Alex. 'It must've taken hours to make everything and put it all together.'

'It takes a while, but not as long as you'd think, and it definitely helps that I've got a contact who sells models and blanks that I can then add to and make more personal so they fit into the theme of the displays.'

'Well, whatever it is you do, they're fantastic; very professional. I'm surprised you haven't been asked to do them for other shops.'

Ed laughed. 'Funny you should say that—'

'Hi, guys.' They turned to see Jasmine and Max smiling at them. 'Awesome displays, Ed,' said Jasmine.

'Thanks, Jazz.'

'They're the best yet,' Max enthused. 'Can't wait to see what you have in mind for the Campion's windows.' Max owned Campion's of York, which had stores in various towns – including Micklewick Bay – its flagship store being in Middleton-le-Moors. The once down on its luck chain was enjoying a renaissance under the ownership of entrepreneur Max and the resurrection of their previous reputation of the place to buy exclusive and discerning gifts.

'I can't wait to get started.' Ed had made no secret of how thrilled he'd been when Max had approached him about designing displays for the Campions' windows, glad to have another outlet for his creativity. His dyslexia still had the knack of making him feel inadequate as far as bookshop-related things were concerned.

When the seats were eventually filled, Florrie joined Leah and Jean at the window which was at the opposite end of the room from Jack and Jenna. It was where they usually stood for readings, tucking themselves out of the way. Ed had hung back by the doorway, ready to dim the bright overhead light when the authors gave him the nod, signalling they were ready to start. The softer lighting lent a cosy, more intimate air to the room, with Jack and Jenna each having a reading lamp angled over their seats as they read.

Florrie noted the tall stool Ed had set by the wall for her dad to sit on during the reading, but there was no sign of her parents, which surprised her. She ignored the flash of concern, telling herself to stop letting her thoughts get carried away, that everything was fine.

She was distracted by Jack and Jenna as they entered the room, both wearing wide smiles. Jack was looking smart in a tweed jacket, navy chinos and checked shirt, while Jenna looked stylish in her familiar girl-next-door way. She was wearing a sweater dress in dusky pink that showed off her curves to their full advantage, while adorning her feet were a pair of black leather knee-length boots. Her warm smile was emphasised by her trademark deep-pink lipstick. The couple were instantly greeted by a warm round of applause from the eager audience.

'Thank you,' said Jack, chuckling. 'Tell you what, I aren't half glad to see you lot've settled down a bit. I was getting a tad worried earlier, you were that wound up. Maybe it's quieter now cos the riff-raff's gone home after having a gander at the windows, leaving the quality folk of Micklewick Bay to spend the rest of the evening with Jen and me,' he joked, laughing even harder when a rowdy cheer went up.

'Ah, so there's evidently still a bit of riff-raff, then.' He gave a mischievous grin. 'Just joking, you're all good folk, and Jen and me are always incredibly grateful for your support, aren't we, love?' He turned to Jenna, affection glowing in his eyes for all to see.

'That we are, Jack. And, before you start throwing any more insults about, I reckon it's time we got this show on the road. Fancy calling our audience riff-raff, honest to goodness.' She shook her head, throwing him a look of mock disappointment that had the audience laughing as Jack's shoulders shook with mirth.

'Right then' – Jack picked up his copy of Jenna's book, waving it at the audience – 'anyone fancy some chocolate cake?'

The laughter continued as the two authors made their way through several chapters of Jenna's wittily written romcom novel, injecting their inimitable style of humour into the reading, not to mention Jack's hilarious facial expressions.

'Their chemistry's amazing, no wonder the audience love them,' Ed whispered in Florrie's ear. He'd slipped beside her just as the audience were greeting Jack and Jenna.

Florrie glanced up at him, the soft lighting of the room casting shadows over his handsome face. Her heart skipped a beat. It was thanks to Ed being bold and asking if Jack would do a reading when they'd first taken on the bookshop almost two years ago that they had these events. The author had stunned them by agreeing to it, and they'd become a regular feature ever since. She reached for Ed's hand, weaving her fingers through his. He glanced down with a smile, making her heart skip another beat.

'Right, I'm afraid it's time to lower the tone and get you all feeling as miserable as sin,' Jack said dryly as he picked up his book of poetry, and turning the couple's attention back to him.

'Is Jenna reading from it?' asked a voice from the audience.

Jenna hooted with laughter. 'I'm not so sure my Geordie accent would work very well in North Yorkshire dialect; I reckon the poetry would lose a canny bit of its impact.'

'Maybe we should give it a try, Jen?' Jack's eyes danced with amusement as he handed her the book.

'Oh, go on then.' Jenna took the hardback, taking a moment to select something suitable. 'Right, I'll apologise in advance, but here goes...' She cleared her throat and made a start.

'Aye, lass, point taken,' Jack said with a cheeky grin when she'd done.

He was halfway through his reading when Florrie's ears were alerted to the sound of raised voices out on the street. From the way Ed and Leah were looking at her, they could hear it, too. Before she could think any further, the shouting grew louder, causing heads to turn in the audience, voices murmuring.

'Ey up,' said Jack, looking up from his book. 'Sounds like summat's afoot outside. We'll give it a couple of minutes, see if it passes.'

But the shouting showed no sign of abating, and a chill started to creep up Florrie's spine. She glanced up at Ed who met her gaze. From the look in his eyes, he was clearly thinking the same as her.

'They're unbelievable,' he said with a groan.

The jangle of the shop doorbell rang out and the shouting was joined by more voices, though these were softer. It was followed by a loud bang then a blood-curdling scream. Florrie's heart started pounding as she and Ed rushed towards the reading room door. She was only half aware of Jack telling everyone to stay calm and remain in their seats, Jenna's voice featuring somewhere in there, too.

Florrie's gaze swept quickly around the bookshop, a bolt of alarm shooting through her when she realised there was no sign of her parents. Her eyes alighted on the door which now stood wide open, making her pulse up its speed. Memories of Dodgy Dick's attempts at sabotaging a previous bookshop event sprang to mind. Surely Ed's parents weren't in cahoots with him and his disreputable cronies in the hope of bullying them into handing over the bookshop?

'Oh no!' The alarm in Ed's voice drew her attention to where he was standing in the doorway, his hand pressed against his forehead.

'What is it?' But he didn't get a chance to answer before he rushed out into the street.

Florrie raced after him, her heart thudding hard in her chest.

Outside, dusk had fallen and a sea fret was creeping in, making the air damp and chilly. She stopped in her tracks, her hand flying to her mouth as her gaze went to where Ed had come to a halt over by the kerbside. Under the hazy glow of the vintage streetlamps, she could make out a figure curled up on the floor, a woman bent over it, Ed's hand resting on her shoulder. It took her a couple of seconds to register what she was looking at.

No! Panic seared through her, making her whole body tremble.

'Dad!' she screamed.

TWENTY-ONE

'Stay there, Florrie! Stay where you are!' That Ed's voice was filled with such concern only added to her fears. 'Don't come over here.'

'Ed's right, you stay there, Florrie.' As distressed as she was, Florrie still picked up the shake in her mum's voice.

She froze to the spot, hot tears scorching their way down her cheeks, her fingers knotted in her hair. Her mind was racing, a maelstrom of confusion, fear overriding her every thought. Her brain was sending her myriad conflicting messages: that she should do as Ed and her mum said and stay where she was; that she should rush over and comfort her father; that if she did so, her panic could risk adding to his distress; that she needed to help; that she should ring for an ambulance; was he conscious? Was he... was he going to be okay? Oh, God! That didn't bear thinking about.

This was the worst kind of awful. She clamped her hand over her mouth as great wracking sobs took over her body. The last time she'd felt this utterly helpless was when she'd found out her mum was ill.

Seconds later, Stella appeared beside her. 'Florrie, what's happened?'

Hot on her heels was Jasmine. 'What's all the shouting about?'

Clocking her friend's tears her voice softened. 'Florrie, are you okay?'

Behind Jasmine, Florrie vaguely registered Alex and Max, both men wearing worried expressions.

'It... it's m–my... d–dad... he's f–fallen... over,' she stuttered, as a shadowy thought floated into her mind, wondering what his fall had to do with all the shouting that had brought them rushing outside.

'I'm sure he'll be okay, flower.' Stella put her arm around Florrie, giving her shoulder a reassuring rub. 'Do you know if anyone's called an ambulance?' she asked, her voice calm and in control.

Florrie shook her head. 'I d–don't kn–know.'

'On it,' said Max, quick as a flash pulling his phone from his back pocket.

'Thanks, Max.' Stella turned to Alex. 'Al, can you go and get the wool throws from the back of the leather chairs in the reading room? We'll need to keep Charlie warm while he's on the pavement.'

'Sure.' Alex shot off.

Florrie turned to see Lark and Maggie, Bear and Nate heading towards her, their faces wreathed in concern, their questions tumbling over one another's. Florrie registered snatches of what they were saying; Jack and Jenna were staying in the reading room with the audience while Leah and Jean were in the bookshop, rather than have people spilling out onto the street while they still didn't know what was going on.

Stella quickly filled them in on what little she knew, her words acting as a catalyst for Florrie. She wriggled free of Stella's arm. 'I need to go to my dad.'

'Florrie, are you sure?' asked Jasmine, gently taking hold of Florrie's arm.

'Dad!' she cried, her voice cracking with anguish as she slipped free from Jasmine's grip. She needed to see him, needed to tell him to be okay, that she loved him.

· · ·

'C'mere.' Ed held out his arms, enveloping Florrie in a hug. She rested her head against his chest, allowing herself to melt into the familiar warmth and reassurance of his embrace, finding comfort in the rhythmic beat of his heart. He hugged her close, pressing a kiss to the top of her head. 'Your dad's going to be okay. I promise.'

After what had happened, Florrie wasn't sure how he could make such a bold statement, but she kept her thoughts to herself and hoped with all her heart that he was right.

They were alone in the bookshop, the audience long since gone, a strange silence hanging in the air, like the aftermath of a heavy storm. Despite their friends offering to stay or run her to the hospital, Florrie had declined, preferring instead to be alone with Ed, hoping to get her thoughts in order, make sense of everything that had happened. They meant well, but she simply didn't have the mental capacity for conversation right now; she felt numb, punch-drunk. But she knew, without question, they'd understand; wouldn't take offence at her not wanting them around her right now.

It wasn't long after she'd rushed to be near her dad, that an ambulance had arrived, the paramedics carrying out the necessary checks before they eased him onto a stretcher and into the back of the emergency vehicle. They'd been cheerfully professional and compassionate throughout. Her mum had travelled to hospital with him. Florrie had been struck by how stunned she'd looked – frightened even – her face drawn and pale as she'd promised to let them know as soon as she had any news. Florrie's heart had gone out to her.

It seemed like a different day.

'Would you like me to run you to the hospital?' Ed asked. 'We could take some stuff for your dad; I expect he'll be kept in overnight. Maybe grab some bits for your mum, too. I doubt she'll want to leave your dad's side till she knows he's okay.'

Florrie nodded into his chest, her tears brewing again. 'That'd be good.' There'd never been any question in her mind about joining her mum, to offer support, to be there when news of her father arrived. She couldn't bear the thought of her mum being on her own with the risk of receiving a devastating diagnosis.

'In that case, why don't we head home now? I can drop you off at your parents' house en route so you can gather some stuff together while I head back to Samphire Cottage and take Gerty for a walk. I'll pick you up when that's done. Sound okay?' he asked, stepping back from their embrace, his hands sliding to the top of her arms as he looked into her eyes.

'It does.' She gave him a watery smile, peering through her tear-stained glasses. How had such a wonderful evening ended up with her dad being in hospital? And though it was by far the worst, it wasn't the only thing that had gone wrong that night: the window featuring the bride and groom had been egged.

Florrie hurried down the brightly lit corridor towards the intensive care unit of Middleton-le-Moors hospital, the smell of disinfectant curling around her nose, an overnight bag for her mum in her hand. Ed was taking long strides beside her, the soles of his shoes squeaking against the floor. He was carrying a bagful of stuff for Charlie.

'It's this way,' she said, spotting a sign for the ITU reception desk and taking a sharp left. Moments later, they pushed open the door of the waiting room where her mum was perched on the edge of a chair, worrying her bottom lip. 'Oh, Mum.' It tugged at her heart to see her usually cheerful mother look so anxious.

Paula jumped up and rushed over, throwing her arms around her daughter. 'Oh, Florrie, lovey, I'm so glad to see you; you too, Ed, sweetheart. Thanks for coming.' Her eyes were wet with tears, and she squeezed her daughter as if she'd never let go.

'How is he, Mum? How's Dad?' Florrie struggled against her own tears. 'Is he going to be okay?'

Paula rubbed Florrie's back and released her from her hug. She sniffed and swiped her fingers under her eyes. 'I hope so. They're doing some tests, lots of them, said something about an MRI scan, what with him being unconscious for a while. They want to make sure he hasn't sustained a serious brain injury.' Her bottom lip wobbled at that, and Florrie reached for her hand. 'He came round in the ambulance; was a bit confused, bless him. I have to say, the medical team have been amazing; so kind, too. One of them even made me a cup of sweet tea, said I looked shocked. He wasn't wrong.'

'Why don't we sit down? You look shattered, Paula.' Ed guided her to a chair. 'I'll go and grab you both a cup of tea while Florrie tells you what's in the bags.'

'That'd be good, thanks, lovey.' Paula gave him a weak smile.

Once Florrie had finished explaining what they'd packed, conversation switched to what had happened when the ambulance had arrived at hospital. 'It all felt surreal, like it was happening to someone else and it wasn't your dad getting wheeled along on a trolley, his lovely face as white as a sheet, God love him.'

A sound from the door made Florrie look up to see Ed through the narrow pane of glass. He appeared to be struggling to open the door. She jumped up and pulled it open for him.

'Here we are,' said Ed, a cardboard cup of tea in each hand. He set the drinks down on the table and pulled a bottle of water for himself from the back pocket of his jeans.

'Thanks, lovey,' said Paula, reaching for a cup.

'Yeah, thanks, Ed.' Florrie pressed her lips into a smile. She'd been waiting for Ed to return so he could hear what she had to say, too; save her mum having to repeat it. 'So, what happened, Mum? How come Dad ended up in hospital? We just heard a load of shouting and then a loud bang followed by a scream? Did you see any of that? Is that why you went out?'

Paula rubbed her brow with her fingers. 'Well, you probably noticed your dad and me didn't make it into the reading room.'

Florrie nodded. 'We did.'

'The reason for that was because he'd started to feel a bit dizzy, what with his labyrinthitis, and didn't want to draw attention to himself in a roomful of people, so we decided to stay put and listen from there.' Paula took a sip of her tea, wincing at the heat. 'Anyroad, we became aware of raised voices outside, followed by several thuds that sounded like something hitting the windows. Just after that, the voices got louder so I told your dad I was going to take a look. Well, you know what he's like. He tried to stop me, said it might not be safe, but anyroad, I told him I'd come straight back in if anything looked dodgy.'

'You should be careful, you know, Mum, especially if there's a chance Dodgy Dick and his cronies are out of prison.'

'Florrie's right, Paula,' said Ed.

'Trust me, lovey, Dodgy Dick and the like are the least of my worries right now.' The look she gave Ed puzzled Florrie, and she wondered if he'd noticed it, too.

'Oh?' Florrie couldn't imagine what she was about to hear next.

'So, when I get outside, I see this tall woman with one of them big cartons of eggs in her hand, and she's yelling at a man who seems to be telling her to stop – no idea who he was; I'd never seen him before, maybe a holidaymaker. Anyroad, she chucks a couple of eggs at him and he scarpers off down the road with egg running all down his head and his arm as he's still shouting at her to stop.'

'What?' Florrie couldn't believe what she was hearing. 'Who does that sort of thing? Surely, that's classed as an assault?'

'Stella'd be able to tell you,' said Ed.

'Mmm, she would,' Florrie agreed, picking up her tea.

Paula heaved a sigh, her eyes still puffy from crying. 'But they weren't the only people out there shouting.' She paused as if thinking how best to present what she had to say next. She pulled an apologetic face at Ed before continuing, 'I'm afraid your parents were there, too. They were having a huge argument, and this tall woman somehow seemed to be involved in it as well; they were all really going for it, hammer and tongs, as they say – like you heard for yourself. I'm really sorry, lovey.'

'My parents? But I thought my father was still in London, and that my mother had gone to join him.'

'Well, they were both in Micklewick Bay this evening, large as life, I'm afraid.' Paula's expression fell.

A thought flashed through Florrie's mind. 'Mum, did this tall woman happen to have dark wavy hair, and was she wearing a brightly coloured velvet coat?' She sensed Ed turn his head to her, felt the weight of his gaze.

'She did, and I tell you what else stood out about her, she had a kind of American accent – it wasn't very strong, but it definitely had a bit of a twang to it. Could've been Canadian, I suppose.' Paula glanced between them. 'Why? Do you know who she is?'

Ed tipped his head back and groaned.

Florrie switched her gaze to Ed. 'Luella,' they said in unison.

'Luella? Who's Luella?' asked Paula, her forehead creased.

'My ex,' said Ed, dragging his hand down his face.

'Your ex?' Paula sat up straight. 'Why would your ex be in Micklewick Bay? And why would she be chucking eggs at the bookshop window?'

'Good question,' Ed said wearily. 'Before you ask, it's got absolutely nothing to do with me. My parents are the reason she's here, whatever bonkers reason that may be.'

'But how did Dad end up unconscious on the pavement?' asked Florrie. She didn't want to go down the route of trying to get her head around what Ed's parents and his ex were plotting, she needed to know about her dad.

'As I said, Ed's parents were arguing and shouting, going at it, right hammer and tongs style. From what I could gather, your father was furious with your mother for something she'd done, but I couldn't make out what. He just kept yelling that whatever it was they were arguing about was her fault. I've never seen two people look so angry with one another.'

Ed shook his head in dismay. 'I'll bet I have.'

Paula gave him a sympathetic glance. 'Anyroad, I went over to them and asked them – very politely – if they would mind keeping the noise down on account of Jack and Jenna's reading, and...' She flicked her eyes to Ed. 'I'm really sorry to have to say, lovey, but they turned on me then, yelling all sorts of awful stuff. The language was strong enough to make your hair curl.'

Florrie winced – she knew from what Ed had said of his parents, they didn't like being told what to do by anyone.

'I'm so sorry, Paula, I don't know what—'

Paula placed her hand on his arm. 'It's not your fault, lovey, none of this is.' She swallowed, taking a moment. 'Anyroad, the next thing I know, Charlie appears beside me, even though I'd told him to stay put. He asks your parents and this Luella what all the shouting's been about, and tells them that they're out of order for yelling and swearing at me. The next thing I know, I hear your dad say he's feeling dizzy, and he topples over which is when he hit his head. I tried to catch him, but I was too late. I'll never forget the sound of his head hitting the ground for the rest of my life, it was...' Her eyes filled with tears and a loud sob escaped her mouth. 'And now poor Charlie's in intensive care.'

Florrie felt emotion leap in her chest. 'Oh, Mum, that must've been awful for you.' She took her mum's hand, squeezing it tight as she fought against her own tears. 'Just take a few minutes before you carry on; have a mouthful of tea.'

Paula nodded as Ed reached for the box of tissues on the table and handed it to her. She smiled her thanks at him.

Dabbing her eyes, Paula continued, 'You're right, it was awful seeing your dad like that. It wasn't at all what I expected to happen. Anyroad, the loud bang you heard was Dawn driving off and hitting the metal rubbish bin when she mounted the pavement – driving like a lunatic, she was. Peter and Luella ran off down towards the station straight after. Didn't bother asking if your dad was okay, or if he needed an ambulance. Didn't seem to care. And now, here we are,' she finished with a shrug.

Ed hung his head. 'I'm so sorry, Paula. I don't know what to say. If my parents hadn't been shouting and carrying on with Luella, Charlie wouldn't be in intensive care. I can't help but feel responsible.'

'It's not your fault, Ed. No one's blaming you, so there's no need to apologise. You're an innocent party in all of this, just like the rest of us. But I do think the stress of all the shouting caused his dizziness at the time.'

Florrie had to agree. She reached over to Ed with her free hand, wrapping it around his. It was an unfortunate state of affairs and she couldn't begin to understand how he must be feeling.

'I can't bear that they're responsible for Charlie being in here, indirectly or not.' Florrie noted the hard tone in Ed's voice, which matched the steely look in his eyes that she'd never seen before. 'What sort of people are they? And it's all about trying to sabotage our wedding so they can get their hands on the bookshop. I'm ashamed I share their DNA. But that's it, I'm done with them. Finished. Once I've told them what I think, I never want to see either of them again – nor Luella, for that matter.'

TWENTY-TWO

Florrie and Ed barely exchanged a word on the journey home from the hospital, each of them lost in their own rabbit warren of thoughts. Florrie gazed absently out of the window, the flicker of streetlights illuminating the car as they drove through the towns that connected Micklewick Bay to Middleton-le-Moors. She could almost feel Ed's guilt building beside her as he focused on the road. At one point, she'd reached across and touched his arm, telling him again that none of what had happened was his fault, reminding him that no one blamed him. He'd responded with a small smile; it seemed he was going to take some convincing.

Oblivious to their torment and worries, Gerty was thrilled to see them by the time they'd got back to Samphire Cottage. The Labrador had clearly recognised the sound of the car and the squeak of the gate as they'd headed up the path, and from the whimpering and clicking of claws on the tiles, she was already on the other side of the door as Florrie pushed her key into the lock. As soon as the door was opened, Gerty shot out, her tail wagging with such force her whole body was wiggling.

'Hello, Gerty-Girl, that's a grand welcome,' Ed said, stopping to fuss her as she danced around his legs. Once satisfied, Gerty then shot over to Florrie.

'Hello, Gerty, it's good to see you, too.' The Labrador's enthusiastic greeting and upbeat energy was a welcome moment of light in an otherwise dark and gloomy evening. 'Come on, lass, let's go inside, it's nippy out here with this mizzle.' The sea fret that had been creeping in earlier had now enveloped the town in a cold, damp fog. Florrie shivered; she'd been feeling chilled right through to her bones ever since she'd seen her dad in a crumpled heap on the pavement.

Once they'd removed their coats, and Gerty had given them a thorough sniffing, apparently intrigued by the unfamiliar smells of the hospital that lingered on their clothing, they headed down the hall and into the kitchen.

Florrie was glad of the warmth of the room, not to mention the familiar and comforting aroma of toast that seemed to be imbued into its walls. She pulled out a chair at the table and flopped onto it. Ed followed suit, while Gerty went to her bed, watching them both. From her expression she obviously sensed something was wrong.

Ed put his elbow on the table and placed his forehead in his hand. 'I just can't believe my parents... they've stooped too low this time... whatever crap they throw at me as a reason for their behaviour, there's no excuse. Knowing them, they'll try to pin the blame onto someone else. They're oblivious to how they look to the rest of the world and, worse, they don't seem to care. Someone needs to hold a mirror up to them; force them to take a look.' He fell back into his seat, his shoulders slumped in defeat. 'I'm so sorry, Florrie.' The pain in his eyes as he looked at her almost broke her heart.

'Ed, please listen to me and believe it when I say neither me nor my mum blame you, okay? You really need to take that on board. Look at it this way, if my parents behaved in a manner you didn't like, would you hold me responsible for it?'

'No, 'course I wouldn't.' He shook his head.

'Well, then, there you are – it works both ways.'

'Fair point.' His shoulders heaved with a sigh, and he raked his fingers through his hair. 'I have to speak to them, make sure they understand. What were they *thinking*, encouraging Luella to come here? It's next-level madness from them.'

'They're clearly desperate to stop us from getting married.'

'It's time they realised their ridiculous antics at trying to split us up aren't going to work.' He blew out another forceful sigh. 'Anyroad, that's enough about them, I just end up going round in circles trying to fathom them out.' He forced a smile. 'How're you feeling?'

'Still trying to take it all in if I'm honest. Hoping that all the tests come back clear for my dad. Worrying about my mum, and hoping she's not getting herself too worked up about him.'

'I get that.' He reached for her hand, squeezing it tight. 'I doubt you'll be feeling hungry, but you've got to eat; how about something simple like scrambled eggs on toast or soup?' Despite their plans, they'd both been too busy to eat before the reading and the quiche was still in the fridge at the bookshop.

He was right, she had no appetite. In fact, she still felt slightly nauseous, but thought it best to have something in her stomach, just in case they had to make a dash to the hospital – not that she wanted to dwell on the reason for that. 'Actually, not that I'm wanting to upset you, what with it being... well... with Luella being responsible for it, but knowing there's a window with a load of dried-on egg waiting for us in the morning, I think I'd rather go for soup, if that's okay with you?'

Ed pulled a face at the reminder. 'Fair point. That's more than fine with me. I suppose we should be thankful the weather's cold at the minute. If it was blazing sunshine, it'd bake the egg to the glass and make it a right nightmare to remove.'

Florrie groaned. 'What a thought.'

While Ed got on with preparing the soup, Florrie headed upstairs, telling herself she'd wait till after they'd eaten before she tackled the slew of texts and voicemail messages that had landed while they'd been at the hospital. The bulk were from her friends, and she knew they'd be okay with waiting until she was ready to reply.

As soon as she reached the small landing, Florrie was struck by a feeling that things weren't right. The air felt different, as if it had been disturbed. *Not this again.* She paused, taking a moment to steady herself. Her eyes went to the door of the spare room and her heart lurched. The door was ajar again, and she knew for a fact it had been left closed that morning; she'd deliberately run upstairs and checked right before they'd left the house. Her thoughts turned over as her pulse raced. Only Ed had been back since then. Logic told her it must be him. Did that mean he hadn't been telling her the truth when he'd said he hadn't ventured in there? She nibbled on her fingernail, not liking the feelings that thought gave her. Why would he lie? Was he looking for something else in there, other than rummaging through her wedding stuff? She immediately told herself that was highly unlikely, considering their discussion the other day.

'Maybe there's something wrong with the catch?' she said softly to herself, pulling the door to until it clicked shut. She pushed it, hoping it would simply pop open, but it stood firm. 'So much for that theory.'

With her stomach twisting, she opened the door and flicked the light switch on. Peering apprehensively into the room, her gaze went straight to the desk, her heart leaping at what she saw. A couple of the drawers were standing open, the pencil pot had been knocked over, and a clutch of papers were strewn across the carpet along with a couple of pens. An icy chill spiked through her. There was no way she was imagining this, and she knew without a shadow of a doubt it couldn't be Ed, it was so unlike him. He never left drawers hanging open, and that aside, his severe dyslexia meant he gave the desk and its contents a wide berth, which was why they referred to it as hers; he left dealing with any correspondence to her. And he would ask if ever he needed any of their documents, knowing how organised she was with their paperwork, saying he wouldn't know where to look. It was the same for her with the shed which she jokingly referred to as his 'man cave', and never crossed the threshold unless he invited her to do so. It was where he made the components of the window displays and she respected his desire for privacy, knowing he wouldn't want to spoil the element of surprise by her catching a glimpse of anything until the windows were finished.

But if it wasn't Ed, who the heck was it? she wondered. Whoever it was, they were creeping around her home without their permission. And they didn't appear to be too concerned about covering their tracks. Unless they'd been disturbed and left in haste. The thought sent a chill running up her spine.

As she stood and wrestled with all of this, nibbling away on her nail, a worrying thought bloomed in her mind. When Dawn was in possession of their house key the other day, could she have had a copy made? There was a kiosk near the station that offered such a service, boasting how a new key could be cut 'while u wait'. It was a big thing, getting a copy of a key made to someone's house without their knowledge or consent; illegal, no doubt. And it was an equally big thing to accuse somebody of doing it. Would Dawn have been so bold as to do such a thing? Florrie asked herself, a reply coming back in a flash. 'Of course she flaming well would! I wouldn't put anything past that woman!' She doubted Ed's mother would even bat an eyelid as she stood waiting for it to be done, telling herself it was something she was entitled to do.

Florrie wondered what it was Dawn was looking for, if she truly had felt the need to come back for a further snoop around their home? Much as she was dreading it, she was going to have to broach this with Ed even though she knew it would add to the reasons for him to fall out with his parents. It wasn't going to be an easy conversation to start, that was for sure, but her worries weren't for Dawn and Peter Harte, they were for her kind, and mild-mannered fiancé; Ed didn't deserve this.

Heading to their bedroom, she took a quick glance around, relieved to see that nothing looked out of place, and her collection of crystals on the dressing table were just as she'd left them that morning. She couldn't begin to imagine what would be of interest to Ed's parents in this room. The attic, however, was a different matter. Along with several bookcases, the compact room, with its view of the sea, also housed a small filing cabinet where they stored their important documents, including the mortgage details of Samphire Cottage, her exam and English Literature degree certificates, and their individual copies of Mr H's will. It also contained the correspondence and documents relating to the transfer of ownership of the bookshop to them as well as details of Jack and Jean's investment. And they didn't keep it locked; they hadn't felt the need to. Until now.

Heading to the attic, Florrie's stomach rolled over as she took in the scene before her: the drawers to the filing cabinet stood open, while a handful of files were cast carelessly over the floor. 'Oh, no!' she groaned. It told her beyond a shadow of a doubt that it was Dawn who'd been creeping around their home, and maybe Peter, too, with him now being in the town. And the only thing she could think they were looking for was documents relating to the bookshop, no doubt hoping they could find a loophole with which to dispute Ed and Florrie's ownership.

She headed back down to their bedroom and dropped onto the bed, feeling defeated. She didn't know how Ed had coped with such difficult bloody-minded people for all these years. They were self-serving, self-absorbed and deluded – or 'delulu' as Leah had put it; lightyears away from her own parents. And she wasn't sure she had the strength to deal with anything else they had to throw at them right now. Her poor dad was in hospital because of stress caused by them, and she couldn't imagine anything worse. They could look around her home for all they wanted. She didn't care. All she was bothered about was her dad making a full recovery, and being able to walk her down the aisle, smiling proudly as he delivered her to Ed's side.

She felt suddenly swamped by emotion as her tears made a bid for freedom. She took off her glasses and sobbed into her hands.

TWENTY-THREE

Florrie was crying so hard, she didn't notice Ed come into the room. He eased onto the bed beside her, slipping his arm over her shoulder and kissing the side of her head. 'I'm so sorry you're feeling sad. I wish I had a magic wand to wave and make everything better.' He held her close, smoothing her hair until her sobs subsided, then eased back and placed his thumb under her chin, tilting her face to him. 'You okay now?' he asked softly.

She shook her head, wiping her eyes with her fingers. 'Not really. No.' She felt exhausted, as if she had a lead weight on her shoulders.

'Has something else happened? Have you heard from your mum? Is your dad all right?'

'It's not my dad, and I haven't heard anything else from my mum, which I guess is good news – at least, I hope it is.' How could she share her suspicions when he was already wracked with guilt about his parents' behaviour contributing to the reason her dad was lying in a hospital bed in intensive care?

'So what's got you all upset again? Did you feel overwhelmed after everything that's happened? It's completely understandable if you did. I feel distressed and worried, and Charlie's not my dad, so I can't begin to imagine what it must be like for you; your mum, too. But you could've told me you were feeling rubbish, I'd have listened, given you a cuddle. You shouldn't be crying on your own.'

Tears sprang to her eyes again, the kindness in his words just about undoing her. *Bite the bullet, Florrie. You have to tell him.* Swallowing hard, she wiped her eyes and steadied herself. 'I think someone's been in the house again.' She couldn't bring herself to name his mother.

'What? No way?' She watched as myriad emotions flittered over his face, his expression suddenly hardening. 'My mother! Again! She's clearly looking for something in particular and not just to have a preview of your wedding dress. It'll be why she was so insistent on coming here to wait for the kettle to be delivered, making out she was doing us a favour when it really offered her the perfect excuse to snoop around our home. I should've known.' His anger appeared to be pushing him on. Florrie hadn't seen him look this annoyed before. He continued, 'Last Friday when you were at the Jolly and she was here, she excused herself to go to the bathroom. She was gone for ages – and I mean, *ages*. When I asked her what had taken her so long, and joked that I'd been thinking of sending out a search party, she told me not to be so rude, and cut me off when I asked if she'd lost something. But all that time, she'd been snooping around, hell-bent on trying to find something – no doubt to do with the bookshop.' He shook his head, his breathing shallow. 'Absolutely unbelievable.'

'I'm sorry, Ed.' Florrie felt the need to apologise for piling yet more unpleasant revelations about his parents onto him.

'You're not the one who should be sorry, they're the ones who should be apologising, not that they ever do. They leave a trail of trouble and distress wherever they go. It's why we had to move around so much when I was a kid.' He brushed his hand over his head, his expression morphing into one of confusion. 'Hang on a minute... she doesn't have a key anymore, she gave it back to me the other day.' He met Florrie's gaze, searching her face.

Chewing on her bottom lip, she hoped he'd put two and two

together, save her the awful task of having to put her suspicions into words.

She didn't have long to wait. 'No way? Surely she wouldn't stoop so low? That's a *massive* thing, having a key cut so you can sneak into someone's house while they're out, without their knowledge or permission...' Ed shook his head, anger radiating from him. 'The worst thing is, I can actually see her doing that.' He pushed himself up from the bed. 'We need to get the locks changed. I'll call Bear, ask if he can get onto it first thing. Once I tell him the reason, I'm sure he won't mind. We need to get one of those doorbells fitted, too, the sort that have a live video link to your phone.'

Florrie looked on as this unfamiliar version of Ed strode out of the room and thundered down the stairs. Seconds later, the front door slammed shut and the house fell silent.

Florrie was sitting in the living room, curled up on the sofa and trying, but failing, to read a book; she'd lost count of the number of times she'd reread the opening paragraph. Her stomach had been in knots since Ed had left their home in such haste, though she'd made sure not to mention it when her mum rang with an update on her father who she was pleased – and relieved – to report was now fully conscious and responding well to the medical team's questions. It had been good to hear her mum sounding a little brighter.

Tiredness had been creeping over her for the last hour, helped by the fire she'd lit not long after Ed had gone out, the exhausting day catching up with her. She glanced over at the clock on the mantelpiece to see it was almost eleven p.m. She and Ed were usually snuggled up in bed together by now; she'd be reading a book, Ed with his AirPods in his ears as he listened to his latest audiobook – like Amery, he'd become a huge fan of R.J. Kingston.

Florrie was gathering her empty hot chocolate mug and paperback together when Gerty jumped up from where she was toasting herself in front of the fire and trotted into the hallway. In the next moment, there was the sound of the key in the door, followed by

Gerty's happy whimpers and the thud of her wagging tail hitting the wall. Florrie was making her way around the sofa when Ed appeared in the door frame.

'Hi,' he said.

'Hi.' Her eyes roved his face, noting he looked pale, drained and dishevelled. There was a look in his eyes she'd never seen before, and not just that, his body language seemed different, too. She didn't know what to make of it. 'Where've you been?' she asked.

'Speaking to my parents.'

The tone in his voice made her heart plunge.

TWENTY-FOUR

Florrie followed Ed to the kitchen, Gerty plodding along behind; she was clearly ready for bed, too. He flicked the light on, then scooped up the kettle – the very one that had caused so much grief with its delivery – and took it to the sink, the sound of cold water splashing into it filling the room.

Florrie's stomach was in turmoil, not daring to imagine what words of recrimination were thrown about in the conversation with his parents, but desperate to hear it all the same.

'I know it's late, but I think it's only right that I tell you what was said.' He pulled out a chair and flopped down onto it. 'But first, is there any news on your dad?'

She opened the cupboard door and pulled out two mugs, which clinked together as she set them down on the table. 'My mum rang, said he was properly awake, which is good.' She relayed what her mum had told her, Ed listening with interest.

'That's great news. Let's hope he'll be home soon.' His mouth tugged into a small smile though it didn't quite reach his weary eyes.

'Yeah, let's hope so.' She was eager to find out about his conversation with his parents. 'Where did you speak with your mum and dad?'

'I tracked them down to my mother's B&B. My father was there, too – and, would you believe, Luella? I got the impression they were trying to get their story straight; the rubbish they came out with didn't match what your mum told us had happened in the street, and I know who I believe. Luella completely denied egging the shop; denied being there at all. All three of them did – it's total rot.'

Florrie listened as she threw a handful of teabags into the pot. She knew who she believed, too, though she held back from saying it out loud. Why would her mum make up such a story? 'Did you mention the key?' she asked.

'I did, and I'm sure you won't be surprised to hear my mother flatly denied that, too. Even had the nerve to feign offence; her over-the-top act was sickening. She demanded to know who else had a key – I didn't tell her – and told me it must be one of them. I decided not to share the small detail of our decision to get the locks changed and one of those doorbells fitted – oh, and I've spoken to Bear; he's calling at the DIY store to get what he needs first thing, said he'd fit them straight away. That should put an end to her snooping.'

'Thanks for sorting that, Ed.' It was more of a weight off Florrie's mind than she'd anticipated.

'And, as you can expect, because she denied having her own key, she pleaded ignorance to the paperwork being disturbed. And when I mentioned her disappearing upstairs for ages last Friday, she said she was just "admiring the décor". Even told me I had a devious mind for thinking she'd go snooping around other people's houses, that I was the one who wasn't to be trusted.'

'Sounds like gaslighting to me.' Florrie poured tea into the mugs, added a dash of milk and slid one across the table to Ed.

'Thanks. Aye, that's what I thought, too. A conversation with them feels like mental gymnastics, if you say something they don't like they try to run circles around you, make you believe you're in the wrong. It's probably why I've always tried to avoid confrontation with them; I can never keep up.'

'Your personality and temperament's more like your grandad's than it is theirs; being easy-going and laid-back is no match for people like your parents who are –no offence intended – fiery and confrontational. It's never going to be a level playing field.' From her vantage point, it was easy to see how they'd taken advantage of Ed's good-natured personality – he'd do what they wanted for a quiet life except for when it came to the bookshop and Florrie. Then he dug his heels in.

'None taken, they are fiery and confrontational,' he said.

'So how did you leave it? What about Luella?' From what Ed had described of their relationship, she knew his ex could be fiery, too, and prone to violent outbursts.

Ed blew on his mug and took a sip of tea. 'I think they were pretty stunned. I mean, they've never seen me so boiling angry before. I ripped into them, didn't hold back, didn't give them a chance to speak; I wanted to make sure they listened, didn't want to leave them in any doubt about my feelings. Thinking about it now, my mother's face was a picture, but I guess it's cos I've never really stood up to them before. Even Luella, who always loved a good scrap, sat there with her mouth hanging open.'

Florrie couldn't help but giggle at the mental image Ed's words had triggered in her mind. 'I almost wish I'd been there.'

'I'm glad you weren't – they still managed to fire back a load of their toxic nastiness. I wouldn't have wanted you to witness that. Dragged my grandfather into it as well which, as you know, is like a red rag to a bull for me.'

Florrie bristled at hearing that. 'Me too. I think I'd have had to pipe up if I heard them say anything bad about Mr H.'

Ed hung his head in his hands, an air of weariness descending upon him as if suddenly defeated. 'Sitting here, listening to myself talking about having the worst sort of blazing row with my parents, all the things *I* said, the spiteful things *they* said, and the way I feel about them, makes me feel incredibly sad.' He looked up, his eyes filled with anguish. 'They're my parents, I shouldn't be feeling this way about them. But the truth is, your mum and dad have been more like parents to me than my own ever have, and I daresay ever will be. Mine aren't interested in what I'm doing with my life, if I'm happy, what my plans are.' He took a shuddering breath. 'In fact, my mum didn't hold back on telling me exactly how she felt. She told me I'd never been wanted, that I was a mistake, that their life plan had no room for children but that she was too far on in her pregnancy to do anything about it. Even my father had the decency to look sheepish at that.'

'Oh, Ed, that was unbelievably cruel. She was way beyond wrong to say that to you.' Florrie rushed over to him, throwing her arms around his shoulders, all the while fighting against the urge to storm down to Dawn's B&B and give her a piece of her mind, no holding back. She kissed his cheeks, saddened to find they were wet with tears.

Sensing her dad's sadness, Gerty jumped up from her bed and rushed over to him, pushing her head into his lap and whimpering.

'You're a good lass, Gerty-Girl.' Ed smoothed his hand over the Labrador's velvety head.

Pulling her chair close, Florrie eased herself onto the seat, taking his free hand in both of hers. 'Let me tell you this, Ed, you're more than wanted here. I love you so much I can't even begin to think how to put it into words, the nearest I can get to it is to say that I love you with every fibre of my body. And my parents mean it when they say you're like the son they never had; they adore you, as did your grandparents. And let's not forget all our friends think you're amazing, they're always singing your praises. Bear thinks the world of you, he told Maggie you're like a brother to him.'

'He said that?'

'He did. And your grandad was over the moon when you got in touch – and don't get me started on how wrong it was of your parents to deprive you both of having a proper grandad/grandson relationship for all those years. But getting to know you all over again gave him a new lease of life, and he got so excited planning his trips to see you in London, he was bounding about like a teenager, singing away to himself.' She chuckled at the memory. 'When he came back it was all, "Young Edward this, young Edward that".'

Silent tears trickled down Ed's cheeks as he listened.

'And then there's Gerty here, she absolutely adores you. You know yourself she makes a beeline straight for you whenever we land back home. I'm definitely chopped liver by comparison.' She was pleased to see that triggered a smile, albeit a watery one.

'Thanks for saying all that, I appreciate it, particularly after what my mother lobbed at me.' Ed sniffed and wiped his face on his sleeves. 'I'm just tired of all their drama. It's never been any different and it's exhausting. My mother's words hurt so much, it felt like having a bucket of freezing cold water thrown over me, but once I'd got over the shock, they actually made me stop and think. They were the wake-up call I needed. Made me realise I don't have to put up with their crap anymore – *we* don't have to put up with their crap anymore – that it needs to end and they need to fully understand that. I should've taken a stand long before now, but...' He shrugged.

'They're your parents, that was never going to be easy. And it's never too late, Ed. The time had to be right for you.' Florrie wasn't sure how he was going to get his parents to fully understand any of what he hoped, especially when their despicable, cruel behaviour was so ingrained, but she was relieved to see he'd finally seen sense instead of simply taking whatever they threw at him.

'I'm going to make an appointment at Cuthbert, Asquith & Co as soon as they can fit me in and see what legal action I can take to keep them from contacting us – Luella, too, especially after the eggs. I doubt a cease-and-desist letter would do any good, they'd just laugh at it and ignore it completely. I think I might need something more formal and legally binding.'

Florrie took a moment, absorbing the implications of what Ed had just imparted. And though there was a new firmness in his voice, his navy-blue eyes couldn't hide the sadness behind his words. 'Are you sure you don't want to take a bit of time to think about it before you head down that route?'

'I don't. I want to get this moving as quickly as possible,' he said decisively. 'Let's not forget their efforts at manipulation stooped to new depths when they got my volatile ex involved, hoping to break us up. No, I'm making a start as soon as possible.'

A thought struck Florrie. 'Did you find out what it was they were arguing about in the street, and why Luella decided to egg the window?'

'When I asked, my father started to tell me, but my mother just shot him down and they ended up arguing again. He kept yelling that it was all her fault and they wouldn't be in "this position" if it wasn't for her.'

'Goodness, I wonder what he meant by that.'

'I doubt we'll ever find out now. And as for Luella and the eggs, she tripped herself up. After denying she was there, she later admitted she'd thrown the eggs cos no one wanted to see our "pathetic" wedding scene. Seemed to find it hilarious, too.

'Wowzers.'

When they finally went to bed, Florrie snuggled in close to Ed and he wrapped his arms tightly around her. They'd been through a heck of a lot over the last few days, but bizarrely she'd never felt closer to him. As a rule, he drifted off to sleep in a matter of seconds and she'd lay listening to the soothing sound of him breathing, but tonight there was no sign of that. She knew he'd be dealing with the encounter with his parents, processing it, waiting for the residual tension to leave his body. She wished she could magic it away. He hadn't deserved his mother's cruel words – no child did, no matter how old they were.

His chest rose as he inhaled deeply, sleep apparently out of reach for now. She snuggled into him even closer and whispered, 'I love you, Ed Harte.'

He squeezed her tight. 'And I love you, Florrie Appleton. You're the best thing that's ever happened to me.'

'I'll take that,' she said with a giggle, making him laugh, too. His words had never sounded more welcome to Florrie's ears.

TWENTY-FIVE
FRIDAY 17TH APRIL

Florrie couldn't help but notice that Ed was still a little subdued as they made their way along the top prom to the bookshop, but it was hardly surprising after what had happened yesterday. In contrast, she was feeling brighter since she'd had a call from her mum that morning, saying her dad had spent a comfortable night and had been cracking jokes with the nurses. 'One of them even asked if he wrote jokes for Christmas crackers cos they're that bad,' she'd said chuckling. 'Your dad thought it was hilarious.' There was no doubting the relief in her mum's voice.

They'd set off early in order to tackle the egged window before the shop opened, a thought that didn't thrill Florrie thanks to its reminder of the previous evening's drama. They rounded the corner of Endeavour Road onto Victoria Square, surprised to see Lark and Nate busying themselves outside the bookshop.

'I wonder what they're doing out and about so early?' A frown creased Florrie's brow, but as they drew closer, they realised their friends had beaten them to their clean-up session.

'Morning.' Lark beamed at them as she wrung out a cloth into the bucketful of soapy water by her feet. 'Thought we'd make a start on this, get it done before you open the shop.'

'Hiya,' said Nate, throwing a smile over his shoulder as he

scrubbed away at the glass. 'Bloomin' pesky stuff this, mind. It's not keen on shifting.'

'That's really kind, but we really didn't expect you to do it. Your hands must be nithered,' said Florrie. 'Let me dump my backpack and I'll come and take over.'

'Yeah, we'll get Gerty in and—'

'We know you didn't expect us to do it, but we wanted to help.' Nate flashed another smile. 'Last night was eventful, and you both had enough on your plate.'

'That's right. You just get yourselves indoors, do what you'd normally do when you get here. We'll carry on with what we're doing,' said Lark, rubbing vigorously at a particularly stubborn spot.

'But we can't—'

'Yes, you can, flower. Let your friends help you,' said Lark, interrupting Florrie. 'We're nearly finished.'

'Maybe you could stick the kettle on? Wouldn't mind a cuppa when we're done,' said Nate.

'No arguments. Go on, scoot, the pair of you,' Lark said firmly, shooing them away, her bracelets jangling.

'Since when did my sweet and gentle friend become such a bossy britches?' asked Florrie, smiling and making Lark laugh.

'Since about two minutes ago when *my* friend wouldn't listen to me.' She grinned, affection soft in her eyes. 'How's Charlie, by the way?'

'Much better, thanks. And according to my mum, he's got the medical team eating out of his hand, making them laugh with his dad jokes.'

'Ah, bless. That's so good to hear, flower. You and your mum must be relieved. That reminds me, I've prepared some crystals for him and a feel-good aromatherapy spritz. Don't let me go without giving you them.'

'Thanks, Lark.' Florrie didn't like to say her dad wasn't exactly what you'd call a believer in the power of crystal healing or aromatherapy oils, but as far as she was concerned, anything was worth trying, even if it had the smallest chance of helping him on the road to recovery. She'd have a quiet word with her mum – who did make use of Lark's crystals and had them dotted around the house – maybe she could slip them somewhere he wouldn't notice and she could give him the odd squirt of the spray when he wasn't looking. That thought made her smile.

The morning had passed in a flurry of activity, with customers calling in to ask after Florrie's dad. News always did travel fast in Micklewick Bay. Florrie and Ed were grateful to Lark and Nate for their hard work; they'd managed to get the window gleaming. No one would think it had been caked in dried-on egg first thing.

Jean and Leah had arrived early, Jean beside herself with worry about Florrie's father. 'They ought to be ashamed of themselves, that pair, causing such a commotion. Dinah and Bernard would be disgusted if they were still here, God rest their souls.' Florrie could only imagine what she'd have to say if she knew Dawn had referred to her son as a mistake.

Soon after, Jack and Jenna turned up wearing matching concerned expressions, Jack with a large basket of fruit in his hands. 'How's your dad, pet?' Jenna asked, rubbing her hand up and down Florrie's arm. Her smiles made a welcome return once Florrie had updated them on his improvement.

'That's grand news, be sure to send him our love,' said Jack. 'We got him this, to help with his recovery, though I reckon he'd rather have a pint of Old Micklewick Magic.' He chuckled, handing over the basket. 'Tell him the next round's on me as soon as he feels up to it.'

'I'll do that, Jack. He'll be chuffed to hear it,' said Florrie. 'And thank you for this.'

'If there's anything we can do, just shout up, pet. We're happy to help in any way we can,' added Jenna.

'Thank you,' said Florrie, touched by their kindness. In fact, she'd been touched by all of their customers' kindness and well wishes that morning. People had fallen over themselves to send their regards to her dad.

'So, Jenna and me have been talking,' Jack said in his gravelly tones. 'And we'd like to do another reading – if it's okay with you and Ed, of course – to make up for last night's being cut short in the way it was. Call it a gesture of goodwill, if you like, in case folk start baying for a refund – not that I reckon anyone would, mind, but you never know.'

'We thought it'd be a way of us showing our support of both you and your dad, too,' Jenna said, smiling kindly.

'Aye, Jen's right. We thought we could make it a bit different, maybe have a bit of a Q&A session. What d'you think?' He looked between Florrie and Ed, his eyebrows raised in question.

Florrie glanced across at Ed, her heart lifting. 'If you're sure, that'd be lovely. Thank you.' There was no doubt in her mind it would go down a storm!

'Yeah, that's really generous of you both,' added Ed. 'Are you sure you can spare the time? I remember you saying you've both got quite a few commitments coming up.'

'We thought maybe after your wedding, when everything's calmed down a bit here for you,' said Jenna. 'You two just name the day and we'll fit it in around what we've got scheduled.'

'You know me, I don't need much of an excuse to lock a load of folk in a room and blather on; can't beat, quite literally, a captive audience.' Jack gave a throaty chuckle, making Florrie laugh.

'And the other reason we're here is to help with tidying the reading room. We thought you wouldn't have had much of a chance with everything that's been going on,' said Jenna.

'Are you sure you've got time?' asked Florrie, touched by their offer.

''Course we have,' said Jack. 'Jen and me'll make light work of it, won't we, lass?'

'Uh-huh, we will that, pet. Come on, let's get cracking.'

. . .

By the time midday arrived, things had calmed down a little. Jean approached Florrie, a pile of Jenna's books in her hand. 'Have you seen the time, lovey? I just mention it since you said you were going to head over to the hospital at lunchtime.' They were in the reading room, putting the last of the stuff away. Jack and Jenna had sloped off upstairs to the tearoom for a bite to eat.

Florrie pushed back the sleeve of her sweatshirt and looked at her watch. 'Ooh, yikes! Thanks for the reminder, Jean, I hadn't realised the time, this morning's flown by.'

'You're not wrong there. And don't feel you have to rush back, Leah and I will manage. And don't forget Jack and Jenna have offered to stay and help. You spend a bit of time with your mum and dad, make sure your dad gets settled in at home and don't give the bookshop another thought.'

'Thanks, Jean.' Florrie gave her friend an appreciative smile, thinking how lucky they were to have such loyal staff.

In their last conversation Florrie's mum had told her that her dad had been moved out of ITU and onto a different ward, and, even better, it looked as though he was well enough to be discharged and free to come home that day. 'They reckon he took a tumble cos of his labyrinthitis, with the dizziness being exacerbated by the stressful situation. He just needs to pass some final checks, satisfy the medical team he's fit to be sent home before they can sign his discharge papers.' Paula had added that, all being well, he'd be free to leave later that morning. Florrie and Ed were going to collect them – Paula had suggested they leave it until lunchtime to head over and allow all the relevant forms to be signed so they could bring Charlie home. 'These things always take longer than you think, with the doctors and nurses being so busy, lovey, and I'd hate to have you hanging around,' Paula had said.

Since then, Ed had been offered an appointment at the solicitors owing to a last-minute cancellation, and though he'd originally declined it, Florrie had sensed his disappointment. The next free slot wasn't until Wednesday of next week, so she'd suggested he call them back and take the cancellation before it was snapped up by someone else.

When they'd woken that morning, she'd been surprised to find he was still dead set on going ahead with his plan to put something legal in place to prevent his parents from causing any further grief. She'd anticipated, after sleeping on it, the heat might have dispersed from his anger a little, and his feelings, not softened per se, but that maybe he'd wake feeling less determined to do so. Instead, it appeared to have galvanised his resolve.

At the hospital, Florrie found her mum in the ward six waiting room in conversation with a doctor. Paula's face lit up when she spotted her daughter. 'Hello, lovey, the doctor's just explaining your dad's aftercare for when we go home, come and join us.' She patted the seat next to her.

Mother and daughter exchanged a knowing look when the doctor left the room. 'Your dad's not going to take too kindly to hearing he's going to have to take it easy for a few more weeks, especially with all the labyrinthitis business he had to put up with before this,' said Paula, scanning the aftercare information in her hand.

'That thought was just running through my mind,' Florrie said.

'Well, since I'll be the one looking after him, and have to watch him like a hawk for the next forty-eight hours, I'm afraid he's going to have to do as he's told,' Paula said firmly. 'If he'd listened to me in the first place, and stayed put like I'd asked him to instead of coming outside, that dreadful commotion wouldn't have got him all stressed. I mean, we'd stayed in the bookshop rather than going into the reading room cos he was feeling dizzy. He should've known better.'

'He'd have been worried about you, Mum, with you going out there, that's all.' Though Florrie was playing devil's advocate, she was well aware her mum was talking this way out of concern for her husband.

'They have a lot to answer for. Things could've been a whole lot worse if he'd caught his head on the side of the kerb… Ugh! Doesn't bear thinking about.' She pressed her fingers against her mouth, her eyes shiny with tears.

Florrie rested her hand on her mum's arm. 'Don't go getting yourself all upset again. Dad's okay, he's going to be fine, so it's not going to do you any good dwelling on what might've happened. I'll have a word with him; he'll have to listen if both of us stress how important it is he rests and follows the doctor's advice.' Florrie had already made a mental note to tell her dad how worried he'd made her mum, she knew that would bother him, make him take heed of their words.

'Thanks, lovey, you're absolutely right.' Paula patted her hand and pushed up a smile.

In the car on the way home, Florrie updated her parents on Ed's situation with his parents – having checked with him beforehand that he was okay with her telling them everything. He'd replied that he was keen for them to have all the details, that way they'd understand his reasons for taking what most people would consider somewhat drastic action against his parents.

'They're a bloomin' disgrace,' said Charlie. 'They don't deserve a lovely lad like Ed.'

'I agree, they ought to be ashamed of themselves. That's the worst possible thing a parent can say to their child. I'm absolutely disgusted. I've a mind to find that monstrous woman and tell her exactly what I think of her. And it wouldn't be much, that's for sure. I don't blame Ed for seeing a solicitor about them.'

'Neither do I,' Charlie chipped in. 'I'm only surprised he hasn't done it sooner.'

'That young lad's put up with them treating him like dirt for so long out of misplaced loyalty because they're his parents, and they've taken advantage of it time and time again. But telling him he was a mistake was beyond cruel and low! What sort of mother does that?' Paula pulled a face of utter abhorrence. 'Those words will stick in Ed's mind for a very long time, poor lad.'

Paula's words triggered an ache in Florrie's chest; the thought of him dwelling on what his mother had said, never being able to forget them, had played on her mind ever since he'd told her. Her mum was right, it was the worst thing a parent could say to their child. She couldn't begin to imagine how that must feel for him. She only hoped Dawn's cruel words would fade with time, taking the hurt they'd caused with them.

'He's better off without them. All they do is give him grief,' Charlie said matter-of-factly. 'Anyroad, he's got us, he doesn't need them.'

'Aye, you're right, Charlie. And, once he has the legal action in place, the peace and quiet will mean he won't regret it. Be sure to tell him we think the world of him when you get back, won't you, lovey?'

'Aye, you do that,' added Charlie.

''Course I will.' As Florrie took the turn for Micklewick Bay, she couldn't make up her mind if Dawn and Peter Harte would respect the legal bindings of an injunction or tear it up and laugh at it. No doubt they'd soon find out.

TWENTY-SIX

As soon as Florrie arrived back at the bookshop, Leah pounced on her with the news that Ed's father had turned up at the shop an hour earlier and that Ed had left with him. Florrie's heart turned over. 'Don't worry, his dad was all calm and quiet, nothing like he was last night,' the assistant said quietly, conscious that customers might hear.

'What about his mum? Was there any sign of her?' Florrie asked, her voice a whisper, her knees like jelly. She felt sick at the prospect of Dawn seizing the opportunity to throw more toxic words at Ed.

'No, and there was no sign of the woman who came in the shop with her the other day either – the delulu one who threw the eggs at the window.'

'Try not to fret, lovey,' said Jean who'd joined them at the counter, evidently picking up on Florrie's troubled expression. 'From what I could see, Peter was looking suitably sheepish, not that it excuses anything. But I got the impression he didn't have much fight left in him after his shameful performance last night; probably burnt himself out. Got short shrift from me, he did, having the brass neck to show his face round here so soon.'

'From the death stare you shot him, Jean, I was half expecting him to turn to stone.' Leah giggled.

'If only I had the power, lovey, I'd be after his despicable wife, too,' Jean said, grimly.

Jean and Leah's voices faded into the background as Florrie's mind went into overdrive, wondering where Ed could have gone with his father, and fretting over what was being said. She hoped they hadn't headed back to Dawn and the B&B. Her thoughts segued to the solicitor's appointment, wondering if it could be connected to that? But she quickly told herself that it was too soon for anything to be put into place in that regard.

Her next thought was that she couldn't remember a time in all the years she'd been connected to the bookshop either as a young customer or employee when Peter Harte had set foot in the premises. It had been his childhood home, but he'd left as soon as he could, and from what Mr H had told her, he'd visited only occasionally when Ed was a small child, which, with her being younger than Ed, she had no memory of. It begged the question why he'd chosen today to return. A ripple of unease crept over her shoulders.

A customer arrived at the counter, bringing a halt to Leah and Jean's conversation and jolting Florrie out of her thoughts. The three women leapt to attention, Leah serving the customer, while Jean went back to restocking the shelves, and Florrie went to hang up her coat in the kitchen. There, she checked her phone and was disappointed to see no calls or texts from Ed which only added to her disquiet. There were, however, a whole slew of messages from her friends asking after her dad, and if she'd be joining them at the Jolly later that night. She blew out her cheeks – with so many other things going on, their weekly get-together hadn't even crossed her mind, but now she thought about it, she felt she should spend the evening with Ed. Some time together, just the two of them and Gerty, would do them good. And besides, she didn't want to leave him alone to brood on his thoughts while she was out enjoying herself with her friends, especially with his mother's heartless words so fresh in his mind.

She fired off a quick joint text to her friends.

> Hi lasses, thanks for your kind words. Dad's out of hospital and doing well – still looks pale tho. Lots to tell you, but I won't be at the Jolly tonight so will have to catch up with you all later. Feeling exhausted TBH, doubt I'd be much company anyway. Have fun & I'll see you soon Fxx

That done, she toyed with the idea of texting Ed deciding a quick message wouldn't hurt.

> Hi Ed, hope all's okay – Leah said your father came into the shop. Just to let you know, Dad's home and doing well. Mum's already driving him potty with all her fussing and rules. He's been calling her Florence Nightmaringale! She thinks it's hilarious! Fxx

Florrie reread the text, her thumb hovering over the send arrow, hesitating before she sent it, wondering if it was appropriate to include chirpy chat about her parents after the way things had been with his? Deciding it wasn't, she deleted it and started again.

> Hi Ed, hope all's okay. I heard your dad came into the bookshop – hope everything's going well with that. Dad's back home and seems much better. See you soon. Thought we could have a quiet night in, maybe get a takeaway if you fancy? Fxx

She'd be on tenterhooks until he returned.

TWENTY-SEVEN

Florrie flipped the bookshop sign to closed and was just about to slide the bolt across when Ed appeared on the other side of the door, making her start. 'Oh my gosh! Ed!' she said, pressing a hand to her chest, feeling her heart drumming beneath her fingers. On hearing her dad's name, Gerty raced over, dancing from paw to paw.

She opened the door and he rushed in, fresh air clinging to him. 'Sorry I took so long,' he said, out of breath and planting a firm kiss on her lips, the force making her take a step back. 'Hello there, Gerty-Girl, it's good to see you, too.' He bent and gave the Labrador a resounding pat, sending her into raptures.

'How are things?' Florrie searched his face for clues.

'I'll share everything with you in a minute, but first, tell me about your dad. It's great to hear he's out of hospital. Shall we head straight home? I can tell you what happened with my dad en route.' His words tumbled out in a rush.

While they were cashing up and getting ready to leave, Florrie brought him up to speed with her father's situation and he'd laughed heartily at hearing Charlie's new nickname for his wife. 'Florence Nightmaringale, I love it!' he'd said. She'd also reminded him that since she'd returned to the bookshop straight from the hospital, the car was parked on Endeavour Road, so their usual walk back, where they dissected their day, wasn't on the cards that evening.

'Ah, 'course, I'd forgotten about that. Let's head home then, I can tell you all over a pot of tea.'

Florrie was pleased and surprised in equal measure that Ed seemed brighter than when she'd left earlier that day. She couldn't begin to imagine what he had to tell her.

'Before I get started on telling you about how things went with my father, I just want to say, I don't want you to give up your Friday night with the lasses on my account.'

Florrie went to object, but Ed held up his hand. 'No arguments. In fact, while I was out, I bumped into Nate and he asked if I fancied grabbing a beer or two at The Cellar tonight. I thought it sounded tempting so I said yes. The other fellas are joining us, too. Bear's coming along after he's dropped Maggie at the Jolly, said his parents have agreed to babysit Lucy, and Jazz's parents are having her brood. Have to say, I'm looking forward to it, they're good blokes.'

'Wow! You have had quite the afternoon, haven't you?' Florrie chuckled, though she wondered if her friends had got their heads together and arranged this in an act of support for Ed – it would be just like them.

'Aye, you could say. Oh, and Bear's changed the front-door lock, here's your new key.' He dropped it into Florrie's hand. 'He couldn't fit one of those doorbells with a camera, though. Said the shop didn't have the one he was after in stock, but there's one on order. Said he'd fit it as soon as it came in.'

'Good old Bear. What would we do without him?' said Florrie.

'Aye, he can turn his hand to anything.' Ed's face turned serious. 'So, getting back to the unexpected visit from my father, I hadn't been back long from my appointment at the solicitors – I'll tell you about that after this – when he turned up at the bookshop. I was so shocked to see him, it took a while for my brain to register it was actually him standing in the doorway. Anyroad, when it finally did click, my first thought was that I had to get him out. I was worried he was going to kick off with round two of all the screaming and yelling, which we didn't need after last night.'

'Oh, blimey, no.'

'You should've seen the look Jean shot him, talk about a death stare.' He chuckled.

'That's exactly how Leah described it.' Florrie laughed, too. 'She said it's a wonder he didn't turn to stone.'

'She's not wrong. I could almost sense the "mess at your peril" vibes radiating from her. I've never seen my father look so taken aback before.'

'Go, Jean,' said Florrie, unable to resist.

'That's what I thought.' Ed grinned. 'So, when I'd got him out on the street, he was at great pains to assure me he hadn't come to argue or fight, but said he had something to tell me. Something that he thought would help explain my mother's recent actions.'

'This'll be good.' The snort that erupted from Florrie took her by surprise and she clamped her hand over her mouth. 'Sorry. Didn't mean to do that.'

'No need to apologise, I reacted pretty much that way myself. And even after hearing what my father had to say, I still don't think anything can explain or excuse what she's done.' He gave a resigned shrug.

'Where did you go to have your chat?'

'Don't worry, I didn't take him back to Samphire Cottage, if that's what you're wondering. After what my mother's been up to there, I wouldn't do that. We walked to the top prom while I worked out where we could have a talk, ended up sitting on one of the benches looking out to sea – well away from my grandparents' bench. I didn't want him and my mother to get wind of that; I dread to think what they might do to it if they knew it was there.'

'Oh, goodness, I hadn't thought of that.' Florrie wouldn't put anything past either of his parents but particularly Dawn with the mood she was in yesterday.

'Neither had I till we got there. In fact, I hadn't even made up my mind where to take him until then, and although he seemed calm, I hadn't forgotten his temper can be unpredictable and I didn't want to risk him kicking off in a coffee shop or anywhere like that if I said something he didn't like, or didn't respond in the way he hoped. I thought somewhere outdoors was the safest bet, and since it was pretty quiet along the prom and the sun was shining, I thought that'd be the best place.'

Florrie could see the logic in that. 'Did he say where your mum and Luella were?'

'My mum was at the B&B and I think Luella was at hers, and looking into getting a train back to London.'

Florrie nodded. Though she didn't say it, she hoped Luella had been successful and was already being whisked very quickly out of town.

'Anyroad, it won't come as a surprise to you that my father didn't offer an apology about what happened last night.' He gave a hollow laugh. 'But he jumped straight into telling me about the latest mess they've got themselves into. Interestingly, he did say he'd told her not to come here when she'd told him she was thinking about it. He said the first he knew of her visit was when she'd texted him from here. He reckons he followed her to put a stop to her plans.'

Florrie bristled that there was no forthcoming apology, especially after what had happened to her dad. And she wasn't so sure she believed that Peter had nothing to do with the drama, but she kept her irritation to herself and, instead, listened quietly as Ed went on to share his conversation with her. Her eyes grew wide as he told her how, without his father's consent, Dawn had invested all their savings – including some money she'd borrowed from a neighbour – into some Bitcoin 'deal' she'd found on the internet. It had turned out to be a scam and she'd ended up losing every penny, with no trace of the company she'd transferred the money to.

Florrie knew it wasn't the first time they'd lost money on unwise investments; it would seem they never learnt from their mistakes. The more she knew of Ed's parents, the more she understood why his grandfather hadn't bequeathed the bookshop to them.

Ed continued, telling her his father had gone on to say how he'd discovered quite by chance that Dawn had developed an online gambling addiction and had kept it secret for over a year. 'But she never quite got on top of her mounting debt which my father thinks contributed to her addiction growing stronger. The worst of it is, since the Bitcoin disaster, she started borrowing money from loan sharks and they've been breathing down her neck – my father's, too.'

'Oh dear. I'm sorry to hear that, Ed.' Florrie's mind went to Jasmine, whose ex, Bart, had been gripped by a gambling addiction and had borrowed from undesirable individuals to feed his cravings. The situation had caused irreparable damage to their relationship and quashed her friend's vibrant spirit for a long time afterwards.

'When it all came to light, my father said she became defensive and diverted attention to the bookshop, ranting and shouting, throwing things about in her usual way, saying it was rightfully theirs, that they wouldn't be in a financial mess if they'd inherited it. Apparently, she blamed him for not standing up to my grandfather, and raged that he'd let everyone walk all over him.'

Florrie's eyes widened. She couldn't imagine Peter Harte letting anyone so much as stand on his big toe without suffering a verbal savaging, never mind walk all over him!

'I know what you're thinking and I agree.' Ed's mouth quirked into a small smile. 'Anyroad, he said once she'd calmed down, she'd told him that she was going to fix things once and for all. Which leads into why Luella is involved.'

'Oh, blimey.'

'My father thinks it was around this time that she bumped into my ex, and on learning that Luella still had… um… still had feelings for me…' Ed scratched his cheek, an awkward expression on his face. He was clearly feeling uncomfortable at sharing this. 'It would seem the two got chatting and apparently hatched a plan to get us back together. I'm not sure of all the ins and outs of it, but what I do know is that when Luella and I became an item again, she was going to make me "see sense" and either hand over the bookshop to my parents or get me to sell it and give the proceeds to them. Oh, and she was going to have a small percentage of the profit as a reward for her trouble.'

'Wow! That's some bold plan.' Florrie couldn't help but laugh, wondering if it sounded as childish and unsophisticated to Ed as it did to her.

'It was fundamentally flawed on so many levels, though. I mean, they seem to have forgotten the need to take my feelings into account. Did they really think I was going to have an overnight change of heart and suddenly switch my affections from you to Luella? That I'd cancel the wedding, and my ex and I would live happily ever after? Let's not forget the fact that you're also a joint owner of the bookshop, and Jean and Jack have shares now. How were they going to get around that? They had a lot of people to convince to go along with their plan.'

'Desperate people take desperate measures,' she said. 'Panic must've skewed your mum's logic, especially if she's been getting hassled by loan sharks.'

'Hmm. Maybe,' said Ed. 'My dad told me he wasn't involved in any of it, and, like I said before, that the reason he came up here was to stop her from going ahead with her plan – he told me he knew nothing about it until Wednesday evening when she'd let slip during a phone call. She'd originally told him she was visiting a friend and when he questioned her, it apparently all came tumbling out. He got on a train the following morning and arrived in Micklewick Bay that afternoon. He reckons the reason he was arguing with her in the square was because she'd told him she was going to crash Jack and Jenna's reading and tell everyone how badly she and my father had been treated by my grandfather in bequeathing the bookshop to us. He'd been trying to talk her out of it which had made her angry and was the reason she'd started to scream at him in the street. It seems your father falling over and hitting his head forced her to abandon her plan.'

'Poor Dad, getting caught up in all of that.' Florrie felt suddenly drained by the situation. She couldn't imagine how Ed must be feeling knowing his mother was responsible for so much drama. All she knew was that it wouldn't rest easy with his mild-mannered personality.

'Oh, and though she still denies it, my father's pretty certain my mother's been snooping around our house in search of legal documents relating to the bookshop. And what's more, he found a key at her B&B with a fob advertising the name of the key-cutting booth at the station. He said it's not the one for her room at the guest house as that's a different type, so he thinks it's the one she's been using to get into our home.' He sat back in his seat and stretched his arms out on the table. 'And there you have it. A potted explanation for my mother's latest display of dreadful, not to mention irrational, behaviour.'

Florrie sat quietly, turning over the information Ed had just shared. There was a lot to take in and make sense of. Her initial feeling was that the whole messy situation sounded like some awful, overly dramatic plot from a soap opera. Her next thought was to wonder if Peter Harte had been telling the truth. After all, he had his own track record of bad behaviour towards his son, not to mention his own father, and she wouldn't put it past him to make things up to suit his own needs. But then again, she told herself, he'd had a calm discussion with Ed two Christmases back, where he'd revealed he had a heart condition. It seemed to have knocked the wind out of his sails and, in fairness, things had been quiet from their end for a while.

But in all that time, it hadn't stopped her from thinking it could all flare up at any moment and her concerns had been proved right. She also felt an unexpected pang of pity for Dawn; getting on the wrong side of loan sharks must be quite terrifying. And in the middle of all this was poor Ed. She couldn't begin to imagine how he must be feeling, especially after the heartless words his mother had thrown at him last night. The thought caused the pity she'd felt for the woman to quickly dissipate.

'Did he mention the things she said to you last night?' She couldn't bring herself to put them into words.

A look of pain flickered over his face, and she instantly regretted asking him. 'I brought it up, and his response was, "you know what she's like" and that I shouldn't take any notice of what she says in temper, that she doesn't mean half of it. Told me she loves me "in her own way", blah-di-blah. Didn't come as a surprise, I have to say.'

'So basically, he just brushed it off?' She shook her head in disbelief.

'Yeah, brushed it straight under the rug with everything else she's said and done; him, too – he's not blameless, he's said and done plenty of unpleasant stuff over the years.'

'Well, you know what, Ed? I don't think there's room under that rug for anything else. I think it's time they took ownership of what they've done instead of acting like a couple of overgrown children having temper tantrums. That, combined with their bullying and intimidation campaigns, is toxic and it stops now! I'm sorry if that sounds harsh, but I've had enough of them treating you like this, and I'm not going to stand by and let it happen anymore.' Florrie could feel her face burn with indignation as a surge of adrenalin hit her bloodstream. She made the decision there and then that she was going to speak to them. She needed to get her thoughts off her chest and hope her words hit their target the way Dawn Harte's had done with Ed. And she wasn't going to hold back.

Conscious of Ed's gaze on her, she steadied her breathing and pushed up a smile.

Ed took her hand, his eyes finding hers. 'Did I ever tell you that you're totally awesome, Florrie Appleton?'

'Not nearly enough.' She grinned, feeling suddenly bashful.

'Well, let me put that right. Florrie Appleton-soon-to-be-Harte, you may only just scrape over five feet tall—'

'Five feet two and a bit, actually.'

'Okay, Florrie Appleton-soon-to-be-Harte, you may only be five feet two and a – *very important* – half inches tall, but I think you've got the biggest heart of anyone I've ever met. Oh, and on top of that, you just so happen to be totally awesome. That do?'

Florrie let out a laugh. 'I suppose it'll do for starters. And I think you're awesome, too, and you have a great, big heart yourself.' They stretched across the table, their lips meeting in a soft kiss that made her heart flutter.

'So, how did it go at the solicitors'?' she asked, dropping back into her seat, glad to hear his laugh again.

'Interesting. Old Mr Cuthbert told me I have a couple of options, the first being a cease-and-desist letter, though I told him I doubted they'd take much notice of that. Mr Cuthbert agreed – don't forget he knows them of old. The next level would be an injunction which would have legal consequences if they ignored it.'

'Ooh, seems quite scary when you put it like that.'

'I know, that's what I thought. He suggested I think about it, discuss it with you, before I make a decision.'

'Oh, okay.' Florrie was pleased to hear Mr Cuthbert hadn't pushed Ed into going for such a drastic course of action straight away, that he'd advised him to give it some consideration.

'I just can't get it out of my head that my mother's temper and complete disregard for other people actually resulted in your dad getting so stressed he took a tumble and ended up in the intensive care unit of a hospital – albeit indirectly.' All trace of his earlier smiles had deserted him, his expression now grave.

Florrie was unsure how to respond. It had been an unfortunate set of circumstances, but all the same, Dawn needed to curb that temper of hers. Her dad may be home and being fussed over by her mum, but the outcome could just as easily have been very different. Not that she wanted to dwell on that.

'He's on the mend now, which is the main thing.'

'Aye, it is. And we're still together, stronger than ever, no thanks to my mother.' He summoned up a smile.

TWENTY-EIGHT

Her chat with Ed meant Florrie was running late for meeting up with her friends at the Jolly. She rushed up to the bedroom, threw off her Happy Hartes sweatshirt and was having a rummage around her wardrobe for something to wear when Ed appeared in the room.

'Why don't I give you a lift down there? Save you having to rush around.'

'It's fine, it's out of your way, and if I get a wriggle on, I won't be that late.' She pulled out a navy sweater dress and slipped it off the hanger before rooting around her drawers for a pair of chunky tights. 'Where the bloomin' 'eck are they?' she said to herself. It was cold out and the walk back would be nippy, so she wanted to make sure she was wrapped up.

Ed unbuttoned his shirt. 'I can drop you off and come back, leave the car here then have a wander to The Cellar. I'm not meeting the lads till eight, so that'll give me plenty of time.'

Florrie pulled out the elusive tights and stood for a moment considering his offer. 'Okay, if you don't mind, it'd definitely take the pressure off.'

'I don't mind at all, it'll save you running there.' He hitched a smile at that.

'It'd crossed my mind I could saddle Gerty up till I remembered we don't have a saddle.' She grinned at him, pushing her foot into the leg of her tights.

'Now that'd be worth seeing, you riding Gerty-Girl like a little racehorse all the way to the Jolly. I reckon it'd turn a few heads.'

'Daresay it might.'

Florrie had found herself looking forward to seeing her friends and having a relax with them. The time since their last Friday night session seemed further away than a week ago; so much had happened in that time. And the salsa dancing lessons didn't even feel part of the same year! How could that be? she wondered.

Florrie pushed open the heavy door of the Jolly, the usual sounds and smells pulling her in with their comfortable familiarity. She felt a wave of relaxation spread through her as she headed across the bar. The folk group was playing a lively, lilting tune, Lobster Harry's unmistakable cackle floating over the notes, while a fire was blazing in the inglenook and kicking out a welcome warmth along with the cosy aroma of woodsmoke. She beamed a smile as her friends waved enthusiastically from their usual table.

'Come and park your bum, missus,' said Maggie, shuffling up the settle to make room for her.

'How are you diddlin', flower?' asked Jasmine, at the top of the table, as Florrie squeezed by her and onto the settle next to Maggie.

'It's good to see you, lovey,' said Stella, reaching for the bottle of Pinot Grigio in the metal chiller and filling a glass before passing it to Florrie. 'There you go, grab yourself a bit of that.'

'Thanks, Stells.'

'How's your dad?' asked Lark. 'It's good to hear he's out of hospital.'

The others all agreed with that, listening as Florrie filled them in, and laughing heartily when they heard Charlie's 'Florence Nightmaringale' nickname for her mum.

'Your parents are so wholesome,' said Maggie, fondly. 'I bet he secretly loves being fussed over.'

'Oh, there's no doubt about that. It's the not being able to do much or get back to work until he's fully recovered aspect that frustrates the heck out of him.'

'I get that. It's the sort of thing that would drive me mad, too,' said Stella. When Stella wasn't in court or poring over a brief, she was going for a run on the beach or enjoying long walks in the countryside with Alex and his high-spirited black Labrador, Fred.

'Shame he's not into reading like you and your mum,' said Jasmine.

'I know, my mum's tried, but he says he hasn't got the patience to sit and read, so he's been watching all his favourite thriller films on Netflix again. He'll have to make sure he gets plenty of rest for now, though.'

'I'll pop up with a coffee and walnut cake, I know that's his fave.'

'That's kind, Jazz, he'd be chuffed to bits with that.' Florrie gave her friend a grateful smile. She paused for a moment, conscious that her voice was dominating the conversation. 'Listen, lasses, I don't want to hog the evening talking all about what's been happening to me. I feel I did enough of that last week worrying about you lot organising me a strippagram.' She was suddenly struck by how simple that worry was in comparison to the drama that had gone on in the week. 'Tell you what, I'd give anything to swap the worries I've had this last week for that one right now. I'd even put up with Ando Taylor and Lobster Harry as the double act you lot teased me about.'

'Just so you know, we can have that arranged at the drop of a hat. Just say the word.' Stella gave her an exaggerated wink, making them all fall about laughing, Jasmine giving a loud snort.

'Talking of Ando,' said Jasmine, in an 'I've got big news' way. 'I do believe he has a lady friend.'

All eyes switched to her.

'What?' said Maggie, incredulous. 'Who? It can't be anyone we know, surely.'

'Hmm. Now this actually rings a vague bell,' said Lark, tapping her finger on her chin. 'Why do I know this?'

'Haven't a clue,' said Jasmine. 'Maybe it's your intuition and you've been picking up vibes that have been floating about.'

'No, it's not that – I'm sure I overheard someone talking about it.'

'Did I hear right?' Stella looked around them in disbelief. 'Please tell me you haven't ditched Max in favour of Ando. I always had a sneaking suspicion you were getting slowly tempted by his offer of dates at his bedsit, swigging Gut Rot and downing out-of-date pickled eggs.'

'Rumbled. Guilty as charged.' Jasmine held up her hands, making them all roar with laughter.

'Come on, Jazz, we know how loved up you and Max are so there's no chance you'll have succumbed to Ando's culinary horrors. Share the deets and put us out of our torture,' said Maggie.

'Well...' Jasmine glanced around, a playful glint twinkling in her eyes. 'Bear in mind that this is second-hand info so I can't guarantee it'll be a hundred per cent accurate. But, from what I've heard, the woman in question has recently moved to Micklewick Bay and by all accounts is a female version of Ando; she loves skateboarding, she dresses like him – a bit grungy – battered leather jacket, ripped jeans and all, has a fairly laid-back attitude to work... You get the picture?'

'That's all very well, but do we know how she feels about Gut Rot and pickled eggs?' asked Maggie.

'That'll be the true test of their relationship. If she likes those two things, then their love's sealed,' Jasmine said with a giggle.

'Ah, poor Ando, don't mock, you lot,' said Lark. 'We all deserve a bit of love and happiness in our lives.'

'Aye, took you bloomin' long enough to realise that, though, didn't it? It's more a case of poor Nate, never mind poor Ando. You had the lad hanging on for years,' quipped Jasmine.

Lark responded with a shake of her head and a bashful smile. 'I had my reasons, as you know full well.'

'Just teasing, flower.' Jasmine gave Lark's arm an affectionate rub.

'Talking of how we all deserve a bit of love, have you seen who's over there?' said Stella, nodding towards a cosy table for two by the window where the curtains were drawn against the night.

They all turned to see Jean enjoying an animated conversation with Amery, her hands wrapped in his.

Lark clasped her hands to her heart. 'Ahh, bless, that's lovely. Jean so deserves having someone to love her and make her feel special.'

A feeling of warmth flooded Florrie's chest. Seeing Jean looking so happy with Amery touched her heart. Her friend was positively glowing. 'It is lovely.' She was glad to see Amery looked as happy as Jean.

'It's just a shame he didn't find her sooner,' said Stella wistfully.

'It's better than not at all,' added Lark.

'Which leads very nicely on to your dad and Louisa,' said Maggie. 'Is their relationship still going from strength to strength?'

The question brought a huge smile to Lark's face. 'I'm thrilled to report they're blissfully happy, and it looks as though they're going to be moving into his new cottage together when all the renovations are done.'

A flurry of 'ahhs' followed, with Florrie saying, 'Silas so deserved to find love a second time around – Louisa, too. They're so well suited. Just think, if he hadn't come to stay with you when he did last Christmas, they might never have got together.'

'As you lasses know, I always say fate has a plan for us all.' Lark's eyes were shining. 'They were always destined to be together, but the time had to be right for both of them, their stars had to align. Just as they have for Jean and Amery.'

'Anyroad, much as I hate to change the subject from a happy one to a not-so-happy one, you were going to tell us what happened after the reading last night.' Jasmine switched her attention from Lark to Florrie. 'It's really good news that your dad's okay, though.' The friends all agreed with that.

Florrie sucked in a deep breath, preparing herself to relive it all. 'So, after Ed and I got back from hospital, we hadn't been in long when he grabbed his coat and pretty much flew out of the door with not a word as to where he was going although I had a pretty good idea...' She continued, telling them everything that had happened including details of the conversation Ed had had with his father that afternoon and her suspicions about his mother snooping around their house. She'd checked with him beforehand that he was okay with this and he'd said he had no problem with her sharing, especially after the performance his parents had put on in the street.

The friends listened, heads shaking in disbelief, occasionally chipping in with the odd question, murmurs of outrage on hearing the cruel words Dawn had hurled at her son.

'It's been a heck of a twenty-four hours for you all, flower,' said Jasmine.

'Just a bit,' said Florrie, her stress levels spiking after reliving it all again.

'How's Ed, after his mother said what she did?' asked Lark. She was the one in the group who had the most sensitive nature and had looked utterly horrified when Florrie repeated what Dawn had said.

'He looked pretty devastated, which is totally understandable. I think it's what made him take a step back and finally see clearly just how bad she and his father have been treating him.'

'Not before time,' Stella said grimly.

'I can't get my head around the woman's dreadful behaviour, from creeping around your home and rifling through your stuff, to screaming in the street, to saying those hideous words to Ed.' Maggie's expression morphed from disbelief to disgust and back again. 'She obviously has no idea what she looks like or how she comes across.'

'I don't think she cares,' said Florrie.

'Even less so with her being desperate for cash,' added Stella.

'What about this deluded ex of Ed's who thinks they're going to run off hand in hand into the sunset? Lucifer or whatever it is she's called.' From the way Jasmine's eyes glittered wickedly, it was obvious she knew exactly what Ed's ex was called. And even Lark had to laugh at that. 'What made her think it was okay to chuck a load of eggs at the window?'

'It's Luella, but I'm not gonna argue with the Lucifer tag, especially after she egged the window display.' Florrie turned to Lark. 'And thanks again for cleaning it all off.'

'No worries, flower.'

'Apparently, she threw the eggs because she was annoyed about the wedding scene, decided no one would want to look at it. He said it's exactly the sort of thing she used to do when they were together; she'd lose her rag and start screaming and chucking things.'

'Well, they say girls choose men that remind them of their father, seems the same thing applies to boys and their mother,' observed Stella. 'Thankfully for him, that changed when he met our Florrie.'

'Aye, Lucifer and Florrie couldn't be more different if they tried,' added Jasmine.

'So that's all my news, I reckon it's someone else's turn now.' Florrie swept her gaze expectantly around the table.

'I'm pregnant,' said Stella.

Four jaws fell open in perfect synchronicity.

TWENTY-NINE

Jasmine stuck a finger in each ear, waggling them in an exaggerated manner. She was the first of the friends to speak. 'You what? Did I hear right or are my lug 'oles deceiving me? Did you just say what I thought you said?'

'Stells? Are you being serious?' asked Maggie.

Florrie's eyes went to Stella's wine glass, noting the liquid was paler than that in the others. Stella caught her looking. 'It's water. I was the first here, told Tim behind the bar I was on antibiotics so couldn't drink alcohol.'

'I'm totally gobsmacked.' Jasmine looked from the glass to Stella in disbelief.

'Aww, Stells, I thought I was picking up something about you, but I was so concerned about Florrie's situation, it totally threw me.' Lark beamed. 'I'm absolutely thrilled for you.'

'How long have you known and when's the baby due?' asked Florrie. 'Oh, and what does Al think?'

'I found out last Sunday when we got home after the salsa lesson. And in answer to your question about what Al thinks, he's over the moon.' The smile on the usually cool Stella's face told Florrie all she needed to know.

'Blimey, I've got so many questions, but I can't even ask them until I've got my head around this shocker.' Jasmine laughed.

'In that case, let me help,' Stella said with an amused expression. 'It's very early days, I'm only six weeks' pregnant, so please, not a word to anyone – naturally, I was desperate to tell you lot! I've calculated that the baby's due at Christmas.'

'Ooh, another Christmas baby, like little Lucy!' Maggie clapped her hands together.

'What does your mum think?' asked Florrie.

'I'm not gonna lie, she was shocked at first—'

'She's not the only one; you've always said you didn't want kids, Stells,' added Jasmine.

'Fair point,' Stella acknowledged. 'But once it sank in, she was thrilled. Me too, actually.'

'Dare I ask how all this is going to fit in with your life as a busy barrister?' asked Florrie. She knew how important Stella's career was to her, and how hard she'd worked to build her practice and her reputation.

'As it's so early in my pregnancy, I haven't discussed it with chambers yet, but at the moment, and after discussing it with Al, I'm going to take a few months' maternity leave, and then go back part-time until the baby starts school. Obviously both Al and I are self-employed so we can work around the baby. My mum's offered to help out, too. She's so excited about becoming a grandma and wants to be hands-on, as does Al.'

'Wow! I can't believe I'm hearing all of this from the woman who thought all kids were the spawn of the devil and to be avoided at all costs.' Jasmine chuckled.

'Apart from yours and Maggie's,' said Stella. 'Your kids are the exception; they're gorgeous.'

'Hmm. They have their moments.' Despite her words, pride shone in Jasmine's eyes.

The night progressed with the friends chattering and laughing. Florrie sat back, glad she'd decided against staying at home. She'd checked her phone and sent her mum a text, asking after her dad, pleased and relieved in equal measure to hear he was doing well. She'd exchanged a couple of texts with Ed, too. He seemed to be enjoying himself with the lads at The Cellar.

When the end of the evening arrived, and Mandy rang last orders at the bar with her good hand, Maggie said, 'So, as you know, we put you on notice that we have another hen do celebration for you planned for Sunday. This one's our Jazz's idea, and all we can say is wear something you'd go for a walk in and wrap up warm – maybe have a waterproof handy.'

'No more clues than that?' asked Florrie.

'Nope,' said Stella. 'Well, other than one of us will call for you at half ten.'

'Ey up, have you seen who's just walked in?' said Maggie, nudging Florrie with her elbow.

They all turned, following her line of sight to see Ando Taylor wearing his usual attire of baseball cap turned back to front, his battered leather jacket and ripped jeans. But what had caught Maggie's attention was the young woman making moon eyes at him.

'I reckon from your description that's her: his paramour,' said Stella, peering around Lark.

'I reckon you're right, Stells,' said Florrie. 'And from the way she's looking at him, I'd say she's got a major crush on him.'

'Doesn't she just?' said Maggie. 'And for once, he's not rolling drunk and making a turkey of himself.'

'Bless, I'm happy for him,' Lark said softly.

'Me too,' agreed Florrie, as Ando looked in the direction of their table and nodded a hello.

'There's a lot of love in the air here tonight.' Lark smiled over to where Jean and Amery were sitting.

Florrie followed her gaze. 'Looks like the stars have aligned for quite a few folk recently.' The friends looked on as Amery raised Jean's hand to his mouth and lay a gentle kiss on it, a collective 'Ahh' following.

THIRTY
SUNDAY 19TH APRIL

An eager knocking at the door set Gerty off barking and charging down the hallway. Florrie glanced at the kitchen clock. It was just after ten fifteen; whichever of her friends had come to call for her, they were early.

'Blimey, someone's keen,' said Ed. He was busying himself replacing the batteries in the fairy lights that decorated the dresser.

'Aren't they just? And you can calm your jets, Gerty, it's not an axe-wielding burglar, it's just one of the lasses.' Florrie chuckled as she padded after the Labrador. As per their instructions on Friday evening, she was dressed as if she was heading out on a walk and just had her pair of sturdy walking shoes to put on.

Grabbing Gerty by the collar and pulling her back, Florrie managed to open the door, her face falling when her gaze landed on the last person she expected to see on the doorstep. Gerty's hackles stood on end as a low growl emanated from her. Florrie felt herself bristle.

'Dawn. What are you doing here?' she said coolly. After what the woman had said and done, there was no way Florrie was going to waste pleasantries on her.

'I've come to see my son.' With a defiant glint in her eye, Dawn took a step forward as if to walk in, but Florrie stood firm, blocking her path along with Gerty.

She wasn't going to bow down to this bully for a moment longer. 'I'm surprised you didn't use the key you copied from ours and let yourself in again.'

Dawn flinched. 'I don't know what you mean, you're being paranoid, and I don't take kindly to being accused of such preposterous things.'

Florrie could feel herself shaking. Confrontation like this was so out of her comfort zone, but her anger towards this woman for what she'd said to Ed pushed her on. The gloves were off! 'We both know I'm not being paranoid, that you've been letting yourself in here and going through our stuff while we were out.'

'What rubbish!' Dawn gave a scornful laugh. 'If you leave your things in a mess, it's got nothing to do with me, I think you'll find it's all down to you.' Dawn folded her arms across her chest. 'Are you just going to keep me standing here on the doorstep? I've already told you, I'm here to see my son. I need to speak to him.' Her eyes flicked to Gerty who was glowering at her.

Dawn's posture only served to make Florrie all the more determined to stand her ground. 'Is he expecting you? Has he invited you here?' A bolt of alarm flashed through Florrie's mind. Had Ed asked his mother here knowing Florrie was going to be out for several hours? As she was wrestling with this thought, she sensed him appear behind her.

'No, she hasn't been invited, and no, I wasn't expecting her.' Ed's voice held a cool tone Florrie hadn't heard before.

'Edward, I want to talk to you.' From the way Dawn barked at him, no one would ever guess she was addressing her son, more like a person she really didn't like. And if Florrie wasn't mistaken, she was sure she detected a flicker of uncertainty in Dawn's eyes, no doubt at Ed's response. It took Florrie by surprise. She hadn't had much contact with her up to now, so wasn't familiar with the woman's mannerisms, but it suddenly struck Florrie that Dawn's style was classic bully behaviour, made up of intimidating body language and overbearing bluff and bluster. And, much as she understood Ed's mother thrived on confrontation and arguments, something told Florrie if ever she was properly challenged, Dawn would become a quivering cowardly mass. What's more, she thought, now would be the perfect time to put that theory to the test – though Florrie wasn't entirely comfortable conducting such a conversation on their doorstep. Somewhere private would have been preferable but there was no way she was going to let Dawn set foot in their cottage. She didn't want to give her the opportunity to dominate them in their own home.

'You need to stop speaking to Ed in that horrible tone. Like you said, he's your son, not some dog you order around.'

Dawn glared at her, her mouth twitching with anger. Florrie was barely aware of the low hum of a car engine as a vehicle made its way steadily down the road, a seagull crying in the distance.

'After Thursday night, I've heard all I ever want to hear from you. Please go back to London and leave Florrie and me alone.'

'Don't be so stupid, boy, we all say things in the heat of the moment. I'm your mother – you can't dismiss me just like that, I won't allow it.'

Gerty's growls grew louder.

'I'm afraid you have no choice,' said Ed. 'I'm done with your bad behaviour. You need to leave here and go back to London.'

Dawn's mouth set in a hard line as she absorbed his words. 'Don't you dare speak to me in that way. Show me some respect,' she said through bared teeth. Gerty inched forward, snarling. 'And get that idiotic dog under control.'

Florrie's anger finally bubbled over.

'You've got a nerve showing up here after those despicable words you said to Ed last night. I'd ask how you can live with your-self for saying them, but I already know the answer: you're cruel and you have no conscience. You seem to think it's okay to bully your way through life, throw a tantrum, stomp over people to get what you want. But worst of all, you've bullied Ed, made him feel worthless and given him the most miserable childhood. You're oblivious to the wonderful, kind-hearted and thoroughly decent person he is, which is in no way down to you.' She paused. Her chest was heaving, her pulse galloping.

'Aye, well said, lass,' said Frank Jessop from two doors up who was passing as he took his terrier, Floss, for her evening walk.

Dawn spun round. 'How *dare* you?'

'Very easily, actually. It's time someone stood up to you and that obnoxious husband of yours,' he said, his voice fading as he continued down the street.

Florrie blinked. *Frank Jessop knows about Ed's parents?*

'You've been talking about me, spreading gossip and lies, turning people against me.' Dawn's accusatory voice pulled Florrie out of her thoughts. She moved her gaze back to Ed's mother to see pure hatred in her eyes.

'Florrie wouldn't say a word. She's not a gossip, she keeps things private,' said Ed.

The whirr of cycle wheels caught Florrie's attention as two teenage boys slowed up on the opposite side of the road, looking over, apparently intrigued by what was happening at Samphire Cottage. It crossed her mind that things weren't exactly private now, there on the doorstep, but all the same, she was undeterred. She might never get another opportunity to stand up to Dawn like this. She made sure to keep her voice low.

'I think you'll find you've got yourself to thank for that. Word spreads quickly in this town and I daresay your display in the square last night has reached quite a few folk by now. Your performance attracted quite a lot of attention.'

Dawn looked ready to explode.

'Well, I wouldn't have had to go to such drastic measures if it wasn't for you stealing the bookshop from under our noses, inveigling your way into Bernard's affections, creeping around him calling yourself "the granddaughter he never had".' Dawn emphasised the words in a mocking voice. 'You ought to be ashamed of yourself. I'm only surprised he left Edward any part of it, that you didn't try to talk him out of that. I bet you were disappointed when he died before you had a chance to convince him to cut Edward right out of his will.' The gleam in Dawn's eyes left Florrie in no doubt that she got a huge thrill out of delivering her unpalatable opinion. It didn't come as a surprise to Florrie – after all, she knew the woman thrived on this sort of thing – but hearing Mr H spoken of in such a way, their mutual fondness for one another mocked and called into question, felt like a knife to her heart. The accusation that she'd stolen the bookshop left her feeling physically sick.

'Mr and Mrs H filled the gap of grandparents for me and I loved them as if they were my own.' She felt her voice wobble as emotion squeezed in her chest. 'And no one was more surprised than me when I heard I'd been mentioned in Mr H's will; he'd never said a word about it to me beforehand. It was totally unexpected and I even tried to wriggle out of it.'

'Shame you didn't try harder then, isn't it?' Dawn said coldly. 'You're nothing but a scheming little gold digger.'

Ed stepped forward. 'Stop right there, Mother. Don't utter another word. A gold digger is the last thing Florrie is and nor is she scheming. She didn't steal the bookshop; we all know the reason my grandfather didn't include Dad and you in his will, despite how much you try to convince yourself otherwise.'

'Where are your family loyalties?' Dawn spat.

Florrie couldn't help the laugh of disbelief that escaped her mouth. Pushing aside her hurt, she said, 'Family loyalties? Who are you trying to kid? You have no loyalty to anyone but yourself. And you're the one who ought to be ashamed of yourself, turning up here like this, no doubt coming to demand money.'

Dawn's mouth fell open, her eyes glittering with rage.

'Yes, we know all about the financial mess you've got yourself into, not helped by your gambling habit.' Florrie felt a prickle of unease at that, wondering if she'd overstepped the mark by bringing up Dawn's addiction. It wasn't like her at all, but she could never forgive this woman for what she'd said to Ed.

'If that's what Peter's told you, then he's lying. He's twisting everything to suit his own narrative, trying to make me look—'

'If you took ownership for what you do, people might have a little bit of respect for you. And what about your plan with Luella? Who are you going to blame for that?' Lucifer, the nickname Jasmine had given Ed's ex last night, shot through Florrie's mind.

'You foolish girl! It's hardly my fault they still have feelings for each other. Anyone can see they're meant to be together. You need to realise you're in the way. Don't think his father and I don't know what you're doing, forcing him into marriage so you'll have an even bigger share of the bookshop. It's clear as day.'

Her words whipped the breath from Florrie's lungs. *Forcing him into marriage?*

'That's not true, Mother, and you know it.' Ed shook his head, an expression of disgust on his face. 'You've gone too far. Like I said, go back to London and leave us alone.'

'Your father and I are here to get what's rightfully ours while there's still a chance, before it's lost forever,' Dawn hissed. 'We've let you get away with playing at being shopkeepers for long enough. You've had your fun, now it's time to do the decent thing.' The malice in her eyes shook Florrie to her core.

'You've done all you could to cause trouble between Ed and me but trying to ruin our wedding is a step too far, as is sneaking into our house and snooping through our stuff. I think all you've done gives me grounds to take legal action against you and make sure you keep away from me, the bookshop and this house.' Florrie's heart was pounding.

Dawn smirked. 'You're a fool to think Edward would stand for that. I'm his mother. Isn't that right, son?' She rolled her tongue over her top teeth, almost daring him to disagree with her.

'The only reason I haven't called the police before now is because Florrie talked me out of it. I'm so disgusted by your behaviour – trying to break Florrie and me up is despicable. Just go.' Ed went to close the door.

'What have I been missing?' came Jasmine's chirpy voice as she opened the gate, making Ed pause. Her friend was bundled up well against the cold, a bobble hat covering her red pixie crop.

'What do *you* want?' Dawn scowled as Jasmine walked past her.

'I'm here to see my friend – she's expecting me.' Jasmine shot her a look to match.

'Hi, Jazz,' said Florrie, her insides churning with emotions, relief at seeing her friend amongst them.

'Come in, Jazz. My mother was just leaving,' said Ed.

Jasmine stepped inside and he firmly closed the door, sliding the bolt across.

THIRTY-ONE

'That woman has some bloomin' brass neck,' said Jasmine, her top lip curling in disgust when Florrie had finished relaying what had happened with Dawn. The two friends were striding purposefully along the top prom, and though the sun was shining and the sky was clear, there was a chilly wind whipping off the sea, making Florrie glad she'd wrapped up well. She hadn't a clue where they were heading or what they were doing that day; she was still reeling from her encounter with Ed's mother and it hadn't crossed her mind to ask.

'Tell me about it. I was just relieved she'd gone by the time we left. I was half expecting her to still be on the doorstep or parked outside when we opened the door.' Florrie hadn't noticed the vice-like grip of a headache that her altercation with Dawn had triggered until Ed had closed the door. And now her head was pounding.

'Let's hope she's got the message. I mean, it sounds as though Ed's been standing up to the pair of them this time.'

'Aye, let's hope so.' Florrie gave a wistful sigh, hoping the fresh air would help chase her headache away. The two friends walked on, stepping aside to avoid colliding with a couple and their two dogs on their morning run.

'Anyroad, that's enough about that old dragon and Lucifer for now.' Jasmine gave Florrie a playful nudge, catching her eye, the pair of them giggling.

'You're right. So, any chance you're going to tell me what you've got planned today?' She'd spotted Jasmine was wearing her backpack but hadn't been told to bring anything herself.

'Well, I can promise you it's got nowt to do with pigs, Ando Taylor or Lobster Harry, so you can rest easy on that score.'

'Phew!' Florrie mimed wiping sweat from her brow, making them laugh some more.

'I'll give you more info when we reach our destination,' Jasmine said, adopting a mysterious tone.

'Okay.'

Taking the turn onto Skitey Bank, the salty sea breeze hit them full on, though the warmth of the spring sunshine took the edge off the cold. Thorncliffe loomed over on the right, the red pantiles of Old Micklewick glowing under the sun's rays. She spotted the bathing suit-clad Goosebump Gals rushing towards the sea for a chilly frolic amongst the waves – it briefly crossed Florrie's mind that they must have added an extra day to their sea swimming routine. She listened as Jasmine updated her on what she and the kids had been up to, their plans to move in with Max. She knew it wouldn't be a decision Jazz would make lightly, but all the same, it had filled Florrie's heart with joy hearing her friend chatter away so happily. If anyone deserved a happy ending, to Florrie's mind it was Jasmine. Not so very long ago she'd been run ragged, trying to make ends meet, being both mum and dad to her children after Bart had passed away in a tragic acci-dent. Not to mention the grief his parents had given her after-wards. It gladdened Florrie's heart to see her friend settled and content.

'Does this mean we might be hearing wedding bells for you and Max soon?' Florrie gave her friend a knowing look. The blush that tinged Jasmine's cheeks was all the answer she needed.

'Just keep it to yourself for now though. We were going to wait till after you and Ed got married, didn't want you to think we were trying to steal your thunder.' Jasmine cast her a bashful look.

Florrie gave a squeal and threw her arms around her friend. 'Oh, Jazz! This is fantastic news. I'm so happy for you! And we'd never think you were trying to steal our thunder. Ed'll be as over the moon as I am when I tell him.' She pressed a noisy kiss to her friend's cheek before releasing her, clutching onto her shoulders. 'I don't want you to keep it secret on my account. It's such fabulous, happy news, I think you should shout it from the rooftops.' Both women laughed at that.

'Are you sure you wouldn't mind?' Jasmine was glowing with happiness.

''Course not. I hope I haven't been giving you all the impression that I'm some sort of bridezilla diva.'

'Anything but, you're mega low-key, which is why we haven't wanted to wade in with our news and look like we're trying to hog the limelight.'

'Neither of you are like that, Jazz. Please don't give it another thought. Like I said, share it with the world.' Florrie beamed at her.

'Okay. We haven't mentioned anything to the kids yet, but just as soon as we do, we'll tell everyone else.'

'Can't wait! I'm so happy for you, Jazz. Max, too. You can tell by the way he looks at you that he adores you, his eyes go all warm and soft.'

'Right, that's it! Give over with the mush!' Jasmine said, her face burning as she gave an affectionate roll of her eyes, making Florrie hoot with laughter.

Soon they reached the bottom prom where Lark, Jean, Maggie and Leah were waiting by the boarded-up café at the entrance to the pier. They were all wrapped up well and wearing wide smiles as they greeted them.

'We're just waiting for Stella, Jenna and Louisa. Hayley sends her apologies, she's had to head back to university,' said Jean.

'Ah, that's a shame,' said Florrie. She'd enjoyed catching up with Hayley at the salsa dancing lesson.

'Here they are,' said Maggie, as a herring gull screeched from its perch on the railings that separated the bottom prom from the beach.

Florrie turned, following Maggie's line of sight, to see Stella, Jenna and Louisa hurrying towards them from the direction of the beach huts.

'Okay, so, I don't know if you remember, but a few weeks ago, you mentioned something you'd quite like to do. In fact, you thought it'd be the perfect Sunday morning activity,' Stella said, sounding more than a little mysterious.

Florrie racked her brains for what she could've said.

'That "perfect Sunday activity" – in case you've forgotten – is...' Lark added a pause for dramatic effect.

Florrie glanced around at the smiling faces looking back at her, the sound of the waves in the distance as the tide slowly crept out.

'A beach clean!' they all chorused.

Florrie clapped her hands to her face. 'Oh my days, I did! How fab that you remembered.' She laughed. They'd been at the Jolly, enjoying one of their Friday night get-togethers, when Florrie had told them how disappointed she and Ed had been by the amount of rubbish they'd spotted on their recent dog walks along the beach with Gerty. It was then that she'd mentioned that she'd quite like to organise a beach clean at some point.

'It's not your average hen party celebration, but we thought you'd like it,' said Lark. 'This one's Jazz's suggestion.'

'It struck a chord when you mentioned it, cos the kids had brought it up the week before,' said Jasmine. 'I think I told you one of Chloe's friends had cut her foot on some broken glass near the rock pools.'

'I remember that! I hope her friend's foot's better. It's a brilliant suggestion, Jazz. And thank you all for wanting to take part.'

'There's something nice at the end, as a bit of a reward for all our hard work,' added Maggie.

'I've just noticed, you're not wearing your hen do bits and bobs from the other night. Don't think you can wriggle out of wearing such classy stuff just cos you're on a beach clean,' Stella said with a joking wag of her finger.

Florrie clapped her hand to her forehead. 'I've left them at home. They're in a bag hanging on one of the coat pegs. We had an unexpected visitor, and I ended up leaving in a rush; the hen do stuff went right out of my mind. I'm so sorry, lasses.' Florrie felt her cheeks flush with disappointment. She hoped she didn't look ungrateful or for her friends to think she'd left them behind deliberately. She was relieved when Jasmine came to her rescue.

'I can vouch for Florrie, she had an unexpected visitor of the *worst* kind.'

'Not one of Ed's parents or his ex?' said Lark, looking alarmed.

'It was Dawn. She turned up about ten, fifteen minutes before Jazz. It was awful, and I'm ashamed to say we had a bit of a barney on the doorstep. People were looking.' She pulled a regretful face. 'I don't think my parents are going to be too chuffed with me when I tell them.' Florrie cringed internally at the reminder of the heated exchange with Ed's mother and the vitriol that had passed between them.

'I'm sure your parents will understand, they know more than most what that woman's like, especially after Thursday night,' said Maggie. 'By the way, how's your dad? Is he still grumbling about Florence Nightmaringale?'

That resurrected Florrie's smile. 'He's good, thanks. Still feeling a bit dizzy, but my mum said he's got his appetite back. And, yes, he was having a good old complain about her, but it was obvious he's still loving having a fuss made over him.'

'Oh, that's good to hear, lovey,' said Jean, wearing a look of relief. It had shaken her badly when she'd seen Charlie unconscious on the pavement.

'If it's okay with everyone, I'd rather forget about Dawn for now and get on with us having a nice time, especially since you've all given up your Sunday mornings on my account.'

Florrie was relieved to find everyone was happy to agree with her request.

'Not a problem, flower. Let's get cracking. But first, you're going to need one of these,' Jasmine said, adding a hint of drama to her voice as she produced a folded litter picker from her backpack with an exaggerated flourish, opening it out and handing it to Florrie. 'And you'll need a pair of these.' She reached into her backpack once more, and waved a pair of cleaning gloves in front of her. 'And one of these.' This time she proffered a black bin bag.

Florrie couldn't help but laugh. 'I see you've come fully equipped.'

'Don't let anyone say we don't take our litter picking seriously,' said Maggie.

'Right, follow me, team!' Jasmine held her litter picker aloft and strode purposefully over to the short run of steps that led down to the beach, the women following, litter pickers in hand.

'I suggest we work our way along to the surf shop, then double back. I reckon that should keep us busy for a couple of hours,' Jasmine called, her voice being buffeted by the breeze. And there's a prize for the person who collects the most rubbish by the time we're done.'

An exaggerated 'ooh' rang out. 'What's the prize, Jazz?' asked Maggie.

'I'll think of something.'

'Why does that make me feel nervous?' said Stella, quirking an eyebrow.

'Hmm. I kind of know what you mean,' said Lark, grinning.

By the time they'd filled their bin bags – competitive as ever, Stella was onto her second one – they were almost back at the pier where they'd met earlier.

'Well done, lasses.' Jasmine's nose was pinched red from the cold. 'Mind, I have to say, isn't it shocking how much rubbish we've collected between us? And who thinks it's okay to leave their baby's dirty nappy? It's not as if there aren't plenty of bins along the bottom prom.'

'I picked up a flip-flop and a trainer – it's one of them expensive brands,' said Jean.

'How about we contact the local press, show them how much we've gathered? It might help draw attention to what a problem it is, and encourage people to take their rubbish home,' suggested Stella.

'I think that's a bloomin' good idea, pet. I wouldn't mind putting my name behind it – not that I'm saying I'm anything special, but I'm quite taken aback by just how much there is, and what folk leave behind,' said Jenna.

After all agreeing that they liked the idea of doing what they could to highlight the problem and welcoming Jenna's offer, Stella rubbed her hands together, a smile spreading across her face. 'So, now it's time for the best part. We need to head this way.' She spun on her heel and pointed in the direction of the beach huts.

It crossed Florrie's mind that even after a couple of hours being blown about on the beach, Stella still managed to look stylish.

The gaggle of women followed, chatting away and coming to a stop at the door of the beach hut – or chalets, as they were sometimes referred to by the locals – Florrie knew belonged to Stella's mum, Alice. It had a special place in her heart since it was where Ed had proposed to her two Christmases back.

They waited while Stella jiggled with the lock before pushing the door open and a welcome wave of warmth rushed at them. 'Brr!' Florrie gave a shiver – she hadn't realised how cold she was until then.

Inside, the tasteful coastal décor of white painted timber-clad walls had enjoyed a temporary makeover in a nod to Florrie's hen celebration. A small table in the compact kitchen area, whose units were painted a smoky blue, had been set with an array of hen party plates, cups and paper napkins, while a chair at the head had been trimmed with a clutch of pink helium balloons emblazoned with the word 'BRIDE'. Pink streamers were festooned along the white-painted beams and a banner declaring 'Florrie's Hen Party 2026' was situated above the small fireplace where a wood burner sat, flames dancing behind its glass. Florrie spotted a group of folded chairs set against the wall, no doubt deposited by her friends earlier.

'We're having a beach hut picnic!' said Maggie. 'Grub, courtesy of the local deli, with yummy cupcakes made by the fair hands of our very own cake-baker extraordinaire, Jasmine Ingilby.'

'So this is why the three of you were coming from this direction when we met first thing,' said Florrie.

Leah nodded. 'We were getting it all set up.'

'Don't let anyone tell you we don't know how to do tacky with flair.' Stella grinned as she pulled off her pale pink Schoeffel bobble hat and swapped it for a deely bopper, its glittery pink hearts bobbing back and forth and making everyone laugh.

'Oh, lasses, this is amazing. Thank you.' Florrie gazed around the well-thought-out space, memories of her Christmas picnic with Ed floating into her mind and flooding her heart with happiness. 'I love these little buildings, it's a shame there aren't more of them.'

'Funny you should say that,' said Stella. 'Al's been briefed to design some more – I think he said the council's planning ten or twelve with plans to lease them out to small businesses. He's really excited about it, reckons they'll be ready next year.'

'Ooh, that does sound good. I love the idea of some interesting little shops down here,' said Maggie.

It didn't take long before the friends had divested themselves of their bulky coats and were getting stuck into the food, the small space filled with their lively chatter and laughter, those in the know mindful of not mentioning Stella's recent baby news. Florrie couldn't deny she was distracted by her argument with Dawn, but she did her best to push it from her mind and allowed herself to enjoy her time with her friends. It helped that Jenna had a whole armoury of entertaining anecdotes and had everyone in stitches, particularly when she was recounting a time at a book awards ceremony and she'd gone up to accept an award for best romcom novel.

'I do love me a heel, but mind, I'm no Posh Spice when it comes to walking in 'em – I'm no posh anything come to think of it, but you lasses already know that,' she'd said with a cackle. 'Anyway, there I am, teetering across the stage in me six-inch skyscraper Jimmy Choos, glammed up to the nines in a silky Grecian goddess frock, complete with *dangerously* plunging neckline – with heavy emphasis on *dangerous*. I've got a massive smile plastered across me chops, and the award's within touching distance. But the next thing I know, me ankle wobbles and I feel meself being propelled towards Jem Jacobs – he's the dish who's presenting the award,' she'd continued, the group's undivided attention on her. 'Everything feels like it's moving in slow motion, and from the corner of me eye I see me beautiful crystal award flying off the podium and go sailing through the air. I do some sort of crazy lunge, hoping to save it but in the process, I wallop straight into poor old Jem, knock him off his feet and land slap bang on top of him with my boobs in his face. I mean, these bad boys aren't exactly what you'd call small.' Jenna had clapped her hands to the generous proportions of said, 'bad boys'. 'Next thing I know, there's a stampede as what sounds like a hundred wildebeest rush onto the stage to help drag me up – once they'd stopped laughing, that is. And the worst of it is, I'm never gonna be able to forget it cos it keeps getting played on those bloomin' programmes of embarrassing moments.'

It had taken several minutes for their laughter to subside and the power of speech to return to the group. Florrie had been forced to remove her glasses to wipe away the tears of mirth that had streamed down her cheeks.

'Ah, my sides are hurting with laughing so hard,' Stella said through her guffaws.

'What a way to go, eh? Death by boobs.' Maggie giggled, her shoulders shaking.

'Could be the title of your next book, Jenna,' Jasmine quipped, her body still wracked by laughter.

'Ooh, yeah, it'd be a whole new genre for me: cosy crime.' Jenna chuckled.

'With emphasis on the cosy,' added Stella, the ensuing peals of laughter bouncing around the beach hut.

. . .

'Thanks for an amazing day, lasses. I've loved every minute.' Florrie beamed at them as they were walking towards the pier. It had been good to put her thoughts of Dawn and her worries about her dad out of her mind for a few hours.

Lark flung her arm around her, kissing her cheek, pressing her head against Florrie's. 'You're welcome, flower. We're super-chuffed you enjoyed yourself. Just one more hen celebration to go and then it's the big day.'

Florrie turned, meeting her friend's pale green eyes, the pair of them exchanging happy smiles. A pulse of excitement rushed through her. She just hoped the situation with Dawn had calmed down by then, leaving Ed and her to enjoy their special day. And it went without saying that she hoped with all her heart her dad was well enough to walk her down the aisle.

THIRTY-TWO
MONDAY 20TH APRIL

'I wonder what today's going to bring, not to mention the rest of the week,' Florrie said thoughtfully as she and Ed set off for work that morning.

'No drama, hopefully,' Ed said, flashing her a mood-boosting smile and squeezing her hand.

They'd had a long chat yesterday, in which Ed had surprised her. He'd told her he'd decided not to dwell on his mother's words, not let them eat away at him. 'The way I see it is I've got two options: I can absorb them, ruminate over them, cling onto them, if you like, until they affect how I feel about myself, influence my outlook on life, which could, ultimately, affect my relationship with you – which isn't what I want. Or I can push them away and tell myself they're the words of a person who's ultimately unhappy with themselves and projecting how they're feeling onto other people. Yes, what she said hurt like heck at the time, but maybe not as much as if such a display of anger was out of the blue and not the norm; my mother's always been an angry person – my father, too – always screamed and yelled and hurled abuse, so, in some way, it numbed the pain; took the sting out of it.'

His explanation had horrified her.

'And you know what's helped me come to this realisation?' he'd asked. When Florrie had shaken her head and told him no, he'd said, 'You, Florrie. You and your parents. Living with you, and getting to know your mum and dad, being welcomed in and treated as one of their own, has made me realise what a proper family's like. How you show your love for one another, how you support one another, the kindness and the care, how you've totally got each other's back no matter what – and I feel included in that – has opened my eyes. And you've all made me feel that I'm *enough*. That I don't have to try to be someone or something I'm not or can never be. And that I'm not the "useless disappointment" my father has referred to me as so many times.'

Florrie's heart had squeezed as she'd listened.

'We're getting married in under two weeks' time, and I want to take the values and the love that your parents have instilled in and bestowed upon you into our marriage and, hopefully, in the not-too-distant future, our own family. I didn't know what true happiness and a feeling of security and being loved felt like until I met you and your parents.' When he'd finished, he'd given Florrie a heart-warming smile and kissed away the tears that had been cascading down her cheeks.

'Feels like we've had a lifetime's worth of drama over the last couple of weeks. I just want to be able to focus on our wedding without any other distractions getting in the way,' she said.

'Well, hopefully, we can, especially if my father can get through to my mother and get her to speak to someone who can help with her addiction; maybe help with her anger issues in the process. It's a relief to know he's finally accepted that we'll never give up the bookshop.'

After Florrie had left with Jasmine yesterday, Ed had contacted his father and told him of his mother's visit and the heated exchange that had ensued. He hadn't been surprised to learn that Peter had already been given his wife's version of events. Ed also hadn't been surprised to hear they were wildly different from what had actually happened. At the end of their conversation, his father had assured him that he'd speak to Dawn and advise her to keep away and bring an end to her campaign to get her hands on the bookshop. Peter had finally realised that if the business ever fell into his and Dawn's hands, it would go straight on the market, and the proceeds would be gone in the blink of an eye. He finally seemed to accept that his son and Florrie were putting all their efforts into making it a success and that it was their efforts that had made it the viable business it was today.

'You and Florrie have worked hard, son. You've both got vision, know what the bookshop needs to make it a success. It's taken me a while, but I can see that now,' he'd said during their chat.

His father's praise had been hard won, and Florrie knew it was taking some sinking in for Ed, who wasn't used to receiving such positive feedback from a parent.

'I keep pinching myself to make sure I'm not dreaming and am going to wake up to find my father's in on the plan, too.'

'Trust me, you're wide awake,' said Florrie, choosing not to add that she hoped his father was being genuine. Despite her new positive mindset, she couldn't deny it was a possibility that his father was fooling him, and she knew Ed would be gutted if it later transpired it was all an act.

They stopped a moment to let Gerty have a sniff of the grass that poked through the railings on the top prom, the tangy sea breeze lifting the ends of Florrie's bob. From their vantage point, it was easy to see the tide was halfway out, lapping around the legs of the pier and the foot of Thorncliffe. The sound of the waves was never far away, even high up on the top prom. The recent weather forecast crossed Florrie's mind. She'd been watching it closely as the wedding drew closer, and her heart had sunk when she saw storms were predicted for later in the week.

'I know it's not great that my father's been diagnosed with a heart problem, but it seems to have made him look at life differently,' Ed said, pulling her out of her thoughts. 'Two years ago, we'd never have been able to have a civilised conversation like that; he'd have been ready to explode on me as soon as I said something he didn't like, no matter how small it was.'

'Without sounding awful, at least some good's come out of it.' Florrie glanced up at Ed to see him looking thoughtful.

'Doesn't sound awful, s'just a shame it hasn't rubbed off onto my mother.'

'Right then, all you need to do is download the app and set up an account.' Bear had popped into the bookshop later that morning. He'd just come from Samphire Cottage where he'd installed the new doorbell. 'The instructions are pretty straightforward, you can select if you want to get alerts if anyone comes to your door, you can even communicate with them if you want to.'

'Thanks, Bear, that's great,' said Ed.

'Yeah, thanks for getting everything sorted so quickly.' Florrie selected the app and waited for it to download to her phone. She wasn't sure she'd need to communicate with anyone, but it would be interesting to see who turned up unexpectedly at their house. Dawn sprang to mind.

'Oh, and you can also play footage from earlier, check if you missed any callers,' Bear added. 'You'd be surprised what it can show up. I know some folk like it when they see wildlife having a wander round their garden during the night.'

'Thanks again, Bear, let us know how much we owe you and we'll settle up straight away.'

'Aye, no worries.' He smiled. 'Right, I'd best be off, I've got a load of fencing to treat with wood stain over at the Millers. I want to get it finished before the bad weather sets in.' With a cheery goodbye he headed out of the shop.

'It's a shame it's come to this because of my mother, but I do think these doorbells are a good idea security-wise. Mind, let's hope we never have to use it for that reason.'

THIRTY-THREE
WEDNESDAY 22ND APRIL

'No way!' Ed said as he was sitting at the kitchen table, checking the doorbell app on his phone. They hadn't been back from the bookshop long and Gerty was having a noisy drink from her water bowl.

'What's up?' Florrie asked as she set the biscuit tin on the table. 'I've got the munchies; can't wait till our evening meal, I'm afraid.' She popped the lid off and helped herself to a chocolate digestive, offering the tin to Ed.

'No, thanks.' He shook his head, turning his phone towards her. 'Take a look at this.'

'What am I looking at?' She peered through her glasses, squinting. 'Oh—' She stopped in her tracks. 'Is that who I think it is?'

'Mm-hm.'

Florrie grabbed a chair and nudged it closer to Ed, before easing onto it. 'Can you play it again? I couldn't see it too clearly with my eyesight being so pants.'

'Two ticks, I'm still getting used to all the settings.' He took a few seconds of tapping on the screen before he said, 'That's it.'

They both watched as Dawn arrived at their gate, her whole demeanour radiating annoyance. Even her resting face was one of fury. She knocked at the door, glancing around her as she waited a couple of moments. When no one answered, she fished around in her bag, brought out a key and went to push it into the lock. Her expression darkened with irritation when she couldn't get it in. She made several attempts, her face growing increasingly angry each time the key failed to fit in the hole, until she became verbally abusive.

'Oh, blimey, she doesn't sound happy,' said Florrie, as a tirade of abuse was hurled at the lock, her ears picking up Ed's name amongst it all, as well as her own.

'She hasn't finished,' said Ed, still holding his phone between them.

Florrie looked on as Dawn lashed out at the plant pot beside the door, knocking it over.

'Goodness, she's got a heck of a temper. I wondered what had happened to the plant pot, especially since it hasn't been windy enough to knock it over.'

When the footage came to an end, Ed turned to her, disappointment hovering in his eyes. 'This is proof that my mother clearly hasn't listened to a word anyone's said to her.'

'At least she couldn't get in. You never know, it might make her take notice,' said Florrie, keen to reassure him. She hoped she sounded more convincing than she felt.

'This has got to stop,' said Ed grimly. He pushed his chair back and got to his feet. 'She's used up all her chances. I don't see why we should have to put up with this, especially with our wedding being so close.'

Florrie watched as he headed out of the kitchen, the sound of his determined strides making their way down the hall. Seconds later came the sound of the front door closing. Gerty glanced over at Florrie and whimpered.

Though Ed had been gone for less than an hour, it had felt more like twice that to Florrie, and her heart leapt when she heard his key in the door. Following Gerty down the hallway, she found him unbuttoning his coat.

'Hi.' Though he smiled, she was struggling to read his expression. He bent and ruffled Gerty's ears. 'Hello, lass.'

'Hi, you okay?' Florrie asked, anxiety squirming in her stomach. She couldn't imagine how awful it must be for him to have to keep tackling his parents about their unreasonable behaviour, not to mention exhausting.

'I am now. Come on, I'll make a pot of tea and tell you all about it.' He hung up his coat then flung his arm around her and kissed her on the cheek as they made their way to the kitchen.

Florrie listened, her hands cradling her mug, as Ed explained how he'd called his parents and told them to meet him at his mother's B&B. There he showed them both the doorbell camera footage of Dawn attempting to gain entry to Samphire Cottage.

'There was no way she could wriggle out of it,' he told her matter-of-factly. 'Not that she didn't have a good old try, mind, but even my father was having none of her rubbish. I told her if she didn't go back to London, I'd have no choice but to take legal action. Left her in no doubt I wasn't joking. Between us, me and my father managed to get her to agree to leave. She packed her bags while I was there and is heading back first thing.'

Florrie let his words sink in. 'And are you sure she'll definitely leave?' She hardly dared hope it could be the end of the trouble Dawn had been subjecting them to; the woman wasn't exactly one for taking things lying down.

'I'm positive. The look on her face told me she knew she was beaten; I've never seen her wear an expression of defeat like that. Though, before I left, she took great pleasure in telling me she wanted nothing more to do with me; that I was no longer her son.'

'I'm so sorry, Ed, that can't have been very nice for you to hear.' Her heart twisted for him.

'It's nothing more than I expected. In fact, I felt surprisingly numb to her words; they didn't upset me at all. I've come to realise they're par for the course with my mother. All I feel now is relief.'

He reached over and took Florrie's hands in his. 'It's over, Florrie. There'll be no more trouble from her – or my father. We're free to get on with looking forward to our wedding. We're all that matters now, you and me.' He raised his hand to her face, cupping her cheek, and touched his lips to hers.

Gerty whimpered from her bed, making them pull apart, the pair of them giggling.

'Ah, bless her,' Florrie said fondly.

'And of course, you matter, too, Gerty-Girl,' Ed said, laughing. 'We could never forget you.'

THIRTY-FOUR
SATURDAY 25TH APRIL

'You're looking very handsome tonight.' Florrie's eyes roved over Ed who was wearing the new sky-blue shirt she'd bought him for his birthday, the colour setting off the deep blue of his eyes.

'Thank you, you don't scrub up so badly yourself.' He crossed the floor, closing the space between them and slid his arms around her neck, brushing his lips against hers.

'Why, thank you.' She chuckled at his choice of words. It was the evening of the final hen party celebration and the only clue she'd been given was to get dressed up. The instructions had thrilled her; it was always a nice change to wear something special. Tonight, she'd opted for an A-line silk dress in a sumptuous shade of midnight blue, splashed with dots embroidered in a sparkly silver thread. It was a vintage piece she'd picked up in Lark's Vintage Bazaar and it was the first time she'd worn it. She was secretly relieved when Stella had told her she didn't have to wear her hen party sash and other items, since where they were bound that evening wasn't keen to attract 'that type' of celebration with the potential for rowdiness – so the restaurant manager had informed her.

'Give us a twirl.' Ed took her hand and spun her round. 'Actually, you don't just scrub up well, you look gorgeous.' He delivered a warm kiss to her lips.

'Mmm. That was nice.'

'Plenty where that came from, if you play your cards right.' His playful grin that followed made her giggle.

'Looking forward to your curry with the lads?' As well as it being Florrie's hen do, it was Ed's stag celebration and the men had a table reserved at the Indian restaurant in Middleton-le-Moors, which was always a favourite.

'Too right. The thought of the delicious food's been tormenting me all day.' He grinned. 'Chicken Tikka Masala. Mm-hm.' He gave an exaggerated chef's kiss.

'Well, at least you know where you're going. I'm still completely in the dark about where we're heading.'

'Ah, don't worry, you'll enjoy yourself, and all I can tell you is that you'll be enjoying some delicious food, too.'

'You tease! You could give me a little more info.'

'Sorry, no can do.' He looked at his watch. 'Ey up, we'd better get a move on if we're meeting everyone in twenty minutes.'

Florrie glanced at the alarm clock on her bedside table. 'Oops, you're right.' She scooped up her shoes, threw her smart navy-blue velvet coat over her arm and grabbed her bag. 'See you downstairs.'

The Cellar was heaving when Ed pushed the half-glazed door open, a babble of chatter spilling out onto the street, the indie-rock track that was playing growing louder.

'There they are, over at the bar,' he said, squeezing his way through.

'I'll take your word for it,' she said, following him. Saturday nights were always popular at the town's microbrewery thanks to its award-winning beers and friendly, welcoming atmosphere.

Arriving at the bar where a line of beer pumps gleamed under the lights, they were greeted by a flurry of hellos from their friends. It had been arranged for them to have a drink together before the men went one way and the women the other for their respective celebrations. They were to have one drink in The Cellar, then the men would climb into a minibus where a driver would whisk them over to Middleton-le-Moors and wait there to bring them home, though Florrie had known none of this before tonight. A thread of excitement wove through their conversation, as the group of friends caught up on their day.

'So, this is the last Saturday night you're going to be able to call yourself Florrie Appleton,' said Stella. 'This time next week you'll officially be a Florrie happy Harte.'

Florrie giggled at that. 'Oh gosh, I know! I can hardly believe it.'

'Exciting times, flower.' Lark flashed one of her kind smiles. 'You're perfect for one another.'

'Thanks, Lark.'

'Let's raise a glass to Florrie and Ed's last Saturday as single-tons,' said Al, holding his bottle of beer aloft. 'Cheers to Florrie and Ed.' The others followed suit, echoing his words.

Waving the men off as the minibus headed out of the square, Jasmine looked at Florrie and said, 'You'll probably be very pleased to know we haven't got far to go. We remembered you saying you'd be happy to celebrate your hen party by having a meal at Oscar's, just the five of us, so that's what we're doing tonight. This one's our Stells' idea.'

'Thought it'd be a good way to round things off.' Stella smiled fondly at her.

'Ah, lasses, I'm thrilled, thank you. I feel like I've been thoroughly spoilt over the last week or so. I might have to get married again, if this is what happens.'

'That's greedy,' joked Maggie. 'Surely, it's Jazz's turn next.'

Jasmine and Florrie exchanged a look that was instantly caught by eagle-eyed Stella.

'Ey up, what's this? Did our Maggie inadvertently touch on something exciting there?'

'Shh! Stells.' Jasmine waved her hand in a bid to get her friend to lower her voice. Even under the muted glow of the streetlights, her blushes were hard to miss.

'What's this?' asked Lark, cottoning on and leaning in.

'I'll tell you once we're sitting down in the restaurant.' Jasmine linked her arm through Florrie's, hurrying them along, no doubt before she got dragged into any further conversation on the street.

Inside the bistro, they received a warm welcome, their shoes clipping over the polished floorboards as they were led to a table in the corner by the window. Florrie glanced around her as she pulled out the bistro-style wooden chair in front of her. Oscar's was one of her favourite places to go for a meal and she loved the typically French décor, with arched mirrors trimmed with fairy lights set above wainscotting painted a tasteful sage green. The wall at the far end, with its exposed imperial-sized bricks afforded the restaurant a rustic quality, while lighting was courtesy of pendant lights with vintage-style bulbs suspended from twisted fabric cable, and candles wedged in old wine bottles sat on the mismatched tables. A selection of old-style crystal decanters filled with yet more fairy lights were dotted around the place along with a variety of quirky memorabilia.

'Oh, wow! Something smells absolutely delicious,' said Maggie, inhaling the mouth-watering aroma of seafood infused with garlic, which was the bistro's speciality.

'Mmm. It does,' agreed Jasmine, just as their server appeared, handing them all oversized menus.

'I think I'm going to have the crayfish salad to start; the thought of it has been torturing me all day,' said Lark.

'Well, I haven't had that luxury, since I only found out where we were going ten minutes ago,' Florrie said dryly, a smile making her mouth twitch.

'The element of surprise will add to the flavour,' Stella said, chuckling, just as the server arrived back at the table with a basket of sliced French bread and a carafe of water.

Once they'd placed their orders, Maggie waited until the server was out of earshot and asked, 'Dare we ask how things have been with Ed's parents?'

'Quiet since they've gone back to London.' Florrie finished buttering her slice of bread and set her knife down. 'It's been reassuring to know Dawn can't sneak into our house again.'

'Did you ever get to the bottom of what she was looking for?' asked Stella.

'No, but we suspect it was probably documents relating to our ownership of the bookshop.' Florrie shook her head. 'I did notice something missing, though. It was when I went to pay the window cleaner from the tin on the dresser – you know how Jed prefers cash. Anyroad, I thought it felt light when I picked it up and when I took the lid off, it was completely empty, not a single penny left. She must've taken it when she had a key to the cottage.'

Jasmine tutted, and Stella asked, 'Do you know how much was in there?'

'Maybe around fifty quid, made up of notes and coins.'

'Thank goodness you stopped her access when you did,' said Lark.

It had made Florrie feel uneasy at the time, and not wanting to risk those feelings returning – despite her determination not to let Ed's parents get her down – and casting a cloud over the evening, she figured a change of subject was on the cards. 'So, have you been getting any cravings, Stells, or going off particular food? I recall Mags saying she went off her beloved bacon butties.'

'Ooh, I did, big time.' Maggie pulled a face at the memory, setting off a flurry of giggles around the table.

'I can't say I'm craving anything yet, I think it's still early days for that, but I'm definitely struggling with the smell of coffee. Even the thought of it makes my stomach turn over.'

'No coffee for us tonight, then, lasses,' chirped Jasmine.

'So, what are you going to do about living arrangements when the baby arrives, Stells?' asked Maggie. 'I mean, you don't actually live together, do you?'

Stella and Alex lived in separate luxury apartments in Fitzgilbert's Landing, a recently converted warehouse that overlooked the newly created marina. Their apartments occupied the same floor and were located opposite one another, so the close proximity had meant they hadn't felt the need to move in together. Until now.

'Well, rather coincidentally, you might recall I told you Al had plans approved for a decent-sized family home on that plot of land he bought not far from Max's place on the cliffs. He'd originally planned to build then sell the house, but the unexpected baby news has thrown a slightly different light on things.' She glanced around the table. 'So he's decided to keep it and make it our family home. We're going to hang on to my apartment, rent it out, and he's going to sell his.'

Florrie observed her friend, delighting in seeing her look so happy and settled. There was no denying Stella's brittle edges had been smoothed since she'd changed her stance on relationships. She'd previously denounced them as being only for fools, that men weren't to be trusted. But meeting Alex had changed all that. He was good for her, as she was for him. He loved her strong, sassy personality and wasn't intimidated by her ball-breaking attitude or her successful career as a formidable prosecution barrister. In turn, she loved his calming nature, how he was slow to anger, knew just what to do or say to soothe her tendency to be highly-strung. It was obvious to all who knew them, they were a good match. He was the proverbial yin to her yang. He'd gained her trust and made her feel safe and secure such that she'd done something she'd sworn she'd never do: she'd opened up her heart to love.

'Wow! You've got it all worked out, the pair of you, haven't you?' exclaimed Jasmine, smiling happily.

'Ah, Jazzy-Pants, that reminds me, I rather got the impression you have a little secret you'd quite like to share with us this evening.' Stella quirked an eyebrow, her eyes twinkling with mischief as she smiled back at her friend.

Colour flooded Jasmine's cheeks. 'Er, I do, yeah. Mind, it's top secret for now. But' – she covered her face with her hands, muffling her voice – 'I feel so embarrassed saying this, but Max popped the question and I said yes.'

The table bounced with excitement as the friends all congratulated her, mindful of keeping the subject secret from other diners, though a squeal did manage to escape from Lark, turning heads nearby and making Jasmine laugh.

'He's taking me to choose a ring next week; says he wants to do it properly and get down on one knee, and all that mushy stuff.' She rolled her eyes affectionately, her cheeks still blazing. 'Then we're going to tell the kids – who've been hounding us to get married anyway. Zak and Connor keep telling us they're desperate to be "proper brothers" as they call it. Then we'll tell everyone else, though my mum and dad already know and are chuffed to bits for us, as you can no doubt imagine.'

'It's fantastic news, Jazz.' Florrie squeezed her friend's shoulder.

'Wow, what a couple of years it's been for us, lasses. Who'd have thought we'd have joined Mags and Bear in the loved-up club?' Stella said, beaming.

'Funny how things slot together, isn't it?' observed Jasmine. 'Look at Jean and Amery. And even Ando's found someone to share his pickled eggs.'

'Ahh, who says romance is dead?' said Maggie, deadpan.

'I think we can say, love is in the air in Micklewick Bay,' said Lark.

'Sounds like a cue for a song,' said Stella, launching into a song with that very title, the others following suit.

THIRTY-FIVE
FRIDAY 1ST MAY – THE DAY
BEFORE THE WEDDING

The first thing that struck Florrie as she opened her eyes that morning was the sound of the rain lashing against the bedroom window and the wind howling around the cottage. It had woken her several times through the night as things had crashed around outside, a car alarm further up the street screeching like a banshee in the early hours. Her heart plummeted. The weather forecasters had evidently got it right: Storm Maida was on its way, wreaking havoc as it charged over the Atlantic, its full impact estimated to hit the North Yorkshire Coast that evening. As if that wasn't bad enough, the local news reports had been getting everyone whipped up into a frenzy the previous evening, with their dramatic warnings of potential flooding. Apparently, it was something to do with a spring tide that was associated with tonight's full moon, or 'flower moon' as they were calling it. Florrie only hoped Storm Maida had blown itself out by tomorrow morning.

'I think we'd better take the car to work this morning. I'm not so sure a walk along the top prom will be quite the refreshing experience we usually enjoy. We'll end up like drowned rats by the time we get to the bookshop,' Ed said, rubbing sleep from his eyes. 'Which means we don't have to leave the house so early, and I can take advantage of having an extra snuggle with you.' He rolled over and pulled her close, wrapping her up in his arms.

Thoughts of the weather leached from Florrie's mind as she melted into the warmth of his kisses.

'It's really going for it out there.' Florrie was peering out of the window in the bookshop door, watching a band of horizontal rain sweep up the square. Someone in a raincoat dashed past, head bowed against the wind, water running off them in rivulets, while a bus rumbled by splashing through the puddles on the road. It was the first time since Ed had unveiled the window displays that there'd been no one standing watching them transfixed – not that Florrie could blame them, they'd be soaked to the skin in a matter of minutes.

'I'm sure the rain will've stopped by tomorrow morning.' Leah gave Florrie a hopeful smile.

'Let's hope so.' Unconvinced, Florrie returned the smile then checked her watch. It was three thirty and the bookshop and the tearoom upstairs had been quiet all day; no one was keen to venture out in such wild conditions. 'You might as well head home, Leah. We're not likely to get a rush on at this time, and the weather's set in for the evening. I can manage what customers we get. Is your car close by?'

'I was lucky, there weren't many people about this morning so I got a spot just outside the bakery.' The bakery was two doors down from the bookshop.

'In that case, get yourself home before things get worse out there.' Florrie made her way across the floor to the counter.

'If you're sure?'

'Positive. We'll still pay you up to five o'clock, it's pointless you hanging around.'

Just as Leah went to object, the bookshop was plunged into semi-darkness as all the lights went out, making the two women start. Gerty looked up from her bed.

'Power cut – all the streetlights are off, and the other shops, too,' said Leah. Florrie followed her gaze to see a gloomy looking Victoria Square on the other side.

'Looks like we'll all be going home.'

The plan for the night before the wedding was for Florrie to stay at her parents' house; her wedding dress and accessories were already there, her having dropped them off in her lunchbreak the previous day. Ed was to spend the night at Clifftop Cottage with Bear and Maggie, Bear being his best man. The couple had planned on having a couple of hours together at Samphire Cottage, grab a bite to eat before they went their separate ways.

The power cut, however, had meant they were unable to reheat the Mediterranean stew her mum had given her when she'd called round yesterday.

'Looks like it's sandwiches by candlelight,' joked Ed as he flicked the switch for the fairy lights on the dresser and dotted tea lights in glass votives around the kitchen. Rain was drumming against the window.

'How romantic.' Florrie chuckled, rooting around the drawer for her head torch. She'd just got her hands on it when her phone started ringing where she'd left it on the table, the screen illuminating the room.

'Hi, Mum,' she said. 'I'm guessing you've got no power either?'

'Hello, lovey, no, we're all in darkness here at the minute. In fact, the whole town's out from what I can gather, I've heard it stretches over as far as Lingthorpe.'

'That's not so good. I'm keeping everything crossed power's restored by the morning.'

'I'm sure it will be. Listen, flower, as you know, we've got a generator but with your dad being out of sorts the way he is—'

'I'm not out of sorts, I'm perfectly capable of rigging up a bloomin' generator,' came Charlie's voice in the background.

Paula tutted softly, lowering her voice. 'Ignore your dad, he knows as well as I do he's been told not to touch equipment like that until he's fully recovered. It's the night before your wedding and there's no way I'm going to let him rig it up and risk him having a dizzy spell in the process. He could fry himself to a crisp!'

'I heard that, Florence-flaming-Nightmaringale!'

'I don't care, you'd be no use to our Florrie if your stubbornness meant you got yourself half frazzled, would you?'

Florrie couldn't help but giggle. Her parents put her in mind of a double act when they were having a good-natured bicker like this.

'Anyroad, I've just got off the phone to Bear, and he's offered to rig up the generator for us. With them having one at the farm, he knows how to set them up. Says he'll stop off at yours and collect you, Ed and Gerty first, then come here, rig up the generator, then head back to Clifftop Farm with Ed. Maggie says Ed can have his tea with them. And you might as well have yours with us, flower.'

'Sounds like you've got it all worked out, Mum.'

'I just wish I could fix the weather for you.'

'Yeah, looking at the forecast, so do I.'

When the call had ended, Florrie relayed the conversation to Ed. While they were talking, his phone had started ringing with a call from Bear. Between them, they arranged that he'd collect them in half an hour.

With their stuff gathered together, the couple stood in the candlelight of the kitchen, shadows flickering around the room.

'The next time we come into this room you'll be Mrs Florrie Harte.' Ed smiled, stooping to kiss her.

Florrie's heart skipped a beat. 'I like the sound of that.' She pushed her hands inside his padded jacket and reached her arms around his waist, tilting her head to look up at him.

'Me too.' He bent to kiss her when there was a loud knock at the door, causing Gerty to leap from her bed barking like she was some highly trained guard dog.

'This is it, then.' Ed smiled. 'I'd better take this opportunity to give you a proper goodnight kiss since I doubt I'll get the chance at your parents' house.'

'Much as I hate to say it, can you be quick? Poor Bear'll be getting soaked on the doorstep.'

'Good point.' He grinned before pressing his lips against hers and making her knees turn to jelly.

THIRTY-SIX
SATURDAY 2ND MAY – THE
DAY OF THE WEDDING

Florrie had barely slept a wink all night, the knot of nerves in her stomach apparently determined to keep her awake with all their twisting and turning, in cahoots with Storm Maida who'd raged on, letting vent to her fury.

It was still dark outside as Florrie pushed her duvet back and tiptoed over to the window of her childhood bedroom, disappointed to see the rain showed no sign of abating and that the streetlights were off, the electricity still not restored. She flopped back down on the bed and picked up her phone, checking the time and to see if she'd heard from Ed – though she wasn't sure on the etiquette, or superstition of bride and groom communication on the morning of the wedding before they got to the place they were to be married. Not that she wanted to tempt fate, especially with the rocky road they'd had to get to this day over the last few weeks. It was still early, not even six a.m. and, much as she felt restless, she knew there was nothing she could do right now but sit and wait until she heard her parents moving about.

With a restless sigh, she reached for her Kindle, hoping to lose herself in the virtual pages of her latest book.

She'd only been reading for a couple of minutes when she was startled to hear the tinkling ring of her mobile phone. She snatched it up to see the landlady from the Jolly's number illuminated on the screen. Florrie's heart swooped; a call from Mandy at this hour wasn't going to be good news, especially since the Jolly was where she and Ed were having their wedding reception.

She swiped to accept the call. 'Hi, Mandy, is everything okay?' Her heart was thumping, her stomach churning as she registered the sound of sloshing water in the background.

'Florrie, I'm so sorry for calling this early, I didn't know what else to do and I don't know how to tell you this, but the pub's flooded and—'

'Flooded? Oh no!' Florrie didn't need Mandy to tell her anything else; the implications were clear as day.

'You wouldn't believe it down here. A combination of the storm and the high spring tide has meant the sea levels are ridiculous — we're wading through about two and a half feet of seawater; can barely see what we're doing.' Mandy's words were coming out in a torrent, stress evident in her voice. 'The bottom prom's flooded, too, water's reached some of the houses in Old Micklewick. No one's getting down here any time soon. I'm so sorry, love.'

Florrie's mind shot to Lark whose cottage wasn't far from the Jolly, hoping it hadn't reached Mariners Row. 'It's not your fault, Mandy. I'm sorry to hear you're having to deal with all of that. It must be a nightmare.'

A weary sigh travelled down the phone. 'You have no idea. As fast as we sluice it out, it flows straight back in. There's just no stopping it.'

'Sounds awful. Is there anything we can do to help?' Florrie's heart went out to her.

'Thanks for the offer, but all we can do is wait for the tide to go out and the rain to ease up. Hopefully we should see a difference in the next hour or so. Mind, even when that happens, everything's too saturated for you to have your reception here. We're going to have to get some industrial dryers in, change the carpets and the covers on the seats. And then there's the electrics to consider... It'll be too dangerous. Again, I'm so sorry.'

'Hey, it's not your fault. Thanks for letting me know, Mandy. I hope you get sorted soon.'

'You too, love.'

Florrie had just ended the call, her mind racing, when there was a tap at her bedroom door and her mum's head appeared. 'You okay, lovey?' From the concerned tone of her voice, Florrie guessed her mum had caught the gist of her conversation with Mandy.

Paula padded over the carpet in her pyjamas, slipping onto the bed beside her daughter.

Florrie rubbed her hand across her mouth, hardly able to believe what she was about to say. 'The Jolly's flooded, Mum. Mandy says we can't have the reception there.' Her bottom lip quivered and her eyes swam with tears. 'Honestly, it's just been one thing after another, what with all the hassle from Ed's mum, Dad ending up in hospital and now this.'

Paula slipped her arm around Florrie's shoulders. 'Oh, lovey, come here. Try not to fret, we'll think of a solution. It's only early, you're not getting married till twelve and the reception wasn't due to start until two; we've got time to get a plan in place.' Paula sat quiet for a moment, and Florrie could almost hear the cogs of her mind whirring. 'What about the tearoom? You could have your reception there. It's the perfect solution,' her mum said, brightening. With the staff being guests at the wedding, it made sense for the bookshop to close for the day, which meant the tearoom had to close, too.

'But what would we do about food and drink? And how can we cook anything without electricity? More to the point, we haven't got any food to cook even if the electricity was on. Everything for the roast dinner's down at the Jolly and Mandy said the bottom prom's not passable so we wouldn't be able to go and collect it.' The word 'disaster' was on the tip of her tongue, but she held back from saying it. If she didn't know better, she'd swear Dawn and Luella had jinxed this day.

'Right then' – Paula patted her hands on her thighs – 'I reckon we should head downstairs, lovey, have a cup of tea and a good think about what to do. Don't you worry, your dad and me will make sure you and Ed have the wedding day you'd hoped for. I just need to get my thinking cap on and work out what we can do about feeding everyone. And thank goodness you and Ed kept guest numbers low – it makes it easier to resolve.'

Florrie gave her mum a grateful smile, resting her head on her shoulder. 'Thanks, Mum.' Nothing ever defeated Paula Appleton, she was a fixer through and through. And Florrie didn't doubt her mum would come up with a solution, though she couldn't begin to imagine what shape that would take right now.

At just gone eight forty-five, the electricity pinged on and a cheer could be heard running around the street where Florrie's parents lived.

'Oh, thank goodness for that,' said Paula, clapping her hands to her face. 'Why don't you go and get yourself in the shower now the electric's back on, lovey? I'll see what I can sort out about the food.'

Florrie went to protest and say that she wanted to help, but Paula was having none of it. 'I'm on it, you go and have yourself a nice shower, leave the fretting to me. I reckon I'll have a plan in place by the time you come back downstairs.'

'Best not argue with your mother, lass, you know what she's like when she's on a mission,' her dad said, giving her a knowing look.

'Okay,' she said reluctantly, feeling guilty leaving the pressure on her mum to come up with a solution.

Florrie had already spoken to Maggie, who had a bird's-eye view of the bottom prom from Clifftop Cottage. On seeing the tide washing over the road, she'd called Florrie to reassure her they'd get Ed to the church on time and would drive the long way round. During the call, Florrie had declined the offer of having a quick chat with him, superstition kicking in and not wanting to tempt fate any further.

. . .

As she made her way downstairs, Florrie could hear her mum talking to someone in the kitchen, and from her tone, she guessed it wasn't her dad. She walked into the room, catching her dad's eye. He gave her a wink and a smile, igniting a small glimmer of hope inside her.

'That's brilliant, thanks so much, Mandy. And best of luck with everything. Bye, lovey.' Paula ended the call and set her phone down on the countertop then turned around to Florrie, a wide smile on her face. 'All sorted, lovey. Your reception's going ahead and everyone'll be getting their roast dinner.'

Relief spread through Florrie along with a surge of love for her mum. 'How? I mean, where will it be? And how can we get a roast dinner sorted in time? All the food's down at the Jolly.'

'The venue is the bookshop tearoom and I've organised a last-minute shopping spree to grab the ingredients; we're going to make sure there'll still be a roast dinner and lovely pud for your wedding guests. I've been on to the butcher's, told them what we need as far as joints of beef are concerned, and I've called the greengrocer's, explained the situation to them and they're putting veggies in boxes as we speak, ready for us to pick up – I spoke to Mandy at the Jolly and she told me all the quantities for everything which was really helpful. Jazz's mum and dad and Stella's mum and Rhys are meeting me in town to collect everything and drop it off at the bookshop. That call was just Mandy confirming she's organised for the chef and staff who'd be working at the Jolly for your reception to be at the bookshop tearoom instead. I just need to ring round the guests and let them know the change of venue.' Paula beamed a huge smile at her daughter. 'Oh – how could I forget? – Jazz has come up trumps with the pudding. She's taken a couple of trays of chocolate brownie out of the freezer so they can start defrosting. She says they can be served with custard, cream or ice cream, which I know there's plenty of in the bookshop's tearoom.'

'Have you met your mother the tornado?' Charlie asked, chuckling as he hugged his mug of tea.

Florrie felt her anxiety trickle away. 'Mum, you're amazing!

Thank you!' She rushed over to her and flung her arms around her neck, battling the tears that were now blurring her vision.

'I knew we'd get it sorted, lovey. And no more tears now, you don't want your eyes all puffy for your wedding day, do you?' Paula stepped back and kissed her daughter on the cheek.

Florrie shook her head, emotion threatening to overwhelm her. 'No, you're right,' she said in a wobbly voice.

'And look, it's stopped raining and the sky's clearing. I think we might be treated to a bit of sunshine by the time you set off for church.'

THIRTY-SEVEN

Florrie had decided against having someone come to the house to do her hair and make-up before the wedding; she'd much rather do it herself. She wasn't one for much make-up anyway, preferring a flick of mascara, maybe a bit of blusher and a smear of lip gloss if she was going somewhere special. She'd bought a new one for today, in a shade she was told would just emphasise her natural lip colour. 'I want to look like myself when I meet Ed at the altar,' she'd said to the young woman on the make-up counter. Her one concession to having a fuss made over her, had been to let her mum straighten her hair for her. Mother and daughter had used the time to enjoy a trip down memory lane, reminiscing about Mr H and all his plotting to get Florrie and Ed together. 'And here you are,' Paula said fondly, smiling at her daughter in the dressing table mirror, straighteners in hand. 'He'd be chuffed to bits.'

'He would, and I can just imagine his happy chuckle and him clapping his hands together the way he used to when one of his plans had worked out.' Florrie felt emotion squeeze in her chest. She took a calming breath and steadied herself. *No more tears, Florrie.*

With her mum heading off to get changed into her mother-of-the bride outfit, Florrie reached for her wedding dress that had been removed from its cover and was hanging on the back of her bedroom door, nerves fluttering in her stomach.

The dress was in ivory raw silk and had a square neckline, three-quarter sleeves and finished just above the ankle. Like the dress on the mini Florrie in the window display it was empire line, though the real Florrie's was trimmed with ivory braid and the bodice was embellished with hundreds of tiny freshwater pearls while a line of fabric-covered buttons ran down the back.

She eased it carefully off its padded hanger and slipped it over her head, the fabric cool against her skin – she'd need her mum to help with the buttons.

Florrie had swapped her usual plain, no-nonsense underwear for a matching set in ivory silk trimmed with a delicate matching lace. She'd teamed them with a pair of hold-up stockings with pretty lace tops. If you couldn't wear fancy underwear on your wedding day, when could you? she'd thought when she was buying them.

Once she'd fastened her simple silver necklace with its small diamond-studded pendant that matched her earrings – they were her 'something old' and had belonged to Florrie's maternal grand-mother – Florrie slipped her feet into a pair of low-heeled Mary Janes in ivory leather, fastening the diamanté buckle. That done, she called her mum to give her a hand with the buttons of her dress and to fasten the clasp of the silver bracelet decorated with clear crystals Lark had given her for her 'something new'. Her 'some-thing borrowed' were two diamanté hair slides from Maggie to secure her veil in place, and her 'something blue' was a tiny blue money spider Lark had sewn into the hem of her wedding dress when she was altering it for her.

With her delicate tiara in place and her veil thrown back, Florrie made her way downstairs where her parents were waiting for her, her mum having hurried back downstairs so she could enjoy the sight of her daughter emerging from her bedroom.

'Oh, Florrie, lovey, you look absolutely beautiful,' exclaimed her mum, her voice wavering as she handed her daughter the small hand-tied bouquet of spring flowers.

'Aye, that you do, lass.' Her dad beamed, pride shining in his eyes.

'You look like a princess,' said bridesmaid Chloe, who'd been dropped off earlier by her mum Jasmine.

'And so do you,' replied Florrie. Chloe was dressed in an ivory silk ballerina-style dress, the bodice decorated with ivory bugle beads, a cashmere shrug cardigan over her shoulders. Her long strawberry-blonde hair, which had been fixed in loose waves for the occasion, was held off her face by a diamanté and faux pearl headband. Florrie could only imagine how proud Jasmine was of her little daughter.

'Ready, lass?' Her dad arrived by her side.

'Ready, Dad.' The pair exchanged a happy smile.

'Let's do this,' cheered Chloe, her chirpy voice puncturing the air of anticipation and making them all laugh.

As the car headed out of the street and set off on its short journey to the church, Florrie found herself lost in her thoughts, not all of them welcome. A happy one was that her dad's health had improved in leaps and bounds since his trip to hospital, and the dizzy spells were less frequent – though the labyrinthitis still hadn't stopped her from worrying about him walking her down the aisle today, knowing he'd be mortified if he had a dizzy turn in front of so many people.

Ed had gone to great pains to reassure her that nothing untoward would happen involving his parents. Luella, he said, had finally got the message loud and clear that their relationship was over, and was now back in London, as were his parents. His father had told him that after everything that had happened, he and Dawn wouldn't return to Micklewick Bay for the wedding. That had triggered conflicting emotions in Florrie who, on the one hand, was enormously relieved to hear that, since their absence guaranteed Dawn wouldn't be causing any trouble. On the other hand, she felt bad that Ed wouldn't have his mother and father there.

When she'd voiced this to him, he'd explained that he thought it was for the best. A further development was that his father had encouraged Dawn to seek help for her gambling addiction. Since she'd returned to London, she'd made an appointment with her GP, who'd put her on a waiting list for addiction counselling. The news had left Ed and Florrie feeling inordinately relieved. It was a start; Florrie just hoped that it would mean she'd leave them to live their married lives together in peace.

'Here we are, lass.' Her father pulled Florrie out of her thoughts. She glanced out of the window to see her mum standing on the church steps with Chloe, the sun doing all it could to push its way through the clouds. Gerty was there, too, in her capacity of second bridesmaid. She was sporting a new cream collar, a basket brimming with flowers that matched Florrie's and Chloe's clenched between her teeth, and as usual, her tail was wagging happily.

Florrie and her dad waited for the organ to strike up, their cue to make their way down the aisle. She could see Ed up ahead at the altar, looking smart in his dark-blue suit and laughing at something Bear was saying in his ear. Suddenly, the opening notes of Wagner's 'Bridal Chorus' echoed around the church, sending butterflies running amok in her stomach. Her dad gave her arm a squeeze accompanied by a proud smile before they began their slow walk down the aisle towards Ed, Florrie glancing from side to side as she went. Her heart gave a happy lilt as she spotted her friends, the women waving excitedly at her and making her giggle. In the pew behind them, she noticed Jean with Amery standing next to her in his capacity as Jean's 'plus one', both looking inordinately happy. With a mix of excitement and nerves building inside her, Florrie was just a few feet away when Ed turned, his face lighting up with the widest smile, sending a tidal wave of love racing through her.

'You look beautiful,' he said, when she was beside him, his eyes shining with happiness.

THIRTY-EIGHT

After the initial drama, the wedding went without a hitch, much to
Florrie's relief.

A cheer rang out when the photographer finally declared that
she was happy with the photos she'd taken as they'd shivered in the
grounds of the church, being buffeted by a chilly breeze that was
struggling to keep the rain at bay. No one wasted a moment and
hurried to their cars and drove to the reception.

Upon their arrival at the bookshop tearoom, Florrie and Ed
were greeted with a rousing round of applause as they took their
seats at the newly created top table. Florrie glanced around her,
thrilled to see the room had been given a thorough wedding
makeover. The tables had been covered with crisp white table-
cloths, while lengths of frothy organza were wrapped around the
backs of the chairs and tied in a bow – no doubt courtesy of Lark
who Florrie recalled had mentioned recently taking a delivery of
such fabric. Spring flowers that matched her bouquet had been
arranged in vases and placed on any available surface, with smaller
versions dotted at intervals along the tables. Florrie was delighted
to see the wedding favours set out on the placemats. She'd commis-
sioned the chocolates in the shape of miniature piles of books from
Becca at the Chocolate Cherub chocolatiers in Middleton-le-

Moors. They'd been placed in book-shaped boxes Becca had sourced specially for Florrie and Ed's wedding. The confectionary had luckily avoided being stranded at the Jolly since Mandy had expressed her concern about them getting damaged owing to the lack of storage space at the pub with all of the wedding paraphernalia taking up so much of it. Florrie gave a grateful smile; she'd have been so disappointed if they'd been ruined in the flood.

Adding to the wedding vibe, fairy lights were festooned from the ceiling and subtle music spilled from the speakers of the vintage radio. The mouth-watering aroma of roast dinner that permeated the air made Florrie feel suddenly ravenous.

In no time at all, plates of steaming food were placed in front of them. Gerty, who'd travelled to the bookshop in the car with Ed and Florrie, was sitting at Ed's feet, sniffing the air appreciatively. The room was filled with upbeat chatter, punctuated with bursts of laughter. Florrie cast her gaze around – she was delighted that the last-minute change of venue hadn't dampened anyone's spirits or taken the edge off the day. She caught Ed's eye and the pair exchanged happy smiles.

When it came to the dessert, Jasmine's chocolate brownies went down a storm, especially since they had been served warm, making the centres extra gooey and luxurious, melting into the warm custard.

Once the food – which had been delicious despite it having been hurriedly prepared – had been devoured, it was time for the speeches. Florrie could feel Ed fidgeting nervously beside her. He'd told her he hadn't officially prepared a speech nor written anything down. He was concerned his dyslexia would make him stumble over his words if he attempted to read from a sheet of paper. He'd already warned her that it might not be a particularly polished affair, but he needn't have worried. As he spoke, it was obvious his words came straight from the heart, his love for Florrie shining through and leaving many of their guests in tears.

'Before I sit down, I have a surprise for my beautiful wife – blimey, it feels good saying that!' he said, making everyone, including Florrie, laugh. He turned to look at her, his eyes warm with affection. 'So, Mrs Harte – feels pretty good saying that, too! – it's no secret to everyone who knows you that you've always been a massive fan of the Brontë sisters, and that *Wuthering Heights* is your favourite novel of all time. Which is why we'll be spending our honeymoon in the Brontë's hometown of Haworth where we'll be visiting what was their home at the parsonage museum. We'll also be taking the Brontë trail, including a trip to Top Withens, and generally getting all "Brontëfied" for a good few days!'

Florrie leapt to her feet and flung her arms around her new husband, planting kisses over his face in a most un-Florrie-like public display of affection. 'Oh, Ed, thank you! I can't think of a more wonderful way to spend our honeymoon!' In truth, they'd had a conversation and agreed that with all of the expense they'd had in setting up the tearoom and making improvements on the bookshop, they'd forgo a honeymoon and take a holiday later when funds allowed. Little did Florrie know that Ed had been secretly planning the Brontë trip to surprise her with, knowing how much it would mean to her.

The excitement continued with the cutting of the stunning cake Jasmine had created for them. It was a three-tiered affair covered in ivory-coloured fondant icing. On the top tier was a pile of three sugar paste vintage-style books set amongst a cluster of hand-painted sugar paste spring flowers. The faux blooms continued down the side, creating a tumbling effect. 'It's a shame we have to cut it, Jazz,' Florrie called to her friend.

Before long, the tables were pushed back against the walls creating space for a makeshift dance floor. Ed led Florrie to the centre of the room as Gabe Dublin's 'My Rose-shaped Heart' poured from the speakers, triggering a cheer from their guests who looked on as Ed held his new wife close, the pair swaying to the music.

'If it's okay with you, I wouldn't mind sneaking out for a few minutes. Won't take long. Sorry to sound cryptic, but I'm sure you'll understand when I tell you the reason. Bear's not drinking so he said he'd be happy to take us in the Landie.'

'Oh, okay,' Florrie said, looking puzzled.

Five minutes later, Bear pulled up at a familiar place on the top prom. 'Here you go, folks,' he said, yanking the handbrake on. 'Take as long as you need.'

Ed reached for a small gift bag at his feet and climbed out of the vehicle, before helping Florrie down.

Dusk was creeping in, creating a golden glow over the sky. Taking her hand, he led her over to the commemorative bench they'd sponsored for Mr and Mrs H. 'I thought we couldn't let our special day pass without checking in with my grandparents.'

Florrie's heart squeezed. 'I love that, especially since your granddad, aka Cupid Harte, played such a big role in us getting together in the first place.'

'As you can see, I came prepared.' Ed pulled out two plastic bags from the gift bag. 'They're not very stylish, but it'll mean we don't get our clothes wet when we sit down.'

'I see you've thought of everything.' She smiled as they both stretched out the carrier bags on Mr and Mrs H's seat and quickly sat down before the wind snatched them up and sent them blowing along the prom. Florrie rubbed her arms as goosebumps pinged over her skin, prompting Ed to remove his jacket and drape it over her shoulders.

That done, he produced two small champagne glasses, handing them to Florrie as he shared the contents of a small bottle of fizz between them. 'We won't stay here long, it's chilly and your dress, beautiful as it is, won't keep the cold at bay, but I thought it'd be nice to toast my grandparents.'

'Absolutely.'

Ed held his glass aloft and Florrie followed suit. 'Here's to you and Grandma, Grandad. I know you can't be with us in person, but I know you'll be looking down at us, smiling that mischievous smile of yours, Grandad. I'm sorry our time together wasn't longer, but I'll treasure every moment.' Ed's voice faltered and he fell silent.

Florrie took his hand, her throat squeezing with emotion as her gaze swept along to Mr and Mrs H's beloved Thorncliffe. Just then, the sun broke through the clouds and a rainbow appeared, its colours softened by the deliciously warm hues of golden hour. 'Look! How gorgeous is that?' she said.

Ed followed her line of sight. 'Oh, wow! It's a double one, see?'

'Lark says double rainbows mean good luck, that they're a sign of new beginnings and where the spiritual world connects with the physical world,' said Florrie. 'Looks like your grandad heard you.'

'Looks like he did.' Ed's face broke out into a smile. 'One last thing while you're listening, Grandad, thank you for bringing me to this amazing woman, you really knew what you were doing when you set that ball rolling.' He caught Florrie's eye and they exchanged a smile. 'And here's to the next generation of Happy Hartes.' He leant towards her and pressed his lips against hers, all soft and warm. 'Love you, Florrie Harte.'

'Love you right back.'

A LETTER FROM THE AUTHOR

Huge thanks for choosing to pick up *A Wedding at the Little Bookshop by the Sea*.

I hope you enjoyed this instalment of the Micklewick Bay series and catching up with Florrie and Ed on the countdown to their wedding! If you'd like to join other readers in hearing all about my new releases and bonus content, you can sign up for my newsletter!

We won't share your email address, and you can unsubscribe any time.

www.stormpublishing.co/eliza-j-scott

If you enjoyed this book and could spare a few moments to leave a review that would be hugely appreciated. It doesn't have to be long, just a few words would do, but for us authors it can make all the difference in encouraging a reader to discover our books for the first time. Thank you so much. If you click on the link below it will take you right there.

This was meant to be the last book in the Micklewick Bay series, which I have to say, made me feel rather sad the further I got into writing it. However, all of that changed when my lovely editor, Kate, asked if I had any ideas for more Micklewick Bay books. I was delighted to be able to say that not only had I outlined a spin-off series, but I'd also got a story that I'd outlined several years ago, but hadn't yet got around to writing. It's based in Micklewick Bay, but I wasn't sure where to place it with the other books. Kate instantly hit on the brilliant idea of making it book eight in the original Micklewick Bay series, which means that although two completely new characters will be introduced, we get to catch up with Florrie and the rest of the friendship group, which I'm so happy about. I've given it the working title of *Snowflakes and Secrets in Micklewick Bay* and it's set for publication in September 2026. It's part of a three-book deal I've recently signed with Storm which takes us right through to 2028. That should keep me out of mischief for a while!

Back to *A Wedding at the Little Bookshop by the Sea*. I was thrilled to catch up with Florrie and Ed, and see how their relationship has strengthened as their love has deepened – not to mention that they finally get their dream wedding, despite the hurdles they faced along the way, not least Dawn Harte. I was keen to show how good friends and a small community can rally round and offer support to one another when faced with unexpected challenges, turning problems into a success story, as they did for Florrie and Ed's wedding. The day had the potential to be a total disaster; however, it was anything but. It's definitely a story for them to tell their grandchildren!

I'm also glad Ed has finally been able to shrug off his insecurity, stand up to his parents and accept that he deserves to be part of a loving family, which is exactly what Florrie and her parents offer. I can't wait to see what the future holds for the newlyweds...

facebook.com/elizajscottauthor

instagram.com/elizajscott

x.com/ElizaJScott1

bookbub.com/authors/eliza-j-scott

bsky.app/profile/elizajscott.bsky.social

ACKNOWLEDGEMENTS

Here's where I get the opportunity to thank everyone involved in getting *A Wedding at the Little Bookshop by the Sea* ready for publication day and beyond.

Of course, I have to start with my wonderful editor, Kate Smith, who is such a joy to work with and deserves the biggest thank you for so many reasons. Not least her insightful edits – always delivered with kindness – and her unwavering support, enthusiasm and encouragement. Whilst we were working on the edits for *A Wedding at the Little Bookshop by the Sea* Kate delivered the very exciting news that she's expecting a baby! And though it means she'll be on maternity leave for publication day, Kate's assured me she'll be cheering our book on from the sidelines, which means such a lot. Her input in *A Wedding at the Little Bookshop by the Sea* has been invaluable and the story is so much better for it. I'll miss Kate enormously while she's away, but I know I've been left in excellent hands with assistant editor, Naomi Knox, and publishing director, Emily Gowers, who I met via a video call and were super friendly. Sending you a huge thank you for always being so lovely, Kate, and many congratulations on your wonderful baby news! xxx

That leads me very nicely on to saying a great big thank you to Naomi and Emily who have been liaising with Kate before taking over the latter part of the Bookshop Wedding editing process.

Sticking with Storm, I must say a great big thank you to the forward-thinking man at the top, Oliver Rhodes, for creating such a wonderful publishing house filled with the kindest team of people. Thanks are also owed to digital and operations director, Chris

Lucraft, for his techy, behind-the-scenes skills in getting my books into the hands of new readers. The ever-patient editorial operations director, Alexandra Begley, deserves a great big thank you for all she does in preparing my books for publication day, as does the equally patient editorial operations assistant, Maheen Mehmood – I do hope the FACs are getting better, Maheen! Many thanks also to head of marketing, Elke Desanghere, for her delightful marketing campaigns, and to publicity manager, Anna McKerrow, for her fab posts on social media. Thank you both so much! I must also mention copyeditor, Shirley Khan, and proofreader, Amanda Raybould, for checking over this book and giving it a final polish before publication day. Once again, book cover designer Rose Cooper gets a massive thank you for creating yet another stunning Micklewick Bay cover. It's utterly gorgeous!

The super-organised Rachel of Rachel's Random Resources gets a huge thank you for setting up yet another amazing blog tour for one of my books. Thanks also to the fabulous book bloggers who have generously signed up for another blog tour. I'm enormously grateful for them taking the time to read and review my books.

As ever, I owe a heartfelt thank you to my wonderful friends and fellow authors, Jessica Redland and Sharon Booth, for their continued support and kindness. I always look forward to our catch-ups over cheese scones and cakes!

I must mention two Facebook groups I feel lucky to be a member of. The Friendly Book Community and Riveting Reads and Vintage Finds are two places where you're always guaranteed to find a warm and cosy welcome. At the York Tea last September, I was delighted to finally get to meet the admins of The Friendly Book Community: Sarah Kingsnorth, Hazel Elkin and Marie Harris. I can't begin to tell you how lovely they are. Although we didn't get the chance to have much of a chat, in that short time we had one heck of a giggle! Thank you so much, Sarah, Hazel, Marie and Sue Baker, for all you do in running these wonderful groups and offering us readers and authors a warm and friendly place for us to pop by.

In fact, I'd like to continue by sending out an enormous thank you to the amazing book community in general whose kindness and support over social media is thoroughly heartwarming.

Of course, I have to say a massive thank you to my wonderful family for their unwavering support and endless supply of cups of tea and ginger biscuits while I'm scribbling away in my writing room. I couldn't do it without you guys. Love you heaps!

A final, and enormous, thank you goes to you the reader. I'm grateful and humbled in equal measure that you've chosen to read my book. Thank you from the bottom of my heart.

Much love,

Eliza xxx